The *Regency*

LORDS & LADIES
COLLECTION

*Two Glittering Regency
Love Affairs*

Miranda's Masquerade
by Meg Alexander
&
Gifford's Lady
by Claire Thornton

The *Regency*

LORDS & LADIES

COLLECTION

The Regency

LORDS & LADIES
COLLECTION

Meg Alexander &
Claire Thornton

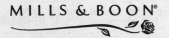

MILLS & BOON®

*First published in Great Britain 2006 by
Harlequin Mills & Boon Limited,
Eton House, 18-24 Paradise Road, Richmond, Surrey TW9 1SR*

THE REGENCY LORDS & LADIES COLLECTION
© Harlequin Books S.A. 2006

The publisher acknowledges the copyright holders of the
individual works as follows:

Miranda's Masquerade © Meg Alexander 1997
Gifford's Lady © Claire Thornton 2002

ISBN 0 263 84426 9

138-0406

*Printed and bound in Spain
by Litografia Rosés S.A., Barcelona*

Miranda's Masquerade
by
Meg Alexander

After living in southern Spain for many years, **Meg Alexander** now lives in Kent, although, having been born in Lancashire, she feels that her roots are in the north of England. Meg's career has encompassed a wide variety of roles, from professional cook to assistant director of a conference centre. She has always been a voracious reader, and loves to write. Other loves include history, cats, gardening, cooking and travel. She has a son and two grandchildren.

Chapter One

"I'll make him sorry he ever offered for me!" With a cry of anguish, Frances Gaysford threw herself upon her bed and burst into a storm of tears.

"That shouldn't be too difficult, Fanny," her twin observed dispassionately. "Just let Lord Heston see you now and he'll cry off at once. The end of your nose is as red as your eyes..."

"Oh! Oh! Unfeeling! I might have known you'd make a joke of it...my own *sister!* You don't care in the least, Miranda."

"I might if I believed in this Cheltenham tragedy. Come to your senses, love. Harry Lakenham will never marry you. Even if he were of age, he won't wed to disoblige his family."

"We are promised to each other..." Fanny raised her head, the drowned blue eyes looking enormous in the delicate oval of her face. "His heart will not change, and nor will mine..."

"But yours has changed three times in the last three months! I have lost count of the men to whom you've sworn undying devotion."

"This time it's different. In the past…well…it was but an illusion. Now I know the meaning of true love."

"Perhaps so. In the meantime, you had best get up and bathe your face. Heston will be here at noon. You have less than an hour to change your dress, which, I may say, is sadly crumpled…"

"I won't see him. I can't. I am not well enough." Fanny's wails increased. "Uncle shall make my excuses…"

"He won't do so for a third time. Both Mr Mordaunt and Sir Patrick Caswell were insulted when you claimed the headache, and then they saw you later at the Opera."

"Could I help it if I felt a little better later in the day? I should not have taken either, in any case…a widower on the one hand, and a middle-aged country squire? I can't think what Uncle was about to allow them to address me."

"He hopes to see us comfortably settled, Fanny. Was that not his object in giving us this Season? Mama could not afford it—"

"I know! Pray do not go on about it. He has been kind, but doubtless he has his reasons…"

"What can you mean?" There was a note of anger in Miranda's voice, and Fanny looked uncomfortable.

"Don't get upon your high ropes!" she said defiantly. "With Father gone, Uncle will not care to have our family foisted upon him. He would marry us to anyone."

"That is both ungenerous and untrue! You might at least see Heston. Uncle does not insist that you accept him…only that you listen to his offer."

"How can I? My heart is broken…" With a gesture worthy of a tragedy queen, Fanny raised herself upon one elbow and covered her eyes with a drooping hand.

Miranda recognised the scene at once. It was part of

the repertoire of the latest actress to take the town by storm.

"What do I care for money or position?" her sister mourned. "I should be happy in a cottage with my darling."

"Stuff and nonsense!" Miranda said decisively. "Sometimes you put me out of all patience with you. You in a cottage? I can just see you feeding chickens and cleaning out the pigs. Remember how you hated life in Yorkshire...the plain food, no new clothes, an outside privy, and the cold? Have you forgot the cold?"

"No, of course not, but it will not come to that. Harry has expectations. All we need is a little time... He will see his grandfather—"

"Do be sensible, Fanny! It will not serve, you know."

"You have always been against him. How can you be so cruel? Why must I be sacrificed to that ugly dotard? Heston is a freak...a mountain...a positive Alp! He has neither manners nor wit to recommend him. Oh, why could he not take you?"

This suggestion was too much for Miranda. Her sense of humour bubbled to the surface. "Fanny, you will be the end of me! Do you believe that this...this monster, as you call him, would make me an ideal husband?"

"Of course not!" Fanny sniffed. "And you need not laugh. I doubt if any man would suit you. You treat them all as if their compliments are meaningless."

"Most of them are, and I won't be taken in by flattery."

"It isn't all false. We are not ill-looking, you and I. When a gentleman expresses admiration it is not kind in you to put him out of countenance by speaking out so plain. You frighten them away, you know."

"I'll try to mend my ways," Miranda promised.

"Now, dearest, do get dressed. Much as I should like to help you, Lord Heston has not offered for me. He has asked to see Miss Gaysford, and you are the elder…"

"Only by twenty minutes. It isn't fair!" Fanny gazed at her twin, a look of speculation in her eyes. "He would not know the difference," she said thoughtfully. "We might play a trick on him, if you were to take my place."

Miranda stared at her. "I wonder that you could suggest it," she said in dismay.

"But we have exchanged places all our lives. It cannot signify for a mere half-hour. It could do no harm."

"I doubt if Lord Heston would see it so. It would be insulting, Fanny. Think of the scandal if we were to be found out? This is no childish game. The scandal would be unbearable—" She stopped. Fanny had given way to a series of hiccuping sobs. They were a certain prelude to an attack of hysteria. She looked up helplessly as her aunt came into the room.

"Why, what is this, my dears?" Mrs Shere gathered Fanny to her ample bosom. "There, my love, pray don't distress yourself. When your sister marries, she will not be lost to you, and you will be wed yourself before the year is out." She stroked her niece's copper curls with a gentle hand.

"I…I'm sorry, Aunt." Fanny lifted a drooping head. "I do not mean to be a watering-pot." The glance she threw at Miranda was one of triumph. Mrs Shere had mistaken one twin for the other, as she had often done before.

Miranda was about to correct her when Fanny caught at her hand. "You will come back at once and tell us what Lord Heston has to say?" she pleaded.

"Of course she will." Mrs Shere beamed upon the twins. "His lordship has arrived, and we must not keep him waiting." She took Miranda's arm and led her from the room.

"Aunt, please wait! I have something to say to you."

"Not now, my love. It must wait until later. This is not the time..." She hurried ahead, along the corridor and down the staircase, pausing only when they reached the door to the salon.

"You were right to wear the white sprigged muslin." She considered Miranda with a critical eye. "It is most becoming. I could wish that these short hairstyles were not so much the vogue, but there, we must be in the fashion. Be kind to Lord Heston," she whispered finally. "Gentlemen, too, can be nervous on these occasions."

She opened the door and led her niece towards the man who stood by the window.

He turned as they entered and came towards her, bowing first to her aunt and then to herself.

Miranda felt a slight twinge of amusement. Anyone less nervous she had yet to see. A sharp glance from beneath his black brows had assured her of that.

She held her breath as she waited for his first words. Would he see through her deception? Then it became apparent that he too had mistaken her for Fanny. As he exchanged civilities with Mrs Shere, Miranda kept her eyes upon the carpet.

At last she nerved herself to look at him more closely. Immensely tall and built in proportion the perfect tailoring of his coat and breeches could not disguise his heavily muscled shoulders and thighs. He moved with the easy grace of an athlete.

Even the most partial would not have termed him handsome. Crowned by a mass of thick black hair, cut in the fashionable "Brutus" style, his face had a vitality of its own. The heavy jaw and a slightly crooked nose merely added character to his expression.

At this moment, that expression was unfathomable as his eyes met hers. She was startled. Hard and bleak as the grey of a winter sea, they roved over her with indifference.

It must be her imagination. She had seen him before, of course. His height alone made him conspicuous in any gathering. His lordship did not dance, and seemed to find no pleasure in feminine company.

"Who is that man?" she had asked her friend, Charlotte Fairfax. She had been half-piqued and half-amused when he had thrown her a single glance and, clearly unimpressed, had turned away.

"Heston? He is one of the richest men in London. Don't cast your handkerchief in his direction, my dear. You would be wasting your time."

"Why is that? Has he a reputation?"

"Not that I can discover, but he is a mis—a mis—well, one of those men who has not time for women. He thinks only of gaming, horses, and curricle racing."

"How very dull of him!" Miranda had watched as his lordship had strolled idly through the chattering throng and had made his way to the card tables in the adjoining room.

"Miranda, never let anyone hear you say so! Heston is a Corinthian and quite at the top of the tree. He is the idol of the younger set and a member of the Four-Horse Club."

"Remarkable! Are we supposed to admire him because he wears a Belcher handkerchief, a nosegay in his driving coat, and a spotted cravat? How ridiculous! It seems more like fancy-dress to me."

"Please, I beg of you…" Charlotte had drawn her

friend into the shelter of an alcove, and had cast an anxious look about her. "Do guard your tongue, Miranda. You must not speak your mind so openly. Someone will overhear you. Gentlemen have their odd notions, and we must accept them."

"I suppose so…" Miranda had given her hand to the gallant who had come to claim her for the quadrille and had promptly forgotten Lord Heston's existence.

It was strange to see him again under these circumstances. She had been as puzzled as Fanny by his sudden decision to call upon their uncle. Fanny had met him once, when he was introduced to her by Harry Lakenham, and had taken him in instant dislike. Why, then, did he wish to offer for her hand? She was deep in thought when her aunt recalled her to the matter in hand.

Mrs Shere rose to her feet. Ignoring Miranda's imploring look, she murmured something about leaving the two young people to get to know each other and left the room.

A silence fell, which his lordship made no attempt to break.

"Won't you sit down, my lord?" Miranda asked in desperation. Standing over her as he did, Lord Heston seemed to fill the room.

"Certainly, madam." Heston took a seat on the other side of the fireplace. "I imagine you can guess why I am here?"

Miranda coloured. "My uncle said that you had asked to speak to me in private. I confess I was surprised…"

She heard an ugly laugh. "Were you? You do not suppose that Lakenham's friends would allow him to contract a *mésalliance* without making some attempt to save him?"

Miranda gazed at him in stupefaction.

"Come, now! Don't play the innocent with me. Will you deny that the boy has been fool enough to promise marriage?"

Miranda found her voice at last. "What has that to do with you?" she demanded. "You are not his guardian."

"True, but I am connected with the family. The details need not concern you. It is enough for you to know that I am here on behalf of Harry's grandfather, Lord Rudyard."

The cool effrontery of this statement made Miranda burn with rage. Heston was insolence personified.

"The decision must rest with Lord Lakenham," she snapped.

"On the contrary, it rests with you. Harry has refused to give you up. Nothing his grandfather could say will alter his resolution…"

"Then, sir, you are wasting your time!"

"I think not. It is up to you to make the break. You must cry off at once. It is contemptible to take advantage of a young man's inexperience. I must appeal to your better nature…"

Miranda gave him a limpid look. "What makes you think I have one? On the contrary, I have a fancy for a title and a fortune." Anger had betrayed her into indiscretion, but she did not care. Who did this pompous creature think he was, issuing demands and insulting her with every word?

"I see!" His voice was soft, but there was an underlying note of menace. "Well…let us get down to cases…how much?"

Fury threatened to choke Miranda, but she kept her eyes upon the carpet. "La, sir, I don't see an objection to the match," she simpered. "My family is perfectly respectable—"

"I know your background," Heston snapped. "You are penniless and your uncle is in trade."

"The money cannot matter. Harry will have a handsome fortune when he comes of age." The great blue eyes peeped up at him through long dark lashes. "As to the trade...well...no one need find out. When Harry and I are wed, I shall not spread it abroad."

"Strumpet! Make no mistake, ma'am, you shall not marry him."

"Who is to stop me, sir? When Harry knows of your visit here, he may insist on elopement."

"Such a marriage would be annulled."

"But think of the scandal, my lord! And then, you know, I might present his family with an heir."

Heston did not mince his words. "The child would be a bastard. Will you saddle yourself with a burden such as that for life? I ask you again...how much?"

"I could not think of such a sordid bargain," Miranda said demurely. "With every tender hope dashed, I might go into a decline... No amount of money would be of use to me if that should happen."

"It might soothe your final moments, madam. They are like to be upon you more quickly than you realise if you do not stop this trifling."

"Threats, sir? I might have known it!" Miranda raised a hand to her brow in one of Fanny's more theatrical gestures. "Your reputation is not unknown to me, my lord. You are said to be the hardest of men, even in your dealing with the fair sex,"

"You may believe it. I have had dealings with your sort before. Every harpy in the country converges upon London in the Season, hoping to entrap some innocent boy. This time you won't succeed."

"No!" She favoured him with her sweetest smile.

"You are mistaken, sir. Harry's letters have made his sentiments clear…"

She heard a muttered curse. "Letters, too? I wonder that the lad escaped his leading-strings. You have kept them all, I take it?"

"Naturally. How could I find it in my heart to part with them? Harry is so poetical. My eyes, so he says, are like the brightest stars in the heavens, and he compares my skin with that of the softest peach."

She heard a snort of disgust.

"Hardly original, madam!"

"But most sincere!" Miranda peeped up at him again, and then wished that she had not done so. His face was dark with anger, and there was a strange glitter in his eyes. For a moment she wondered if she had gone too far, but his lordship's insults had made her reckless.

"We are wasting time," he announced. "Tell me what price you set upon your charms. Shall we say five thousand pounds?"

She managed a coquettish laugh. "Does Lord Rudyard set so little store upon his family honour?"

She was unprepared for what happened next. Heston was out of his chair in a single lithe movement. Her chin was gripped in an iron hand and the harsh dark face came close to hers.

"Amazing!" he said softly. "The face of an angel, and a heart as hard as that of any common doxy. Aye, you're a beauty, you little vixen. I suppose you must peddle your wares."

Miranda struck out sharply and caught him full across the face. The imprint of her fingers showed up clearly on his cheek, but he merely laughed. She lifted her hand again, but this time he caught her wrist with such force that she gave a cry of pain.

"Temper!" he reproved. "Let us not turn this interview into a common brawl. You would have the worst of it, I promise you. Now, madam, pray consider. Lakenham is not the only catch in London. With money you might buy a house in which you and your sister might...er...entertain without the trouble of a husband."

As the implications of his speech came home to her, Miranda flushed to the roots of her hair. She reached out blindly and caught up a heavy vase, but he was too quick for her. The pressure of his fingers forced her to put it down.

"Insulted, my dear? I had not supposed it possible. Pray do not feel obliged to throw this delightful object. Your uncle would find your behaviour somewhat eccentric."

"You are despicable," Miranda cried. "You came here under false pretences. My uncle would never have received you or allowed you to be alone with me had he not believed that you intended to make me an offer."

"Have I not just done so?" His face was bland as he resumed his seat.

"You worm! You Corinthian! How dare you suggest that way of life to my sister and myself? Words cannot express what I should like to say to you."

"True! The title of Corinthian is, you know, regarded as a compliment. Perhaps your vocabulary is a little lacking in force?" He was very much at his ease as he lounged back in his chair.

Miranda longed to wipe the sneer from his lips. "I wonder that you did not make your offer to my uncle," she said in icy tones. "You may regard him as a counterjumper, but he would soon have disabused you of the idea that I am a—"

"A lightskirt?" he supplied helpfully. "I had considered such a course, Miss Gaysford, but I had not met you then. I decided to give you the benefit of the doubt, not knowing if your uncle was aware of Lakenham's entanglement. For all I knew, you might have been some simple country miss who fancied herself in love with him."

"You do not think so now?" There was a dangerous sparkle in her eyes.

"Not for a moment." Again she heard the ugly laugh. "It is more likely that you are all in this together…your aunt…your uncle…and your sister."

Miranda felt that she must explode with rage. How she longed to crush him…to grind her heel into that mocking face. She wanted to strike at him, to wound him as he had wounded her. He would pay for these insults, no matter what the cost.

"Silent, my dear? Am I to suppose you robbed of speech? A temporary condition only, I feel sure. I am prepared to give you a little time to consider my proposition."

He rose then and strolled over to the window, apparently convinced that the outcome of this meeting would be as he wished.

Miranda's mind was racing. She should have ordered him out of the house, but she longed to pay him back in his own coin. Yet how was she to do it? Oh, if she could but see this proud and arrogant creature grovelling at her feet.

Suddenly, the solution flashed into her mind. It would be dangerous, but it was worth it just to see him squirm. For once this haughty member of the nobility would find himself at a loss. A little smile lifted the corners of her mouth, but when she looked at him her face was composed.

"You are mistaken, sir," she told him. "My aunt and uncle know nothing of this matter. They do not accompany us into Polite Society."

"I had supposed as much." Heston's sneer grew more apparent. "I wondered how you got the entrée, but I supposed there are enough impoverished gentlefolk about to introduce you at a price."

"Quite so! Alas, when one is of indifferent breeding, it is necessary to make shift as best one can." Something in her voice made him eye her with suspicion, but her expression told him nothing. "Only my sister knows of Harry's attachment to me."

"Hmm! Well, that is of little consequence. You may change your mind, I suppose."

"My sister will wonder at it. You were right in thinking that we are penniless, she and I, and it is true that our mama hopes that we shall marry well enough to restore the family fortunes."

"That, at least, is honest," he said grudgingly. "Your ambitions are no worse than those of many another in the marriage market."

"Oh, you do understand. I felt sure you would when I explained." Any member of Miranda's family could have warned Lord Heston of the danger in that charming smile, but his lordship fell into the trap.

"I may have been a little hard on you," he admitted. "My remarks were not those of a gentleman, and for that I crave your pardon."

"They are forgotten." Miranda beamed at him. "I could not take the money, sir, even had I wished to do so. How might I have come into possession of such a large sum?"

"I see that it might have been a problem." He smiled

at her, and Miranda was satisfied. He would not smile for long.

Heston resumed his seat. "Give up Lakenham," he pleaded. "With your beauty, half the men in London will offer for your hand."

Miranda dimpled. "Are you referring to my starry eyes and my peach-like skin, my lord?"

"Now you are making sport of me. Harry was a fool to put his sentiments in writing. If these young sprigs would learn to avoid the pen, much trouble might be avoided."

"How right you are! Perhaps the letters should be burned...?"

"That would be generous, indeed! Now, I do not mean to be offensive, but if you will oblige Lord Rudyard in this matter you may consider me your servant, ma'am. I will do my best to further your...er..."

"My career?" she said innocently.

"I was about to say your ambitions. I am not without influence—"

"Pray say no more!" Miranda waved his words aside with an airy gesture. "You have persuaded me. I shall give up Harry Lakenham."

He came to her then and raised her fingers to his lips. His relief was apparent.

"I had hoped that you would see the good sense of such a course," he told her warmly. "Harry will mourn his loss for a time, but the young are resilient. I shall invite him to my place in Warwickshire—"

"Before our wedding, my lord? There will not be much time."

Heston frowned. "Have you not this moment assured me that you will give him up?"

"I have, and I meant it. I was not speaking of Harry,

my lord. I have decided to make you the happiest man alive…I accept your offer of marriage.'' Modestly she kept her eyes upon her folded hands.

He was silent for so long that she thought he had misunderstood her. Then he spoke.

''I made you no such offer,'' he said quietly.

''That is not my understanding, nor my uncle's. You said all that was proper to him, I believe, when you asked his permission to address me. I must suppose that you gave him some indication of your circumstances and went into the matter of a proper settlement?''

''I see that I have underestimated you, Miss Gaysford. In answer to your question, I did not explain my circumstances to your worthy relative. There seemed to be no need—''

''Of course not! How very stupid of me! Your wealth is common knowledge, is it not? How foolish I should be to pin my hopes upon a young man not yet in possession of his fortune when I might have the use of yours. I daresay you could buy and sell Lord Rudyard. Is that not correct?''

Heston bowed. ''There is one small point which you may have overlooked. How are you to coerce me into making you my bride, or is that an indelicate question? Will you tear your gown and accuse me of rape, or have you some other plan in mind?''

''There will be no need for such dramatics, sir. We have made an excellent start. This household is at present agog to know the results of our tête-à-tête.''

''I see! I might have had second thoughts, upon reflection. Had you considered that?''

''You, my lord? I think not! You are known to be a man of firm resolution. Alas, so is my uncle. He is an

Alderman, as you must know. I fear he would advise me to sue for breach of promise.''

Miranda felt a little breathless even as she spoke those hasty words. Heston had goaded her beyond endurance, and now she had gone much further than she had intended. She had hoped only to shatter his composure, to crack that icy mask of hauteur, and to pay him out for his offensive remarks. She felt a twinge of panic. To threaten such a man was the height of folly and she knew it. She waited for the explosion which must follow.

''Breach of promise? That would never do!'' Somehow his calm words frightened her more than if he had shouted at her.

She looked up to find that he was smiling. It was more terrifying than anything she could have imagined. Though his lips were curved in a wolfish grin, there was no amusement in his eyes. They were as hard as stone. He reached out and pulled the bell-rope. Then he issued a swift order to the servant who came in answer to his summons.

''Ask Miss Gaysford's family to join us,'' he said briefly. Then he strode over to Miranda and pulled her to her feet.

''So you would try a fall with me, would you? Don't say you haven't been warned. I'll teach you a lesson you won't forget...''

His arms slid about he and he kissed her with such force that the breath was driven from her body. Miranda struggled wildly, but she was powerless against his strength. She clenched her teeth as he tried to force her lips apart, arching away from him until she thought her spine must crack.

He released her only as the door opened to admit her aunt, her uncle, and a startled Fanny.

Clamping her to his side with an arm that felt like a band of iron, he turned to face them.

"You may wish us happy," he said pleasantly. "May I present the future Lady Heston?"

Chapter Two

Amid the babel of congratulations, Miranda was conscious only of Fanny's stricken face. An imperceptible shake of her head brought her sister to her side. On the pretext of kissing her, Fanny drew her to the window-seat.

"Miranda, how could you?" she murmured brokenly. "You know I cannot marry him."

"Nor shall you! It is a fate I would not wish upon my worst enemy. Don't look so startled. I'll explain later."

Her mouth was bruised and swollen, but she managed a crooked smile as Heston came towards them with two glasses of champagne. He accepted a third from a nearby servant and turned to Alderman Shere.

That gentleman advanced towards Miranda, his rubicund face glowing with pleasure. He took her hand and drew her to her feet. Then he raised his glass.

"To the betrothed couple! My dear young people, we wish you all the happiness in the world!"

Miranda swayed. This could not be happening. Events had moved with the speed of some dreadful nightmare from which she must awaken.

Then Heston slipped a hand beneath her elbow, holding her upright by main force. "Until tomorrow, dearest," he said tenderly. "Your uncle and I have much to discuss...settlements...the announcements in the morning papers..."

Miranda gazed at him in horror. He could not mean to continue with this farce. Her eyes pleaded with him to release her...to make some excuse...but his expression was impassive.

What had she done? She must have been mad to think that she could worst him. She felt that she had opened Pandora's box, only to let out all the evils in the world. She had put herself in Heston's power, and she could think of no way to escape.

"Dearest, you look a little pale," he murmured with exaggerated concern. "It is the excitement, I expect. I shall leave you in the care of your aunt..." He pressed a chaste kiss upon her cheek.

His lips seemed to burn her skin, but she did not flinch, although she longed to jerk her head away. Heston's smile was jovial as he took her uncle by the arm and left the room.

"My dear love, what a match for you!" Mrs Shere embraced her niece.

It was all too much. Miranda burst into tears.

"There...his lordship was quite right. How thoughtful he is! You are overwrought and it is not to be wondered at. The future Lady Heston? Your mama will be beside herself with joy. It is more than even she had hoped for you."

Miranda could not speak, and her aunt began to look a little anxious. "Will you not lie upon your bed for an hour or two? Perhaps a tisane...and a hot brick for your feet?"

"Thank you...I am being foolish, I expect, but I do feel a little strangely." Miranda dabbed at her eyes.

Fanny, too, appeared to be suffering from shock. She put her arm about her sister's waist and hugged her.

"Let us go upstairs and then you may rest," she said.

"What a pair you are!" Mrs Shere regarded her nieces with a benevolent eye. "This is an occasion for rejoicing, not for tears. Ah, well, I know how close you are. You will not care to be separated, even by marriage. Off you go! I will send up your luncheon on a tray, and you shall not stir from your room until this evening."

"Miranda, what has happened?" Fanny swung round upon her twin as soon as they were alone. "I was never so shocked in all my life when I heard that you had accepted Heston. How could you betray me so?"

"I didn't," Miranda told her dully. She ached all over and was convinced that when she slipped out of her gown her arms and shoulders would be black and blue. "That brutal creature! He should be whipped at the cart's tail!"

"But...but...you are betrothed to him."

"No, I am not," Miranda snapped. "He tricked me...at least I think he did. Oh, Fanny, I am so confused...I don't know what happened. I was hoping to frighten him, you see."

Fanny gasped. "You must be mad! What did you say to him? What have you done? You lost you temper, didn't you? When you fly into alt, you never guard your tongue!"

"Nor does he. If you must know, he did not come to make you an offer at all."

"Then why did he ask to see me alone?"

"He came to buy you off. Harry has been to see his

grandfather, who will have nothing to say to the connection. Heston is Lord Rudyard's envoy, come to save his grandson from a fortune-hunting harpy who is tainted by the smell of trade.''

Fanny's face grew scarlet. ''Cruel!'' she whispered in a failing voice. ''Has he persuaded my darling to give me up?''

''No, he has not.'' The sight of her sister's distress fuelled Miranda's sense of outrage. ''You had best hear the whole of it, Fanny. You won't like it, but I feel you should know what Heston was about.''

Her recital was interrupted at frequent intervals by Fanny's moans and sobs. It was not until the letters were mentioned that she raised her head.

''There are no letters,'' she wailed. ''Harry has never written to me. When he picks up a pen, he cannot think of anything to say.''

''It is of no importance. I offered to burn the letters in any case when I offered to give him up.''

''You did that? Then my life is over...'' Fanny buried her head in the pillow and gave way to despair.

''At nineteen? Really, Fanny, where is your spirit? You cannot think I meant it?''

''Heston must have been delighted!''

''He was, but his delight lasted for no more than thirty seconds.''

''I don't understand you. How could that be?''

''His rapture was short-lived when I said that I would marry him instead—''

Fanny screamed. She was on the verge of a strong attack of hysterics, but Miranda held her hands.

''No, listen to me. I meant it only as a joke. Well, not perhaps a joke, but I could not bear his insults. I wanted to pay him back, to shock him out of his smug complacency.''

''Oh, do not say so! I cannot bear it. What folly to defy a man like that! He had not even offered for you...for me, I mean.''

''I pretended I thought he had. I even—''

''Even what? There cannot be more!''

''I'm afraid there is. I mentioned...er...an action for breach of promise.''

Fanny lay still. Her face was white to the lips. ''Then we are ruined. Have you no sense at all? Heston is the most ruthless creature alive. Have you not heard what is said of him? A threat is merely a challenge.''

''I know it now. It was a stupid thing to do, but I had no idea that he would take me at my word and move so fast. You were all in the room before I had time to think.''

''What did you expect?'' Fanny's voice was bitter. ''Did you imagine that he would flee the house with his tail between his legs? You do not know him. He will be revenged on all of us. And when the announcement appears in the *Gazette,* Harry is sure to call him out.''

Miranda was dismayed. ''I hadn't considered that. Can you get a message to him?''

''What can I say? He will think me faithless...and all we needed was a little time.''

''Ask him to call this evening. If we can contrive to leave you alone, you could explain—''

''Explain what? That I am to marry a dotard?''

''Heston isn't exactly a dotard, Fanny. He can't be more than thirty, but that is beside the point. You are not going to marry him. Can Harry keep a secret? You might tell him what has happened.''

''Tell him the whole, you mean?'' Fanny grew

thoughtful. Then her eyes began to sparkle. "He would think it a famous jest, and it would throw Lord Heston off the scent. If only he may not discover that he is betrothed to the wrong person. When Harry comes of age in December he may do as he pleases...it would give us the time we need."

"You must warn him to be careful. He must appear to be broken-hearted. Still, loving you as he does, he must wish only for your happiness."

The twins exchanged a glance of pure mischief. Then Fanny's face clouded.

"What of you?" she asked. "Can you support Lord Heston's company for a time?"

"I intend to do so. For the moment he believes that he holds the upper hand, but I shall find some way to crush his...his pretensions."

Miranda had recovered her composure and now she began to dwell with pleasure upon the delightful prospect of seeing Lord Heston grovelling at her feet, begging for mercy.

Quite how this desirable state of affairs was to be achieved she had no idea, but she would think of something.

"Do be careful, dearest," Fanny pleaded. "You are so reckless when you fly into the boughs, and Heston is a dangerous man. There is a sort of black glitter about him...about his eyes, I mean."

"His eyes are grey," Miranda said shortly. "He thinks himself a god, you know. A Corinthian, forsooth! What has that to say to anything? He may be a famous whip, and the idol of a pack of silly boys because he boxes at Gentleman Jackson's saloon, and can afford to buy his clothes from Schweitzer and Davidson. I have seen no evidence of honour or of a pleasing character in him.''

"That is what I mean. He is unscrupulous. Oh, love, I fear he means to harm you.''

"He won't so do,'' Miranda told her stoutly. "Now you must write to Harry without delay. Ellen will take it for you. There is not much time if you wish to avoid a duel.''

This terrifying thought was enough to send Fanny to her desk at once. When Ellen came up with a tray she was told to slip out with the message during the afternoon.

"I do feel hungry.'' Miranda lifted the lid from a tureen of asparagus soup and began to serve her sister.

"I don't know how you can eat.'' Fanny pushed her plate away. "This is all such a tangle. Heston cannot mean to marry you.''

"Of course not! He intends to frighten me. Would he wed the niece of a mere Alderman...a nobody? His pride would not allow it. Well, he will learn. This nobody will prick the bubble of his conceit. These chicken patties are delicious...won't you try one?''

Fanny was persuaded to nibble at a little of the food and to take a glass of wine. Then, worn out by the events of the last few hours, she fell asleep.

Miranda took up her book, but she could not read. Heston's lightning reaction to her attempt to worst him had shaken her to the core of her being.

She drew a hand across her swollen mouth, as if by doing so she could wipe out the memory of that brutal kiss.

She had never been handled so roughly in her life. The man was a monster. He must have known that she was merely teasing him, but he had not spared her.

She slipped out of bed and walked over to the mirror. Dark bruises showed up clearly on her milky skin. He would be made to pay for each one of those marks, and pay in full.

She wondered if he would go ahead with his plan to announce the betrothal in the morning papers. If so, the world would take him for a fool if he mistook the name of his bride-to-be. Then she frowned. That solution would not serve at all. She and Fanny shared the same initials.

Fanny had been christened Melissa Frances, whilst she had been named Miranda Ferne. Not for the first time she wondered what had possessed their mother to indulge in such flights of fancy.

It could not be helped. Miss M. F. Gaysford might be either of them when the name appeared in the *Morning Post* and the *Gazette*.

In any case, it was important that Heston should continue to believe that he was betrothed to Fanny. She would play out his charade for the present. Meantime, Fanny might grow out of her infatuation with Harry Lakenham. That would be the ideal solution. Then she herself could cry off from her supposed engagement, and let the world believe that she had jilted Heston.

Even so, she felt dispirited. Nothing had worked out as she had hoped.

She and Fanny had been in transports when their uncle had offered them a Season. It was true that they had enjoyed the balls, the drums, the routs, visits to the Tower to see the King's Beasts, the Grand Firework Displays and the Balloon Ascents, yet not all the efforts of Lady Medlicott, the faded gentlewoman who was their chaperon, had served to produce the type of offer upon which their mama had set her heart.

If only Mrs Gaysford had not been so taken with the story of those Gunning girls. The famous Irish beauties had taken London by storm more than fifty years earlier. Elizabeth Gunning had married the Duke of Hamilton, and Maria Gunning had become the bride of the Earl of Coventry. Mrs Gaysford could think of no reason why her own girls should not enjoy similar success.

Instead, Fanny had fallen in and out of love with a succession of young officers, dazzled by their splendid appearance in their regimentals, and not one of them a suitable match for her.

Her own heart had remained untouched. Such offers as had come their way had been from middle-aged worthies, warm enough in the pocket to overlook a lack of dowry, but scarcely calculated to arouse the interest of two lively nineteen-year-olds.

She laid aside her book as her aunt entered the room.

"That's better." Mrs Shere looked with approval at Fanny's sleeping figure. "Your sister will be more herself when she awakens. The excitement was too much for her, and it is not to be wondered at. Who could have supposed that Lord Heston would offer for her?"

Miranda managed a faint smile. "It was surprising," she agreed. "Ma'am, may I ask you something?"

"What is it, my dear?"

"Would you object if Lord Lakenham were to speak to Fanny alone...that is, if he calls upon us?"

Mrs Shere looked mystified.

"The thing is that he has conceived a *tendre* for Fanny. It is but calf-love, yet it would be kind if you could allow her to tell him herself of her betrothal."

Miranda felt ashamed of herself. It was not at all the thing to be deceiving this gentle woman who had been so kind to them.

"I don't know, Miranda. I cannot think that Lord Heston would agree to such an interview…" Mrs Shere was clearly troubled.

"Ma'am, he need not know. If Lakenham were to call, you would not turn him away?"

Mrs Shere smiled. "You know your uncle better than that, my dear. No military man is ever refused admittance to this house. Shere is only too well aware of what we owe to Wellington's armies."

Miranda kissed her aunt's cheek. "How good you are," she said warmly.

Her kiss was returned, and Mrs Shere patted her cheek. "It will be your turn next," she announced. "Then how happy your mama will be. Your uncle has sent off to her already with the news, but Fanny must write too."

"So soon?" Miranda was startled. Events were moving so fast that they were overtaking her.

"Of course, my love. She must not read it first in the *Gazette*. That would be most improper. We shall not make the announcement until she has given Fanny her blessing. You had best wake her. Were you not to go to the play tonight?"

"I think we should cry off," Miranda told her. "I doubt if Fanny will be up to it."

"You are right. A quiet evening at home would be best. I will send a message to Lady Medlicott, and your uncle will be pleased. He wishes to speak to Fanny about arrangements for her marriage."

Her parting words did nothing to reassure Miranda. She was becoming entangled in a web from which it was growing more and more difficult to free herself. At least she had ensured that Fanny would be at home if Harry came in answer to her summons.

* * *

Later that evening she and Fanny walked into the dining-room, dressed alike in pale blue muslin. Alderman Shere greeted them with a beaming smile.

"You are both in looks tonight," he announced. "Alike as two peas in a pod! I'm blessed if I know how Lord Heston could tell you one from the other."

Miranda stiffened. It was merely one of their uncle's endearing jokes, but it was uncomfortably close to the truth.

"Well, well," he continued. "Come and sit you down. We have much to celebrate. Fanny, you are a lucky girl. I confess you might have knocked me down with a feather when his lordship called on me. The finest catch in London, and he has offered for you."

Fanny's enchanting smile peeped out. She dimpled as he chucked her under the chin.

"That's a good girl," he said approvingly. "Those sparkling eyes tell me all I need to know. Swept off his feet, was he? My dear, I hope he will make you happy. I was a little worried at first, if the truth be known. I had heard him spoken of as high in the instep and a cold fish, but you have not found him so, I imagine."

His eyes twinkled as a blush rose to Fanny's cheeks.

"Nay, I won't tease you further. Now you shall take a glass of wine." He signalled to the footman and sat down.

Though not as wealthy as many of his friends, the Alderman kept a good table, and prided himself upon the excellence of his cook.

He made short work of a dish of mushroom fritters, followed by a slice or two of tongue braised in Madeira wine. This was followed by a serpent of mutton with green peas. A succulent pigeon pie was waved aside in favour of a curd pudding.

To Miranda, the meal seemed endless. She looked across at Fanny and frowned a warning. Her twin was trying without success to hide a feeling of suppressed excitement. Miranda hoped that her aunt and uncle would put it down to the supposed betrothal.

She took a little of the delicately flavoured Floating Island pudding. It was one of her favourites, but tonight she found it tasteless. She sighed with relief when Mrs Shere withdrew, leaving the Alderman to his port.

"Aunt, the drawing-room feels so warm. May I open the windows?"

"Certainly, my dear. On a night like this we shall not take a chill."

Miranda threw open the long French doors and walked on to the terrace with Fanny by her side.

"Will Harry come tonight?" she murmured in an undertone.

Fanny nodded. "He told Ellen that he would. Oh, this is famous!"

"Is it? I don't like to deceive our aunt and uncle."

Fanny pouted. "You haven't changed your mind already? You will go ahead with our plan?"

"I won't fail you," Miranda said with some asperity. "There is the door-knocker. It must be Harry."

As Fanny disappeared into the drawing-room, Miranda pressed her fingers to her burning cheeks. What on earth was she to do?

For a moment she was tempted to make a clean breast of the whole, in spite of her promise to her sister. Yet it could serve no useful purpose. Reproaches would be heaped upon the twins from their mama, to say nothing of the humiliation which must fall upon her relatives. She was forced to admit it...she was caught in a trap of her own making.

When the door opened to admit Harry Lakenham and his friend, John Helmsley, both girls made their curtsies. Then Miranda walked over to the spinet. "Aunt, shall I play for you?" she asked.

"Would you dearest? That would be pleasant, and if Mr Helmsley would be kind enough to turn the music for you…? Lord Lakenham, I fear I am sitting in a draught. Might I ask you to close the window a little? Fanny will explain the catch."

Miranda threw her aunt a look of gratitude as Fanny and her lover moved out to the terrace. They were gone for so long that Mrs Shere grew agitated.

Miranda looked up at John Helmsley. "Will you forgive me, sir?" she said. "I am a little tired tonight."

She closed the instrument and walked towards the window. As she peered into the night she caught a glimpse of Fanny's gown, pale against the darkness of the shrubbery. Harry Lakenham and her sister were locked in each other's arms.

Miranda walked towards them. "Are you quite mad?" she hissed. "You will ruin everything."

Harry seized her hand and kissed it. "Thank you!" he said in fervent tones. "You have saved us!"

"I shall not be able to do so if you continue to behave so foolishly. For heaven's sake, take care, my lord. Don't forget that you have your part to play in this."

Miranda grasped Fanny's arm and led her sister back indoors. They were followed by Harry who was striving to give the appearance of a rejected lover.

"Dear boy!" Mrs Shere said fondly. "You will not desert us, even though Fanny is to wed? You are always welcome here, you know."

Harry sighed, but his eyes were dancing, and Miranda took him to task at once.

"Do you take your leave," she urged in an aside. "You look like the cat with its paw in a pot of cream."

Obediently he signalled to John Helmsley and they moved towards the door. There he blew her a kiss behind her aunt's back, laughing as she frowned at him.

"Have I missed our guests?" The Alderman walked through from the dining-room. "You should have called me, wife."

"They could not stay, my love."

The Alderman beckoned Fanny to his side. "Lord Heston agrees that we must wait to hear from your mama before the announcement appears, but the world will learn of your good fortune before the week is out. Don't trouble your head about settlements and so forth. I have undertaken to discuss those with him. You will not find him ungenerous, I believe."

Fanny nodded as he beamed at her. Then he settled himself more comfortably in his chair, legs planted firmly apart, with his plump little hands resting on his knees.

"There is one other thing," he continued. "You are not to trouble your head about the cost of bride-clothes and the other female fripperies which you'll need. Those shall be my gift to you. We shall send you off in style."

Fanny looked uncomfortable, but she murmured her thanks and kissed him, colouring as she did so.

"No need to be embarrassed about it," he told her kindly. "I could wish I might do more, but sadly, dowries are beyond my means—"

"Sir, you have been more than generous," Miranda broke in swiftly. "You have your own boys to consider. Is not George to transfer from a line regiment?"

Her uncle nodded. "I must set up Frederick, too, when he is done with Oxford…"

"You must be very proud of them."

"Aye! I want to give them a better start than I had myself." He looked across at her aunt. "Still, we haven't done so badly, Emma, have we?" A look of affection passed between them, and Miranda sprang up to kiss them both.

How unjust it was of Heston to sneer at these good people. They were more honourable than he would ever be. Her determination to humiliate him grew even stronger as she looked at their two lined faces.

She said as much to Fanny when they were alone.

"I hope you know what you are about," her twin said doubtfully. "Harry was delighted. He says that Heston needs a set-down, but I cannot help but fear for you. I wish that you may not get yourself into a scrape."

Miranda stared at her in disbelief. "I am already in a scrape," she cried. "I should never have agreed to take your place."

"Thank heavens you did so. Had Heston insulted me as he did you, I should have fainted on the spot. I did not tell Harry the whole of it, but he was already planning an elopement."

"Fanny, you would not! Think of the scandal...the disgrace! It would break Mama's heart, and my uncle would blame himself for not taking better care of you."

"Well, it need not come to that if you will but keep Heston occupied." Fanny drew her bedgown over her head and began to tie the ribbons of her nightcap. "He must not know the truth until we are safely wed, so do take care not to betray yourself."

"Heston cannot wish for my company," Miranda said with decision. "I doubt if he would consider it amusing to take me about." In that she was mistaken.

* * *

Both girls were sitting by the window on the following morning when a high-perch phaeton drew up at their door. Heston threw the reins to his tiger, and ran lightly up the steps.

Miranda felt sick with apprehension, but apart from her heightened colour there was little to betray that emotion when Heston was shown into the room.

She took her sister's hand as they rose to greet him. She and her twin were dressed alike in white sprigged muslin with blue ribands in their hair. This was the test. Would he be able to tell them apart?

To her astonishment, he did not hesitate. He strode straight towards her and took her hand.

"My love!" he uttered in throbbing accents. "An hour apart from you seems like a lifetime..." He drew her to him, kissed her fingers, and pressed a chaste salute upon her cheek.

She longed to free herself, but with Mrs Shere's indulgent eyes upon her she was forced to submit to his caresses.

"Make haste, my love," her aunt urged gently. "If Lord Heston hopes to take you for a drive, he will not wish to keep his horses standing."

"Quite right, ma'am!" Heston bowed to indicate his pleasure at her understanding. "Sadly, the phaeton is unsuitable for more than one passenger, but you have no objection to my taking your niece to the Park?"

"Of course not! We have promised ourselves a shopping trip to Bond Street." She glanced at Fanny. "You will enjoy that, will you not, my dear?"

Fanny's smile of agreement was unconvincing. She had nothing to say either to her aunt or to Lord Heston.

"Miss Gaysford, have you seen the Elgin Marbles? They are very fine, I assure you. Perhaps on another occasion you may care to accompany us to the British Museum?''

Fanny murmured an inarticulate reply, which caused her aunt to stare, but she was saved from further embarrassment when Miranda reappeared.

''Charming! Quite charming!'' His lordship put up his quizzing-glass to inspect the neat little figure who stood before him. ''How well that shade of bronze becomes you! The bonnet, too! It is quite a triumph! I shall be the envy of every man in town.''

''You are too kind, my lord.'' Miranda gritted out the words through clenched teeth, feeling rather as if she were a slave on sale in an Arab market.

''Not at all! My words come from the heart!'' With a bow to the two ladies, Heston gripped her elbow and ushered her from the room.

He handed Miranda up into the phaeton, and dismissed his tiger. ''I shall not need you, Jem.''

Miranda was at a loss to account for the astonishment on the lad's face, but Heston did not appear to notice it. He took the reins and turned the splendid pair of chestnuts south in the direction of Piccadilly.

That thoroughfare was crowded, but, as Miranda soon realised, his lordship was capable of driving to an inch. With careless ease he avoided the press of hackney carriages, a stately landaulet, and a smart barouche.

He stopped for a crossing-sweeper, moved on and then was forced to swerve as a curricle, clearly in inexperienced hands, shot out from the southern end of Bond Street.

Heston did not hesitate. He was past the plunging horses in an instant as Miranda gasped.

''My apologies, ma'am. I trust I did not frighten you.

The town is overfull with the arrival of the Allies for the Gala Celebrations.''

"You did not," Miranda told him with more dignity than truth. Her knuckles were white as she gripped the side of the vehicle.

"Liar!" he said smoothly.

"Did you seek my company merely to insult me?" Miranda's face was pale. The day was warm and the stench in the streets was overpowering. She began to wish that she had provided herself with a nosegay to counteract the vile odours, but she had not done so. The near-collision had disturbed her, and suddenly she felt sick.

"You will feel better when we reach the Park," Heston predicted. "London can be trying on a hot day. Bear up, my dear. When we are settled in Warwickshire, I shall not insist that you come to town again."

"Warwickshire?" Miranda was perplexed.

"My country seat. Had you forgot? With your children about you, you will not yearn for the pleasures of the capital."

"My children?"

"Naturally. Why do you look surprised? I am hoping for a full quiver, as the saying goes. At least four boys and perhaps a girl or two. I won't promise to keep you company in the Season, but you will not mind that."

Miranda eyed him with acute dislike.

Chapter Three

"My love, must you give me dagger-looks?" Heston continued smoothly. "Have I said something to offend you?"

Miranda did not answer him.

"Lost your tongue? You surprise me! Yesterday you had so much to say. Must I crave your pardon for being so indelicate as to mention the main purpose of our marriage? I had not thought your sensibilities quite so nice. You are not, I must hope, of a frigid disposition?"

"No, I am not! How dare you speak of such things to me?" Miranda cried hotly.

"There must be no misunderstanding between husband and wife." Heston's tone was sententious. "The physical side is, after all, an important part of marriage." He looked down at her then, assessing her from head to toe, and Miranda flushed to the roots of her hair, feeling naked beneath his gaze.

"There! I have put you to the blush. How unforgivable of me!" With a cynical grin his lordship drove his phaeton into Hyde Park. "Do you think you could manage a smile or two, my dear? My friends must not be led to believe that we have quarrelled at this early stage in our relationship.''

Miranda tried to compose herself. Anger threatened to overwhelm her, but her voice was calm as she replied, ''I shall play my part, my lord.''

''Of course you will, and very prettily, too.'' Heston bowed and smiled as he slowed the horses to a walking pace, and threaded his way past other carriages.

Thankful to find his attention diverted from herself, Miranda looked about her. She was not too green to realise that the passers-by included the cream of Polite Society. She saw a look of surprise on several faces, and wondered why everyone was staring so. She was not long kept in ignorance.

A cavalier reined in beside them and swept off his hat.

''Adam, you sly dog! I might have known...''

''Might have known what?'' his lordship answered mildly.

''That you are not the misogynist we suspected. Here you are, with the loveliest girl in London—''

''Ah, yes. May I present my cousin to you, my dear? This is Thomas Frant.''

Miranda was disarmed by the cheerful smile with which the young man greeted her. He was short and stocky, but he had a pleasant open face. A dusting of freckles across his snub nose emphasised a pair of bright blue eyes.

Miranda gave him her hand.

''I won't say I'm surprised,'' Thomas told her gaily. ''Who could resist you, ma'am?''

''Who, indeed? My love, you have made yet another conquest.'' Heston gathered up the reins and prepared to move on, apparently oblivious of the effect of his tender words upon his cousin.

Thomas caught him by the arm. "Adam, you ain't thrown the handkerchief at last?" he said in awed tones.

"You may believe it!" Heston replied. "As you said yourself, my dear Thomas, who could resist such beauty?" He gazed down fondly at Miranda as he spoke.

"Good God, Adam!" Thomas was brought to his senses by the cool expression in his cousin's eyes. "Beg pardon, ma'am. I meant no offence...but Adam ain't in the petticoat line, not as a rule, I mean."

"You have said quite enough. In confidence, Thomas, Miss Gayford and I are recently betrothed. You will keep it to yourself for the moment...?"

"Of course! Of course!" Thomas was so astonished that he grabbed sharply at his reins, causing his mount to jib. "Not a word! You may rely on me." He moved away.

"I hope we may," Miranda said in scathing tones. "Did we not agree, my lord, that no one was to know of our betrothal, until my mother had been informed?"

"You feel she may object? Oh dear, I hope not. You see, Thomas, charming though he is, is possibly the worst gabster in London. He is incapable of keeping a secret."

"You knew that, and yet you told him?"

"A lamentable oversight on my part...due, perhaps, to my longing to acquaint the world of our happiness. Will you forgive me, dearest?"

Miranda's anger threatened to overcome her. Heston was taunting her, utterly sure of himself. He would soon learn that he had met his match.

"Of course!" She smiled up at him. "I am so happy

to know that you care nothing for the opinion of the *ton.*'

Heston raised an eyebrow. "Would you care to explain yourself?"

"I was thinking only of the possible consequences to you, of such a connection, sir. I'm sure you understand me. The betrothal of such a notable Corinthian as yourself to a mere nobody, moreover one who is related to a cit? I fear it may have a sad effect on your position in society."

Heston laughed aloud. "If you believe that, you will believe anything. My credit will survive the worst *mésalliance.* I am known to be eccentric, and I do as I please, as I hope to prove to you."

Miranda turned her head away. Yet again this unpleasant creature had managed to have the last word. She was still fuming when they were hailed by a well-known voice.

"Lakenham, by all that's holy!" Heston drew his carriage to a halt. "How are you, my dear boy? What a surprise to find you here! I had not thought that you rose till noon."

"I could not sleep." Viscount Lakenham was much in danger of overacting, Miranda thought to herself. She wished him elsewhere with fervour as he looked at her with a mournful expression.

The boy was a fool, and Heston must be sure to see through his pretence of abject despair. She stole a fleeting glance at her companion, to find him all concern.

"Liverish this morning, are you?" Heston said cheerfully. "Take my advice, my lad, and change your wine merchant."

Lakenham threw him an angry look and was about to address Miranda.

"No, you shall not delay us," Heston protested. "Miss Gaysford finds the heat oppressive. I have promised to take her home. My regards to your mother." He whipped up his horses and left the Park by the West Gate.

"Harry looks somewhat subdued," he remarked idly as they rejoined the traffic in Piccadilly.

"Are you surprised, my lord?"

"I had not thought to see him so dejected merely because you are in my company. You have not found his jealousy excessive?"

"Sir, he knows the truth. My aunt allowed me to tell him of our...of our betrothal."

"You assured me yesterday that she was unaware of Harry's infatuation."

"She was...but my sister explained to her that it was but calf-love, scarce worth a mention. We...I thought it best that he should learn the news from me."

"Hoping to save his skin, my dear? You may be easy in your mind. I shall not allow him to call me out. In any case, I doubt if he would be so foolish."

"You are a marksman too, Lord Heston? How very splendid! You put all my acquaintance in the shade..."

"Ah, yes, but then your acquaintance is not large, and, dare I say it, a little questionable?"

Miranda did not rise to the bait, though it took a supreme effort not to do so. She gave him an innocent look, thinking as she did so that if she were a man she would have called him out herself for that remark.

"Quite so!" she murmured. "But now that I am to rise in the world, your friends will be mine, I trust. It can only be an improvement." Her tone left him in no doubt that she did not think so for a moment.

To her fury he laughed again.

"Well done!" he said. "A palpable hit, my dear. I must learn not to lead with my chin when sparring with you."

Miranda did not trouble to reply. Instead, she gazed at the passing scene which never failed to fascinate her. Piemen shouting their wares, flower-sellers and a group of quarrelling jarveys striking out at the beggars who barred their way, all contrasted sharply with the fashionable exquisites who lounged along the pavements. Women dressed in the height of fashion lounged in their barouches, accompanied in many cases by their beaux, riding alongside.

Heston was hailed again and again, and Miranda found herself subjected to many a hard stare, both from the occupants of the carriages and their companions.

"You seem to be creating something of a stir today, my lord," she murmured wickedly.

"I cannot claim the credit for that. Much of it is due to you. Did I not say that every man in London must envy me? Think what a furore you will arouse at the play tonight."

"I do not intend to visit the play this evening," she told him stiffly.

"No? What a disappointment for your sister and your aunt! They were looking forward to it."

"You asked my aunt?" Miranda was astonished. She had not supposed that Lord Heston would care to be seen with someone so far beneath him in status.

"Naturally...and your uncle, too. You must not think me lacking in courtesy, my dearest. Sadly the Alderman has another engagement, but your aunt felt free to accept my invitation."

Miranda's mouth set in a mutinous line.

"I do not care to go."

"But you will, my dear, you will. That is, unless you decide to plead the headache. That would be unworthy of you. I had not supposed you capable of cowardice."

Miranda's eyes flashed and her chin went up, but they had arrived at their destination, and she had no opportunity to utter the angry words which sprang to her lips.

Heston handed his reins to the groom who came down the steps towards them and handed Miranda down from the phaeton with great solicitude.

"Until tonight, then?" Oblivious of the passers-by he saluted her with a tender kiss upon her cheek and sprang back into the carriage.

Miranda stalked indoors without a backward glance, to find that Fanny and Mrs Shere had returned from their shopping expedition. The hall was littered with bandboxes and parcels.

"Did you enjoy your drive, my dear?" Mrs Shere did not wait for an answer. "We have been so busy you would scarce believe it! Pray come upstairs and see what we have bought for you. How fortunate that you and your sister are the same size and colouring. What becomes one of you must suit the other…"

Still chattering, she led the girls upstairs.

"See now, is this not delightful?" She held up a gown of sea-green gauze over an underslip of satin.

"It looks expensive," Miranda said doubtfully.

"It was, but your uncle will not care for that. He is not a penny-pincher, and we must consider what is due to Lord Heston." She began to rifle through the other boxes, drawing out filmy undergarments, long kid gloves, silk stockings and handkerchiefs trimmed with Valenciennes lace.

Fanny was in raptures when she found herself the

proud possessor of a matching gown. She flung her arms about her aunt and kissed her.

"There, it is little enough, my dear girl. It will cheer you up, I hope, and your uncle likes to see you dressed alike. You both look so charmingly together…"

Miranda tried to smile, but such generosity served only to depress her spirits further. She longed to end the deception, but she could not find the courage to do so.

Fanny was quick to sense her mood.

"Was it very bad?" she asked when Mrs Shere had left them. "Surely Heston did not continue to insult you?"

"What makes you suppose that he will give up now? His lordship is enjoying himself, knowing that I cannot escape."

"Harry said that he had seen you. We met him in Bond Street."

"Fanny, you must speak to him. He should not have sought us out. You are fond of telling me that Heston is a dotard, but he is far from being feeble-minded, I assure you. Harry's manner was such as to make him question me later, and should he ever suspect that we have changed places…"

"Harry thought he gave a very good performance as a rejected lover," Fanny said defensively.

"Perhaps he should be on the stage! It would be better if he returned to his grandfather for a time. He is sure to give us away."

"No, I won't be parted from him!"

"Very well, but you must both be more discreet. You can't be seen together. Lord Heston intends that Harry shall sever all connection with our family. It won't serve if he thinks that you are now the object of his attentions."

"I suppose I may meet him in company?" Fanny sulked.

"If you do so, pray take care! Last evening, for example, if anyone but myself had found you in the garden, all would have been lost. I won't go on with this charade if you don't play your part."

"I thought you wanted to punish Heston."

"I do, but you must help me. The insults were addressed to you, you know."

"Oh, very well!" Fanny dismissed the matter from her mind, and began to peacock round the room with a shawl of Norwich silk thrown about her shoulders.

"There is another thing," Miranda added quietly. "I cannot like all this expense. Uncle cannot well afford it."

"Of course he can! Did he not insist? And Aunt Emma enjoyed herself so much this morning. She tells me that she has always longed for a daughter. I don't see how you can stop her."

"We might mention that Mama would wish to be consulted."

Fanny stared. "Have you written to her?"

"I have not," Miranda said with a heavy heart. "I don't know what to say."

"Well, Uncle will think it strange of you. You might mention that Heston has offered, and that you hope for her blessing. You may be sure it will be given. Nothing could be more certain."

"And what then?"

"Why ask me? You were so set on getting back at Heston. Surely you have some plan?"

"I have not, and well you know it. As far as I can tell I am simply getting deeper into the mire."

"You'll think of something," Fanny told her comfortably. "After all, you always do. We have been in scrapes before and you have got us out of them."

Miranda was not attending. "Fanny, don't you find it strange that Heston never mistakes us one for the other?" she said thoughtfully. "He came to me at once this morning."

"Nor does Harry," her sister replied. "Have we not always found it so in men who care for us? Oh, I see what you mean..." Fanny looked startled.

"Exactly so! Heston must be the exception. Do you suppose that he can have noticed the mole behind my ear? It is the only difference."

"He must have done. He seems to see everything. I must confess he frightens me. His eyes are so penetrating...they seem to look into my mind."

"I hope you are wrong. I would not have him know what is in my mind."

"Let us forget him," Fanny cried impatiently. "Shall we wear our new gowns tonight?"

"That is Aunt's intention, I believe."

"She was pleased to be included in the invitation. She refused at first, you know, but Lord Heston can be most persuasive. He insisted..."

"And why not, pray? The world may consider that Aunt Emma married beneath her, but her birth, like our own, is unexceptionable."

Fanny began to giggle. "I love you when you get upon your high ropes, dearest. Have you told Lord Heston of our worthy connections?"

"No, I have not!" Miranda snapped. "I intend to make him squirm. Let us see if he can carry off this affront to his consequence."

She looked at her sister and dimpled. "If I thought that Aunt Emma would permit it, I should try to look as vulgar as possible, with plumes, and feathers, and gauds. I should even paint my face..."

"Miranda, you wouldn't?" Fanny was shocked. "Aunt would send you to wash it off."

"I know." It was with regret that Miranda abandoned the idea. "But Heston need not think that he will find me biddable, hanging upon his every word as if it were...were the laws of the Medes and Persians..."

"I expect he has never heard of the Medes and Persians and nor have I. What have they to do with anything?"

"Nothing, love. Let us go down. We shall be late for luncheon."

She was thoughtful as she toyed with a dish of buttered eggs, and took so little of a proffered platter of cold meats and salad that her aunt was moved to protest.

"My dear, this will not do! If you go on in this way you will be naught but skin and bone, and that will not please his lordship."

Obediently, Miranda allowed herself to be helped to another slice of beef from the sirloin, and forced herself to take a little of the Celerata cream which followed.

At last Mrs Shere rose from the table, announcing that she planned to rest for an hour or two, and indicating that the twins should follow her example.

"But, Aunt, we intended to go to Richardson's, to change our library books," said Fanny. "That is, if you have no objection."

"Very well, but you shall take the carriage, and Ellen must go with you. Now do not dawdle about, my dears. I believe that you should lie upon your beds for at least an hour before you dress this evening."

Both girls kissed her and went upstairs to put on their bonnets.

"I could wish that Aunt did not treat us as a couple of dowagers," Fanny grumbled. "Where is the harm in walking on such a pleasant day?"

"I expect she was thinking only of our comfort. In any case, it will give you more time to find another of those dreadful Gothic romances." Miranda's eyes twinkled. Fanny's passion for romantic fiction had made her the butt of their elder brother's jokes for years.

She was too preoccupied with her own search for something to read to pay much attention to Fanny when they reached the library. She had taken out much of the stock already, including *Evelina* by Fanny Burney, and the works of Samuel Richardson. Her eye fell upon a copy of *Tom Jones,* but then she decided against it. Aunt might not approve. The book was considered too explicit to be thought suitable reading for an unmarried girl, even though the author, Mr Fielding, was a magistrate.

Poetry? No, she was no admirer of Lord Byron, though his works were all the rage. *Ivanhoe* looked promising, and there could be no objection to any of the works of Sir Walter Scott. She would lose herself in the story, and it would help her to forget her present troubles.

"I will take this," she said decisively "Have you found anything, Fanny?"

There was no reply. Fanny had disappeared. Miranda was untroubled, thinking that her sister had wandered into another part of the shop. Then she saw Ellen. Their abigail was standing by a deep recess and her furtive expression warned Miranda that something was amiss.

As she approached she heard the murmur of voices. Anger threatened to consume her as she recognised that of Harry Lakenham.

"You may wait in the carriage, Ellen," she said sharply. As their maid scurried away, Miranda walked towards the lovers.

They were standing in the shadows, oblivious of all about them. Harry's arm was about her sister's waist and her head was resting on his shoulder.

"I see now why you were so anxious to change your library book, Fanny. When did you make this assignation?" Miranda's tone was so cold that Fanny fired up at once.

"It is not an assignation," she cried hotly.

"What else would you call a clandestine meeting? Did I not beg you most particularly to take care?"

"It is all my fault," Harry intervened. "I persuaded Fanny when we met this morning. Do not be cross with her. It is I who deserve your censure."

Miranda ignored him. "You had best return to the carriage, Fanny, but before you go I have something to say to both of you. If Lord Lakenham appears at the play tonight, I shall not help you further."

"You would go back upon your word?" Fanny stared at her in consternation.

"You have not kept yours. I mean it, Fanny. I will put an end to this ridiculous charade."

Pausing only at the counter to record the loan of her book, she marched out of the shop.

Aware of the coachman on the box, Miranda did not trust herself to say more until they reached the privacy of their bedchamber. Then she swung round upon her twin.

"How could you deceive me so?" she demanded. "Have you no sense at all? Suppose Lord Heston had seen you?"

"There was no danger of that." Fanny's face was

sullen. "Harry said that he was gone to Tattersall's to look at bloodstock. You do not suppose that he spends his time in libraries, do you?"

"I have no idea how he spends his time, nor do I care, but he is not blind. You know how gossip travels among the *ton*. Any of his friends might have seen the pair of you together."

"It was unlikely," Fanny protested. "Harry is no reader, nor are his friends…"

"Then how strange that he should enter a library…it must give rise to comment."

"Suppose it did? I am supposed to be you. Heston could not take exception…"

Miranda eyed her twin in disbelief. "You think not? Heston would no more countenance a match with you than with me."

"He can't forbid a mere friendship. Harry might have sought me out to comfort him for his loss…"

"And we all know what that can lead to. You put me out of all patience with you. I meant what I said. If Harry appears tonight, you may say goodbye to all your hopes."

"He won't," Fanny sulked. "You made it clear that he must not, though I do not see how you can stop him."

"You don't? I could cry off from this supposed engagement, Fanny, having mistaken my own heart. It happens every day, and it must come to that in the end."

"Not yet, I beg of you!" Fanny began to whimper. "I will be good, you'll see."

"Very well, but don't be such a watering-pot." Miranda looked at the clock. "I shall take Aunt's advice and rest for an hour. You had best do the same. I suppose you had no time to choose another book?"

In silence Fanny held out *The Mysteries of Udolpo* for her sister's inspection.

Miranda smiled. ''That will do very well,'' she said. ''Better to frighten yourself with that than with thoughts of Heston's anger if he should discover how we have deceived him.'' She picked up her own book and was soon deep in the story.

Before she knew it, it was time to dress and not all her worries could quite destroy her pleasure in her new gown. It was a perfect fit, and over the slender column of the under-dress the pale green gauze whispered softly to the ground, caught at the bosom with matching ribbons.

She gazed at the mirror-image of herself as Fanny twisted and turned before the glass.

''Have you ever seen anything so beautiful?'' Fanny whispered reverently. ''We have never worn anything so expensive!''

Miranda grimaced. ''We did not pay for the gowns, I must remind you.''

''I know it, but may we not enjoy our finery just for tonight? Oh, if Harry could but see me now...''

''You must pray that he does not,'' her sister told her sternly. She frowned at Fanny and was about to repeat her warning when Mrs Shere came to find them.

''Why, Aunt, how fine you are this evening!'' Fanny caught the older woman by the shoulders and turned her round. ''You will put us in the shade...''

Mrs Shere shook her head in a disclaimer, though she was pleased. Her dark grey silk was trimmed at the neck with rows of French lace, and she carried a shawl of the same material. The garment was beautifully cut, and it did much to disguise the outlines of her ample figure.

''Nonsense, my dear, you are too kind. I admit that,

before we married, your mama and I were used to have
a fondness for the latest modes, but I have grown stout,
I fear.''

''No, ma'am, Fa—my sister does not exaggerate.''
Miranda caught herself before she made a fatal slip.
''You look charmingly...that gown is so becoming...''

She felt that she was babbling in fright. She had come
so close to giving herself away. Would Aunt Emma notice?

''Well, we owe it to Lord Heston to appear at our
best,'' Mrs Shere told her. ''Most certainly he cannot
find fault with either of you, my dears. I have not seen
you look so well before. The gowns were a good choice,
were they not?''

''They were,'' Miranda kissed her warmly. ''I hope
that our uncle will be pleased with the results of his
generosity.''

''He is gone out to dine,'' her aunt announced. ''Lord
Heston invited him, you know, but he felt that he owed
it to his lordship's consequence to refuse. I was a little
undecided on my own account, but Heston insisted.''

''And why should he not?'' Miranda cried. ''We may
not be of noble birth, not persons of consequence, but
we have some pretensions of gentility, and our family is
respectable.''

''Of course, my love! You must not think me insen-
sible of our connections, though my family has cast me
off...''

''More fool them!'' Miranda cried inelegantly.
''There are no better people alive than you and my un-
cle... To spurn you just because you married for love...?
It is past all bearing.''

''It is an old story, and we shall think no more about
it at this present time,'' Mrs Shere said firmly. ''Now,

my dears, we must go down. We have not allowed ourselves much time to dine, and Lord Heston will be here
at eight.''

Again Miranda felt slight panic, but she crushed it
firmly. Why should she be afraid of Heston? The afternoon had given her time for reflection, and all that was
necessary was to treat him with the civility due to his
position. Sadly, he had the most unfortunate habit of
throwing her off balance with a word or the lift of an
eyebrow. His spurious tenderness in the company of others was hateful to her. She knew his true opinion of her
character.

He might have made a fortune on the boards, she
thought scornfully. His acting rivalled that of Edmund
Kean.

When he arrived she looked at him askance, though
honesty compelled her to admit that no fault could be
found with his appearance. He was dressed *de rigueur*
in a black swallow-tailed coat and satin knee-breeches
with silk stockings. A splendid waistcoat of watered silk
softened the severity of his garb, but apparently he had
no other modish leanings. The bosom of his shirt was
unadorned by a frill.

Miranda stiffened as he bent to salute her cheek. She
turned away, but he stayed her with a hand upon her
arm.

''My darling, this betrothal gift is unworthy of your
beauty, but I beg that you will accept it.'' He handed
her a long flat box.

Miranda did not attempt to open it, so he took it from
her and threw back the lid to reveal a fine string of
perfectly matched pearls.

Mrs Shere gasped and Fanny's eyes grew round.

"I trust the necklace pleases you," his lordship murmured. "Will you wear it tonight?"

Miranda looked at the gleaming pearls. Their sheen was such that they seemed like living things, sending her a warning.

Chapter Four

Miranda closed the lid of the box with a snap.

"My lord, you are most generous," she said smoothly. "But I cannot wear the pearls. We are not yet officially betrothed. My mama has not given her consent."

"Dearest, you must not refine too much upon the matter." Mrs Shere looked startled. "Nothing is more certain than that she will give you her blessing..."

"Even so..." Miranda would not be swayed.

"Try them at least," his lordship pleaded. "Here, let me clasp them about your neck." He caught up the necklace and led her to a mirror, turning her to face it, his hands resting lightly on her shoulders.

"There!" He fastened the clasp, his fingers lingering upon her skin.

Miranda flushed as she looked at his dark face beside her own. Although his hands were cool they seemed to burn her flesh. She shuddered. There was a curious expression in his heavy-lidded eyes, and it turned her knees to water. She caught her breath.

"Very pretty!" To her relief her voice sounded calm. "Another time perhaps, my lord?"

"As you wish, my dear." Heston returned the pearls to their box and laid it on the sofa-table.

He did not speak to her again until they reached the theatre, reserving his attention for her aunt. That lady answered him politely, but she was quick to admonish Miranda when his lordship spoke to Fanny, careful of her comfort as he led her to a seat with a good view of the stage.

"Dearest, that was not well done of you to refuse to wear his lordship's gift." Mrs Shere sounded reproachful as she drew Miranda aside.

"I'm sorry, Aunt, but I could not think it right. It must have given rise to comment, and all eyes are upon us as it is."

Miranda spoke no more than the truth. The appearance of the twins with their aunt in Lord Heston's box had resulted in a buzz of speculation from all parts of the theatre. They were the cynosure of all eyes, and she felt ready to sink with embarrassment as lorgnettes were raised and quizzing glasses levelled in their direction.

Lord Heston seated himself beside her. In her opinion he was much too close, and for one awful moment she thought he intended to lay a casual arm along the back of her chair. Surely he could not be so lost to all sense of propriety?

"My darling, I trust that you are perfectly comfortable?" he enquired in a solicitous tone, which did not deceive her for a second.

A sharp retort rose to Miranda's lips, but she bit back the angry words, aware that her aunt must overhear her.

Heston smiled, knowing that he could taunt her with impunity, and that she was powerless to reply.

She turned her attention to the stage, but later she could recall neither the title of the piece, nor the names

of the players. The presence of the man beside her filled
her mind to the exclusion of all else. What had she done?

It was all very well to promise herself that she would
pay him back for all his insults, but his reaction to her
attempt to worst him had been both swift and unexpected.

What could he hope to gain by taking her at her word?
She stole a glance at him to find his eyes upon her. His
sardonic gaze held her own and she felt her colour rising.

"Puzzled, my dear?" he said gently.

"Not at all, my lord. The piece has a simple plot."
She pretended to misunderstand him, but she saw the
flash of white teeth in the semi-darkness as he laughed.

"Has it? You must tell me about it later...it is not
perfectly clear to me." He lapsed into silence once more,
leaving Miranda to her own thoughts.

They were not pleasant. Not for the first time she felt
a stab of panic. Matters had gone much further than she
had intended. It had not occurred to her that Heston
would be so quick to call her bluff, but who could have
supposed that this haughty creature would insist on a
betrothal, however false his intentions? And then to appear with her in public, and to offer distinguishing attention to her sister and her aunt? It was not to be borne,
but for the moment she could see no way to extricate
herself from her predicament.

During the interval, her composure was severely tried
as Heston's friends descended upon the box. Miranda
knew one or two of them by sight, and also by reputation, but neither she nor her sister had been introduced
to them.

His lordship was quick to remedy the omission, and
Miranda found herself the subject of a number of spec-
ulative glances, especially from the ladies.

"Is she Heston's latest flirt, do you suppose?" The play was about to resume, and Miranda heard the careless words as the door to the box was closing.

Fiery colour stained her cheeks, and she felt ready to sink with embarrassment. The reply did nothing to restore her composure.

"What else? Heston isn't the marrying kind, and even he would not present a bird of paradise to you, my dear."

Miranda pressed her hands to her burning face. Thankfully, Heston was speaking to her aunt and had not heard the muttered exchange.

"Forgive me, ma'am, but are you quite well? May I bring you a glass of wine?"

Miranda looked up to find that she was being addressed by a gentleman in a military uniform which she did not recognise. There was a slight but attractive foreign accent in his voice.

Realising that she had been too preoccupied to notice him earlier in the press of introduction, she bent her gaze upon him, striving in vain to remember his name.

The young man brought his heels together and bowed.

"Alexei Toumanov at your service, Miss Gaysford. You may not have caught my name. I am with the Tsar of Russia's entourage. May I be of service to you?" A pair of gentle brown eyes looked down at her with an expression of concern.

"You are very kind, but it is nothing," Miranda said quickly. "I found the heat a little oppressive, that is all, Count Toumanov." She sipped gratefully at the proffered glass of wine, thankful that she had at least remembered his title.

As the curtain went up once more, he slipped into a chair beside her after a questioning look at Heston.

His lordship chuckled. "Alexei, you are a complete hand. Was it your intention to usurp my place?"

"Not at all, my dear Adam, though you did invite me to join you."

"So I did! Now, was it a mistake, I wonder?" Heston threw a pointed look at Miranda, which she ignored.

She found herself wondering at their obvious friendship. It was clear that the two men were on easy terms, and it puzzled her. In the Count's presence Heston had dropped his supercilious manner, and for the first time she saw something of his charm.

As the play resumed he stopped his banter and took a chair behind her, slightly to her left.

Miranda felt indignant. Did he intend to spy upon her? The look he had given her when he found the Count beside her had spoken volumes. Did he imagine that she intended to try her wiles upon his friend? It was apparent that she was not to be allowed to indulge in any conversation which he might not hear.

During the next interval she was glad to have the opportunity to confound him.

"Do you ladies care to walk about the corridor?" the Count enquired. "I believe that you would find it cooler there…"

Miranda rose at once and laid her hand upon his arm. With a mischievous smile at Heston the Count took Fanny upon his other side and left the box.

Mrs Shere had no opportunity to do more than look a little dismayed, for Heston was drawing back her chair and offering to escort her.

The crush in the passageway was excessive, but the Count was quick to lead them to a seat in a deserted alcove from where they were able to watch the fashionable crowd about them.

"I doubt if I have ever seen so many people," Fanny exclaimed. "Where have they all come from?"

"Many are foreigners, as I am myself," Count Toumanov explained. "The Allies intend to celebrate their victory over Napoleon in extravagant style. It is a little hard upon the inhabitants of this city."

"Oh, no, they will enjoy it, Count. There is not a seat to be had along the processional route, you know." Miranda gave him her enchanting smile.

"But you, at least, will see it, will you not? I cannot believe that Heston has not made arrangements."

"He has not told us of them," Miranda said demurely.

"Then you must allow me. There will be no difficulty, I assure you."

"Quite unnecessary, Alexei!" Heston had come up to them with Mrs Shere upon his arm. "You have spoilt my surprise, you villain!"

Unperturbed by Heston's reproof, the Count grinned at him. "You will not blame me for trying, Adam?"

"Not at all, but you will have enough to do, my friend, upon the great occasion. We shall look down upon you from the comfort of our seats as you clatter along behind your master's carriage. I shall feel for you, of course. It cannot be comfortable to wear all your finery for any length of time."

"You are speaking to a man of iron, my dear sir. Later I hope to dance the night away. Ladies, may I beg that you will partner me?"

Fanny was thrown into confusion. "I do not know, Count Toumanov."

"As yet our plans are undecided," Miranda broke in firmly.

"Then I must beg Adam to decide them for you."

The Count's enthusiasm was infectious. "Come, Adam, what do you say? May we not make up a party?"

"I see that I shall have no choice," his lordship murmured. "Leave it with me, and I shall get in touch with you."

With that the irrepressible Alexei had to be contented. With great good humour he led the ladies back to their box and stayed with them until the play was over.

"You are well acquainted with the Count, my lord?" Mrs Shere enquired as the carriage took them home.

"A boyhood friend, ma'am. We lived in Russia for some time. My father was attached to the Tsar's court."

"I see." Mrs Shere looked thoughtful, but she did not pursue the subject, although Miranda suspected that she was disturbed by the young man's evident admiration for the twins.

Her suspicions were confirmed when Mrs Shere made a point of leaving her alone with Heston when they reached the house.

Fanny was inclined to linger by her sister's side, unwilling to abandon her to his lordship's less-than-tender mercies, but Mrs Shere would have none of it. She took Fanny by the hand and led her from the room.

"Well, my dear, another triumph for you! Count Toumanov was smitten to the heart." Heston gave Miranda a lazy look. "I wish you might have heard his raptures when we were alone…something about eyes that a man could drown in… He cannot decide if they are blue or violet."

Miranda gave him an angry look.

"He was right, of course," his lordship continued. "For my own part, I am sure that they are violet. They darken when you are furious, did you know it? A pity that Alexei cannot see beneath that innocent appearance to the heart beneath.''

''I wonder that you dared to expose him to my evil influence,'' Miranda retorted.

''I intend to dare much more than that.'' Heston moved to stand in front of her. ''Now, my love, may I claim what is due to your prospective husband?''

Before she could protest he caught her to his chest and his mouth came down on hers. Miranda felt a dizzying sensation. His lips were soft, warm, and most insistent as they found her own.

She had vowed earlier that if he ever tried to kiss her again she would not struggle. Her strength was useless against his own, and she had no wish to find herself once more covered in bruises. She let herself grow limp and unresponsive in his arms.

Heston held her away from him. ''New tactics?'' he said in a soft voice. ''They will not serve, my dear. Let us try again...'' He picked her up and carried her to a sofa. ''I see that you demand finesse.''

Miranda found herself upon his knee. ''The servants...'' she gasped. ''Have you no sense of propriety, sir?''

''None whatever,'' he said equably. He lifted her hand to his lips, turned it over and kissed the palm. Then his mouth travelled upwards along the inside of her arm.

Miranda found the butterfly kisses strangely disturbing, and a new sensation possessed her as he began to caress the back of her neck with the fingers of one hand.

''Please!'' She tried to push him away.

''Please what? You must tell me how to delight you, dearest.''

To Miranda's horror his hand travelled from her waist until it cupped her breast. She tried to strike out at him and found herself helpless as both her wrists were gripped.

"No, no, my little termagant!" he reproved. "Pray do not struggle. To enjoy love, it is necessary to relax."

"Love?" she spat at him. "You call this love? How dare you insult me so? I might be no better than one of those creatures who were peddling their wares at the Opera House tonight!"

"You recognised them, did you? It was only to be expected. Tell me, my dear, how do their ambitions differ from your own?"

Miranda looked at the mocking face. If he kissed her again, she would bite through his upper lip. Sadly, he seemed to have no such intention. He set her upon her feet, and rose to take his leave.

"A word of warning, Miss Gaysford! Count Toumanov is not for you. In future, I must beg of you to save your charms for me."

He was gone before she could reply, but her anger knew no bounds.

Her temper was not improved when she was confronted by her aunt. Mrs Shere took one look at her face, and tried to heal the breach.

"You could not expect Lord Heston to be pleased, my love," she murmured. "Count Toumanov was most particular in his attentions. It was not wise to encourage him."

"I did not encourage him," Miranda snapped. "Heston invited him. You would not expect me to be less than civil to his friend."

"There are degrees of civility, dearest, and the young man seems volatile..."

"He was very kind to me and, Aunt, I am not yet betrothed, whatever you may think."

"Very well, I shall not interfere, but do take care. This is a splendid match for you. You must do nothing to overturn it."

Miranda kissed her aunt goodnight and sought the sanctuary of her bedchamber. There she found Fanny waiting for her.

"What is Heston about?" her twin demanded. "Did you see Aunt Emma's face when she saw the pearls? They must be worth a fortune!"

Miranda glared at her. "Do you suppose their cost would weigh with him? Doubtless he hands out similar trinkets to his lightskirts every week."

"That is hardly fair," her sister protested. "I have never seen him in the company of a woman, and nor have you. That is why our appearance in his box tonight created such a stir."

"Of course we have not seen him with a woman. The type of female he prefers would hardly be thought suitable to hang upon his arm at the Opera."

"You mean...you think he is a libertine? Oh, love, that can't be true. He is thought to be a cold fish."

"I assure you he is not." The colour rose to Miranda's cheeks. "And if he had kissed you you would know it."

"Oh, dear! I had not thought that he would press his attentions on you in that way..."

"Why not? He intends to punish me for daring to stand up to him. What better way than to take advantage of the fact that we are supposed to be betrothed?"

"That is not the action of a gentleman."

"Great heavens, Fanny, what kind of person do you suppose that we are dealing with? Heston is under the impression that he can walk on water, and I intend to disabuse him of that idea."

"You are grown very hard," Fanny ventured.

"Is it surprising? Heston would bring out the worst in anyone. He misses no opportunity to give me a set-down. Do you know that he actually warned me... warned me not to encourage Count Toumanov?"

"But, love, the Count was very attentive to you."

"To both of us, Fanny, and he meant no harm. It was a pleasure to speak to such a gentle and entertaining person. There was no need to keep up one's guard, as I am forced to do with Heston."

"It would be hard to find two people less alike than his lordship and the Count," her twin agreed. "Their friendship is surprising."

"Monsters are few and far between, thank goodness! There cannot be another such as Heston. Beside him anyone must seem charming."

"But he did give you the pearls, Miranda. Why would he do that if he dislikes you so?"

"It was simply another attempt to put me out of countenance. To frighten me, he will carry this deception as far as he dare go."

Fanny hesitated, twisting her handkerchief between her fingers. "And how far will he go?"

She looked so pale that Miranda stared at her.

"What do you mean?"

"I am afraid of him," Fanny said simply. Slow tears rolled down her cheeks. "Do you think that he intends to marry you? I could not bear it."

Miranda went to sit beside her and slipped an arm about her sister's waist. "What nonsense!" she said in a rallying tone. "Would his lordship wed a nonentity? He would not give the idea a moment's consideration. Oh, I know he thinks his position unassailable, but he would not care for the humiliation. He has no such thought in mind. In any case, not even he could marry without his bride's consent.''

''I hope you may be right.'' Fanny dabbed at her eyes. ''But I fear you are mistaken in him. He does not care for the opinion of the world, else he would not have spoken to Uncle, or agreed to the announcement being made.''

''There is that, of course.'' Miranda looked thoughtful. ''But he thinks himself safe enough. He knows that I shall cry off, but I shan't do it yet. This is a test of nerves, my love, and I intend to win it.''

Fanny shuddered. ''Heston is playing some deep game, I know it. Suppose you have misjudged him? He must intend to marry before he is much older...there is the question of an heir, you know. For all we are aware, he may decide to wed you simply for that purpose.''

''Stuff!'' Miranda was out of all patience. ''Have I not explained that he cannot force me into marriage?''

''He thinks that he need not do so. Does he not believe that you want a title and his fortune? How will he guess that you plan to cry off?''

Miranda felt dismayed as the truth of her sister's words came home to her, but she forced herself to smile.

''He must intend to cry off himself, possibly at the last moment. Come, Fanny, in your wildest dreams you can't think that he would care to wed me. Mutual dislike is no basis for marriage. His life would be hell, and he must know it.''

''So would yours,'' her sister said dolefully. ''He could shut you away in the country, and I should never see you again.'' She began to wail.

''For heaven's sake, do stop!'' Miranda cried. ''What would you have me do? Am I to confess the whole and take the consequences?''

Fanny raised her head. She looked shamefaced. "I'm sorry," she murmured. "I must suppose that you know what you are doing, and Harry and I are so grateful for your help. Perhaps it will all work out as you would wish."

"Of course it will! Now, Fanny, we must go to bed. It's very late and I have no wish to look hagged tomorrow. Heston must not think that he is robbing me of my sleep."

It was a sensible suggestion, but sleep did not come as easily as Miranda hoped. Fanny's words had disturbed her more than she would admit, and it was not only her sister's remark about being shut away in the country, which echoed Heston's threats, made earlier in the day.

What was it Fanny had said? Something about his lordship playing a deep game? Try as she might she could not guess what it might be. Fanny must surely be mistaken, and yet a tiny doubt remained.

What had started as a simple hoax had now turned into something very different, and not only her sister and herself were involved in it. Their mama, their aunt and uncle, Harry Lakenham and Heston himself were all entangled in the deception.

Miranda's face burned. She could never lift her head again when the truth came out. She must have been mad to let matters go so far, but it was no use repining or wishing the events of the last few days undone. There was no going back. The only time she might have told the truth was at the end of that first ugly interview with Heston, and that would have put the cat among the pigeons with a vengeance.

She must go on, but how was she to support this dreadful farce for what might be several months? Her only hope lay in Fanny's volatile temperament. Fickle in her affections, it was more than likely that her twin would discover a passion for someone who pleased her more than Lakenham, before that young man attained his majority.

London was crowded for the coming celebrations, and Heston had made it clear that they were to mingle in the highest circles. Surely there was someone who might take her sister's fancy. With that hopeful thought, Miranda fell asleep.

The following day she was tempted to plead exhaustion as a means of keeping to her room, but Heston's taunt of cowardice had stung. He should never be allowed to think that of her. She dressed quickly and accompanied Fanny to the breakfast-room.

As she sat down she cast an anxious look at the pile of letters beside her uncle's plate. It was only when he had finished reading them that she allowed herself a sigh of relief.

"Uncle, is there nothing from Mama?" she murmured.

"Nay, love, we cannot hope for an answer yet. It is too soon, but do not be fretting yourself. Your match with Heston must be all that she has hoped for...more, in fact. You will have her blessing, I am sure of it."

Miranda gave him a feeble smile, feeling relieved that she was to be spared from the announcement for one more day. Her hopes were not to be realised. Later that morning her uncle burst into the room, with a young man close behind him. He was waving a missive, and as she looked at him her heart sank. His beaming face confirmed her worst fears.

"There now! You may set your mind at rest, my dear.

Here is your mother's letter, brought to us by your brother's friend.''

Miranda nodded to Richard Young, wishing him still in Yorkshire. He was a neighbour and she knew him well, but what was he doing in London? It was sheer bad luck that he had been on hand to act as her mother's messenger.

"How kind!" The irony in her tone was not lost upon her twin and Fanny threw Miranda a warning glance as she moved to greet their visitor.

"It was indeed! Very civil, sir, I must admit," said Alderman Shere. "Now you shall meet my wife, and you will join us, I hope, for luncheon?"

Richard blushed, but he was easily persuaded. He came towards Miranda and handed her another billet.

"This one is for you, Miss Gaysford." He looked from one twin to the other, an anxious frown upon his face. "I have it right, I hope?"

"Thank you, Richard." Miranda held out her hand for the letter. It was not mere courtesy which stopped her from begging leave to read it there and then. She could guess what it contained, and the thought of her mother's inevitable raptures filled her with despair.

Her aunt was quick to urge her not to stand on ceremony. "Mr Richard Young will excuse us if your uncle tells us what your mother has to say. He must be in her confidence already." She smiled and nodded at the young man. "We are so excited, my dear sir. Who could have hoped for such a match for Fanny?"

Richard smiled and bowed. "Ma'am, you are right. Mrs Gaysford is delighted for her daughter."

All eyes were on Miranda as she opened the letter. The single sheet of paper was covered on both sides with her mother's untidy scrawl, but she could not make out a word of it. The letter had been crossed and re-crossed so many times that it was undecipherable. Mrs Gaysford must have written it with the intention of sending it by the mails.

"I'm sorry, but it is a little difficult to read." She handed it to her uncle, who raised his eyebrows and gave it to her aunt.

"Now isn't that just like Letty?" Mrs Shere exclaimed. "She was hoping to save you money, George. What does she say to you?"

The Alderman's eyes twinkled. "Mine was written in less haste. Shall I read it to you?"

They sat in silence as he began to do so. Mrs Gaysford had been so overcome by the prospect of her elder daughter's brilliant match that the page was filled with superlatives. Her tears of happiness had blotted out several words, but he was able to assure Miranda that all the blessings in the world were called down upon her head.

Miranda squirmed inwardly, and her dismay increased tenfold when Lord Heston was announced.

"My lord, we have splendid news for you!" The Alderman hastened to greet him. "We have heard from my sister-in-law, who sends you every good wish for your future happiness. She has given her consent to your betrothal."

"Splendid news indeed!" Heston gripped the older man's hand, but his eyes were on Miranda's face. In their grey depths she detected a look of triumph. It was no more than the impression of a moment. Then he turned as Richard Young was introduced to him.

"My dear sir, we have much to thank you for. We had not hoped for such an early reply. My darling, your cup of happiness must be full.'' With an outstretched hand, he drew Miranda to his side.

As his lean fingers gripped her own, Miranda longed to draw away. He sensed it, and his grasp tightened.

''At last!'' he murmured tenderly. ''Now the announcement may be made, and the world shall know of our joy.''

Chapter Five

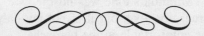

Miranda coloured and her uncle began to tease her. He could not know that her rosy blush was due to anger rather than embarrassment. As Heston slipped an arm about her waist, kissing her hand before saluting her cheek, her rage increased.

"Now, now, there is no cause to be shy, my girl! We all understand his lordship's feelings, and we'll have no ceremony here. You will join us for luncheon, my lord? Quite informal, you know, and Mr Young is to join us."

"Sadly, I have another engagement," Heston told him smoothly. "I came merely to ask if Miss Gaysford will drive with me this afternoon?"

There was no way that Miranda could refuse, though she threw a desperate glance at Fanny.

"Aunt, were we not to drive along the processional route to the Guildhall?" Fanny broke in swiftly.

Mrs Shere looked startled. "No, no, you are mistaken. I cannot recall that I mentioned such a thing…"

"Nevertheless, it is a splendid idea! Perhaps the Elgin marbles first, and a drive through the city later? You will all accompany us, I hope."

"My lord, you cannot wish for such a large party on

your drive?'' Mrs Shere shook her head, but she was pleased.

Heston chuckled. ''You are all consideration, ma'am, but lovers do not expect always to be alone—that is, until they are married.''

''Then, if you are sure...?''

''Did you not tell me that your phaeton takes no more than two?'' Miranda's tone was hostile.

''Very true, my love, but it is not my only carriage. You will be comfortable in the barouche.''

Miranda did not argue further. Naturally, Heston would have more than one carriage. Most probably he has six, she thought bitterly.

''Shall we say four o'clock, then?'' Heston was all courtesy as he consulted Mrs Shere.

Mrs Shere smiled her assent, but when he had gone she drew Miranda aside.

''My dear, you must try to be a little more amenable. Gentlemen prefer to see a smiling face, you know. Now I do not mean to scold. Let us go in to luncheon.''

The reproof was gentle but Miranda felt disturbed. She had allowed her dislike of Heston to betray her into incivility. More worrying than that was her mother's swift acceptance of her supposed betrothal. She groaned inwardly, yet what else had she expected? A feeling of depression seized her, but she forced herself to take part in the conversation of the others, hoping that her low spirits would pass unnoticed.

As always her aunt had provided an excellent meal. Conscious of Mrs Shere's anxious scrutiny she took a little of the asparagus in butter sauce, and a slice or two of a fine York ham.

As one course followed another, she pushed the food

about her plate, hiding it as best she could beneath an Italian salad.

Fanny was chattering happily to Richard Young, and from their conversation Miranda learned that her mother and her brothers and sisters were in good health, and looking forward to her marriage.

"Shall you be wed in Yorkshire?" Richard asked. "Your mother wishes to know."

"I have no idea," Miranda told him helplessly.

"Of course not!" The Alderman broke in at once. "How could that be? Lord Heston will wish the ceremony to take place in London, as befits his consequence. My sister-in-law will come to us, together with her family."

"We have not yet decided on a date," Miranda faltered.

"If I don't misjudge his lordship, it will be sooner rather than later." Alderman Shere gave his niece a mischievous smile. "Heston is head over heels in love with you, my dear, and he does not strike me as a man who is prepared to wait for his happiness."

Miranda felt an uncomfortable churning in the pit of her stomach. "There is no hurry," she protested.

"Perhaps not for you, my dear child, but gentlemen have different ideas..." He left it there, but her aunt was not so tactful.

When the meal was over and Richard Young had left them she came into the drawing-room. A glance sent Fanny hurrying away.

"Now, dearest, I must speak to you," Mrs Shere said firmly. "You have surprised me. One might think that you did not care to fix Lord Heston's interest. The match is not distasteful to you, is it?"

Miranda hesitated. She longed to tell her aunt of her

deception, but the words would not come. She shook her head.

"Very well, then. You know us well enough, I hope, to believe that we should not wish you to engage yourself to someone you dislike. Is that not so?"

Too stricken to speak, Miranda nodded.

"My dear, you are very young, and you have led a sheltered life in Yorkshire. I doubt if you understand the full extent of your good fortune. Heston is the finest catch in London..." She paused as Miranda frowned.

"Well, perhaps that is an unfortunate expression. I should not wish you to think me mercenary, dearest, but the comfort of a fortune is not to be denied."

Miranda looked at her with swimming eyes.

"There now, you shall not be distressed, but we must face the facts. Consider your mama, my love. She was cast off by her family, as I was myself, for marrying beneath her."

"Papa was not beneath her. He was a scholar..."

"Of course, but he had no money. I was more fortunate. George is comfortable, if not wealthy. However, that is not what I intended to say. Do you not see that if you do not go on with this betrothal...if you were so foolish as to give Lord Heston a dislike of you...well then...you would face a second Season?"

"We could not ask that of uncle," Miranda muttered.

"He would do it gladly, but it rarely serves. There is a certain stigma attached to young women who do not 'take', as the saying goes. Too many hopeful maidens are keen to step into their shoes."

Miranda felt unable to reply.

"Well, there it is." A comforting arm stole about Miranda's shoulders. "Do not take my words amiss, my child. I think only of your happiness, and I would a thousand times see you shy rather than unbecomingly bold, but perhaps you should be a little kinder to his lordship.''

Miranda promised to do her best. She dressed with care that afternoon, in an effort to please her aunt.

When Heston arrived she greeted him with every appearance of pleasure which, though assumed, caused him to regard her with suspicion.

She dimpled at him, realising suddenly that to play the part of a loving bride-to-be would baffle him more than covert hostility. If he could play the fond lover, so could she. She would beat him at his own game.

As they drove towards Bloomsbury, Miranda hung upon his lordship's every word, simpering and smiling in what she hoped was a perfect imitation of a shy but excited maiden charmed by the attentions of her lover.

Fanny's face was a study in perplexity, but Mrs Shere looked with approval at Miranda, pleased to think that her words of censure had been heeded.

With the easy address of a man of fashion Heston drew both Fanny and her aunt into conversation. He seemed to know everyone of note in London, including the Prince Regent.

''Have you visited Carlton House?'' he asked.

Miranda suspected him of offering them a setdown. He knew as well as she did that an invitation from the Prince would be unlikely to reach the home of Alderman Shere.

''Alas, we do not move in such exalted circles,'' she said demurely. ''Nor have we been to Almack's.''

It was an effort to forestall what she imagined would be his next question, and she would not have her aunt distressed.

Mrs Shere had suffered a bitter disappointment when she was informed that not even Lady Medlicott could obtain the coveted vouchers for her nieces. The highborn Patronesses of that august establishment had not looked kindly upon the hopes of her penniless relations, without even a title to recommend them.

"You haven't missed much," Heston said indifferently. "It's a barn of a place without a shred of comfort. Why everyone flocks to King Street to eat stale bread and butter and drink orgeat and lemonade, I can't imagine."

Mrs Shere could have told him. Almack's was the recognised marriage mart for members of the *haut ton*. Lord Heston might despise it, but for lesser mortals the possession of an entry voucher was prized more than gold. Those unfortunates who were excluded might only consider themselves upon the fringes of society.

"Is it true that they dance only country dances?" Fanny murmured.

"They are moving with the times at last," his lordship said with heavy irony. "Quadrilles and waltzes have been approved, so I understand."

"But that would not affect you, my lord." Miranda gave him her most enchanting smile. "You do not dance, I think?"

The heavy-lidded eyes looked down at her, and then his harsh face softened into an expression of what she recognised as spurious tenderness.

"Dearest, I could be persuaded to waltz," he told her in a sentimental tone. "The thought of holding you in my arms…"

"La, sir, you will put me to the blush." Miranda opened her fan and hid behind it. "We are not alone." She was careful to avoid Fanny's eye.

It was not until they were standing amidst the statuary brought from Greece a few years earlier that Fanny managed a word alone with her.

"Sister, what are you about?" she asked. "You are so unlike yourself that even Aunt must notice, and as for Heston…"

"I'm trying to annoy him," Miranda chuckled. "At least he is confused."

"So am I. You will give him a strange impression, and Aunt must wonder at your odd behaviour."

"Aunt will be pleased. She told me only this morning that I should be more…er…forthcoming."

"Oh, you make me so cross!"

"Do I, love? You must try to bear it. I'd planned to spray myself with the cheapest, most obnoxious perfume I could find, but sadly there wasn't anything suitable in the house."

Fanny threw up her eyes to heaven and went to join the others.

Heston was pointing out the features of the sculptures to her aunt, and in spite of herself Miranda was drawn to listen to his story of the difficulties involved in bringing them to England.

"And they were shipwrecked, do you say? Lord Elgin must have been distraught. We heard that he gave an enormous sum for them."

"Something in the region of seventy-four thousand pounds, ma'am, but look at the craftsmanship. These wine-bearers are from the north frieze of the Parthenon in Athens. They are the work of Pheidias."

Miranda was enthralled as they strolled from one group of figures to another.

"They are very fine, are they not?"

She had moved away from the others, and was startled to find that Heston was beside her.

"They are quite wonderful," she breathed. "The marble almost looks like living flesh, and see how the draperies flow about the figures. Pheidias must have been the finest sculptor in the world."

"They are not all his work, so it is believed." The grey eyes gave her a penetrating glance. "Other splendid artists worked upon the Parthenon and the temple of Nike Apteros, but their names are lost to us."

"It seems such a pity that they should have been torn away from their original sites..."

"You think it wanton destruction?"

She nodded.

"So do I." For once the mocking note was absent from his voice. "But since we have them here, we must make the most of the pleasure that they give us. There is some talk of buying them for the nation."

"Will that happen, do you suppose? I do hope so. At least they would be preserved."

"I am happy to hear that you approve." His eyes were warm as he looked at her, and Miranda gave him an answering smile before she remembered that she was acting out of character for the part which she intended to play.

"La, sir, I can have no opinion on the subject," she simpered.

Heston took her arm and led her behind an enormous group of charioteers.

"Let us have no more of that," he chided softly. "You are so much more entrancing when you are yourself, Miss Gaysford. For a time you had me believing that your mother's blessing had brought about a change of heart, but I realise that it is not so."

Miranda crimsoned, too mortified to answer him, and furious when she heard a low laugh.

"A good try, but unconvincing," he announced. "To play a part successfully, one must be consistent."

"As you would know, my lord."

"You think I am playing a part," he said in mock surprise. "Dearest, my heart is at your feet..."

She was spared the need to answer when Fanny came to find them.

"Aunt is a little tired of standing, Lord Heston. She is sorry..."

"Not at all! It is I who should apologise. I have been remiss in not considering the length of time we have been here." He went at once to order the barouche.

"Shall you wish to go directly home, ma'am?" he asked when they were seated in the carriage. "We may take our drive on another day, you know."

"No, no, I would not spoil your pleasure for the world," Mrs Shere protested. "It is just that my feet are inclined to swell..." She paused, uncomfortably aware that the great Lord Heston could have no possible interest in her complaints.

"That can be a trial, ma'am. My own mother suffered in a similar way. She found that lying flat, with her feet raised at an angle, was of the greatest help to her."

Miranda was astounded. Clearly there was an unsuspected side to his lordship's character. She could not have supposed it possible that he could be so kind in his concern for her aunt. She was forced to admit that his sympathy was unfeigned. What a mystery he was. This man who was said to have no interests other than in horses and in gaming had also surprised her that day with his love of art, and his knowledge of history.

* * *

As they drove through the Park, she was conscious once again of the unwelcome interest of the fashionable exquisites who strolled along the footpath arm in arm. Other carriages slowed at their approach and she saw avid curiosity on the faces of their occupants. She shrank back into one corner of the barouche, praying that the ordeal would soon be over.

"I have never before seen such crowds in London," Mrs Shere said brightly. "But it was only to be expected. The end of the war with France is certainly a cause for celebration."

"Let us hope that the celebrations are not premature, ma'am." Heston's face was grim.

"What can you mean, my lord?" Miranda was startled into speech. "Napoleon has abdicated and is in exile."

"On Elba?" Heston laughed. "If you suppose that the man who has conquered most of Europe will relinquish power so easily, you are more of an optimist than I."

"But what can he do? He was stripped of everything. His titles, his possessions, his armies…"

"The man is a genius…a magician, if you like. He was an idol to his men. He has only to land in France again, and the Little Corporal will have an army at his back."

"Pray do not say so!" Mrs Shere grew pale. "My eldest son is with Wellington, my lord. I could not bear to think of him in danger yet again."

"Aunt, it will not come to that." Miranda threw an angry look at Heston. "Napoleon is well guarded. How could he escape?"

Her words of comfort cheered her aunt a little and she began to draw Fanny's attention to the passing parade of fashion. Miranda seized the opportunity to speak to Heston.

"Pray do not frighten my aunt with your ridiculous notions," she said in a cool tone. "How could you be so tactless?"

He gave her a penetrating look in which there was more than a hint of sadness.

"Tactless, perhaps," he said in a quiet voice, "but the notion of an escape is not ridiculous, my dear. Elba is close to the southern coast of France, and the Emperor still has many adherents. For twenty years, as you know, he was accounted the saviour of his country."

"I can't think why," she retorted sharply. "Unless it is considered admirable to lose so many men in battle."

"Have you forgotten the Napoleonic Code?"

"No, I have not." Miranda was about to launch into a spirited discussion when she caught her aunt's eye and subsided.

"An interesting subject," Heston observed. "Perhaps we might continue with it later?"

Miranda nodded, though the look of astonishment on Mrs Shere's face was mingled with disapproval. In her view, ladies left all discussions of political matters to their menfolk, who were so much better able to understand them.

It was some comfort to think that Heston had not patronised her. He had not told her not to bother her pretty head about such things, which was the usual reaction from the gentlemen she knew. But then, he was no gentleman. Her lips curved in a tiny smile. For once she found herself in charity with him. He had seemed to be quite interested in her point of view.

* * *

This did not save her from another lecture from her aunt later that day.

"My dear, I did not like to see you pick up Lord Heston in that hey-go-mad way when he spoke of Napoleon," she scolded. "Such matters are not for ladies to understand. You would not have him think you a blue-stocking?"

"I doubt if he thinks that, Aunt Emma."

"He cannot have been pleased to hear you speaking out so boldly. I thought he must have given you a set-down, and you would have deserved it."

"He seemed quite interested in my views," Miranda told her mildly. "But I shall not speak of such things again unless he should desire it." She changed the subject with a coaxing smile. "In any case, I do not think he will attend the Grand Masquerade at Vauxhall. We were to go with Lady Medlicott, if you recall."

"But not without a male escort, my love." Mrs Shere looked shocked. "You must give up that plan. I can't think that his lordship would approve."

Miranda was tempted to announce that his lordship did not own her, but she bit back the hasty words.

"Richard Young has offered to accompany us. He is come to London to see the sights, Aunt, and we have known him all our lives. Mama would not object..."

Mrs Shere shook her head. "It is to be hoped that you know what you are doing, dearest." It was a dismal echo of Fanny's words. "I cannot like your manner with Lord Heston. You do not appear to realise the extent of your good fortune."

Miranda kissed her cheek. "Lord Heston is not an ordinary man," she said with perfect truth. "I am learning to understand him. Believe me, he will not cry off." She crossed her fingers behind her back.

"You may be right, but it is easy to push good nature too far." Mrs Shere sighed, and then a thought struck her. "Your mama approves of Richard Young, you say? Has she hopes of him for your sister? What is his background?"

"Richard is just a country gentleman. He is the eldest son of the local squire and our good neighbour." She smiled. "But you shall not raise your hopes, Aunt Emma. Mama aims higher than Richard for my twin."

"Your sister makes no push to fix any gentleman's interest," Mrs Shere said sadly. "And, with the Season well advanced, most of the eligible gentlemen are committed. Will you have a word with her, my dear? Any advice would come better from you and be more readily acceptable. As I say, a second Season is never so successful. The novelty of a new face is gone, and other girls are more admired."

"I'll do my best," Miranda promised.

"That's right, my love. You, at least, have exceeded your mother's fondest hopes."

Miranda went to fetch her twin, thankful that she had escaped with only the mildest of scoldings. To hear Heston described as good-natured had shaken her a little, but she could not deny that he had been charming to her aunt.

"Thank heavens you had the sense to ask Richard to escort us to the Masquerade," she told Fanny. "Aunt was about to forbid us to go. Of course, Lady Medlicott must accompany us."

"Even that will be better than today." Fanny's face was sullen. "I can't think what possessed Heston to drag us off to look at a heap of broken stones. I thought I must die of boredom... How Harry would have stared to see us there!"

"I expect he would. Sculpture is not to everyone's taste, but I enjoyed the visit."

"Did you? I thought that you were still acting for Heston's benefit. I thought I should burst out laughing."

Miranda was silent.

"And then all that dreary talk about Napoleon! So dull! In Heston's company you have more to bear than I imagined. He has no conversation…"

"He doesn't gossip, Fanny, if that's what you mean. I suppose if he had entertained us with the latest crim. cons. you would have approved?"

"He moves in the Regent's circles. He might have told us the truth about the Princess Charlotte's broken engagement to the Prince of Orange, or if the Regent really is a bigamist. I confess I'd like to know if he had married Maria Fitzherbert before he was wed to Caroline of Brunswick."

"You put me out of patience with you, Fanny. It would be most improper of Heston to discuss such matters when he is in a privileged position to know the truth of them."

Fanny stared at her. "I thought you hated him? Why do you defend him now?"

"I am not defending him. I am defending the principle that it is wrong to discuss confidential matters, especially when they refer to a friend."

Fanny was not satisfied. "Are you beginning to think better of him? I didn't think you'd change your mind so quickly. Have you forgot his insults?"

"No, I have not! For heaven's sake, Fanny, let it rest! I have enough to trouble me. I can't think what I am to do if the announcement should appear in the *Gazette* tomorrow…" Her words served to silence Fanny.

* * *

But the next edition of the *Gazette* did not carry the news of the supposed betrothal, and Miranda could not disguise her relief. The announcement must have arrived too late to be included, but Mrs Shere was disappointed.

"Perhaps it is for the best," Miranda soothed. "Now there can be no objection to our going to the Masquerade with Richard."

Her aunt looked doubtful. "Dearest, I am persuaded that his lordship would not like it. You should ask his permission first."

Miranda kept her opinion of this suggestion to herself.

"Lord Heston is at Carlton House today," she pointed out. "And, Aunt, we shall wear our dominoes as well as our velvet masks. No one will recognise us."

"Very well then." Mrs Shere gave her permission for the outing with some reluctance. "But you must not stay too long."

"We shall be home by midnight," Miranda promised. "And with Richard to take care of us, we cannot come to any harm."

This prophetic statement proved to be untrue. The crowds at the Vauxhall Gardens were immense and it was difficult for the four members of their party to stay together. Lady Medlicott, an incorrigible gossip, insisted upon chatting to those persons whom she recognised, whilst Richard was diverted by the Grand Display of Fireworks.

"Oh, there is Harry!" Fanny cried out in delight. "Will he know me, do you think?"

Miranda threw her a glance filled with deep suspicion and Fanny pouted.

"I did not know he would be here," she insisted. "Don't glare at me, Miranda! This is a chance meeting."

"Obviously!" Miranda looked at Harry's companions. In addition to one or two gentlemen, there were a couple of well-known Incognitas.

Fanny's face grew pale. She had been about to rush over to her lover, but the sight of the high-flyers had stopped her instantly. A hand flew to her mouth.

"Oh no, he could not..." she whispered. Then she swayed and seemed about to faint.

"Don't you dare!" Miranda hissed. "Do you wish to make a spectacle of yourself and me? Those women may have nothing to do with Harry. You must forget that you have seen him in their company."

"How could I? Miranda, I must know." Before Miranda could stop her, she rushed to Harry's side.

It was the height of folly, but worse was to come. Fanny tore off her mask and confronted her lover with accusing eyes. His look of surprise changed to one of dismay, and he led her away from the others into a side turning, off the main promenade.

Miranda plunged after them, but the impetus of the crowd carried her far beyond the little group as it surged towards the Water Spectacle which was about to begin.

"All alone, little lady? You must not lose your footing." To Miranda's horror, an arm slid about her waist, and she caught a glimpse of gleaming teeth beneath a mask.

"Let me go!" she cried. "How dare you?"

"Unhand the lady, sir!" Suddenly Richard was by her side. His face was flushed, and his eyes were bright with anger.

"Out of it, stripling! This prize is mine." Her captor shouldered Richard aside as he tightened his grip upon Miranda's waist. Then he swung round. Richard had gripped his shoulder, and a bunched fist gave notice of his intentions. Next moment a blow from her attacker's cane felled Richard to the ground.

"Now let me see your face, my pretty!" A rough hand swept Miranda's hood from her hair and began to untie the strings of her mask.

As she fought him, Richard shook his spinning head, gathered himself and launched another attack upon the man who held her.

This time he was tripped and landed on his back. Miranda screamed as she saw the flash of light upon a gleaming blade. The innocent-looking cane was a swordstick and its tip was now against Richard's throat.

"You are in need of a lesson, my friend. A scar upon each cheek will remind you of this night—"

"He is unarmed!" Miranda cried wildly.

A circle had cleared about them as the crowd moved back. For a frozen moment Miranda stared at the spectators.

"Will no one help me?" she begged. A murmur of disgust was the only reply. No one was prepared to face the swordsman, much as they disapproved of his actions. She could see Fanny's ashen face on the outskirts of the group, and beside her Lady Medlicott was on the verge of collapse.

"Cowards, all of you!" Miranda shrieked. She took a step backwards and kicked her attacker sharply behind the knee. Her silken sandals were too soft to injure him, but he swung round with a curse.

"Hell-cat!" he growled. Then his face changed as his raised arm was caught in a bone-crushing grip. He gave a yelp of agony, and the weapon clattered to the ground.

"You! I might have known!" The contempt in Heston's voice brought an ugly flush to the man's face. He scurried away, helped along by a kick to the seat of his breeches.

Chapter Six

Heston looked at Miranda. "All right?" he asked.

Miranda nodded. She was shaking so violently that she thought her legs would not support her, and she felt incapable of speech.

Heston reached down to help Richard to his feet.

"My lord, I'm sorry!" The younger man was white to the lips. "What must you think of me? I made the poorest showing as an escort for the ladies."

"You did very well." Heston's harsh, dark face softened for a moment as he smiled. "An unarmed man has no defence against a weapon such as this." He picked up the discarded sword, and then he turned to Miranda.

"I think we should leave, my dear," he said mildly. "We have provided quite enough entertainment for these bystanders. Where is your sister?"

"I saw her over there with Lady Medlicott." Miranda pointed with a trembling finger.

"Ah, yes!" His lordship took her arm and led her through the rapidly dispersing crowd.

Lady Medlicott had been supported to a nearby seat. She looked very ill. Fanny was chafing her hands, but there was no sign of Harry Lakenham.

"Mr Young, will you be good enough to take her ladyship home? I will bring her to the carriage…"

"A pleasure, sir!" Richard was eager to make amends for his previous failure to take care of them. "Shall I take Fanny and Miranda, too?"

"That will not be necessary. Count Toumanov and I will see them home."

"Oh, I did not see you." Miranda turned to find Alexei Toumanov by her side.

"Hardly surprising, ma'am. You had more than enough to occupy you." The Count smiled, but Miranda felt ashamed. What must Heston and his friend think of her? To be discovered in such circumstances was the outside of enough. She looked up at Heston, but his face was inscrutable.

"How…how did you find us, my lord?" she murmured.

Heston took her arm and led her ahead of the others, supporting Lady Medlicott upon one arm.

"Later, my love." With exquisite courtesy he handed her ladyship into the carriage with his wishes for her swift recovery, and the express hope that she would soon forget the ugly incident.

Lady Medlicott was no fool. She nodded, aware of his wish that she should not speak of it.

Fanny had regained her colour. As the carriage drove away, she smiled up prettily at Heston.

"How fortunate that you were here tonight," she cried. "I had not supposed you to like masquerades, my lord."

His penetrating eyes scanned her face. "I don't," he told her bluntly. "Mrs Shere advised us that you were come to the Vauxhall Gardens."

"We had thought you occupied at Carlton House,"

Miranda faltered. "I did not expect that you would call on us this evening."

"Obviously not!" It was clear that he was furious. "Have you no sense, madam? How came you to be separated from your party?"

"Don't speak to me in that tone, if you please! If you must know, I was carried along in the crush."

"Really? Without your sister?" Miranda knew that he did not believe her. "On our way in we passed Lakenham. Had you an assignation with him?"

"No, I had not! I am surprised that you could think it. He knows of our...of our betrothal." She was speaking the truth, but a blush rose to her cheeks.

"Don't play games with me, my dear. If I find that you have been deceiving me, you will regret it. You asked how I found you? It was simple. When we saw the disturbance, I guessed that you would be at the centre of it."

"No, no, Adam, that is coming it too strong! Ignore him, Miss Gaysford! Adam is so tall. He looked above the crowd and saw your hair." Count Toumanov had come up to them and was attempting to heal the breach. "He is angry because you were in danger."

Heston glared at him, and then he began to laugh. "There is some truth in that," he admitted ruefully. "But I meant what I said. Trouble has an unerring way of finding you, my love. It is a sobering thought."

Miranda would not be mollified. She turned to the Count. "I hope we have not spoiled your evening," she said. "This has all been most unpleasant for you. It will give you a sad opinion of London."

"Not at all!" Alexei bowed. "Our only disappointment was in not finding you at home. That is one reason for Adam's sour expression. We had hoped to take you to the Piazza for some supper."

"Famous!" Fanny clapped her hands. "I should like that above anything."

"But you cannot wish to go after such an experience?" Heston's eyes were on Miranda. "I believe we should take you home. It must have been a shock...?"

"It was, but I am quite recovered." Blue eyes locked with grey. "You need have no fears for me, my lord. I do not plan to faint."

"As you wish." His tone was casual, but she saw the spark of something like admiration in his look. "The carriage is by the gates." Again he took her arm and led the way, leaving Fanny and the Count to follow.

"Tell me, where did you learn your street-fighting, dearest? It came as a surprise to me, though I have always been aware that you have unsuspected talents."

"I can't think what you mean." Miranda said stiffly.

"Must I explain?" He looked down at her dainty silken sandals. "Let me give you a word of advice. That kick to the back of the knee is more effective when you are wearing stouter shoes, but it served its purpose. Foolish, of course. If he had struck you, you might have been badly injured. I think I must teach you rather better. Your previous tutor left much to be desired..."

"My brother did not think that I should ever be in such a situation," she cried hotly.

"Then I must suppose that he does not know you very well. Personally I have no such sanguine hopes."

Miranda did not trouble to reply to this gibe. A thought had struck her.

"That man. You know him, do you not?"

"I know of him," he corrected. "An ugly customer, my dear, with a string of scandals behind him. It was no

surprise to find him here, hoping to find a companion
for the night.''

Miranda flushed to the roots of her hair.

''Surely he could not imagine that I...that I...?''

''That you were available? Why not? You were apparently unattended and he saw his chance. Men are not
saints, you know, and you are a prize worth the taking.
Your face is likely to be your downfall, madam, unless
you take more care.''

''I did not know that such things could happen,'' she
protested. ''No gentleman would thrust his attention
upon a woman in that brutal way.''

She heard an ugly laugh. ''What an innocent you are!
Do you know nothing of the reputation of this place?
These gatherings in the Vauxhall Gardens offer oppor-
tunities for many a lightskirt to find a rich protector.
Your aunt should have forbidden this expedition.''

''How dare you criticise her? She could not have
known the truth of what you say, and I...well, I insisted
upon coming here.''

''That does not surprise me in the least. I hope you
have learned your lesson.''

''I have learned what cowards people are. Not a man
in the crowd would lift a finger to help us.''

''You forget...the man was armed. Courage is of little
use against a sword.''

''It did not stop you, my lord.'' Miranda spoke without thinking. Then she coloured a little.

''Ah, yes, but then, you see, I took your assailant by
surprise. You had diverted his attention.''

''Even so, it was a brave thing to do, and I thank you
for it. It was unforgivable to draw on Richard as he
did...he threatened to scar his face, you know.''

''He would have done so without a second thought.

Stroud has something of a reputation as a sadist. Not only was he blackballed at Brooks and White's, but he is barred from many...er...houses of ill repute. A girl was killed upon one occasion, I understand.''

Miranda shuddered.

''Now I have shocked you. You must forgive me, but I wished to make the danger clear to you.''

''It is clear enough, my lord. I shall not visit this place again,'' Miranda said firmly, forgetting for the moment that had he forbidden her to do so she would most certainly have defied him. ''It is hateful.''

''Not altogether. The concerts and the entertainments can be delightful if one is in a party, and uses a little common sense.''

Miranda flushed again, but she did not argue, although it was not entirely her fault that she had found herself isolated from the others.

''Even so, I hope that you will accept my thanks,'' she murmured.

''I could do no less for my beloved.'' The mocking note was back in his voice as he handed her into the carriage.

His lordship did not appear to notice her annoyance. He chatted amicably to Fanny and the Count as the carriage bore them towards the Piazza, and Alexei was quick to extol the excellence of the food.

Then Miranda's ears pricked up.

''Mr Richard Young is an old friend of yours?'' Heston's question was apparently casual, but there was something in his tone which warned her of his interest.

''He is a neighbour of ours in Yorkshire, and an old friend of my brother,'' she said shortly.

''We have known him all our lives,'' Fanny intervened. ''He is come to London for the celebrations.''

"You are fortunate in your friend. He does not lack courage. Do you suppose that he would care to join us to see the Regent's procession?"

"That would be kind." Miranda turned to him, her face alight with pleasure, and surprised something in his expression which she had not expected to see there. She blinked, feeling that she must have been mistaken. It was almost a look of tenderness.

The twins had not previously visited the Piazza, and they were suitably impressed. Their supper was all that the Count had promised but, though Miranda joined in the light-hearted conversation, she felt troubled. The incident in the Vauxhall Gardens had shaken her, but it was not that.

Heston was beginning to fill her mind to the exclusion of all else. She strove in vain to remember how much she had disliked him, but honestly compelled to admit that she might have been mistaken in his character.

A teasing remark from the Count recalled her wandering thoughts. Knowing of her impending betrothal he was accusing her of daydreaming and being lost in love.

"Adam, you are a lucky dog!" he announced. "You have captured the heart of one of the two most beautiful girls in London." As he spoke, he took Fanny's hand and raised it to his lips. His smile was full of mischief. "I must pin my hopes upon capturing the other."

Fanny coloured, but she was not displeased by the young Russian's evident admiration.

Miranda's spirits sank. Heston could only be annoyed by this flirtation, innocent though it was. To her surprise, his face was bland as he looked at the other couple.

"You may find it more difficult than you imagine," he said softly.

A moment of panic seized Miranda. It was a strange

remark. Her discomfort was increased by the level look his lordship gave her. How much did he know? Surely he could not have guessed at the deception? It was impossible.

Later that night she tossed and turned as she lay in bed, unable to sleep. Heston did not trust her. He had made that clear. Yet he had warned her not to encourage the Count.

Why had he brought his friend along on that particular evening? Perhaps he imagined that Harry Lakenham would transfer his attentions to her sister. Alexei Toumanov must have been invited as a diversion, but she could not be sure. Suddenly she was tired of the whole ignominious business. She should never have become involved.

Heston was not the monster she had thought him. Common sense told her that. After all, it was not so dreadful for a man to wish to rescue a friend from a designing female. If the truth were to be told, it was admirable.

As for his insults, well, she had brought most of those upon herself. Not for the first time, she bemoaned her hasty tongue.

She was not entirely to blame, although she had been persuaded into this stupid hoax against her better judgement. The fact that she had sought to protect her sister was no excuse.

Lord Heston had been hasty, too. He had misjudged her from the start. Sadly, that was no comfort now. Somehow it seemed important that he should think better of her as their acquaintance grew.

In this last day or two she had seen him in a different light. He had been kind to her aunt and also to Lady

Medlicott. She had been surprised, too, by the wide range of his interests. His conversation was stimulating, and on more than one occasion she had forgotten her dislike of him as they discussed particular topics.

Miranda tossed off her coverlet and turned her pillow, pressing her cheek against the cool linen. Yet still sleep would not come. Something deeper was disturbing her and at last she was forced to face the unpalatable truth. Tonight at the Vauxhall Gardens, her heart had jumped when she found that massive figure by her side, and it was not simply the fact that he had rescued both herself and Richard.

Later, as they supped at the Piazza, she had been aware of no one else. She could recall neither Count Toumanov's conversation nor that of her sister, and the other diners were merely a blur.

Only one thing stood out clearly in her mind, and that was the harsh, dark face of Adam Heston as his heavy-lidded eyes gazed down at her. She knew every detail of those features, the black brows, the acquiline nose, the clean line of his jaw, and the curve of his lips.

Her face grew hot as she recalled his kisses. His mouth had been warm upon her own as he held her to him, and the remembered scent of soap, sweet clean linen and the outdoors came back to haunt her.

She closed her eyes, pressing her palms against them as if by doing so she could shut him out of her mind. It was ridiculous. The last thing she needed was to fall in love with that formidable creature. He despised her. She must remember that, holding on to the thought as if it were some kind of talisman.

All she needed was the firm resolution to keep him at a distance, but in her present situation that was impossible. If only Fanny would fall out of love with Harry

Lakenham she might manage to extricate herself from her predicament. She could then announce that she had mistaken her own heart and cry off from her supposed betrothal.

She had meant to chide Fanny for leaving her to run to Harry's side in the Gardens. Now she realised that her sister had said nothing of that meeting. It was strange. In the usual way Fanny was so open.

Miranda had expected tears and sulks. Fanny, she knew, had been shocked to see her lover in the company of such birds of paradise, yet later she had not even seemed subdued. Her enjoyment of the rest of the evening had been obvious.

Miranda looked at the sleeping figure beside her with a mixture of love and exasperation. Then she sighed. Perhaps it was as well that her twin could sleep so soundly, untroubled by the chaotic state of their affairs. She would make a few discreet enquiries in the morning. Upon that thought she fell asleep herself.

She had no opportunity to carry out her plan to question Fanny. The arrival of their aunt with the *Gazette* drove any such idea out of Miranda's mind.

"See, my love. The announcement is here in black and white!" She brandished the paper under her niece's nose.

Miranda took it from her with a shaking hand. She had expected it, but somehow the words leapt out at her, larger, blacker, and more final than she could have dreamed. Heston had been given all his titles, but it was her own name which burned into her mind.

"Now at last we can make plans," Mrs Shere announced happily. "You must dress at once, my dearest.

His lordship is sure to call within the hour. I'll send your maid. Will you wear the French sprigged muslin?''

Miranda nodded, but her heart was thumping in a most alarming way, and she felt a little sick. With an effort she controlled her nausea and slipped out of bed.

The news had awakened Fanny. As their aunt left the room she looked across at her twin.

"Are you all right?" she whispered. "You look so pale…"

Miranda took refuge in a sharp retort. "Why did you leave me in the Gardens?" she demanded. "You should not have gone to Harry, and well you know it. If you'd had any sense at all, you'd have pretended not to see him.''

"I could not do it, Miranda. I had to know what he was doing with those awful women. You need not scold. You would have done the same yourself.'' Fanny began to sulk.

"No, I should not. We all know that gentlemen have convenients in their keeping, but we need not recognise them.''

"I didn't speak to them. Harry took me away…he wished to explain that the…er…lightskirts were with his friends.''

"That may be true, but you need not have taxed him with it there and then. Suppose Lord Heston had seen you? He did meet Harry later.''

"But not when he was with me," Fanny told her in an injured tone.

"Even so, he asked if I had arranged an assignation. I said not, but I doubt if he believed me.''

"Does it matter? You were with Richard when Heston found you.''

"I was, indeed! And what he must have thought I

can't imagine, with Richard lying on the ground and a swordsman standing over him.''

"That was not my fault," Fanny pouted.

"You can't escape all blame. Had our party stayed together, the man would not have dared approach me.''

"It seems I can do nothing right. Perhaps you have forgot that Lady Medlicott stayed behind, chatting to her friends, and Richard was watching the fireworks?''

"That isn't the point," Miranda cried impatiently. "The whole thing might have been avoided if you had shown a little more conduct.''

Fanny shrugged her shoulders as she sipped her morning chocolate. "We came to no harm." Her face brightened. "Was it not splendid at the Piazza? I am so glad that the Count and Heston came to find us. I did enjoy our supper, and I was even in charity with his lordship. He was not angry, was he?''

"He was furious," Miranda told her shortly. "And with good reason.''

"Why should you care?" Fanny gave her sister a curious glance. "Was it not your intention to annoy him?''

"Not by risking Richard's neck, and making a spectacle of myself.''

"Don't be such a crosspatch!" Fanny nibbled at a roll. "Alexei Toumanov is a character, isn't he? Do you like him?''

Miranda swung round on her.

"For heaven's sake, don't set your sights on him," she cried. "Heston has already warned me not to encourage the Count.''

"Naturally, you may not, but the same cannot apply to me. They came to invite us both to supper. That was an odd start in Heston if he did not wish his friend to know us.''

Miranda had thought much the same herself, but she was not prepared to discuss the matter.

"What of Harry?" she demanded. "Is your affection for him fading already?"

"Of course not!" Fanny looked uncomfortable. "Yet I may not see him. You said as much yourself, and I won't wear the willow else Aunt would notice my low spirits."

It was the most transparent of excuses for Fanny's clear delight in the Count's obvious admiration.

"Stuff!" her twin said rudely. "Fanny, if you bring more trouble down upon our heads, I shall wash my hands of you." With that threat she swept out of the room.

For the rest of the morning the knocker went incessantly as notes were delivered to her uncle's door by hand. All bore good wishes for her future happiness.

Miranda was leafing through a pile of cards and invitations from members of the *ton* who had not previously acknowledged her existence when Heston was announced.

"You, too?" He grinned at her as he looked at the scattered pieces of pasteboard on the table. "Today we are the most popular pair of lovers in London."

Miranda turned her head away. Her lips were trembling, and for some unaccountable reason she was on the verge of tears.

"Come for a drive with me," his lordship suggested gently. "The air will do you good."

Miranda shook her head. Then his hand cupped her chin and forced her to look up at him.

"Courage, my love! Yesterday you faced a swordsman. You will not tell me now that you cannot bear the scrutiny of the Polite World?''

The great blue eyes looked too large for her pale face, and Heston dropped a kiss upon her nose.

''Get your bonnet!'' he insisted. ''My devotion will wear thin if you keep my horses waiting.''

His teasing restored her spirits a little.

''Don't worry,'' he promised. ''I shall not throw you to the wolves. All you need do is smile and bow and look delightfully as you always do. I will take care of the rest.''

His kindness brought fresh tears to her eyes as she hurried away. She would never understand him. At one moment he could be hard and ruthless, so secure in his pride and arrogance that she found it easy to detest him. His concern to help her through the coming ordeal was far more difficult to bear. Fanny had suspected him of playing some deep game, but what it was she could not begin to guess, and nor could Fanny.

As she settled a gay little hat upon her copper curls, she began to regain her composure.

''Charming!'' he announced as she rejoined him. ''I like the jaunty feather.''

Miranda felt far from jaunty as they drove into Hyde Park. Their appearance was the signal for a crowd to surround their carriage, and she found herself the centre of a large group of well-wishers.

Astonishment was plain on many faces, and she fell prey to acute embarrassment. Most probably these people imagined that Heston had run mad to offer for a bride so far beneath him.

''Cheer up, my love!'' he whispered. ''No one will say it to my face, but they are all happy to see a confirmed bachelor caught by the foot at last.''

That was not true of all his lordship's acquaintance.

"We have not met before, I think." A matron in an ornate turban signalled to her coachman to pull up. She eyed Miranda with undisguised hostility. "Where have you been hiding your betrothed, my dear Heston?"

Miranda flushed to the ears. The cold words had made it sound as if there were something shameful in her which Heston had been at pains to hide.

The girl beside her was as scarlet as Miranda. She held out her hand. "I hope you will be very happy," she murmured in a voice choked with mortification.

"Thank you." Miranda smiled. "Is this your first Season?"

"It is!" The matron answered for her daughter, as she tried to stare Miranda down. "We do not see you at Almack's, Miss…er…Miss…?"

"Miss Gaysford," his lordship supplied helpfully. "My apologies, ma'am. I should have spoken more clearly. I had forgot your difficulty in hearing well."

It was a crushing setdown, and it had the result which Heston had intended. An alarming purple flush stained the woman's face, and her several chins began to wobble as she sought for a reply. Words failed her. She poked her coachman in the back with the tip of her parasol, and with a last dagger-look at Heston she was borne away.

Miranda had difficulty in keeping her countenance. Her shoulders were shaking as she made an unsuccessful attempt to turn a chuckle into a cough.

"Something amuses you, my dear?" Her companion looked down at her. His expression was as bland as usual but his eyes were twinkling.

"I fear you have made an enemy for life, sir. The lady will not soon recover from such a snub."

"You may be right. It is a lowering thought, but I shall try to bear it. It would not do to fall into a fit of the dismals…"

His words were too much for Miranda, but she made a last attempt to hide her amusement.

"You were not kind," she reproached.

"Neither was she. An ill-natured creature, Lady Eddington, and well known for her vicious tongue."

"I liked her daughter," Miranda ventured.

"Amabel?" his lordship shrugged. "A pleasant girl with a heavy cross to bear in such a mother. I pity her future husband with a dragon for a mother-in-law."

Miranda was silent, but his next words filled her with dismay.

"Tell me about your own mama," he said. "Is she like you or like your sister?"

"My lord?"

"I wished merely to know what I am to expect, my dearest." His smile filled her with acute foreboding. He could not be serious. He intended no more than she to go through with the marriage. Miranda stiffened. It was just another attempt to frighten her.

"I don't quite understand you," she replied in a cool tone.

"I think you do. You and your sister are so unlike, are you not?"

Panic seized Miranda. Was Heston beginning to suspect that he had been deceived?

"We are thought to be identical," she babbled. "Few people can tell us one from the other."

"How odd!" he mused. "I do not find the slightest difficulty in doing so. It is something about the eyes, I think."

This was dangerous ground. Miranda cast about wildly in her mind for some way to change the subject.

"You have not answered my original question," he reminded her.

"Oh, you mean in her nature?" Miranda made a quick recover. "Mama is more like Fa—like my favourite sister."

Heston did not appear to have noticed the slip, but Miranda's blood ran cold. She had come so close to giving herself away.

"Then I have nothing to worry about." Her companion did not look at her, but his lips twitched.

"Do you mean that as an insult, sir? It is unworthy of you." Miranda spoke with some heat, hoping that a quarrel would divert his lordship's attention from this perilous topic.

Heston would not be drawn.

"It was meant as a compliment," he told her smoothly. "Your sister is of a sanguine temperament, I believe."

"You don't mean that at all! You think her silly and frivolous and flighty!" Miranda stopped in dismay. Swift in defence of her twin, she had allowed her annoyance to lead her into saying more than she intended.

"Don't you?" he asked mildly.

"How dare you! You do not know her in the least."

"Then I crave your pardon. I must get to know her better…" He stopped as a cavalier on horseback came up to their carriage to offer his congratulations.

Miranda sank back thankfully against the cushioned seat. She had been reprieved, but for how long? Was Heston playing with her as a cat might play with a mouse before the kill?

That morning he had almost trapped her into betraying

herself, and she found his veiled remarks deeply disturbing. If he should carry out his promise to get to know Fanny better, she could place no reliance upon her twin's ability to deceive him. If he pushed Fanny far enough, the result might be a hysterical outburst in which everything would be revealed.

Her face showed nothing of her inner emotions. She smiled prettily at the compliments offered to her, and by the time the horseman moved away she had regained much of her composure.

"Do you dine at Carlton House tonight, my lord?" she asked.

"Unfortunately, yes. The Prince is giving a dinner for the Tsar and the King of Prussia. To refuse the invitation would be to give offence."

"You do not enjoy these gatherings, it would seem."

"The food is beyond reproach, and the music excellent." There was a cynical note in Heston's voice. "That is, if one enjoys a 'descent into hell'."

"My lord?"

"A favourite saying of the Prince's guests, my dear. The heat throughout the house is suffocating."

"I had heard that the Prince is afraid of draughts, but surely the interior is very fine? A friend described one of the chandeliers as looking like a shower of diamonds."

"It was probably almost as costly. You will go there, naturally, and you may see for yourself. The Regent will wish to meet my bride-to-be."

Miranda heard his words with dread. This was the worst blow of all. How could she appear at Carlton House under false pretences? It would likely be considered treason and she would end up in the Tower.

A shaky laugh escaped her lips.

"I like the idea of going there no more than you do," she protested.

"You will find that you have no alternative," he told her lightly.

Chapter Seven

The thought of deceiving the heir to the throne effectively destroyed the last traces of Miranda's peace of mind. Her face whitened to the lips and she could not speak.

"Come now, pray do not look as if you have seen a ghost! Prinny is no ghost, in fact very much the opposite. You will find him charming. It is his greatest gift." Heston took her hand and raised it to his lips.

In the ordinary way Miranda would have snatched it away, but now she left it in his grasp, her fingers tightening instinctively. He responded to the pressure, and then he released her to take up the reins once more.

"Chin up!" he said. "All is not yet lost, I assure you."

It was an odd remark, and it struck her forcibly. Distraught though she was, she could not let it go unchallenged.

"You speak in riddles, sir." She gave him a look of deep suspicion.

"Hedgehog!" he reproved. "I meant merely that you will enjoy a meeting with the Regent and his friends. He is a cultivated man, and a great patron of the arts, the best since Charles I.''

As he had intended, Miranda's attention was diverted.

"But he is hissed and booed by the public whenever he appears, my lord."

"Are you surprised? The English distrust an intellectual. In the public mind, hunting is more to be admired than sculpture, gaming rather than an interest in literature, and the work of the finest artists is not to be compared with an afternoon at the races."

"But the Prince does all those things," Miranda pointed out.

"He did. He has not hunted for some years, and he was never more popular than when his colours appeared on the racetrack. The scandal was unfortunate...he gave up racing on the spot."

"Scandal? I had not heard of it."

"It happened more than twenty years ago. His horse, Escape, was said to be the finest on the turf. It failed one day at Newmarket, and the odds against it shortened to five to one. Next day it won with ease, and both the Prince and his jockey, Chifney, were thought to have made large sums of money. The Prince was told that if Chifney rode for him again, no gentleman would start against him."

"But surely it was not true? The Prince would not stoop to cheating?"

"Of course not! It was just malicious gossip. Chifney published a vindication some time later, but the Prince had vowed that he would not race again."

Miranda gave him a curious glance. "You like him, don't you?"

"I do. Admittedly, he is his own worst enemy. The public sees him preoccupied with expensive trivia, his dress, his passion for building and redecoration, but how else is he to spend his time? He is excluded from the serious business of governing the country."

"He has a good friend in you, I think." Miranda smiled at her companion, quite forgetting her previous fears.

"I can give him little else but friendship," Heston murmured. "So much has gone amiss for him."

Miranda was silent. It would have been presumptuous to comment upon matters of which she knew so little.

"Much of it is due to his disastrous marriage to the Princess Caroline." Heston seemed to be speaking more to himself than to her. "One could wish that Mrs Fitz-herbert had been born a Protestant princess."

"But the people sympathise with the Princess of Wales," Miranda protested. "She is cheered when the Prince is hissed and booed."

"The public do not know her." Heston's face was sombre. "Few of them can have considered what it must be like for a cultured and fastidious man to be wed to a hoyden who is not even clean in her person, and whose way of life is such that not even the most liberal-minded can condone it."

"She may not be entirely to blame," Miranda ventured. "It is said that she loved someone else before she was married to the Prince."

"So did he!" Heston looked down at her then, with a strange expression in his eyes. "What deep pits we dig for ourselves when in the grip of strong emotion. It is as well to guard oneself against such follies." His mocking tone annoyed her.

"You can be in no such danger, sir," she told him coolly.

"Very true, my dear. The more tender emotions are not quite in my style, or in yours, I believe."

"How well you are getting to know me, sir. You have expressed my feelings perfectly." She turned away, so that he would not see the glitter in her eyes. He thought her hard and mercenary and she could not bear it.

"I'm happy to know that you won't suffer because I am forced to leave you for a day or two," Heston said lightly. "The Prince is to go to Oxford to receive a loyal address and I am invited to form part of his entourage."

Miranda looked her surprise.

"He has earned it," Heston replied to her unspoken question. "He is an honorary Doctor of Civil Law, and has founded two university readerships, among other things."

"How long will you be away?" Miranda's first feeling of relief was tempered by a sense of disappointment, which she did not care to examine too closely.

"Am I to suppose that you will miss me?" Heston's smile did not reach his eyes. "How touching!"

"I doubt if I shall go into a decline, my lord."

"I doubt it, too. Until our next meeting, then?" He had drawn up before her uncle's house, and sprang down from the phaeton to help her to alight.

She turned to bid him farewell, but he took her arm and accompanied her indoors.

"I must pay my respects to your aunt," he said.

That lady was descending the staircase as they entered the hall, and Heston greeted her with the utmost courtesy, explaining as he did so that he would be out of London for a day or two.

"I expect that you would like to take your leave of each other in private," Mrs Shere said kindly. "There is no one in the salon at this present time…"

Heston's eyes sparkled with amusement, but Miranda had no alternative but to accompany him. She stalked ahead of him and tossed aside her hat.

"That's right," he murmured. "Delightful confection though it is, the veil is something of an obstacle."

Next moment she was in his arms and his mouth came down on hers.

Miranda had promised herself that the next time he kissed her she would not respond. If she stood quite still, this demanding creature would soon grow tired of making love to a statue.

It was easier said than done. The touch of those warm lips was producing a most alarming sensation in the pit of her stomach and turning her limbs to jelly. Insensibly she relaxed within his arms.

"Let us sit down," he said. He slipped an arm about her waist and led her to a sofa. Miranda stiffened as he took a seat beside her. Then she turned her face away.

"Shy, my love? That will not do..." His lips grazed her cheek. "What a tease you are!" He began to kiss her eyelids, and then he pressed his mouth against the hollow of her neck. "Must you be so cold?"

"Please, my lord...you really must not..." She tried to fight a sudden urge to throw her arms about his neck and hold him to her. She wanted to press her cheek to his, to trace the curve of those smiling lips, and to stroke that thick dark hair.

Then he found her mouth again and the world was lost. Her pleasure was such that she felt powerless to resist him. She found herself responding with a passion that startled her.

When he released her, she could not look at him. Nothing in her experience had prepared her for the emotions which now threatened to overwhelm her.

She was trembling and made no effort to resist when he took her in his arms once more.

"So there is fire beneath the ice?" he murmured. "I had suspected it." There was no trace of mockery in his voice as he turned her face to his. "Blushing, my love? There is no need. It is nothing to be ashamed of, rather to be delighted in."

"Please go!" Miranda choked out the words. She felt ready to sink with mortification.

It was not until later when she was alone that his curious reaction struck her. It seemed that he had understood that this was her first experience of true passion. Yet that could not be true. Heston despised her as a mere adventuress...a fortune hunter. Was it likely that in that role she would be unversed in the ways of love?

She was still lost in thought when her aunt came to find her.

"Don't look so sad, my dear. Lord Heston will not be gone for long." Mrs Shere patted her hand.

Miranda managed a reluctant smile. "It is not that," she said.

"What then? Has something happened to disturb you?"

"Oh, Aunt, I feel so worried. Heston says that he will present me to the Regent."

"Is that all? Love, I must imagine, has driven all thought of protocol from his lordship's mind."

"What do you mean?"

"Dearest, you cannot appear in the presence of royalty before you have been formally presented at Court."

Her aunt's words went some way towards restoring Miranda's peace of mind, but it was quickly shattered.

"I have been considering the matter," Mrs Shere said

thoughtfully. "Lady Medlicott is not quite the person to sponsor you. Perhaps we should consult his lordship…"

"Yes, let us do it." Miranda was anxious to change the subject. "Richard has promised to call on us tomorrow. He has promised to take us to see the Balloon Ascent in Hyde Park…"

"Should you be going about so much without Lord Heston? I cannot think he would approve. If you had but seen his face when he called here last night and found you had gone to the Vauxhall Gardens…"

"His lordship can have no wish that I should stay indoors, Aunt Emma. In any case, I should not heed him if he had."

"My dear girl, think what you are saying!" Mrs Shere was scandalised. "In a few weeks time you will promise to obey him…"

"But not yet! In any case, he has not forbidden it. A pleasure outing in an afternoon is unexceptionable."

"Oh, dear, I suppose so, though I could wish that you were not so headstrong, dearest. You speak out so freely, and the way you take decisions in such a determined way is not quite—"

"Ladylike?" Miranda kissed the older woman with a rueful smile. "Aunt, I have had to make decisions all my life. Mama will not do so."

"I know it. Your mama is lost without a husband to guide her. She has had to rely so much upon her children, but now all will be changed. What a comfort it will be to her to be able to ask our dear Lord Heston for advice. Such a sensible man, and most good-natured, too!"

It was clear that his lordship had won the heart of at least one of Miranda's relatives.

"Do you think so?" she murmured.

"Of course, my love, and your uncle is much taken with him. Perhaps I should not say so, but we had heard that he was excessively proud and disagreeable. We both feared that you would find him so, and not even the prospect of a splendid match could be allowed to weigh against your future happiness."

Miranda was silent.

"You can't think what a relief it was to find that gossip had lied," her aunt continued. "I am persuaded that jealousy has much to do with it. His lordship's manner is charming…so courteous! He must be a model for any gentleman. Only the most depraved could take against him!"

A smile touched the corner of Miranda's mouth. She had not previously considered herself a monster of depravity, and she had most certainly taken against him.

"Aunt Emma, I must believe that you think Lord Heston perfect," she teased.

"Don't you, my love?" Mrs Shere saw the amusement in Miranda's expression and she returned the smile. "Well, perhaps not perfect," she admitted. "A saint would be difficult to live with, but one can't fail to admire his character." She looked steadily at her niece. "You don't know him well, as yet, my love. I don't expect transports of affection, but you think well of him, I hope?"

"He puzzles me," Miranda said with perfect truth. "I wonder if anyone would grow to know him well." She saw her aunt's troubled expression and hastened to amend her words. "You are right, of course, the more I am in his lordship's company the more I realise that much of what is said of him is unjustified. He is not a mere gamester, with no interests beyond his horses."

Her aunt kissed her. "You are growing up, my dear.

You will not take it amiss if I tell you that at first I thought you much more frivolous than your sister? Now I see that I was mistaken..." She patted Miranda's cheek. "Enjoy your outing with your friend."

Left alone, Miranda's thoughts were troubled. It was becoming more and more difficult to play the part of Fanny. The twins were so different in character, and Mrs Shere had noticed it. She herself had spoken without thinking when she had mentioned the need to make decisions for her mother. Fanny had never done so. She must make an effort to indulge in charming nonsense, to giggle, and to be light-hearted. She had never felt less like indulging in such behaviour.

A sense of relief swept over her as she stepped into the carriage the next day. Fanny knew the truth. There would be no need to dissemble with her twin.

As for Richard, he was too excited by the prospect of seeing his first Balloon Ascent to notice that Miranda was not her usual self.

"I have never enjoyed myself so much in all my life," he announced happily. "I wish you had been with me yesterday...the city was ablaze with light. It is the illuminations, you know...at night it looks a different place..."

"And so wonderful!" Fanny told him earnestly. "I could not go back to live in Yorkshire ever again. When one has lived in the capital the rest of England seems so...so provincial!"

"It's all very well to be here for a celebration," Richard said defensively. "But, Fanny, it does smell vile, and I can't say that I care much for the crowds."

"It isn't always like this." Fanny was in the mood to quarrel. "The foreigners are everywhere..."

"They won't be here for ever," Miranda intervened. "Richard, you are looking very fine today...quite the town beau, in fact."

"This rig?" Richard glanced down at his yellow pantaloons with assumed indifference. His brocade waistcoat was so brightly patterned that it was dazzling to the eye. Above it, his stiffly starched shirt-points rose almost to the middle of his cheeks, making it difficult for him to turn his head to left or right.

"It don't do to look the country cousin," he explained defensively. "I'd stand out like a sore thumb here in London."

"Whereas in that waistcoat you are all but invisible," Fanny giggled.

Richard's face fell. "Do you think it too much?" he asked anxiously. "M'father said I might buy what I chose."

"It looks very well." Miranda frowned at her sister. "Quite the latest thing, in fact. I'm sure you looked about you to see what others are wearing before you visited the tailor."

"Oh, I did, and he told me that it was all the crack, you know."

"Then you may be easy in your mind." Miranda smiled at him. His garments were expensive, and she felt sure that he had been persuaded into parting with a great deal of money in his efforts to become a gentleman of fashion. She would not spoil his pleasure for the world, although she felt sure that the shirtpoints in particular were causing him discomfort.

"Well, it would not do for Yorkshire." He grinned at her a little consciously. "But one must be in the correct way of things."

Miranda nodded her agreement. She had always been

fond of him. Good-natured to a fault, he, more than any of her brother's friends, had been the one to take the twins' part in any of their scrapes. Scorned by the other boys, who refused to have mere females take part in their adventures, Richard had raised no objections. He bore the expostulations of his friends with great good humour, but he would not be swayed.

She looked at him with renewed affection. He was hung about with fobs and an expensive tie-pin gleamed in the folds of his cravat, but he did not quite achieve the appearance of a dandy, which was clearly his intention.

Miranda suspected that he had chosen his present rig knowing that he was to escort them, and wishing to do them credit.

"Are any of your friends in London?" she asked kindly.

"No, but I am putting up at Grillon's, and I made a new acquaintance. He is a famous fellow. We went to see the wild beasts in the Tower, and to Astley's Ampitheatre..." He did not think it prudent to mention the cock-fights to which his new friend had taken him, nor his visit to Gentleman Jackson's saloon to watch that gentleman sparring with other devotees of The Fancy. Ladies were not interested in such exciting sports.

He saw her worried look and smiled at her. "He is not an ivory-turner. You may have no fears on that score."

Miranda felt relieved. In the short time she had spent in London, she had heard stories of the men who lay in wait for gullible boys, leading them to ruin in the many gaming hells which had sprung up in the capital.

At that moment she was hailed by Charlotte Fairfax.

"Do you go to the Ascent?" her friend called out.

The twins nodded in unison.

"Then may we go together? We must walk from here, you know, and I want to talk to you." Charlotte's face was alive with curiosity as she dismissed her brother.

Young Fairfax needed no urging to be relieved of his charge. He handed his sister down from their carriage and, with a bow to Miranda's party, he went off to find his friends.

"Wretched boy!" Charlotte said with feeling. "I wish you might have heard the fuss he made when Mamma said that he must bring me."

"Brothers are all the same," Fanny agreed. "It was only Richard here who would ever allow us to go about with him when we were children."

Charlotte looked at their escort, a question in her eyes. "This gentleman is not your brother? I had supposed..."

"Richard is a family friend." Miranda made the necessary introductions. Under the cover of the ensuing civilities, Fanny tugged at her elbow.

"You will not fly into the boughs if we see Harry, I hope? He is quite likely to be here today."

"Of course not! We can't prevent him from going wherever he wishes, but pray do not slip away with him. It is a different thing if you meet him in company."

"You two are the outside of enough!" Charlotte teased. "Now which of you am I to congratulate upon your betrothal?" She turned to Richard. "Do you find the same difficulty, sir? If you have known Fanny and Miranda from childhood, perhaps you can tell them apart?"

Miranda froze, and beside her she felt her sister stiffen. It was true that Richard knew them as well as their own family.

She should have thought of it before. It was no more

likely that they could deceive Richard than that they
could deceive their own brother. Yet he had handed her
the letter from her mother with no more than a moment's
hesitation, clearly believing that she was Fanny. It was
that which had lulled her into a sense of false security.
She held her breath, waiting for the blow to fall.

"We have not been much in each other's company
for these past few years," Richard said easily. "I was
at Oxford, Miss Fairfax. Meantime, the twins have
grown even more alike. Sometimes they confuse me,
too."

Miranda looked at him with gratitude in her eyes. He
met her own with a level gaze and only the faintest of
smiles. It was enough. He knew of the deception, she
was convinced of it.

Fanny took her arm. "You must wish my sister happy,
Charlotte. She is the fortunate bride-to-be."

Charlotte threw her arms about Miranda. "Sly creature!" she chaffed. "We had not the least idea...why, I
almost fainted when I read the announcement. I would
not believe it! Lord Heston of all people! I thought it
must be some mistake when you had both taken him in
such dislike."

Miranda gave her an ironic look, and Charlotte's hand
flew to her mouth. "Oh, my stupid tongue again... I
should not have said that. Indeed, I wish you happy."

"I know you do." Miranda rescued her from her confusion. "We had best go, or we shall miss the ascent."

As they strolled through the crowds to get a better
view, Miranda allowed Fanny and Charlotte to go ahead.
She fell into step with Richard.

"Thank you," she said simply.

"For what?"

"I think you know quite well. When did you guess?"

"When I brought the letters."

"But you gave Mama's letter to me, and it was addressed to Fanny."

"Your uncle made it clear that he thought that you were Fanny. It was not up to me to correct him."

"You must be wondering…!"

"I wondered if you were in a scrape again. It wouldn't be the first time…"

She heard a low chuckle.

"This time it isn't so amusing, and it is all my fault. If I hadn't lost my temper and said things which I now regret, we should not be in this situation."

"You will not tell me that Fanny had no hand in it? I should not believe you."

Miranda hesitated.

"You need not tell me if you don't wish, you know, but if there is anything I can do…?"

"There is nothing anyone can do, I fear. Sometimes I long to turn tail and run back home."

"That isn't like you. You were always the one with the lion heart. Can you not think of a way to put matters right?"

"I wish I could. Meantime, I feel wretched to be deceiving everyone in this way. Oh, Richard, I should not—"

"You should not worry so. Neither you nor Fanny would do anything really bad. I know you well enough for that. It will all come right, you'll see…"

With these words of comfort he took her arm and caught up with the others.

They had found a vantage point beside the roped-off enclosure from which the balloon ascent was to be made. The silken globe was already tugging at its moorings in the breeze, the brilliant colours gleaming in the sunlight.

At each corner men held tightly to the mooring rope, whilst some argument seemed to be taking place beside the wicker basket which was to hold the occupants.

"How many will it hold?" asked Charlotte.

"Two, or possibly three, I should imagine." Richard eyed the proceedings with interest.

"Oh, no!" Fanny's eyes were upon one of the men at the centre of the argument. He was muffled to the eyes, but she had no difficulty in recognising Harry Lakenham. "He cannot be planning to go with them."

"I fear he does. Fanny, please." Miranda gripped her sister's arm. "You must not go to him."

"I will! I will! He is sure to be killed...I know it..." Fanny's voice had risen to a shriek and several people turned to look at her.

"Don't worry, they will not take him if he is inexperienced. Is he a friend of yours?" It was a casual question, but something in Richard's tone caused Miranda to throw him a sharp glance. His eyes were on Fanny's face, and in that moment he betrayed himself.

Miranda groaned inwardly. This was yet another complication and one which she could well do without. She could not doubt that Richard was in love with Fanny, and he could not fail to be hurt. Suddenly she felt fiercely protective towards him.

"Pull yourself together, Fanny!" she urged. "See, they have turned Harry away..."

It was true. As she watched, the two intrepid flyers climbed in the basket and signalled to their assistants. Harry had been motioned to one side with a couple of stalwarts between himself and the balloon. They jumped out of the way as the ballast was thrown out and the wind filled the silken dome. As it began to rise, Harry saw his chance. He dodged the men and leapt for the basket, catching at a trailing rope, already high in the air.

As the crowds watched in horror, Fanny crumpled at Miranda's feet. She fell to her knees beside her sister, but Richard was there before her. He lifted Fanny tenderly in his arms.

"We must get her home at once," he said.

Miranda nodded dumbly, but she could not take her eyes from the struggle taking place above her head. As she watched, Harry gained the rim of the basket, causing it to sway alarmingly. Then he was pulled to safety inside. Next moment he was on his feet again, waving cheerfully to the onlookers below.

Miranda heard a murmur of disgust from those beside her.

"Doubtless he did it for a wager," one man said. "But he might have killed them all. I have no patience with such folly."

Miranda was in complete agreement with his sentiments, but Fanny was her more immediate concern. She followed Richard through the press of people with Charlotte by her side.

"You will come home with us?" she asked Charlotte. "We shall never find your brother in these crowds, and we cannot leave you here alone."

Charlotte herself was pale and trembling. "I feel quite faint myself," she admitted. "If Lord Lakenham had fallen... It does not bear thinking about."

"Then don't think about it. It was the most stupid thing I have ever seen, and I don't propose to give myself a fit of the dismals over Harry Lakenham's idiocy. It would have served him right if he had fallen and broken a leg."

"He was more likely to have broken his neck." Charlotte shuddered and was still trembling as their carriage reached its destination.

"You are back early," Mrs Shere began as Miranda stepped into the hall. Then she saw Richard with Fanny in his arms. "What is it? What has happened?"

"My sister fainted, and Charlotte is not well. There was an accident during the Ascent, but no one has been hurt…"

"Bring her in here and put her on the sofa, poor child. Miss Fairfax, do sit down! You shall take a glass of brandy."

Charlotte took a glass from Richard's hand, sipping at the spirit with a small moue of distaste. It soon restored her, and she cast an anxious look at Fanny, who lay inert upon the couch.

"Here, my love!" Mrs Shere forced a little of the brandy between her niece's pallid lips. "This will make you feel better."

Fanny had recovered consciousness in the carriage, but she had not uttered a word since her collapse. Now her eyes met Miranda's in a heart-rending plea for reassurance.

"Tell me the worst," she murmured at last. I must know…even if he is dead."

"Lakenham is not dead, though he deserves to be," Miranda told her sharply. "I know that his stupid action was a shock for you, as it was for all of us. Charlotte almost fainted too." She looked a warning at her sister as she spoke. In her present state of near-hysteria, Fanny was only too likely to betray herself. "Let me take you to your room…you should have rest and quiet."

"That will be best," Mrs Shere agreed. "If Mr Young will be good enough to see Charlotte home? My dears,

I can't believe such folly! Apart from all else, it has quite ruined your outing.''

Miranda caught Richard's eyes. With his usual courtesy he had agreed at once to escort Charlotte home, but his normally cheerful expression had disappeared and she knew the reason why. Fanny's outburst had convinced him that she was in love with Harry Lakenham.

Miranda was quick to caution Fanny when they were alone.

''I know that you could not help fainting. It was a terrifying experience, but, Fanny, do take care what you say. Aunt Emma must have wondered…''

''I could not help it. I was sure that Harry must have been killed. You would not lie to me? He is really safe?''

''The last time I saw him he was waving to the crowd with all the effrontery in the world, and it did not make him popular. Everyone realised that he might have killed others beside himself.''

''It was just a high-spirited prank,'' Fanny pouted.

''You did not think so at the time, and I doubt if it would have seem so to the widows of the men he might have destroyed.''

''You never make allowances for him. He is young…''

''He is, indeed, and, in my opinion, far too light-minded to think of getting wed. I'm not surprised that his grandfather is against it. Had you been a duchess, with the largest dowry in the world, Lord Rudyard must have been of the same opinion.''

Slow tears rolled down Fanny's cheeks. ''I love him…'' she said brokenly.

''Well, I don't admire your choice. If you married

him, you would not have a moment's peace of mind. A handsome face is no substitute for common sense.''

''I don't expect you to understand. You have never fallen in love...''

''When I do, it won't be with a man like Harry Lakenham.''

''Then I'm surprised you didn't take that fat old creature who offered for you when we first came here. Surely he was staid enough for you?''

''Mr Norton?'' Miranda smiled. ''He was a little too staid, even for me. Oh, Fanny, I don't mean to criticise. No one can tell where their heart will lead them...''

She grew silent. For some reason the memory of a harsh, dark face swam into her mind. Heston would be a rock, a man upon whom any sensible woman might rely. It was strange how that penetrating gaze could soften into a smile which had the oddest way of making her heart turn over. She brushed the treacherous thought aside. How could she reproach Fanny further when her own fancies were just as wayward?

''Won't you rest?'' she begged. ''Richard had promised to return this evening to see how you go on.''

''I won't come down. If he wishes, he may call again tomorrow.'' Fanny turned her face away. ''I wish that life were not so dull at present. You have forbidden me to see Harry, and Count Toumanov is away at Oxford.''

''Haven't you had enough excitement for one day?'' Miranda teased gently. ''Would you like me to sit with you this evening? I could read to you, or we might play cribbage?''

''You need not! I don't care to listen to any more lectures.''

''As you wish.'' Miranda was losing patience. She changed quickly and left the room before she was tempted to utter words which she might regret. It was useless to argue further. She would abandon Fanny to her sulks.

During supper she was obliged to relate the day's events again for the benefit of her uncle.

The Alderman's face grew dark with anger. "That young man needs taking in hand," he announced. "Such folly! When Lord Rudyard gets to hear of this escapade the lad will be sent to the country on a repairing lease, and high time too."

"It was very bad," Mrs Shere agreed. "But I fear that young Lakenham has been indulged too much by his grandfather. His mother and father are both dead—"

"That is no excuse! How true is the old adage 'to spare the rod and spoil the child'."

"He is a charming boy," Aunt Emma ventured.

"Too charming!" came the gruff reply. "That has been his undoing... Now let us speak no more of it. It will ruin my digestion."

This dire prediction did not affect his appetite and he made an excellent meal. As usual, Mrs Shere left him to his port and led Miranda through into the salon.

She was playing a favourite song upon the spinet when Richard was announced. Miranda closed the instrument at once, and walked towards him.

"Your patient is better, I trust?" He bowed to both ladies as his eyes searched their faces.

"My sister is much recovered from her fright, though she is tired. She will not come down this evening, but she will be glad to see you in the morning."

Richard hid his disappointment with a good grace. He did not refer to the incident again, confining himself to an exchange of pleasantries, and a remark about the mock battle on the Serpentine which was to take place during the following week.

It was not until Mrs Shere was called out of the room that he spoke of the subject closest to his heart.

"I have no right to ask," he told Miranda. "Do not answer me if you think it indiscreet, but has Fanny formed an attachment for Lord Lakenham?"

"Mere calf-love," Miranda said briskly. "I suspect that it is a youthful infatuation on both sides. If I am not mistaken, it will come to nothing."

"I must hope that you are right." His eager look dismayed Miranda. "I do not ask from a mere vulgar curiosity. The thing is…well…I have always been fond of her, even when we were children. I felt that she needed protecting, you see."

"You are right," Miranda told him drily. "And more from herself than from any outside influence."

He smiled at that. "You were always the strong one, Miranda. It's hard to believe that you are twins."

"Fanny has many qualities that I lack."

"I doubt if that is so." He coloured to the roots of his hair. "Seeing her again after so long…well…I won't deny my feelings. I had hoped to ask her to become my wife."

"Dear Richard, how good you are! Fanny is a lucky girl, if she did but know it."

"But she must not know of my wishes, at least for the moment. I would not have her feel awkward with me, or obliged to say…to say…"

"To refuse you? No, you are quite right. Let her get over this youthful passion. If I know her, it will not take long."

"You think your mama would not object to my offering for Fanny? She seems to believe that both of you should marry well.''

"How could she object, my dear Richard? You are the son of one of her oldest friends. As to marrying well…in my opinion, Fanny could not do better than to wed a man with such a loving heart as yours. Mama will be satisfied with the thought of my own match." Miranda looked a little conscious as she spoke, but Richard did not notice.

"Indeed, I wish you happy, Miranda. I cannot doubt it. Lord Heston is such a splendid fellow, isn't he?"

Miranda gave him a mechanical smile. She nodded, thinking as she did so that Richard might be the answer to her prayers. If he and Fanny were to make a match of it, she would be free to cry off from her own supposed betrothal. The prospect should have cheered her, but she found it unaccountably depressing.

Chapter Eight

Richard was an early visitor on the following morning and Fanny greeted him with unaffected pleasure. She had recovered from her fright and was disposed to regard with a kindly eye any visitor who promised an opportunity to chatter and make plans for the coming week.

Now she dimpled as she welcomed him, drawing him aside to sit with her by the window.

Miranda regarded them with some anxiety. To flirt with any personable young man, even a childhood friend, was as natural to Fanny as breathing. Thank heavens Richard understood her. It would be cruel to raise his hopes by leading him on in that careless way she had.

Richard caught Miranda's eye, and a faint smile curved his lips. Inwardly, Miranda blessed him. His face betrayed nothing of his inner turmoil. To all appearances he was his usual amiable self. He knew very well that Fanny's lively manner did not indicate a change in her feelings for him.

"More visitors!" Fanny jumped to her feet and looked out of the window. "Why, it is Charlotte and her brother! Now we shall be gay!"

She abandoned Richard and hurried to greet her friends.

"Are you recovered, Charlotte? What a fright we had! I thought that I should die of terror!"

"So did I!" Charlotte's manner was still subdued. "I cannot forget the sight. Last night I could not sleep. Mama is furious. She had intended to write to Lakenham's grandfather, but now she says that she will speak to Lord Heston instead, rather than worry the old man."

"Lord Heston?" Miranda was surprised. "What can he do?"

"He acts in some way as Harry's guardian. He is not, of course, but there is a connection. Heston is Lord Rudyard's godson. You did not know of it?"

Miranda shook her head.

"Heston keeps an eye on Harry to oblige his grandfather. Lord Rudyard is said to be a martyr to gout. He can no longer get about as he was used to do."

"I see." Miranda grew thoughtful. Much that she had not understood before was now becoming clear to her. She had wondered why Heston should take so keen an interest in Harry's affairs. His concern had seemed to her to go far beyond the claims of friendship.

She sighed. Even had Heston been in London on the previous day, she doubted if he would have been drawn to attend a Balloon Ascent. In any case, Harry was no longer a child. Heston could not be expected to watch over him as if he were still in leading-strings.

Her irritation grew. Harry Lakenham, like her sister, sailed through life with little regard for the peace of mind of those about them. When she next saw him, she would give him a piece of her mind.

The opportunity came at once. They had not been sitting for more than a few moments when the door was opened cautiously and Harry's laughing face appeared.

"Must I throw my hat in, Mrs Shere?" he cried.

"Come in, you wicked creature!" Mrs Shere strove to preserve a stern expression, but Harry was a favourite of hers. She was not proof against his charm. "I should send you about your business. It is certainly what you deserve...frightening us as you did!"

Miranda was furious. Harry must be mad to come here. She could not look at him. Instead, her eyes flew to Fanny's face, and was dismayed by what she saw there. Fanny's heart was in her eyes. In another moment she must betray herself.

Miranda stepped in front of her twin and greeted Harry with cold civility.

"Are you very angry with me?" he said penitently. "You look so severe, Miss Gaysford. I confess I am quaking in my boots..."

"That I must doubt, my lord!" Miranda stepped aside and allowed him to make his bow to Charlotte and her brother.

Then he moved to Fanny's side. "Helmsley tells me that you are the person who suffered most from my ill-judged behaviour," he said softly. "Indeed, I am sorry for it. Will this make amends?" He handed her a small parcel.

Fanny could not answer him. Her hands were shaking as she busied herself with the wrappings.

"Let me!" He took the packet from her and opened it to reveal a book of poems. "They are by George Byron," he explained. "I remembered that you liked his work."

"Thank you." Fanny's reply was almost inaudible.

"You feel more yourself, I hope?" Harry continued

eagerly. "I should have called last evening to see how you did, but we landed far out in the country and I did not see Helmsley until midnight."

"Then you were not injured?" Fanny murmured. "Oh, if you only knew how much I have suffered!"

"It was the sudden shock which overcame your nerves," Miranda broke in quickly. "Charlotte was in much the same case and so were many others..." She picked up the book of poems. "I had not imagined that you were a lover of poetry, Lord Lakenham." It was a desperate effort to change the subject.

Harry grinned at her. "I'm not," he said frankly. "Can't understand what the women see in the fellow. All these romantic vapourings... He's naught but a poseur...sleeps with his hair in curling papers."

"That can't be true," Mrs Shere protested. She, too, was an admirer of the noble lord. "It is simply malicious gossip."

"Upon my word, it is the truth. M'friend called on him one morning and saw it. Byron admitted that he was as vain of his ringlets as a girl. Begged Scrope Davies not to speak of it, of course, but the joke was too good to keep it to himself."

"You will ruin my niece's pleasure in her book," Mrs Shere reproached. "No matter what is said of Lord Byron, there is still his poetry, which I find most uplifting."

"Are you an admirer of his work?" Richard addressed Miranda in an effort to keep the conversation away from dangerous subjects. He had supported his introduction to Harry Lakenham with perfect civility, but there was an indefinable air of tension in the room.

"He is not quite in my style, though the fault must lie with me, I fear." Miranda smiled at him. Byron had spoken to her on one occasion, drawn by her beauty and clearly expecting to be met with the same adulation which he regarded as his due from the female sex. She had been unimpressed, finding this lion of London society so self-centred as to be a bore. He had soon moved away in search of a more appreciative audience.

"Have you missed Heston? He is at Oxford with the Prince, I hear..." Harry's eyes danced with mischief as he teased her.

Miranda resolved to pay him back in his own coin.

"Lord Heston returns to town today, so I understand. Doubtless he will wish to seek you out without delay."

"I expect so, if only to give me a roasting..." Harry pulled a comical face. Then, undeterred by this warning of Heston's displeasure, he grinned. "He'll be full of stories. The Prince is a wit, you know."

"We heard that the Regent has a humorous turn of phrase," Mrs Shere agreed.

"It's clever, but not always kind." Harry began to laugh. "He described the Marquess of Wellesley as a Spanish grandee grafted on to an Irish potato. The Wellesleys are of Irish stock, as you know. It was so apt. Richard Wellesley is a stiff old stick."

"Yet the Duke of Wellington thinks highly of his brother, I believe. It is said that the Marquess is the cleverer of the two." Richard spoke quietly, but Harry Lakenham looked up.

"My dear sir, you sound like Adam Heston..." He was smiling, but there was a challenge in his eyes. His careless gossip had not met with universal approval and it did not please him.

Miranda turned to Charlotte. "Shall you watch the procession to the Guildhall?" she asked quickly. "Heston has promised that we are to go..." The rest of her words died upon her lips when the door opened and the subject of her conversation walked into the room.

At the sight of his tall figure, Miranda's heart began to pound. She could not decide if this disturbing sensation had arisen from joy or fright.

As always, Heston's face was impassive, but by now she knew him well enough to realise that he was very angry. She rose and went towards him.

"I am glad to see you, my lord," she said with perfect truth. It was strange, but there was something so dependable about him.

"Are you, my dear? I am glad to hear it." He kissed her hand and then her cheek.

"We did not expect you this morning," she continued brightly. "Here you find us talking about the procession to the Guildhall..." She prayed to heaven that he would not give full vent to his displeasure in the presence of her aunt.

"I see." His indifferent gaze roved from one face to another as he greeted the assembled company with his usual civility, albeit with some reserve.

It was enough to persuade Charlotte and her brother to take their leave. Richard was about to follow them when Heston stopped him.

"Mr Young, you have not forgot that you are to join our party?"

"Your lordship is very kind. I had not forgot—indeed, I am looking forward to it." Richard bowed and walked towards the door.

"Wait, I will go with you..." Harry made as if to join him.

"Must you rush away so soon?" Heston's gentle words stopped Harry in his tracks.

"I have just remembered an appointment." Harry's face was the picture of guilt.

"An urgent appointment, I am sure... Will you wait upon me, say, at six o'clock? I shall be expecting you." Heston's tone made it impossible for Harry to refuse. He gulped, nodded, and hurried away.

"My lord, you will not be too hard on him?" Mrs Shere pleaded. "It was just a boy's trick. Lord Lakenham did not think that it might have serious consequences."

"You are too generous, ma'am." Heston gave her a faint smile. Then his frown returned. "That is Harry's problem...he never considers the consequences of his actions until it is too late. I have been at fault. I should not have agreed to his coming to London, but that is easily remedied."

"What do you mean?" Fanny spoke so sharply that Mrs Shere shot her a quick look of reproof.

Heston bent his penetrating gaze on Fanny. "Harry must return to his grandfather," he announced. "I had thought him grown to manhood, but he is still a thoughtless child. In the country he may fall out of trees and into the river without harming others."

Fanny gasped and burst into tears. Then she fled from the room.

"Oh, dear! My lord, you must forgive my niece. Her nerves are on edge since yesterday. Poor child...such a shock. I must go to her..."

Heston waited until the door had closed behind her.

"And how are your nerves, my dear?" he said smoothly. "I heard that you had fainted in the Park."

"No, I did not!" Miranda snapped. "It was my sister who was overcome..."

"Curious! But then I expect that you are made of stronger stuff...I won't say I'm surprised."

Miranda did not answer him.

"What does surprise me, however, is to find Lakenham here this morning... No doubt you will tell me the reason?"

"He...he came to apologise," Miranda stammered. "My sister and Charlotte Fairfax and many other ladies felt ill when they saw Lord Lakenham in danger of his life."

"Touching! But then, you have such tender hearts, have you not? It has always been a source of some amazement to me that you ladies form such attachments for gentlemen with rakish tendencies."

"Harry is not a rake," Miranda cried hotly.

"He is well on the way to being so. Harry is a lightweight, and well you know it."

"Do I?"

"I think so. I have never imagined you to be a fool. You think me hard, perhaps? Let me assure you that if Harry stays in London, not satisfied with forming an unfortunate attachment, he will also fall into the hands of ivory-turners and will lose his patrimony as soon as he comes of age."

"That must be a source of anxiety to you," Miranda said with a touch of irony.

"It is." Heston ignored the sarcasm. "I have known men die before the age of thirty, ruined by drink and gaming." There was no trace of mockery in his voice and Miranda felt ashamed of her outburst.

"I know that it can happen," she agreed.

"Well then, my love, we are in charity with each other once again, I hope? I have some news for you. My mother longs to meet you. Next week she will come here from Warwickshire…''

''Your…your mother?'' Miranda eyed him with dread.

''Of course. Why should you be surprised? I have a mother, you know. I did not spring to life fully formed, like some character of old.''

''You have not mentioned meeting her before,'' Miranda said faintly.

''I was not sure that she would come to London. She is an artist, and painting is her life. I thought perhaps a quiet dinner in Brook Street, to include your aunt and uncle and your sister, if that would please you?''

Stunned by this news, Miranda could only acquiesce.

''It will give you an opportunity to see your new home. You may like to make some changes to the furnishings, but I will leave that in your hands…''

Miranda looked at him in desperation. ''My lord…''

''No, don't talk! We have been parted for too long.'' He drew her to him and sought her lips.

''Please, you must not!'' she protested.

''But I must! Kiss me, dearest! I have thought of you each waking moment since I saw you last.''

''Humbug!'' she cried fiercely.

A quiver of emotion disturbed the calm of Heston's expression, and his shoulders began to shake.

''How unkind!'' he reproached in a bland tone. ''At our first meeting you struck me. Now you throw my words of love back in my face… I am beginning to believe that I am betrothed to a termagant.''

Miranda was strongly tempted to inform him that he was not betrothed to anyone, but she bit back the angry words.

"I am aware that you find our situation amusing," she retorted.

"Oh, I do, my dear, I do! I haven't been so entertained in years. You are a constant joy to me. I had begun to believe that there wasn't a woman in London possessed of any spirit...and you have always some surprise in store for me."

"I shall try not to disappoint you in that respect." Miranda spoke with feeling. She had a number of surprises in store for this self-assured creature. Her eyes began to sparkle. Then she recalled how quick he was to sense her every mood. She stole a glance at him, but he was regarding her with that false expression of tenderness which she disliked so much.

"I doubt if you could ever disappoint me, even if you would," he murmured in sentimental tones as he slid an arm about her waist. He drew her to him, and then his hand stole up her spine. As he began to stroke her neck, little shivers of delight swept over her. He bent his head and kissed her beneath her ear.

"Must you always stiffen when I touch you?" he whispered. "Relax, my love. You will enjoy it more." He took the small pink lobe between his teeth and nibbled at it gently.

Miranda did not pull away from him. Insensibly she was losing the power to resist his caresses, but she made a last determined effort. There was something she had to say.

"My lord, may I ask you something?"

"Anything, my dearest!"

"I have been thinking. Would it be wise to send Lord Lakenham out of London in disgrace? He is high-spirited. It may persuade him to do something foolish."

Heston released her and rose to his feet. There was a curious glitter in his eyes.

"You think that he might yet elope? How could that be, my dear, when you are promised to me? Or do you still have a *tendre* for him?"

"Of course not! I was never in love with Harry—" Miranda's hand flew to her mouth. She had betrayed herself at last. Now she waited for the explosion of wrath and demands for explanations which must be sure to follow her outburst.

"I did not think you were...not for a moment. On your part it was a business arrangement, was it not? My hope that you will not cry off from our engagement must lie in the fact that my fortune is greater than his."

The cruel words struck Miranda like a blow to the heart. Tears stung her eyes, and her mouth was trembling.

"You may believe what you will," she whispered.

"What else can I believe? You made your position very clear. You shrink from my caresses and you answer my attempts at tenderness with insults."

"Tenderness? From you? Sir, you shall not think me a fool. I know very well what you are about."

"I wish that I could say the same, my love."

His words were casual enough, but they filled Miranda with dread. How much did he suspect? She hardly dared to look at him, but when she did so he appeared to be absorbed in studying the intricate pattern carved into the lid of his snuff-box.

"You speak in riddles, my lord. I do not understand you..."

"You will come to do so, I suspect, though it may take a lifetime. You do not find it a lowering thought to consider the trials ahead of you?"

Miranda had recovered her composure. She gave him her most enchanting smile. "I shall do my best to bear them," she said sweetly.

"You do not lack courage, as I have observed before. Will it carry you through an evening at Almack's?" He produced two of the coveted vouchers and laid them upon a table.

"You wish me to make an appearance there? Well, I suppose that I must do so. You will not wish me to be exposed to further insults from your friends."

Heston looked mystified and then he laughed. "You are referring to Lady Eddington? She is no friend of mine. I thought merely that you might like to satisfy your curiosity about the place, and Alexei finds it amusing."

"You will invite Count Toumanov?"

"Only if you do not object. I believe you find him entertaining…" His voice was bland.

"I find him charming." Miranda gave her tormentor a hostile look. "He is so kind."

"A worthy trait of character! Would that I could lay claim to it…sadly, I am irredeemable."

"In that, at least, we are in agreement, sir. When is this visit to Almack's to take place?"

"If Alexei is to join us, it must be tonight. Those hallowed portals are open only on Wednesdays, and by next week he will be gone."

"He returns to Russia?"

"Unless his master gives him leave to stay. It is unlikely." Heston looked at his watch. "Much as it distresses me, my love, I must tear myself away from your side for the moment."

"I will try to bear it, sir."

Heston grinned at her. "Always the hard word, my dearest? Until this evening, then…shall we say at nine?"

Miranda walked to the door and opened it a trifle. He would not attempt to kiss her again in full view of the servants. When she looked up at him she saw his mocking smile.

"Minx!" he chided. "That would not stop me, but you may have your way. Don't worry about Harry Lakenham, by the way. I could not send him out of London, even had I wished to do so. I am not his guardian, but I'll give him a dressing-down he won't forget. What his grandfather may decide is something else."

Miranda was thoughtful as she made her way upstairs to Fanny. Heston was the most extraordinary creature she had ever met. She needed time to think…to understand her own emotions…

In the course of the last hour her feelings had fluctuated wildly. At the sight of his tall figure she had experienced an unguarded moment of joy. It had been followed almost at once by dread of his reaction to the sight of Harry in her company.

Then she recalled the words which had hurt her so. She closed her eyes in agony. Heston had made his opinion of her only too clear. He considered her a fortune-hunter, no better than the expensive Incognitas who swarmed about the capital.

He had not made the best of bargains, either. At least those harpies gave value for money, and it was not unreasonable of him to expect the same from her.

Her face burned. If he only knew how she had longed to melt into his arms, to return his kisses, to trace the curve of that mobile mouth… She dared not. It was much too dangerous. Only by keeping him at arm's length could she hope to carry out her plan.

But what was that plan? With every day that passed her motives grew more hazy. Her own honesty compelled her to admit that Heston was right in his judgment of Harry's character. She herself had given him no reason to think well of her; in fact, she had been at pains to do the opposite. Why should she object when he accused her of being what she had claimed to be?

She entered the bedchamber to find Fanny staring at the ceiling.

"Has Heston gone?" her twin demanded.

Miranda nodded.

"Of all the rude, arrogant, overbearing men in the world, he must be the worst," Fanny cried. "How dare he speak of Harry so?"

"He had some justification," Miranda pointed out.

"I don't know how you can defend him. Harry was right...he needs a setdown. To threaten to send my darling away as if he were a naughty child? I tell you— Harry will not go."

"Lord Heston is not his guardian. He has no power to banish him from London, so he tells me."

"He did not give me that impression," Fanny sulked. "Did you get round him, then?"

"There was no need. The decision rests with Harry's grandfather. Heston will speak to Harry, of course, as someone must do."

"Pompous creature! One might suppose that he had never been young. Lord Rudyard, I suppose, will get a full report from him?"

"I doubt it, Fanny. Heston, whatever his faults, does strike me as a tattle-tale. Others will be ready enough to put Lord Rudyard in possession of the story."

"It must come to the same thing," Fanny mourned.

"Harry will be sent away and we shall never see each other more."

"You still feel the same about him?"

"Of course I do. I know you think me fickle, but yesterday, when I thought Harry dead, I knew I could not live without him."

"Luckily he is still alive and so are you. Now do cheer up. Heston has obtained two vouchers for Almack's for us."

"You are not serious?" Fanny brightened up at once.

"Indeed I am. We are to go this evening. Heston has asked Count Toumanov to make up our party. That is, if you feel well enough…?"

"I would not miss it for the world!" Fanny jumped out of bed, a beaming smile upon her face. "We must tell Aunt Emma. She will be so pleased."

"You feel you can bear Lord Heston's company, then?" Miranda asked wickedly.

"I shall ignore him. The Count is so charming. I shall leave you to put up with Heston's rudeness and sarcastic comments."

"Thank you so much! It promises to be a very pleasant evening…"

Fanny regarded her twin. "You seem to deal together," she said. "He never takes his eyes off you."

"I hope you are mistaken. He worries me, I will admit. I am beginning to wonder if he suspects."

"Nonsense! How could he?" Fanny waved the suggestion aside. "What are we to wear tonight?"

Her final decision required more than an hour of serious consideration, but at last she settled upon a gown of spider-gauze, with ribbon braces.

"Our zephyr cloaks will go well with this toilette," she announced. "Do you think them suitable?"

Miranda nodded absent-mindedly. She had taken little interest in the selection of gowns which Fanny had paraded for her approval. Heston filled her mind to the exclusion of all else.

Was he playing some deep game? It was becoming more and more impossible to doubt it. He had taken her so far along the road to matrimony that she could see no escape.

Yet he could not mean to go ahead with it. A fortune hunter, tainted by the smell of trade, and penniless into the bargain? No, it was impossible. He was planning some hideous retribution. Perhaps he intended to leave her at the altar, the butt of the Polite World. Or at best he might jilt her even earlier, and go abroad.

In her own heart she did not believe him capable of either of those actions, but the alternative might be worse. Surely he could not intend to marry her and punish her for the rest of her life? She pushed the thought aside. She was allowing her overwrought imagination to overcome her common sense.

She went to find her aunt.

To her surprise, that lady found herself unable to give the proposed visit to Almack's her unqualified approval.

"Your sister should rest," she announced. "She is not yet recovered from the shock of her experience yesterday."

"The invitation has raised her spirits, ma'am."

"Well, of course, we must all be delighted by the vouchers, but..." Mrs Shere hesitated "...my dear, I cannot think it right that you should appear there in the company of two young men, and without a chaperon. Lady Medlicott does not have the entrée. She could not go with you."

"Heston did not mention the matter, and, Aunt, as you well know, he is a law unto himself…"

"Not at Almack's, dearest. Why, Willis turned away Wellington himself because he was wearing pantaloons instead of knee breeches…the rules are very strict."

"It is not quite the same thing. Heston is my… er…betrothed. That must make all perfectly respectable." Miranda looked a little self-conscious as she spoke, but her embarrassment went unnoticed.

"I don't know, I'm sure. Still, dear Lord Heston will always behave with propriety. You and your sister may go, my dear, though I believe that I should mention it to him."

In the event, there was no need for Mrs Shere to undertake this duty. When Heston appeared, resplendent in black coat, satin knee-breeches, silk stockings and buckled shoes, he was quick to assure her that Alexei's sister, the Princess Chaliapine, would be happy to undertake the role of chaperon.

"Her husband will be with her, ma'am," Alexei told her with a smile. "Between us, we shall take good care of the young ladies."

Mrs Shere beamed at him. She had a soft spot for a handsome young man, and Alexei was a dazzling figure in his dress regimentals.

Even so, there was no comparison between the two men, Miranda thought to herself. Heston lacked Alexei's classical features, and he was so large that he might have appeared clumsy. Yet he did not. There was some quality about him…an air of physical grace, perhaps?

Above all, a certain air of authority in his bearing drew all eyes, making the man beside him seem insignificant.

Chapter Nine

When they reached King Street, the guardian of Almack's, the great Willis himself came forward to greet them.

"Welcome, my lord!" He made a low obeisance. "This is an unexpected pleasure..."

Heston nodded an acknowledgement, chatting amiably as the ladies removed their cloaks.

"Is my sister arrived yet?" Alexei enquired. "She is the Princess Chaliapine."

Willis bowed again. "I believe that you will find the Princess in the ballroom, sir. May I take you through?"

"Great heavens! We'll never find her in this crush." Alexei gazed about the crowded ballroom.

Yet their arrival had not gone unnoticed, and a laughing girl soon appeared at his side. She was accompanied by a burly man much older than herself. He was dressed in Russian military uniform, and Miranda guessed from his insignia that he must be a high-ranking officer.

"Xenia, may I present the Misses Gaysford to you and the General?" Alexei took his sister's hand and kissed it. "You have heard me speak of them, I know."

"Very often!" the Princess teased. Then she turned to his companions and held out both her hands.

"How delightful! And I am to be your chaperon? I could not wish for prettier charges, and I shall not be too strict, I promise."

Even the General smiled at that. It was clear that he was devoted to his lovely wife. So slender as to seem ethereal, the Princess yet bore a strong resemblance to her brother with the same clear ivory complexion, a full mouth which revealed perfect teeth when she laughed, and large almond-shaped hazel eyes. Her gown of creamy silk was cut with the simplicity which showed the hand of a master couturier, and it formed an ideal background for a necklace of the largest diamonds Miranda had ever seen. The overall effect was that of some exotic creature from another world.

In the face of such splendour Miranda felt ill at ease, but the Princess was quick to banish her shyness. She was perfectly unaffected and natural in her manner, and her charm was such that Miranda warmed to her at once.

"Adam, you are the luckiest man in London," the Princess announced. "I might have guessed that you would steal away one of these two beauties for yourself. There is no need to wish you happy, my dear friend. You cannot fail to be so." She took Miranda's hand.

"I am so glad to meet you," she went on. "Alexei has spoken often of the lovely Gaysford twins. I see now that he did not exaggerate."

"Princess, you are too kind," Miranda murmured.

"Not at all! It is quite true. Have you met the Patronesses yet? They are quite formidable. Such *grandes dames!* But you must not be afraid of them."

"I do feel nervous at the thought of meeting them," Miranda admitted.

"But you have brought Adam here. That must most certainly be a mark in your favour. In the ordinary way he shuns the place, and they do not care to be ignored, you know. Now here comes Lady Castlereagh. See if she does not make a fuss of him."

Miranda looked up as the wife of the Foreign Secretary bore down upon them. This high-ranking lady was not only married to the leader of the House of Commons, she was the second daughter of the Earl of Buckingham, and centuries of authority showed in her bearing.

"So, Heston, you have deigned to visit us at last?" Her mock severity left his lordship undisturbed.

"As you see, Emily. May I present to you my bride-to-be and her sister?"

Both girls made their curtsies, and were rewarded by a bow from her ladyship.

"Charming!" she murmured. "Heston, you never cease to astonish me!"

A quiver of emotion disturbed the calm of his lordship's expression. "You flatter me, ma'am. I had not thought it possible."

"Wicked creature! Do you think to put me out of countenance?"

"I should not dare to attempt such a thing. It would be useless."

Lady Castlereagh smiled. Then she turned to Prince Chaliapine and his wife, keeping them in conversation for some minutes.

Alexei had moved aside with Fanny, and Miranda found herself alone with Adam Heston.

"Well, is this temple of fashion all that you expected?" He looked down at her with a question in his eyes.

Miranda gazed about her. The room was crowded and

both men and women were ablaze with jewels which caught the light and dazzled the onlookers. Toilettes of great magnificence adorned the persons of the ladies, showing to advantage against the regulation costumes of such gentlemen as were present.

"Everyone looks very fine," she admitted cautiously. "But I had not expected such a crush."

His lip curled. "My dear, this place is considered the seventh heaven of the beau monde. To receive an invitation is to achieve the peak of happiness, whilst to be excluded can only mean despair."

"I wonder why?" Miranda murmured, half to herself.

"I have wondered too. There is a desire to mix in "select" company, as some would have it. One must dance and gossip in the best company, after all, and it is a recognised marriage mart."

She looked up sharply. Was this yet another gibe? She would never know, for Heston's attention was fixed upon the doorway. Following his gaze, she saw Harry Lakenham in the middle of a group of friends.

Her companion uttered a low exclamation beneath his breath. "Damn the boy!" he said savagely. "He did not say a word to me. Did you tell him of our visit here?"

"No, I did not!" Miranda snapped. "We have not seen him since we knew that we were to come to Almack's. What is more, my lord, you will please not to use that tone with me!"

He was about to reply when Princess Chaliapine rejoined them.

"Do you like to dance?" she asked Miranda. "It is my passion, but they have strange notions here. The quadrille is not yet allowed, although I hear that Lady Jersey is considering it. We must be satisfied with the old En-

glish country-dances, and those energetic Scottish reels.
It is a pity, as I so love to waltz.''

''Would you cause a scandal, Xenia?'' The harsh,
dark face softened as Heston smiled down at her.

''I shall not have the opportunity, my dear. I doubt if
the musicians have ever heard of it.'' She allowed herself to be led away by the gallant who had come to claim
her hand.

''Shall you care to join them?'' Heston asked.

''I think we are too late, my lord. The sets are made
up.''

''Good evening, Miss Gaysford.''

Miranda turned to find Harry Lakenham at her elbow.
She recognised the man beside him as Heston's cousin,
Thomas Frant.

''Ma'am, I'm happy to see you again,'' said Thomas.
''I shall hope for a dance this evening—that is, if Adam
will allow it.''

''Mr Frant, I shall be happy to partner you,'' Miranda
replied.

Thomas looked startled by this evidence of indepen-
dence, but he took her card and marked it for a Scottish
reel.

Miranda did not glance at Heston. He did not own
her, she thought fiercely, and she would dance with
whom she chose. She half-expected some caustic remark, but his lordship was addressing Harry.

''Is not Almack's a little tame for you?'' he said. ''I
had not thought to see you here tonight.''

''We came for the gaming.'' Unconcerned, Harry
grinned at him.

''You may have done so,'' Thomas announced, ''but
I intend to dance. Some fine-looking women here tonight, saving your presence, ma'am. Who is that gor-

geous creature over there...the one with the diamonds worth a ransom?''

"That is the Princess Chaliapine," Heston informed him in repressive tones. "The General standing by the wall is her husband."

Thomas sighed. "Ain't it always the way? The beauties are snapped up before you can say 'knife'. Will you introduce me, Adam? The General won't object if I ask her for a dance..."

"Ain't she a little above your touch, old boy? Dancing ain't your thing, you know. You caper like a farmer's boy," Harry told him frankly.

"Good of you to say so!" Thomas had stiffened. "You ain't much of a hand at it yourself."

Heston sighed. "Come, my dear, let us leave these two young cockerels to their quarrelling."

He led her through the throng and into the supper-room. There he found her a seat in a secluded corner.

"May I bring you something to drink?" he asked. "Sadly, I fear it is a choice between orgeat and lemonade."

"I should like some lemonade, my lord."

"Very wise! Are you hungry?" There was mischief in his eyes as he asked the question.

Miranda shook her head, but when he returned he carried a plate which he set before her with an air of triumph.

"Positively Lucullan!" he announced as he inspected the food through his quizzing-glass. "Do pray note the interesting way in which this bread and butter has curled at the edges. It must be concern for the health of the patrons here. Fresh bread is thought to be so bad for the digestion."

Miranda's sense of humour got the better of her. She looked up at him with laughter in her eyes.

"You did warn me," she admitted.

"I could not be sure that you believed me. Now, my dear, you must not be shy. I shall not blame you if you fall upon this feast with ravenous appetite."

"My lord, you are a most complete hand. Suppose one of the Patronesses should hear you?"

"I should be banished at once, and thereby cast into obscurity."

Miranda giggled in spite of herself as she pushed the plate away. Then she remembered. She must not allow herself to be charmed into being in charity with this formidable creature, even though his wit amused her.

"We should rejoin the others," she murmured. "My sister will be wondering what has become of me."

"Will she? I had supposed that perhaps Alexei might divert her thoughts from more pressing problems."

Miranda shot a suspicious glance at him, but his expression was bland.

"Well, I should like to dance," she said hastily. She was on dangerous ground and she was anxious to change the subject. Heston would be unable to speak to her throughout the country dance.

"And so you shall, my love." He held out his arm and she had perforce to take it.

They took their places in the next set, and once again her companion succeeded in surprising her. He moved through the figures with a grace peculiarly his own.

"You told me that you did not care to dance," she accused as they joined hands.

"That depends upon my partner." He looked down smiling at her upturned face, and something in his eyes made her heart turn over. In her confusion she missed a step.

"Careful!" he whispered. "We are the cynosure of all eyes."

"I beg your pardon, sir. I was not attending…" Her eye fell upon the couples in the adjoining set. Surely that was Fanny with Alexei, and this must be her second dance with the same young man.

As the music stopped, she moved to her sister's side. "Pray don't dance with the Count again," she whispered in a low tone. "It must give rise to comment."

"Don't be such a prude, Miranda! You are become as stuffy as Heston himself. I may not speak to Harry, and now I may not dance again with Alexei. Do you intend to make my life a misery?"

"Of course not, but you will not wish to lose your voucher. The Contess Lieven has been watching you…"

Fanny looked dismayed. "I meant no harm," she sulked.

"I know it, but you must choose from another of your beaux. There are enough of them, if I am not mistaken…"

Fanny brightened. "I did dance with Mr Frant, but he trod upon my toes, and Alexei is such a perfect dancer."

"He is not the only one. Why not give your hand to Mr Rushton? He has been hovering about you for this age."

Fanny smiled prettily upon the gallant who had pursued her from their entry into the ballroom, and crowned his happiness by giving him her card.

Satisfied that a crisis of ill humour had been averted, Miranda turned her attention to the dancers.

The Princess Chaliapine was so graceful, she thought in admiration. Light on her feet, she executed entrechats with consummate grace as Thomas Frant endeavoured to keep up with her.

Inspired by her example, Thomas sprang into the air, determined to be a credit to his partner, and to emulate her performance. It was then that disaster struck. Thomas landed in a heap upon the ballroom floor. He made a quick recover, but his face was scarlet as the music ended.

Beside her Miranda was aware of Harry Lakenham, convulsed with laughter.

"Shouldn't have tried it, dear old boy," he choked out as Thomas came towards him. "You ain't the build. Getting fat as a flawn."

A picture of injured dignity, Thomas did not take this chaffing in good part.

"Lakenham, you will apologise for that remark," he said stiffly. "Otherwise you may name your friends."

"For laughing because you landed on your rump? Come off it, Thomas…"

"I don't like your tone, and you may not speak such words to me. I take it you ain't afraid to meet me?"

Harry's face changed. "Do you accuse me of cowardice?" he said quietly.

Miranda gasped. She could not believe what she was hearing. What had started as a simple joke had turned into a quarrel and now into something much more serious. Desperate to avoid what promised to turn into a duel, she threw a glance of appeal at Heston.

Her plea was just too late. He had already stepped between the combatants.

"Stop this, you idiots!" he said in icy tones. "Will you make yourselves the laughing-stock of London? Harry, you would do well to keep a still tongue in your head. And Thomas, as for you, if you cannot take a joke against yourself, it is a poor business. You had best shake hands and forget this nonsense. For one thing, you embarrass the ladies.''

For a full minute Harry continued to glare at his challenger. Then he laughed and stuck out his hand.

''My fault entirely, Thomas. Shouldn't have liked it if you'd said the same to me. I need to have my head examined... Will you forgive me and accept my apology?''

Thomas took the proffered hand. ''My fault too, old thing. I must have looked like a grounded whale. Can't blame you for laughing...thing is, I felt a fool.''

''I expect you turned your ankle, sir,'' Miranda broke in swiftly. ''It is easily done, and very painful. I did the same myself on one occasion...''

''Did you, Miss Gaysford?'' Thomas brightened. He had felt the humiliation keenly, but now Miranda's words in some way restored his dignity. ''That must have been it. I'll take care not to slip again.''

''Then you may beg pardon of these ladies, both of you. Take yourselves off to the gaming rooms, for heaven's sake. We've seen enough of you for one evening.''

This command was enough to quell any argument, and with Heston's severe gaze fixed upon them both young men made their apologies and disappeared.

Behind her Miranda heard a tired sigh. Fanny's face was drained of all colour, and she was clutching at Alexei's arm.

''Will you excuse us?'' she asked. ''I find I have torn a flounce. My sister will help me pin it up.''

Heston gave her an ironic look, but he made no comment as she seized Fanny's hand and led her through the crowd to the nearest retiring-room.

Once there, she swung round upon her twin.

"Do pull yourself together," she urged. "If you are to faint whenever Harry takes one of his odd starts, your secret will soon be common knowledge."

"I didn't faint," her twin protested in a low voice.

"You were on the verge of doing so. Take care, or you will betray us both. As for Harry, I am out of all patience with him. I could box his ears. How you can bear...?"

"I can't." Fanny turned her face away.

"Oh, love, I'm sorry, but his behaviour is too bad."

"I know it. It is so lowering, to be always on pins, wondering what he will do next."

Miranda was surprised. She had expected the usual fierce defence from Fanny, coupled with excuses for Harry's folly. A tiny flicker of hope stirred in her heart. Perhaps Fanny was beginning to grow out of her infatuation. She picked up her sister's card and studied it.

"We should go back to the others," she said quietly. "Your next partner will be searching for you, and I'm sure you don't want the suicide of a disappointed beau upon your conscience."

Unresisting, Fanny allowed herself to be led back to the ballroom.

As Miranda had predicted, her next partner was waiting to claim her twin, but Heston was quick to intervene.

"My dear sir, will you excuse Miss Gaysford?" he said mildly. "She has the headache...I expect it is the heat."

Overcome by being noticed by the famous Corinthian, the young man murmured a wish that Fanny might soon recover, and bowed himself away.

Miranda looked at Fanny, but her sister was too dispirited to take exception to the summary dismissal of her partner.

"Do you wish to go home?" his lordship asked. His tone was gentle, and Miranda threw him a look of gratitude.

Fanny shook her head. "I am quite well, my lord, but if we might sit down…"

"Of course." Heston led them to a vacant sofa by the wall. "You will perhaps like to watch the dancing for a time."

The Count was dancing with his sister, his skill clearly matching her own.

"They make a handsome couple, don't they?" Miranda was anxious to draw Heston's attention from her sister's woebegone expression.

"Indeed they do. Looking at Alexei now, one could not guess less than two years ago he was with Platoff's Cossacks, driving the French from Russia."

Fanny's ears pricked up.

"He never speaks of it, my lord."

"No, he would not. No one who took part in that terrible campaign cares to recall the horrors witnessed by both sides, but Alexei was decorated more than once."

Miranda shuddered. Even in Yorkshire they had learned of that fearful winter of 1812, when the French armies, which had conquered most of Europe, had been defeated by the Russian snows and the bravery of the men who were determined to defend their homeland.

The Cossacks, she knew, had appeared as avenging hordes from the wide and icy wastes, falling upon the starving and retreating French to wreak appalling havoc. Then, ghostlike, they had disappeared, only to return when least expected.

"The Count looks too young to have seen such sights," she murmured half to herself.

"It changed him, as such experiences must do..." Heston rose to greet two of his acquaintances who came to offer their congratulations on his betrothal. They were among the many to whom Miranda had been introduced that evening.

"I shall never remember half their names," she whispered to Fanny.

Her sister was not attending. Alexei had returned to her side, and there was hero-worship in her eyes.

"Tell me about Russia," she begged. "Oh, I do not mean to remind you of the war, but the cities must be very fine."

"You would like St Petersburg, Miss Gaysford." He began to speak of the wonders of that city, and Fanny hung upon his every word.

"Do you care to dance again, my dear?" Heston's eyes rested upon Fanny and the Count, and then returned to Miranda.

She consulted her card. "The next dance is to be a Scottish reel, I believe. I am promised to Mr Frant."

Heston laughed. "Do you think he will venture upon the floor again after his mishap? If he does, I must commend his courage, and your own."

"His courage is not in question," Miranda replied. "Here he comes..."

Thomas looked a little self-conscious as he stood before her. "Perhaps you will not care to partner me?" he ventured shyly. "I shall understand—"

"Nonsense, I am looking forward to our dance." Miranda allowed him to lead her out. "You will not trip again, you know. It happens very rarely."

Thus encouraged, Thomas began the reel with great

enthusiasm, bounding high in the air, but without attempting the more intricate flourishes. He acquitted himself well and, when the dance was over, he was flushed with pride.

"There, you see! Did I not tell you? I knew you would enjoy it."

"I had a splendid partner, Miss Gaysford. I say, you really are a brick! Adam is a lucky dog, and I shall tell him so."

When he took her back to Heston, it was to find that the Princess Chaliapine had rejoined their little group.

"Adam, can you spare Alexei?" the Princess asked. "Chaliapine is called away, and I need an escort home."

"We, too, should be going." Heston looked a question at Miranda and she nodded her assent. "Don't worry, I will see the ladies home."

"But I fear I have broken up your party." The Princess looked so penitent that Miranda smiled and shook her head. "You are quite sure? I promise to make it up to you when we meet again." With that, she took her brother's arm and went in search of her carriage.

"She does not care to see me in Alexei's company," Fanny murmured in an undertone.

"Hush!" Miranda felt uncomfortable. She looked at Heston, but he was engaged in conversation with a friend. "Is that so wonderful? You should not have danced with him so much. It cannot have gone unnoticed."

Miranda was quite sure that it had not, but the Princess had been too well bred to comment upon this social gaffe.

Such criticism was enough to send Fanny into the sulks and she was silent on the journey home. Once indoors, she excused herself with a plea of exhaustion,

leaving Miranda to explain away this uncivil behaviour.
She was about to speak when Heston forestalled her.

"Your sister is not herself tonight?"

"Lord Lakenham has given her another shock, I fear.
She was frightened, as I was myself, when he quarrelled
with Mr Frant. I could not believe that they would call
each other out over such a trivial matter."

"Men have fought for less," Heston said indifferently. "Once the actual challenge has been made, it is
almost impossible to draw back."

"But that is ridiculous!" Miranda began to pace the
room. "There can be no need to accept a challenge…a
man of good sense would let it go unheeded."

"And be accused of cowardice? I see you have not
heard of General Thornton, who was excessively fond
of the dance. Theodore Hook gave him the title of "The
Waltzing General", to which Thornton took exception.
When they quarrelled Hook insulted him further, but
Thornton did not call him out. He was accused of cowardice and asked to resign from his regiment."

"What nonsense! At least you, my lord, put a stop to
the quarrel tonight before it could go further…I was so
thankful."

"Were you, my dear?" Heston took her hands and
drew her to sit beside him. "I am delighted to hear that
I have won your approval at last."

Miranda was silent.

"It may surprise you to hear that I am entirely of your
own opinion in this matter. Too many men have lost
their lives over incidents of little consequence."

She looked up at him then. "It does surprise me,"
she told him frankly. "I doubt if I shall ever understand
you."

"Did I not tell you it would take a lifetime?" He

dropped a kiss upon her nose. "Now what is it in particular that you do not understand?"

"I don't know. It's hard to explain. You mix in the highest circles, and yet you do not seem to share the opinions of Polite Society."

"Because I do not care for Almack's, and I disapprove of duelling? It's true... I may yet become a social outcast...it is a lowering thought."

Miranda could not repress a smile. "You are impossible!"

"So I'm told. Now I must go, my love. It is late and you are looking tired."

"Thank you so much, my lord. There is nothing more heartening than to be told that one is looking hagged."

"I did not say that." He wound a finger around a copper curl and tugged it gently. "You could not look other than beautiful, but must you always be as prickly as a porcupine?" He began to stroke her cheek.

Miranda jumped to her feet. "Sir, will you take a glass of wine?" she asked hastily.

"That would be delightful." His face was bland. "I confess to feeling parched. Those fearsome liquids which were served tonight are sufficient to decimate the population. You will join me, I hope?"

Obediently she filled two glasses and took a seat as far away from him as possible.

"Tell me about your sister," he said suddenly. "Her nerves are sadly on edge, I fear."

Miranda eyed him nervously. What was the reason for this sudden interest in Fanny? Was he too afraid that she would become involved with Alexei Toumanov?

"She...she is sometimes a little high-strung, my lord. She was delicate as a child. Mama was always afraid that she would lose her."

"I see. Yet nowadays she looks the picture of health."

"Oh, yes, she is quite recovered. She grew out of her childish ailments…"

"But old habits die hard, and you continue to indulge her?" Heston gave her a quizzical look.

"Of course not!" she replied hotly. Then she blushed at the lie. "Well, perhaps we do, a little…but, sir, you must not think ill of her. She has a loving heart."

"And you?" He drew her to her feet. "What of your own heart?"

Miranda could not answer him. He was so close, and suddenly she felt breathless. Beneath the fine cambric of his shirt she could feel the beating of his heart, and his nearness made her tremble. She hung her head, not daring to look at him. Then a long finger slid beneath her chin and he raised her face to his. His mouth came down on hers and the world was lost.

When he released her she clung to him, afraid that her limbs would no longer hold her upright. He kissed her again, and this time so tenderly that the tears sprang unbidden to her eyes.

"I wish you felt that you could trust me," he murmured gently.

Miranda stiffened in his arms. "I don't know what you mean," she cried in confusion.

"Oh, yes, my dear, I think you do." With those words he left her.

Chapter Ten

Miranda walked upstairs unsteadily. Coming as they had done at the close of a passionate embrace, Heston's final words had robbed her of all hope of sleep.

She allowed a drowsy Ellen to undress her and dismissed the girl. Then she slipped into a dressing-robe and sat by the window, gazing at the gaily illuminated streets with unseeing eyes.

Heston suspected something. He had made that clear when he had invited her to take him into her confidence. She longed to do so, but it was impossible. How could she trust him? To divulge her secret would mean that she would lose him for ever.

And that she could not bear...not now, when all her happiness lay in his hands. Her own honesty compelled her to admit the truth. She loved him dearly, and would do so for the rest of her life.

She could not think how it had happened. She had hated him so at first. Now the very sight of his tall figure heightened all her senses. In his company the world became a different place, so wonderful that until now she felt she had been blind to all its glories.

Yet it was all so hopeless. A tear rolled down her

cheek. Her deception could not be hidden for ever, and when it came to light he would believe the worst of her.

It was too much to bear, especially as he too seemed to have changed in his attitude towards her. On one or two occasions his gentleness had surprised her, and more than once his manner had been almost tender. Perhaps she had imagined it.

Either way, it did not matter. She had no hope of winning his love. It was true, she did not understand him. Why did he persist in continuing with this mock betrothal? They had gone so far along the road to marriage, but he could not mean to go through with it at the end.

She buried her flushed face in her hands. She knew it now. She longed to be his wife, but a future with a man who held her in contempt could only be a living hell.

A disturbed night left her heavy-eyed and listless and brought a comment from her uncle on the following day.

"You must not overdo it, my dear child," he reproached. "Burning the candle at both ends, I fear. I must speak to his lordship."

"We shall not see him today. His mama arrives from Warwickshire, so he will be engaged. He has asked if we will dine with them in Brook Street as she will wish to meet my family. That is, if you agree."

"Naturally, my dear. We must not be lacking in observance to her ladyship, but to be correct they should dine here first."

Miranda summoned up a spurious show of enthusiasm. She would not have her uncle think that she was ashamed of her relations.

"I'll send a note to Brook Street," the Alderman assured her. "In the ordinary way I would not suggest it, but Lord Heston ain't in the least top-lofty, in spite of all that's said of him. He makes himself at home here, though I doubt if he's ever set foot in Bloomsbury before.''

"You are mistaken, sir. He knows the Museum well.''

"Is that so? Well, the gentry have their own ideas of entertainment. At least her ladyship need not fear our food. She won't get a better dinner in London. I'll speak to the cook at once.''

"Shall I do that?'' Mrs Shere asked anxiously.

"No, Emma, not on this occasion. No expense must be spared.'' He went off happily, humming with pleasure as he considered the feast which he intended to lay before his honoured guests.

"My dear, you should have a quiet day.'' Mrs Shere patted Miranda's hand. "Why not read your book? It always takes you out of yourself, as I well know. How many times have I asked you something, and you have not heard me? We shall deny all visitors for this morning.''

"Pray do not do so, ma'am. If Richard calls, I think we shall be glad to see him. He is a restful person.''

"As you wish, my love. Is Fanny still asleep?''

"I believe so. She was very tired when we came home…''

"We must take better care of you. Alas, it is always the same at the start of an engagement…so many invitations and congratulations, and so much to be done. You have not fixed a wedding-date?''

"Not yet.''

"Well, I must suppose that Heston wishes to consult with his mama. And then, you know, we must make arrangements for your own mother to bring the family up to London for the ceremony…''

Suddenly Miranda could bear no more. She excused herself on the thin pretext of searching for her book.

Fanny was still asleep, so she picked up the thick volume and returned to the salon, intending to curl up on the window-seat for the next few hours.

Mrs Shere gave her an anxious look. ''My dear, I have been thinking. If you were to take up tatting, it would help to pass the time...''

Miranda chuckled. ''Aunt Emma, you have seen examples of my tatting. You can't believe that I have a gift for it?''

''Well, then, perhaps some tapestry work? You might cover the dining-chairs in your new home.''

''No, no, you cannot wish that upon Lord Heston. Ma'am, we should have no guests. Who would sit on them?''

Her aunt was forced to smile. ''They are suitable occupations for a lady,'' she said half-heartedly. ''But there, my love, you had always a lively sense of fun. Perhaps you are right.'' She went away to oversee the running of her household, and Miranda was left in peace.

As her aunt had predicted, she was soon lost in her book, and though roused at times by the sound of the front door-knocker, no visitors were allowed to disturb her.

It was time for luncheon before Fanny came to find her. A night's rest had done much to restore the spirits of her twin, and now she sparkled with vivacity.

''I vow I have never laid so long abed,'' she cried. ''I have missed all our morning callers. Tell me, who has been to see us?''

''Aunt is guarding us today.'' Miranda smiled. ''No one has been admitted.''

''Oh, how dull! I had wished to see Alexei, that is, if

he called, but perhaps I have not missed him. There is still the rest of the day..." She stood by the window, gazing along the street.

"I half-expected Richard," Miranda admitted. "I asked that aunt Emma should not send him away."

"Did you?" Fanny's tone was indifferent. "Well, better his company than none at all, I suppose."

"How can you say such things? I know quite well that you are as fond of him as I am."

"Richard is well enough in his way but, when I compare him with Alexei, I confess that he seems dull. Miranda, did you ever hear anything so exciting as the story of the Cossacks when the Russians fought the French? And to be decorated twice? Alexei is a hero."

"I agree, although there are degrees of heroism, you know. I have felt often that it must be difficult to be a non-combatant, held by other ties of duty."

"You can't mean that! I don't agree at all!" Fanny's eyes grew dreamy. "How I should love to visit Russia...to see St Petersburg...to skate on the frozen lakes...and to drive in a troika through the snow, wrapped in wonderful furs."

"And outrunning the wolves if possible?"

"There you go again! Sometimes I think you have no soul. You are always so prosaic."

"I have a keen imagination, Fanny. Shall we go down to luncheon?"

It was clear that Alexei's heroism had raised him even higher in her sister's estimation. Miranda suspected that Harry Lakenham now appeared to be no more than a foolish boy in Fanny's eyes.

She hoped that it was so. With Fanny cured of her infatuation, all might yet be well. A rueful smile curved her lips. It was a vain hope and she knew it in her heart.

Fanny now showed every sign of transferring her affections to the handsome Count Toumanov, but Miranda doubted if he had thoughts of anything more than a light flirtation. Such protestations of devotion were common currency in Polite Society and were not taken seriously by girls with more experience than her sister.

Fanny, as she knew of old, would build them up in her imagination until she had convinced herself that she and Alexei were in the throes of a *grande passion*.

Miranda could only comfort herself with the thought that the Tsar and his entourage would soon return to Russia. Little harm could come to Fanny in the next two weeks.

She looked across at her twin, and then she thought of Richard. Dear Richard! He was far from being the shining knight on a white charger who appeared in Fanny's dreams. How could he compete with a handsome warrior, resplendent in a military uniform, who had taken part in so many dashing adventures?

If only he could rescue Fanny from a burning building, or snatch her from the path of runaway horses. Miranda's sense of humour bubbled to the surface, and she laughed aloud. There seemed little likelihood that any such desirable events would occur in the near future.

"There, my love, you are much better for the rest, as I knew you would be. I am glad to see you more yourself again. Will you not share the joke with us?" Mrs Shere said fondly.

"It was nothing, Aunt Emma...just a silly fancy... Do you go out this afternoon?"

"I think not. I have just been saying that I have obtained a copy of Ackermann's *Repository of Fashion*. I thought that we might look at it this afternoon. It will take some time as there are a full four hundred and fifty plates to study if we are to decide upon your bride-clothes.''

Fanny clapped her hands. ''Famous!'' she cried. ''We shall like that above anything...''

''It can do no harm to look at it.'' Miranda threw her twin a warning glance. ''But, Aunt, we have so many gowns. We shall never wear them in a twelvemonth. It would be extravagant to order more.''

''Do not let your uncle hear you say so. Your bride-clothes are to be his present to you.''

Miranda murmured her thanks, but she was determined that the Alderman should not be put to any more expense on her behalf.

This resolution was sorely tried as the ladies examined the coloured plates. Tempting visions of the latest fashions appeared before her eyes. Charming light dresses in both white and coloured sarsnets, chamerry gauzes, muslins and tiffany were all suggestions for the summer. Many of them were trimmed with gold or silver fringe. Most had short puffed sleeves, but all were caught high beneath the bosom with matching or contrasting ribbons.

''Pray look at these dear little hats!'' Fanny exclaimed in delight. ''They are so unlike my own poke bonnets. They just sit on the back or the side of the head, and this one, with the plumes of feathers, is the most ravishing of all.''

''I declare! We shall be spoilt for choice. My dears, do examine the shoes. They are charming.''

Obediently Miranda looked at a selection of demi-boots in satin with gilt buttons, black kid shoes with a yellow underlay, and similar versions in a blue and black print.

Fanny was exclaiming over white silk slippers with self-ruching and binding.

"These would be my choice," she said with longing.

"Of course! They would be just the thing for heavy snow…" Miranda teased.

"But, my dear, we shall have no snow before November at the earliest." Mrs Shere was mystified. "And it is not yet the end of June."

"I am just funning, Aunt, but you will agree that white silk is not very practical?"

"It would quickly soil, but that cannot be a consideration when you become Lady Heston. Perhaps this grey silk, with the lower part of black leather, is a better choice? You may not have much time, you know, once your wedding date is set, and nothing is more trying than to be rushing about at the last moment. It quite ruins all ones pleasure."

Thus pressed, Miranda had an inspiration.

"You will not take it amiss, ma'am, when I tell you that Heston has decided views upon a suitable toilette? Perhaps I should consult him before making a decision?"

"Has he, my dear? I confess you have surprised me. I had not thought that gentlemen took much interest in such matters, preferring only to see the results. Still, his lordship is so elegant himself. I expect that you are right. He will advise you on what is suitable for the life you are to lead."

Miranda gave an inward sigh of relief. It would be wrong to involve her uncle in spending money upon a wedding which would not take place. Such conduct would be inexcusable.

But so much of her conduct had been inexcusable, she thought sadly. Even if Fanny was in the way of falling out of love with Harry Lakenham, it would not help her own disastrous situation. How could she confess the truth to Heston?

She was roused from such dispiriting thoughts when Richard was announced. He had forsworn his former dress in favour of a blue coat with brass buttons, leather breeches, and immaculately polished top-boots. His shirt-points no longer reached half-way up his cheeks, and he looked much more comfortable.

After the usual civilities had been exchanged he looked at Mrs Shere.

"Ma'am, I was wondering… If you do not object to travel in a hackney carriage, you might like to drive out to the Park this afternoon with Fanny and Miranda."

"My dear boy! What a happy thought! We should enjoy a breath of air, but there is no need for a hackney." She pulled at the bell-rope and ordered her own coach.

"Off you go, my dears, but put on your pelisses. I think it is not warm enough for just a spencer."

As Fanny hurried away, Miranda begged to be excused.

"I should like to sit quietly for a time," she said. "Will you forgive me if I do not join you?"

Mrs Shere gave her an arch look. "I understand perfectly, my love. You will not wish to be abroad in the town if Lord Heston should chance to call."

Miranda coloured. "I doubt if he will do so," she replied. "He did not speak of it last evening."

"Well, well, one never knows! In any event, you will not be lonely. You may keep your uncle company. He will soon be home…"

They had not been gone above half an hour when the Alderman returned from the city.

"Aha! You have caught me playing truant from my

business, my dear.'' Mr Shere looked so like the picture
of an errant schoolboy that Miranda smiled.

"Let me guess,'' she teased. "You were worried
about the plants in your glasshouse.''

"I admit it. In the summer months, you know, they
need more care, and some must be watered twice a day.
I leave instructions, but John is inclined either to drown
them, or to miss one or two.''

Miranda laid aside her book. "Will you let me help
you? I can't tell exactly when the time is right to water
them, but if you were to tell me...''

"It is just a matter of experience.'' He looked doubtfully at her figured muslin gown. "You will not wish to
soil your dress...''

"I shall be careful,'' she promised.

"Very well, then.'' The Alderman removed his coat
and followed her into the garden. Once there, his progress to the glasshouse was delayed incessantly as he
paused to examine one or other of his extensive collection of exotic plants and shrubs.

"It is a pity the garden is so small,'' he sighed. "I
have been thinking...perhaps I should buy a villa on the
outskirts of the city, with more ground.''

"I suspect that in your heart you are a countryman,
sir.'' Miranda gave him an affectionate look.

"Your aunt would agree with you. She claims to be
a gardening widow as it is...but I cannot resist a new
plant. They are mighty expensive, though. I heard that
the Marquess of Blandford gave five hundred pounds for
a rarity.''

"So much?''

The Alderman winked at her. "I haven't yet fallen so
far from grace. Now let us see how we go on in here...''
He opened the door to his glasshouse. "Hmm, it is as I

thought. Take up this small pot, my dear. Do you feel how light it is? That tells you that it is in need of water. With more experience one may know by simply tapping the pot…''

Miranda picked up a watering-can.

''No…no…not that way. Set it in this bowl of water until the soil darkens. That way you will not get moisture upon the crown.''

He moved about among his treasures, murmuring an occasional instruction to her until he was satisfied that all was well. Then, as they were leaving the glasshouse, his eye fell upon a tangled jasmine by the door.

''Dear me, this will not do! It has fallen away from the support and will come down if we have high winds.'' He took a small knife from his pocket and cut some small lengths of twine. Then, with infinite care, he began to tease out the winding tendrils of the plant.

Miranda sat upon a rustic bench and watched him. It had always been a source of amazement to her to find that his chubby hands could be so gentle. Totally absorbed in his task, he had forgotten her for the moment.

She found it soothing just to sit there, not speaking, yet grateful for his presence. There was something about his solid figure which was comforting, and she could forget her troubles for a time.

Suddenly she was aware of being watched. Looking up, she found to her surprise that Heston was standing not three yards away, his eyes intent upon her.

''My lord, we did not expect you today,'' she cried in confusion. She rose to her feet, scattering the knife, the lengths of string, and the ball of twine. Her heart was pounding in the most alarming way.

Heston bent to retrieve the fallen objects, apologising

as he did so for telling the servant that there was no need to announce him.

"Quite right, Lord Heston! You need stand on no ceremony with us…indeed, I hope that you will not. But now, as you see, you have caught me in all my dirt, so I won't offer to shake hands." The Alderman looked delighted to see his unexpected visitor.

"I see that you are busy, sir. That is a fine jasmine, and the scent is so powerful, is it not?" Heston put out a long lean hand to examine one of the leaves.

"It is a good variety, my lord. Repton recommends it…"

"You know his work? I wonder if you believe, as I do, that he will change the nature of gardening in this country?"

"He has some very fine ideas. I make use of some of them here."

"So do I, Mr Shere. Perhaps you may care to visit me in Warwickshire, where he did some work for me?"

The Alderman's eyes were bright with interest. Heston had hit upon the subject closest to his heart.

"You are most kind." He bowed. "You received my note, Lord Heston?"

"Indeed I did. We shall be honoured to dine with you tomorrow, though I should warn you that my mother is not much accustomed to company. By her own choice she leads a somewhat solitary life…"

"She will not object to coming into Bloomsbury?"

"My dear sir, it is quite her favourite part of London. When she visits the capital, which is not often, she spends her days in the Museum. Sometimes I have suggested that she might take up residence there…"

The Alderman laughed heartily. "It would be uncomfortable to live among the antiquities, I should imagine, although I have not seen them. My lord, will you excuse me? I shall get a roasting from my wife if she discovers that I have received you in my present state.'' He hurried into the house.

"Your mother is well?'' Miranda ventured when she and Heston were alone. "I trust she did not find the journey trying?''

"I doubt if she noticed it.'' Heston grew thoughtful. "She is not quite in the common way, you know, and she is very shy. To be in company is a torture to her. I think I need not ask, but, my dear, may I beg you to be kind to her?''

"You are quite right. You need not ask that of me,'' Miranda answered gently. "Shyness is an affliction which those who do not suffer from it find hard to understand.''

"Yet you do and I think that you have never been shy in all your life.''

Her enchanting smile peeped out. "You may have noticed, sir, that I find it difficult to keep a still tongue in my head when I have strong opinions upon a subject.''

"Yes, I had noticed,'' he agreed drily. "On occasion there can be a certain…er…paralysing frankness about your conversation.''

Miranda flushed to the roots of her hair. Was he referring to that dreadful interview when she had announced herself ready to become his bride? She felt ready to sink with embarrassment, and she would not meet his eyes.

He looked at her bent head and his lips twitched with amusement. "No answer for me? I can't believe it! I was congratulating myself upon winning for my bride the only girl in London who does not look at me as a terrified rabbit might gaze upon a stoat.''

''Now you are gammoning me,'' she murmured. ''That can't be true, my lord.''

''Indeed it is! I have pondered upon the matter. It is so disheartening that on occasion I have been tempted to put a period to my existence...''

Miranda repressed a giggle. ''How astonishing!'' she replied in a demure tone. ''There can be no reason for this strange effect you have upon the ladies. After all, sir, your manner is so engaging on first acquaintance.''

''Minx! That's milled me down.'' He took a seat beside her and smiled down at her upturned face. Miranda's heart turned over.

''You...I mean...it was good of you to invite my uncle to see Repton's work on your estate,'' she said hastily. ''Gardening is his passion.''

''I guessed as much. He and my mother will deal together famously. In her painting she has recorded every flower in the grounds.''

''I wish I had her gift, but I believe it to be inborn.''

''You are right. One can acquire a certain facility, but there can be no comparison with the work of a true artist.'' He looked about him. ''All this is very pleasant and comfortable.'' He drew her head down to rest upon his shoulder. ''I have a confession to make,'' he said.

''Yes, my lord?'' Miranda was startled, and she stiffened. Was he about to tell her that he knew of her deception? A moment's reflection convinced her otherwise. Heston would not be sitting here at his ease if that were the case.

''I met your aunt and your sister in the Park. I came here in the hope of finding you alone.''

''I see,'' she answered faintly. ''Was there some reason, sir?'' She prayed that he would not start to question her or ask her again to trust him.

"Need you ask?" His fingers tickled the back of her neck, and a shiver of pleasure ran down her spine. She ought to pull away from him, to make some excuse to go indoors, but she could not. His caresses were beginning to produce such sensations of delight that she was losing all power to resist him.

"My uncle is pleased that you and your mother have agreed to dine with us tomorrow," she whispered. It was a last desperate effort to divert his mind from this seductive love-making. "You seem to have changed your mind about his ill intentions..."

Heston held her away from him and looked deep into her eyes. "In these past few days I have changed my mind about so many things," he told her. Then his lips found hers and once again she was swept away into a world where only they existed.

When he released her her head was spinning, but his next words brought her back to reality with a jolt.

"May I hope that you too have changed your mind?" he asked. "Or do you still intend to punish me, my love?"

Miranda stared at him in horror. He must have seen through all her plans. Racked with despair, she could think of nothing to say to him.

Then providence came to her aid in the shape of Fanny, who came tripping down the path.

She stopped short at the sight of Heston.

"Why, my lord, I did not expect to see you here," she said. "I thought you had a pressing engagement..."

"I had," he told her smoothly.

Fanny looked at her sister's face and then at his. What

she saw there brought a look of astonishment to her face. It was quickly hidden.

"Then I must beg your pardon for disturbing you," she faltered.

"Lord Heston was just leaving," Miranda told her. "Did you enjoy your drive?"

"Oh, yes. After you left, Count Toumanov stayed on with us, sir. We set him down at the Imperial Hotel in Piccadilly. Is it not strange that the Tsar should choose to stay there, rather than at Carlton House?"

Heston laughed. "After the cold of the Russian steppes, the Tsar may have found the heat at Carlton House somewhat stifling. The Prince is afraid of draughts, even in the height of summer, and the windows are never opened."

"But does not the King of Prussia stay there, and General Blücher, too?"

"On their own terms, Miss Gaysford. I hear that they sleep on army cots, rather than in the luxury of canopied beds."

"How very odd of them!" Fanny was about to question him further when Miranda gave him her hand.

"We shall not detain you further, sir. It was good of you to call in answer to my uncle's note."

She saw the laughter in his eyes, but he accepted his dismissal with good grace.

"Miranda, you do not fool me for a moment," Fanny began as soon as he had left. "I have suspected for some time that you don't dislike Heston as you once did."

Miranda was silent.

"Why don't you answer me? Surely you cannot have a *tendre* for him?"

"Would it be so strange?" her twin said slowly. "I believe I have misjudged him…"

"Oh, pray don't say so! He means you harm, I know it! To make you fall in love with him...what better way to injure you?"

"I don't think that of him."

"Then you are a fool! You will not tell me that he holds you in regard? Think of the things he said to you."

"I can't forget them."

"Then how can you care for him?"

"I don't know, except that he has changed, and so have I."

"Then you had best go on with this remarkable betrothal, and I wish you joy of him." Fanny's face grew bitter.

"You need not do so. He will never marry me. How could he when the truth is out?" Her anguish was too deep for tears and she turned away.

Chapter Eleven

Fanny did not broach the subject again. She was tempted to do so, but the closed look on Miranda's face warned her against it.

Instead, she set herself the task of diverting her sister's thoughts into lighter channels, and Fanny could be charming when she chose.

"Will you not read aloud to me?" she coaxed. "I have finished *The Mysteries of Udolpho,* whilst you are still reading *Ivanhoe!*"

"But I am halfway through the book. You will not understand the story."

"You could tell me the beginning. Perhaps we might go to the library tomorrow..."

"Do you mean to meet Harry Lakenham again?" Miranda asked.

"Of course not. I have not seen him, so you need not be suspicious." Fanny gave her a bright smile.

Miranda was satisfied. Her sister was incapable of dissembling. It was clear that Harry's star was fading, or Fanny would not look so cheerful.

"Very well then. In any case, the library will be

closed tomorrow. Have you forgot the Procession to the Guildhall?''

''But that is not until the following day.''

''So it is. I must be dreaming...tomorrow is the day when Lady Heston is to dine with us.''

Fanny looked uncomfortable. ''I'm sorry for what I've done, believe me, especially as...''

''As you no longer think of marrying Harry Lakenham?'' Miranda said steadily.

''Well, you see, I am not sure...he has behaved so badly, as you said yourself.''

''Is it not rather late to be convinced of that? I wish you had discovered it before we found ourselves in such a tangle.''

''It's easy to make a mistake,'' Fanny pouted. ''You have done the same with Heston.''

''So I have. There is no point in recriminations, is there?''

''At least you are free to cry off from your supposed betrothal, if that is what you wish.''

Miranda lost her temper. ''You think it will be easy? When he is coming here tomorrow with his mother?''

''She may take you in dislike and forbid the match.'' Fanny's brow cleared. ''That would be the obvious solution.''

''I intend to make sure that she does not take me in dislike. Heston has asked particularly that we make her welcome, and we shall do so.''

''You are very anxious to oblige him.''

''In this particular case I am, and I expect the same from you. None of your tricks, remember! You will be civil to her, if only for Uncle's sake.''

''I shan't forget my manners,'' Fanny sulked.

"Make sure that you don't. I warn you, Fanny, I won't put up with any of your nonsense!"

Fanny grew more conciliatory. When Miranda spoke in that particular tone it was time to retreat.

"Is Lady Heston very *grande dame?*" she asked. "Did Heston tell you anything about her?"

"Only that she is shy and does not go much into company…"

"How odd! I mean, with her position in society and all her wealth, one might suppose…"

"She is an artist…a gifted painter."

"Well, that is something. Better a Bohemian than a fearsome dragon like the Countess Lieven. Did you see the high-nosed way she looked at us at Almack's?"

Miranda gave up. "Do you wish to hear the story of *Ivanhoe* or not?" she snapped.

Fanny subsided. "More than anything," she said meekly.

The candles were guttering in their sockets before Miranda laid aside the book. Then Mrs Shere appeared.

"Not abed yet?" she reproached them. "I saw your light and wondered if aught was amiss."

"We were reading, Aunt. I beg your pardon…we have been wasting the candles."

"As if that mattered, my dear child. Still, it is late, and we shall have a busy day tomorrow. You will need your rest."

She kissed the twins and left them to their slumbers, but it was a long time before Miranda fell asleep. The thought of meeting Lady Heston filled her with dismay, and it was long after midnight when she closed her eyes.

On the following day the household was astir at an early hour. Amid the bustle Miranda sought out her aunt.

"Is there anything we can do to help?" she asked.

"Perhaps the flowers, dearest girl? The cook tells me that we have no milk...I might have expected it. Milk has been so difficult to come by with all these people in the city. As for the linen...it has not yet been returned. Those washerwomen leave our orders to put those of the foreigners first. I will look out some more just in case..." She hurried away.

Miranda decided to leave the flower arrangements until later in the day. They would wilt in the sultry heat.

The day before her stretched out endlessly, and she was glad to accompany Fanny to the library. It would help to pass an hour or two.

Luncheon that day consisted of cold meats and salads and she was glad of it. Her appetite seemed to have deserted her. When it was over, she took Fanny with her and went into a chilly pantry which normally did duty as a flower-room. John had plunged the cut blooms up to their necks in water to keep them fresh.

She and Fanny began upon their task, but even that did not take long. Afterwards the hours seemed to crawl. It was the oddest thing. In Heston's company the time flew by, but without him the hands of the clock refused to move.

"What are we to wear tonight?" Fanny asked. "I suppose we must be very fine."

"Your white gowns with the French bead edges would be suitable," Mrs Shere suggested. "And perhaps a small wreath of flowers in your hair?"

"I think I'd prefer a ribbon," Miranda answered hastily. The flowers would make her look too much like a bride.

"As you wish, my love. The ribbons should match the blue tiffany sashes, and you will wear your pearls tonight, I hope? You would not have his lordship think that you despised his gift, and yet you have not worn it.''

Miranda nodded her assent. There was no way she could refuse. Mild panic seized her as she thought of the woman she was to meet that evening. How many others would be drawn into this deception before it ended? And how she disliked herself for going on with it.

When the twins came down that evening Mrs Shere inspected them with approval. Miranda was wearing her pearls, much against her own inclination. Beautiful though they were, she felt that they must burn her skin and brand her for the trickster which she felt herself to be.

''I have not seen you in better looks, my dears,'' Mrs Shere said kindly. ''Now, tell me what you think of the dining-table…''

They accompanied her into the panelled room. In the soft candlelight, the huge silver epergne which formed the centrepiece glistened with reflections. Beside it stood small pillars holding wreaths of trailing plants.

Miranda caught her breath. ''How lovely!'' she exclaimed. Then something about the table settings caught her eye. ''Aunt, the servants are mistaken. They have laid for eight, and we are only six.''

''Did I not tell you? I vow that today my head has been in such a spin that I forgot. I have invited Count Toumanov and also Mr Young. Eight is such a comfortable number for a dinner, and we could not have four ladies and two gentlemen.''

Fanny's eyes began to sparkle. ''How clever of you, Aunt!''

''Well, you know, my dears, I thought it might take

away any little awkwardness which might occur. Lady Heston is well acquainted with the Count, and she will like to have a friend here. As for Mr Young, he is always welcome, and Lord Heston seems to think well of him.''

"So he should!" Miranda cried warmly. "Richard need not fear to be in any company.''

"Of course not, dearest!" Mrs Shere patted her hand. "You must be calm. To meet one's future mother-in-law is always an ordeal, but she cannot fail to love you as Heston does himself.''

There was no time to say more, for at that moment Richard was announced. As he came towards them, Miranda blessed him. Dear Richard, always so calm and pleasant, and so dependable. She gave him her hand.

"How do you go on?" he murmured in an aside. "This cannot be very pleasant for you.''

"It is hateful," she replied. "But I have no choice.''

"There is always a choice, Miranda, though you may not care to make it…''

"Oh, don't," she cried in desperation. "Please don't! If you only knew…''

She looked up as the rest of the party was announced, allowing Heston to take her nerveless hand in his. Then he led her forward.

"This is my bride, my dear Mama. I hope you will love her as I do.''

Miranda sank into a deep curtsy, hardly daring to look up at the woman who stood before her.

When she did so, she was reassured. Lady Heston was very tall, but so thin as to make her son seem larger than ever. There was little resemblance between them, except for the raven darkness of their hair and brows. In place of hard grey eyes, her ladyship's were of a blue so dark as to appear violet. What struck Miranda most was the peculiar sweetness of her expression, combined with a certain reserve.

"I am glad to meet you," Lady Heston murmured in a musical voice. "Adam is so happy, and I must thank you for it."

Miranda shot a fleeting glance at Heston, but he was regarding them with an air of benevolence. She could hope for no help from that quarter. She felt a surge of indignation. How dare he claim to love her when both he and she knew that it was untrue? When it came to deception, she was not the only one who had cause for self-reproach.

She felt even worse when Lady Heston took her hands and kissed her, knowing what it had cost this shy and sensitive woman to make such a gesture of affection.

"Ma'am, you are very kind," she said in a low voice. "Adam tells me that you are an artist, with an interest in flowers and plants. My uncle shares that interest. You might care to see his collection...?"

"Will you show it to me later?"

"It would by my pleasure, Lady Heston, but my uncle is the expert. I have little knowledge, and could not give you the Latin names."

The Alderman had been listening to their conversation. Now he stepped forward with an offer to take her ladyship into the garden.

Miranda sighed with relief. She had no wish to enter into a private conversation with Lady Heston. Her ladyship might appear to be reserved and even diffident, but loving her son as she did her perception would be keen. She must soon discover that all was not as well as it might appear to the less interested observer.

Fanny was deep in conversation with Count Toumanov and Richard was chatting to her aunt. Miranda stood by the long windows watching Lady Heston as the Alderman trotted beside her down the garden path.

"Did I not say that they would deal famously together?"

She turned to find Heston by her side, and frowned at him.

"Now do not look black at me," he reproached. "What have I done to deserve it?"

"You need not have claimed to love me," she replied with strong feeling. "We both know that it is not true."

"You must forgive me," he told her smoothly. "It was but a natural desire to set my mother's heart at rest. She disapproves of arranged marriages, with no serious attachment on either side. I fear she regards them as a certain path to disaster."

"She is quite right," Miranda said hotly.

"Do you think so, my dear? You have surprised me yet again…" He gave her a dangerous smile. "I had not supposed that your affections were engaged. Am I to hope that you are learning to think of me with kindness?"

The colour rose to Miranda's cheeks, and for the moment she was robbed of speech. She turned away from him, throwing a pleading glance at Richard as she did so.

He came to her rescue at once, leading Mrs Shere to join them, with the expressed desire to pay his respects to Lord Heston.

His lordship was all civility, but his lips twitched.

"What should we do without our childhood friends?" he murmured to Miranda. Then, in his usual easy manner, he began to speak of the Prince's recent visit to Oxford.

"The Regent was well received there?" Mrs Shere

enquired. "I fear that he is not always treated well in London, and I cannot think it right that the people should behave so ill as to hiss and boo him, when perhaps they do not understand..."

Heston bowed. "The visit was a great success, ma'am. His Royal Highness is popular in that city. In his speech he said all that was gracious."

"It was a great occasion." Alexei brought Fanny over to join them. "Two hundred persons dined at the Radcliffe Camera." His eyes twinkled. "There were lighter moments, Mrs Shere, in spite of all the gold plate. General Blücher enjoyed the wine to such an extent that later he got lost in search of his lodgings."

They all smiled at that.

"And my master insisted upon strolling down the High Street afterwards to see the candles shining a welcome in every window. He may be Tsar of All the Russias, but the spectacle pleased him immensely."

"He is thought to be extremely handsome, is he not?" Fanny's eyes shone. "How I look forward to seeing him tomorrow."

"Where will you be?" Alexei asked eagerly. "I shan't forget to wave to you as we pass."

Heston was explaining the exact position of their vantage point when his mother came up to him. Her arms were filled with flowers, and she was smiling.

"See how spoiled I am," she murmured, "I feel so guilty... Mr Shere has stripped his garden for me."

"Let me take them, your ladyship." Richard stepped forward and relieved her of her burden. "Should they go into water?"

Mrs Shere signalled to a footman, who bore the blooms away. Then the Alderman returned, and Lady Heston went to him at once.

"I have done more damage than a plague of locusts, my dear sir. I must hope that your garden will recover…"

The Alderman waved her apologies aside. He was glowing with pride. "Happy to have pleased you, ma'am. As I say, some of the roses are cuttings from the Empress Josephine's collection at Malmaison. A friend was good enough to bring them over."

"I have seen them only in paintings by Pierre-Joseph Redouté until today."

"By next year they will be well established. I shall hope that you will come to see them. The Gallicas, in particular, should be very fine…" He was about to launch into a discourse upon his favourite topic when Mrs Shere caught his eye.

"Well, well, I must not be a bore upon this subject," he said cheerfully.

At that moment the gong sounded and they went in to dine.

In spite of her aunt's efforts, Miranda had feared that the atmosphere at the dining-table must be strained. As she glanced about her, she sensed with some surprise that it was not so.

Seated at the Alderman's right hand, Lady Heston had clearly found a friend. She was chatting to him without the least trace of reserve.

Seated at the other end of the table his wife had Lord Heston by her side, and he at once engaged her in a conversation which touched upon the Prince Regent's courtesy in translating General Blücher's speech in German for the benefit of the General's English audience.

Miranda turned to Richard, who was seated on her right.

His eyes were fixed upon Fanny, who faced him across the table, and was absorbed in listening to the Count.

"Take heart!" she murmured inaudibly. "She is quite recovered from her previous infatuation."

"And in the way to falling into another one?" His face was sad. "How can I compete? I can't appear in a splendid uniform, or tell of my adventures. There isn't much adventure to be found in Yorkshire."

"The Tsar and his entourage will leave next week," Miranda told him. "You have heard of the old saying that out of sight is out of mind?"

Richard brightened visibly. Then his face fell.

"There will be someone else, with more to offer than I."

"Stuff! You shall not think so poorly of yourself."

She might have gone on, but the conversation became more general. Peace with France was to be proclaimed on the twentieth of June, and later that week the Fleet was to be reviewed at Portsmouth.

"Shall you go there, my lord?" The Alderman addressed himself to Heston. "It will be a fine sight."

"I believe so, sir. I'm not yet sure if I shall accompany the Prince, but Alexei will go, of course." He glanced across at his friend with a slight smile in his eyes. "It won't be a favourite occasion for him. He is the worst of sailors."

"You are right!" the Count shuddered. "Give me a horse beneath me rather than a rolling deck. The motion of the sea is the worst sensation in the world. Shall you go to Portsmouth, sir?"

The Alderman shook his head and laughed. "We shall content ourselves with the mock battle on the Serpentine in August."

"Very wise, if I may say so. Is it not to be a recreation of the Battle of Trafalgar?"

Fanny clapped her hands. "Oh yes, and it is to be exact, down to the cannon and the rammings, and the smoke. Someone told me that the crews are to be dwarfs, to make the ships seem larger."

"The Regent does nothing by halves, ma'am." Heston turned to Mrs Shere. "He intends that the celebration of the first centenary of the House of Hanover shall be an unforgettable spectacle."

"I cannot blame him," Mrs Shere replied. "It will be a grand occasion, and the more so because we shall have our feet on dry land. I share your dislike of the motion of the sea, Count Toumanov. I cannot be easy even in harbour."

"Dry land is much to be preferred," Alexei agreed. "Alas, I shall not see the battle. We return to Russia after the Fleet Review."

Fanny's face fell. "Oh, no!" she began. Then a sharp look from Miranda silenced her. Her sister's obvious disappointment went beyond the bounds of propriety.

"You do not stay on?" she asked. "We shall all be sorry to lose you."

"It is not for another two weeks or so. Meantime, there is much to see and do. I have not yet visited the Temple of Concord, or the Chinese Pagoda…"

A general discussion of these wonders relieved Miranda of the need to speak overmuch herself. She had eaten little of the splendid meal, although the Alderman's cook had lived up to his reputation.

White almond soup with asparagus had been followed by a fine turbot with a side dish of fish quenelles in bouillon, and another of tiny vols-au-vent filled with shrimps, as well as a salver of whiting.

There was something for every taste, from salmis of duckling in wine and epigrammes of chicken to ham braised in Madeira and a baron of beef.

Miranda looked about her. Her own lack of appetite had gone unnoticed due to the Alderman's concern that Lady Heston should eat more. Smiling, that lady shook her head.

"I seldom dine on more than a single course," she protested. "But I must compliment you upon your chef. Everything is so delicious. It will put our own man upon his mettle, I assure you."

Heston was quick to agree with her. He, at least, had done full justice to the meal, as had Alexei and the Alderman himself.

Heston looked at Miranda's plate. "Have you been influenced by George Byron?" he teased in a low voice.

"I don't understand you, sir."

"It is one of his little foibles. He dislikes to see women eat, preferring to think of them as ethereal creatures."

"What nonsense!" she cried warmly. It was enough to persuade her into accepting a serving of summer fruits in jelly.

"You are not an admirer of the noble lord," he asked carelessly. "I thought I saw a book of his upon your table the other day."

"That belongs to Fa—to my sister. Lord Lakenham gave it to her." Miranda could not look at her companion. Once again she had come so close to giving herself away.

Apparently he had not noticed the slip. "Lakenham gave her a book?" He looked incredulous.

"It was a peace-offering," she explained hastily. "He

was sorry to have caused her to faint at the Balloon Ascent.''

"Very civil of him," Heston said smoothly. "If he continues in his present ways, he will be forced to buy up half the books on sale in London. Don't you agree?''

"I have no idea. We have not seen him, sir." It was a curt reply and she flushed. She had warned Fanny to be civil to their guests, and now she herself was guilty of rudeness.

Heston waved aside the cheeseboard and changed the subject. "We shall not stay late this evening. Tomorrow we must make an early start if we are to get through the crowds before the procession begins.''

She nodded as Mrs Shere broke in with a question about the arrangements for the following day.

Miranda turned to Richard.

"I believe I shall go back to Yorkshire after the Parade," he said. He looked so disconsolate that her heart was wrung with pity.

"Pray don't leave just yet," she begged. "Your father will spare you for another week or two…''

"But will it do any good?" he sighed. "Fanny does not look at me.''

Miranda frowned a warning at him. Heston had sharp ears. If he heard Fanny's name on Richard's lips, all would be lost.

"Give her time!" she insisted. "You heard the Count. In two weeks' time he will be gone, and that will be your opportunity.''

"I hope you may be right." His face cleared a little. "I'll stay if you feel that I have the slightest chance of winning her.''

"Of course you have," she encouraged. "Would that I could discover a monster for you to slay…''

She smiled at that, though he looked rueful. "I know you think her foolish, but I love her so. I would care for her, you know, and she would have all she could desire. Once away from London, she will be different."

"I agree," she told him quietly. "Perhaps it was not the best idea for us to come here. Mama was delighted and Uncle believed that it would be an opportunity for us but things have gone so sadly wrong."

Richard pressed her hand. "Are you quite sure of that?" he asked.

"I'm afraid so. I can see no way out of our difficulties that will not hurt the people I love best."

His face was grave, but he pressed her hand again. "I believe you to be mistaken, and that all will yet be well for you."

She was about to deny his words when Mrs Shere rose from the table and the ladies withdrew to the salon.

"Do you like music, your ladyship? Both our girls play so well upon the spinet..."

Miranda threw her aunt a glance of gratitude. She had been wondering what on earth she was to say to Lady Heston if they should find themselves tête-à-tête.

A pleasant smile of encouragement sent her to the instrument, with a gloomy-looking Fanny beside her.

On the pretext of searching through the music, she managed to have a private word with Fanny.

"For heaven's sake, smile!" she urged. "Would you have everyone notice that you dislike the thought of Count Toumanov going away? They may imagine that you have a *tendre* for him."

"London will be so dull without him," Fanny sighed.

"Then we had best go back to Yorkshire."

This dire prospect startled Fanny. "You cannot mean

it! How can you say such a thing? You cannot leave Heston, can you?''

''No, I can't, and well you know it. Now turn the music, and try to look as if you are enjoying it.''

Subdued, Fanny did as she was bidden and Miranda began to play a favourite piece. As always, she found the music soothing, and it as not until she reached the final bars that she was aware of being watched. She looked up quickly to find Lady Heston's eyes upon her. In their depths she saw a question, or was it her imagination?

Their aunt beckoned to the twins. ''Come and sit down with us,'' she said. ''My dear, we have been discussing a date for your marriage.''

Miranda froze. Why had she supposed that matters could not possibly grow any worse? She stared from one face to the other, but it was Fanny who broke the silence.

''Must it be just yet?'' she asked in a hollow voice. ''There is so much to be done, and Mama will wish to make arrangements to come to London...''

''Naughty girl! You must not put difficulties in your sister's way, my dear child.'' Mrs Shere turned to her ladyship. ''You must forgive my niece, ma'am. The twins are so close that they dislike the thought of separation, one from the other.''

''That is perfectly natural,'' her ladyship agreed quietly. Her thoughtful gaze rested upon Miranda's face. ''There is a special bond between twins, so I understand, and you are identical, are you not?''

''Yes, your ladyship.'' Miranda sat down suddenly, clenching her hands as she waited for the next blow to fall. It came soon enough.

''We have decided upon the first week in September, if Lord Heston agrees. That will give us more than two full months to make our preparations, and allow plenty of time for your mama to come down for the ceremony.''

Fanny dared not argue further, and Miranda could think of nothing to say. To protest would be unthinkable. How could she disgrace her aunt and uncle by announcing her decision to end her betrothal at this moment?

She prayed that something would happen…anything to extricate her from her present predicament.

Her prayers were answered briefly when the door opened and the gentlemen came to join them.

Mrs Shere rang for the tea-tray.

''Your ladyship, if you will be kind enough to ask Lord Heston for his views?''

''Upon what, ma'am?''

''We have been speaking of your marriage,'' his mother told him. ''We thought perhaps the first week in September? Is that agreeable to you?''

''Much too far away!'' He grinned at her. ''But if it suits my bride, then her wish is my command.''

He sat down beside Miranda and took her hand. ''What do you say, my dear?''

She knew then that she must end this hoax without delay, but this was neither the time nor the place. She kept her eyes fixed firmly upon the carpet.

''It shall be as you wish,'' she said.

Chapter Twelve

As Heston had promised, the company did not stay late, but Miranda was only half-aware of their leaving.

She felt that she was drowning in deep water, and reality no longer had a meaning for her. She was drifting as though through a dream from which she must awaken. Even her own voice sounded strange to her.

Fanny and Richard watched her with concern. They alone knew how she was suffering. They stood together in one corner of the room, and Fanny's lips were trembling.

When they were alone that night, she flung herself upon the bed and wept as if her heart must break.

"Don't cry!" Miranda told her quietly. "It can serve no purpose."

"But what will you do?" her sister wailed. "I did not think it would come to this…"

"What did you expect? When one is betrothed, marriage must follow."

"But you are not betrothed!"

"Sadly, I am, and everyone knows it." Miranda felt like an automaton. She was moving about the room, taking off her gown and her undergarments and even the ribbon in her hair, but she was not aware of it.

"But you can't marry Heston...you can't."

"No, I can't. I won't cheat him to that extent." Something in her voice made Fanny look at her, and then she began to weep afresh.

"You love him, don't you?"

"Yes I do. I had not intended it, but there it is."

"Then, dearest, you must wish to marry him. If you love him, would it not be possible...to go ahead with it, I mean?"

Miranda's smile was a ghastly travesty. "You think I should deceive him further? Sometimes I wonder what you must *think* of me. I won't do it, Fanny. Tomorrow I shall tell him everything."

Fanny paled to her lips. "Oh, please, you can't! He will blame me, I know it. If you must cry off, why not start a quarrel? That would give you the excuse...and then no one would need to know—"

"Your part in this hoax, or mine? I might take your advice if I thought that it would serve, but it won't."

"Why not?"

"You don't know Heston as I do. He would see through it in a moment. Sometimes I think that he suspects already."

"How could he?"

"I don't know. It is the things he says and the way he looks..."

"If he loves you, he will not care, and he must do so or he would have taxed you with it."

"If he loves me?" There was no amusement in Miranda's laugh. "Fanny, you know what Heston thinks of me. He has made his opinion only too clear."

"Then I think it wrong of him to pretend to love you,

especially to his mama. He is guilty of deceit, as much as any of us.''

''It really doesn't matter as to who is most to blame. The point is that I must put an end to it. We can't go on like this and I shall tell him so in the morning.''

''Oh, please, you can't! Not tomorrow, I beg of you…everyone will be there to see the Procession and I could not face them all. We shall be disgraced and sent back home at once.''

''It can't be helped.''

''Yes, it can! I think you are being very selfish, Miranda. I do not care to be sent away from London. Alexei has only a few more days with us, and you might think of me instead of yourself.''

This remark caused Miranda to gaze at her sister in stupefaction. Words failed her for the moment.

''Besides, you will think of something…some other way to free yourself,'' her sister announced. ''You spoke of telling Heston that you had mistaken your heart. Would that not be better than to shame us? You must consider Aunt and Uncle.''

Miranda was silent.

''Won't you wait a little while?'' Fanny coaxed. ''It is not as if you were to be wed next week. September is a full two months away… In the meantime, anything might happen.''

She looked a little conscious as she spoke and Miranda's heart sank. Surely Fanny did not expect an offer from Count Toumanov? It stiffened her resolve to put an end to the hoax without delay, but there was much to consider in her sister's pleas.

She grew thoughtful. A scandal must be avoided if possible. She had been badly shaken to hear that a date was to be set for her wedding, but as her composure

returned she knew that it was panic which had overwhelmed her. Her plan to confess everything to Heston
had been born of desperation and a feeling of being
trapped.

"There may be another way," she admitted with reluctance. "I can but try...a quarrel might serve."

On the following day she was given no opportunity
to carry out her scheme. The household was astir at an
early hour, but the Strand was already crowded as the
Alderman's coach bore them towards the building which
was their destination. Their progress was slow, but they
arrived at the appointed hour.

Heston had used his influence to reserve a series of
rooms with long windows which would give them a
splendid view of the Procession. Nothing had been neglected for their comfort, from easy chairs to tables laid
for a late breakfast.

His mother was already seated by a window, sketching the scene before her and Heston was chatting to
Richard Young.

He turned as they entered and came towards them
with a smile.

"We shall have some hours to wait," he said. "Will
you take some refreshment?"

He was the perfect host, apparently casual, but Miranda noticed that his eyes missed nothing which might
add to their pleasure in the occasion.

How could she possibly quarrel with him? Miranda
thought in despair. He neither did nor said anything
which she could take amiss. In any case, this was not
the occasion upon which to carry out her plan. She gave
up all thought of it for the time being and began to enjoy
herself.

Whatever the future held, she would forget her troubles for this one day. It might be the last occasion upon which this man whom she loved so much would look at her, if not with love, certainly with admiration in his eyes.

That she could not mistake. When their meal was over, he came to her and took her hand.

"Unfair, my love!" he murmured softly. "How can you tease me so?"

"My lord, you speak in riddles. I do not understand."

"Don't you, my dearest? Can it be possible that you do not know how delicious you look today? It is a severe test of my self-control. I want to take you in my arms and kiss you here and now."

"Please, my lord...someone will hear you." The colour rose to Miranda's cheeks, but she was glad that she had chosen to wear her new walking-dress of French cambric, with a charming Oldenburg hat. She was not immune to flattery, although it was mortifying to be forced to admit it.

"Now I have made you blush," he teased. "Will you always do so?"

Miranda's face grew warm. She did not pretend to misunderstand his meaning.

"Sir, I beg that you will not continue with this conversation. Do you wish to provoke me into quarreling with you?"

He laughed and patted her hand. "No, I won't do that. Did you think to escape me with a quarrel?"

With these thought-provoking words, he moved away to speak to Mrs Shere.

Miranda stayed where she was, frozen into immobility. It was as she had feared. Heston seemed always to be able to read her mind.

"You are very quiet." Richard slipped into the seat beside her. "I can't say that I blame you."

"No, it is all getting out of hand, and I don't know how to put and end—"

"Do you wish to?"

Miranda looked up in surprise. "You know that I must. I am so ashamed of all the lies and the deceit."

"That's understandable, but Fanny tells me—"

"Fanny should not gossip," she cried in anger.

"She did not tell me anything that I did not already know," he told her gently.

"Oh, Richard, is it so obvious that I love him?"

"It is to me, but then I've known you since you were a child. What of Lord Heston?"

"He wishes only to punish me. I tricked him into this betrothal, in a way."

"I doubt if there is a soul alive who could trick him into anything." Richard looked at her with smiling eyes. "You misjudge him, my dear."

"I don't think so. What other reason could he have?"

Richard laughed aloud. "Neither you nor your sister could claim the prize as the ugliest women in London," he chaffed.

"There are others with more beauty."

"But none with the same spirit as your own. Oh, I'll admit that you might have angered him at first, but has it not occurred to you that he might have changed his mind?"

"I wish it might be so," she faltered. "But I cannot believe it."

"Then you must be blind. Do you think him a man of honour?"

She looked at him dumbly. Then she nodded.

"So do I. It would be beneath him to seek to harm

you." Richard spoke with conviction. "Don't do anything foolish, I beg of you. In time all will be well."

"What are you trying to say?"

"If you will have it straight, I believe Lord Heston loves you."

For the first time a little flame of hope burned in Miranda's heart. Then she shook her head.

"That isn't possible, but even if it were true it cannot help me. How could I accept that love knowing all that I do? No marriage can be built upon a lie."

"It might be built upon love, as I hope my own will be... Do you hear the cheering? The Procession must be close."

He led her over to the window and settled her in a chair as the clatter of horses sounded in the distance.

The Procession was a tribute to the Prince Regent's love of splendour. First came a company of the Eleventh Light Dragoons in their uniforms of blue and buff, and they were followed by a number of carriages bearing the officers of the Prince's household. Then came those of the foreign generals, and the state carriages of the Regent's brothers, all of them Royal Dukes.

It was all a feast for the eye, and the number of dignitaries seemed endless. All the members of the Cabinet were there, together with the Speaker, in splendid isolation in his own coach. Then came a troop of Horse Guards, their accoutrements glittering in the sunlight as they preceded the Royal officers of state and certain of the foreign suites.

The Regent himself looked sullen, and even the presence of his popular allies did not prevent the crowd from booing and making cat-calls as his eight cream horses drew the State Coach past.

"Shame on them!" Mrs Shere cried indignantly. "To-day, at least, they might have honoured him."

"He does not look as if he is enjoying himself," Fanny murmured. "It must be galling to hear the cheering for the others. But, Aunt, he is enormous, positively gross, in fact. What a disappointment!"

"Fanny, remember where you are!" Miranda hissed. "I hope that Lord Heston did not hear you."

Fanny was not attending, for at that moment the Tsar's procession came into view.

"At last!" she cried in high excitement. "Here come the Russians and the Tsar himself." She clasped her hands in rapture. "He is everything I had expected...tall and slim...and so handsome. Some may think him dandified, but I do not agree..."

A murmur of amusement went around the room, but Fanny did not notice.

"Where is Count Toumanov? I do not see him, and he promised to ride upon this side." She leaned out of the window, peering anxiously at the cavaliers below.

"Dearest, do take care," Mrs Shere pleaded. "You must not risk a fall."

Fanny was oblivious of the danger. She leaned out even further. "There he is!" She began to wave her handkerchief and was rewarded when Alexei looked up briefly and grinned at her. "Does he not look splendid, and see how well he controls his horse?"

"Yes, yes, my love. Now do pray close the window, or her ladyship may take a chill."

It was unlikely on that pleasant summer day, but Fanny obeyed her, unconscious of the fact that her conduct had gone beyond the bounds of propriety.

"How I should like to have attended the banquet!"

she cried. "I wonder that Uncle could not have obtained an invitation for us."

"He will tell us all about it later!" Miranda was aware of her aunt's dismayed expression. Fanny's present behaviour was the outside of enough. She shuddered to imagine what Lady Heston must think of such a lack of restraint.

Apparently her ladyship had not noticed. She was preoccupied with her sketching and seemed lost to all else.

Heston touched her lightly on the shoulder. "Do you care to stay here for a while?" he asked. "I shall not be long, but I must see the ladies home."

Richard offered at once to perform that office for him, but Heston shook his head.

"Then I shall bear her ladyship company, if she will permit," Richard said shyly.

"How very kind of you!" Lady Heston had taken a liking to this quiet young man who seemed so diffident. "Then I shall not mind how long Adam is away. Now tell me, Mr Young, do you feel that I have captured something of the atmosphere today?" She held out her sketchpad to him, and came over to Mrs Shere.

"Will you come to Brook Street with your nieces whilst Adam is in Portsmouth?" she asked. "We must learn to know each other better, but first I hope that you will bring the Alderman to dine. Shall we say three days from now?"

Mrs Shere thanked her, and the ladies took their leave. Fanny continued to chatter brightly on the journey back to Bloomsbury, but when Heston had left them her aunt took her to task.

"It grieves me to say so, but I was ashamed of you today, my dear. How could you behave so ill? That hoydenish way you leaned out of the window, and called to Count Toumanov? I could not believe my ears.''

Fanny looked startled and dismayed. ''I did not think—''

''Then it is high time that you began to do so. How could you disgrace your sister in that way? What your mama would have said I can't imagine.''

''Pray don't be cross with me.'' Fanny's eyes filled. ''I was so excited...''

''Well, it will not do. I cannot help but notice that you are either in high alt, or down in the cellars, my dear girl. Such nervous excitement is not good for you. I wonder if I should write to your mama?''

''Please don't!'' Fanny began to cry in earnest. ''I didn't mean to be so bad, and I will try to be better.''

As always, the sight of tears had their usual effect upon Mrs Shere's tender heart. She laid a comforting hand on Fanny's arm.

''It is the thought of your sister's marriage which has disturbed you so, I think. But you will grow used to the idea, believe me. Now dry your eyes, my dear one. Lady Heston did not seem to notice your behaviour and for that we must be thankful. Dear me, I must confess that I find her somewhat odd. To be drawing at such a time is most unusual.''

''She has been so kind,'' Miranda ventured.

''To be sure she has. You are fortunate in your mother-in-law, my love. I doubt if she will take the trouble to interfere in anything you may wish to do.''

Miranda forced a smile. ''She is devoted to her son, my dear ma'am. His wishes will come first with her.''

''But of course. With his father dead, he is the head of the household, and so capable. Dear Lord Heston! How very lucky you are, my dear.''

Miranda had reservations upon that point. Luck was the last word she would have used to describe her present situation, but she murmured a feeble assent.

When their aunt had left them, Fanny rounded upon her.

"You might have supported me," she complained in an injured tone. "Aunt Emma was so cross and you did not say a word in my defence."

"If she had not done so, I was about to speak to you myself," Miranda told her grimly. "Aunt was right...you embarrassed both of us."

"Oh, you are grown as high in the instep as Heston himself... I do not know you any more. Are we to sit like statues, unsmiling, and without a word to say? That may be your idea of fun, but it is not mine."

"No one asks that of you, but can't you see how you expose yourself to gossip?"

"As if I cared!" Fanny tossed her head. "Since you have known Heston you are changed. You were used to be light-hearted. Now all you care about is the proprieties—"

"That isn't true! But we aren't children any more. What passed for high spirits long ago in Yorkshire is not acceptable in Polite Society, and you know how tongues can wag." Miranda sighed. "Sometimes I think that members of the *ton* have nothing else to do."

"I have done no harm," Fanny sulked. "Lady Heston did not notice, and his lordship does not know that I exist."

"Don't be too sure of that!" Miranda warned. She knew that it was not so. Nothing that her sister did or said escaped Heston's notice. That penetrating gaze rested frequently upon her twin and she had seen speculation in his eyes. His apparently casual manner hid a mind that was razor-sharp, and it never ceased to worry her.

Fanny bridled. ''What has he been saying to you?'' she demanded. ''He need not think to criticise me, for I will not have it. It seems I can do nothing right. You are all against me, except for Richard. He is the only one who does not say a word except in kindness.''

''Richard is very fond of you.'' It was an incautious statement in view of the fact that Miranda had promised not to reveal his true feelings for her sister, but Fanny was unmoved.

''I know that. He is fond of both of us. When we were small I was used to wish that he were my brother, instead of Jonathan and William. He did not torment us as they liked to do.''

''He is the best of creatures,'' Miranda said warmly. ''It is a pity…'' She stopped in confusion. She had been on the verge of saying too much, but Fanny was not attending.

''I think I have behaved quite well,'' she announced. ''I did not make the least fuss because Alexei cannot visit us this evening.''

''How could he possibly do so? The celebrations will go on until the early hours, and he is in attendance upon the Tsar. He did not come to London just for pleasure, as you know.''

''Well, I think it most unreasonable of his master to keep him at his duties for so long.''

''How fortunate that we are not in Russia! You would probably be beaten with a knout for that remark.''

''You may make a joke of it, but he did promise…at least, he suggested a party after the Procession on the night we met, if you recall.''

"It was only a suggestion. There was nothing definite settled, and his duties must come first."

"I suppose so. Oh dear, how dull we are this evening!"

"Well, I, for one, have had enough excitement for one day. We made such an early start this morning, then all the crowds, and the Procession. After supper I shall seek my bed."

This suggestion met with approval from her aunt. Mrs Shere's eyes searched Miranda's face, then she nodded to herself with a strange little smile of satisfaction.

"What is it, Aunt Emma? You are looking positively conspiratorial. Have you some secret plans for us?" Fanny could not hide her curiosity.

"I have a surprise, but you are not to know of it until tomorrow."

Not all Fanny's wheedling could persuade her to reveal her secret before the twins retired.

Fanny returned to the subject at breakfast on the following morning.

"Now do pray tell us, Aunt," she coaxed prettily. "I vow I have not closed my eyes all night for wondering."

"What a story! When I looked in upon you, you were sound asleep!" Mrs Shere glanced from one twin to the other. "Very well, then. We are to go for a drive, but I shall not tell you our destination."

"How exciting! I love a mystery!" Fanny clapped her hands. "What are we to wear? Must we be very fine?"

"We may be out for quite some time, so perhaps your Sardinian blue pelisses with the matching bonnets, and an extra shawl for warmth. And your parasols against the sun?"

Miranda chuckled. "I see that this is to be a serious

expedition, ma'am, if we are to go from one extreme of temperature to another.''

"There is no harm in being prepared against the weather," her aunt reproved. "It may be high summer, but in this climate one can never tell... The morning is fine, but before the day is out we may have rain, or even blazing sunshine.''

"Are we to be out all day?" Fanny's face clouded, and Miranda threw her a warning look.

Fanny must not raise objections to the outing, however much she hoped that the Count would call. Aunt Emma may have believed that Fanny's behaviour on the previous day was just high spirits, but she would not be deceived for long.

And only Fanny could believe that Alexei would offer for her. To be seen to throw herself at the young man's head would bring down Mrs Shere's severest disapproval upon her. It would be the last straw as far as their aunt was concerned. She would write at once to their mama.

And much good that would do her, Miranda thought ruefully. However unlikely the chance of such a thing occurring, her mother would be in raptures as the thought of having a Countess in the family.

Her frown quelled Fanny's objections for the moment, although she heard a few mutterings of rebellion as they tied the ribbons of their bonnets.

"I can't think why we must be out all day," Fanny complained. "I believe it will be too tiring, but I suppose we may come home if I am not feeling well.''

"To make an instant recovery if Count Toumanov should happen to call? You will do no such thing! Aunt has arranged this outing for our pleasure, and you will do nothing to spoil it.''

"You always think the worst of me," Fanny complained in an injured tone. "You are becoming such a crosspatch."

Miranda was tempted to inform Fanny that her behaviour would try the patience of a saint. Instead she turned the conversation to their new bonnets.

"I like these curled plumes, don't you?" she said. "I wonder how they managed to dye these feathers to the exact shade of blue?"

Fanny looked at her reflection in the glass and gave a nod of satisfaction.

"They are pretty," she agreed. "Though I wonder if we should not wear the new small hats instead?"

"Aunt Emma suggested bonnets." Miranda began to laugh. "They are more likely to protect our faces from either snow or blazing sunshine."

Fanny picked up her shawl. "I wonder where we are to go? I thought we had visited almost everywhere of interest. Pray heaven it is not to be another outing to the Museum!"

"I doubt it. I did not see any parasols unfurled in there, nor gentlemen in fur hats."

They went downstairs together to find Richard waiting for them in the salon.

"Oh, is it you?" Fanny murmured. "We are to go out today, you know."

"And I am to accompany you. Mrs Shere arranged it with me yesterday…"

That was not the full extent of Mrs Shere's arrangements. The next arrival was Lord Heston, attired in a riding coat, buckskin breeches, and gleaming Hessians. He took Miranda's hand.

"Beautiful as always!" he murmured. "You are ready, my dear?"

"Why, yes! I did not know that you were to come with us, sir."

"With *you*," he corrected. "Shall we go? I do not care to keep my horses standing."

"But my aunt intends to travel in the family coach..." Miranda looked across at Mrs Shere for confirmation, and was surprised to see a conspiratorial smile again.

Still chuckling, her aunt proceeded towards her own coach and stepped inside. She was followed by Fanny and then by Richard, and the carriage set off along the cobbled street.

"I hope you know our destination, my lord, for I do not." Miranda allowed herself to be handed up into Heston's racing curricle. She was somewhat mystified by these curious travelling arrangements. There was room and to spare for both herself and her companion in the coach. Perhaps Heston preferred to drive himself upon this strange expedition.

"I know my own, and yours." Heston's expression was enigmatic and suddenly she felt sudden panic. Her aunt's coach had turned to the left at the far end of the street, but his lordship guided his team to the right.

"What are you about?" she cried. "Surely we should follow them?"

"Why should we do that? They are not going in our direction."

"You will please to stop at once. How dare you trick me in this way? I did not agree to spend the day with you...my aunt will be distraught."

"I doubt it, dearest one. She knows of my intention."

"And what is that, my lord?"

"Why, I have kidnapped you! Sadly, only for the day, but I believe that we should make the most of it."

"And you arranged this with my aunt? How could she agree to such a plan? I can't believe it!"

"But you must. She thinks you too much in your sister's company, and so do I. It is a strain on both of you."

Miranda's fury knew no bounds. "My relations with my family are none of your concern," she cried. "You dislike Fa—my twin. You have made that clear, but you do not understand, and nor does my aunt."

"I think we do," he told her calmly. "I have no wish to come between you and your sister—"

"You could not!" she burst out.

"That may be so, but confess it. Shall you not enjoy a drive to Richmond? It is peaceful there, away from the noise of the city. Both your aunt and my mother thought you in need of rest."

Miranda was about to fly at him. Then she recalled her ladyship's sweet smile. That gentle person must have seen her inner torment. She had been about to inform Heston of her strong dislike of being discussed in her absence, but she checked the angry words.

"That was kind of her. I had not thought—"

"That you were looking 'hagged'? That is your own expression, I believe? No, my love, you could not look other than ravishing, but there is an expression in your eyes. Sometimes, I have thought…" He left it there, and Miranda did not answer him.

No purpose could be served by either admitting or denying his words. She leaned back against the cushions as he took the road to the west.

Chapter Thirteen

For a time he drove in silence, a fact for which Miranda was profoundly thankful. She had no wish to return to the topic of Fanny and herself, and to comment upon the weather or the charm of the countryside through which they passed held no appeal for her. It was the type of trivial conversation which Heston would find trying, though why she should care for that was puzzling.

She smiled to herself. On occasion she had noticed how his eyes would glaze with boredom when faced with a gabblemonger. At least he could not accuse her of that.

She was intensely aware of his strong hands on the reins as he sprang his team of matching chestnuts. He seemed at one with the splendid animals, never pushing them too hard, or dragging at their tender mouths, yet allowing them to cover the miles to Richmond at a spanking pace.

It was always a pleasure to watch an expert, she admitted to herself, and he was right. To escape from the city with its crowds and its fearful stench was exactly what she most needed on a day like this.

"My compliments, ma'am! You are no chatterbox!"

He drew the curricle to a halt at a small inn. A groom materialised as if from nowhere, and Heston threw him the reins.

"Glad to see your lordship! It's been some time!"

"Too long, Ben! How do you like my cattle?"

The groom ran an appraising eye over the team.

"You ain't lost your eye for bloodstock, sir, and that's a fact," he grinned. "Shall I stable them?"

"Just for a few hours, if you please." Heston took Miranda's arm and led her into the inn.

There he was greeted with evident pleasure by the landlord.

"Ah, Flodden, there you are. You kept your private parlour for us?"

"As if you need to ask, my lord!" The man bowed low, but there was no trace of servility in his manner. As he straightened Miranda was aware that she was the object of scrutiny from a pair of sharp blue eyes.

"My dear, this is Flodden. He is an old friend of mine." Heston clapped their host upon the shoulder. "Now, you old rascal, where is Annie? I must make her known to Miss Gaysford, who is to be my bride."

Flodden was clearly startled by this news, but he made a quick recover, leading them through into an inner room where the table was already laid for two.

"You will take a glass of wine, my lord, to clear the dust?"

"Champagne, I think. The occasion calls for it..."

As Flodden limped away Miranda saw that he was badly crippled. One leg was bent at an awkward angle, and his left arm was almost useless. His short stature and slight build, as well as something in his walk, made her suspect that he had been a jockey.

When he returned he was accompanied by a buxom

woman who was twice his size. The contrast between them was incongruous, but there was a certain dignity in Mrs Flodden's bearing that commanded respect rather than amusement.

She flushed with pleasure as Heston rose to greet her.

"Well, Annie, how do you go on? Still ruling the roost with an iron hand?"

Mrs Flodden smiled at this sally, but she shook her head in reproach. Then she made her curtsy to Miranda.

"Now, tell me, how is Mary? No further setbacks, I hope?"

"Not since your lordship sent the physician down from London. She hopes to see you, sir, to thank you herself."

Although Miranda had never succeeded in putting Heston out of countenance, the older woman's words clearly embarrassed him.

"I'll come at once," he said quickly. "Perhaps Miss Gaysford will like to remove her coat and bonnet."

Miranda's curiosity was aroused. She followed the landlord's wife to an upper room where she found all in readiness for her to wash away the dust of travel.

"Have you known Lord Heston long?" she asked.

"For many years, ma'am, and what we should have done without him I don't know."

Miranda looked up, a question in her eyes, but Mrs Flodden would not go on.

"Ma'am, we are forbidden to speak of it. You saw how Lord Heston looked when I tried to thank him for his goodness. I fear that I disobeyed his wishes..." She handed a towel to Miranda. "Will you excuse me?"

She hurried back to her kitchen, clearly preoccupied with thoughts of the meal already in preparation.

Miranda made her way downstairs. Her untouched

glass of champagne stood upon a side table, the bubbles still rising to the surface. She took a sip or two, realising suddenly that she was both thirsty and hungry.

Now that she was alone she had leisure to look about her. The place was spotless in the brilliant sunshine which flooded through the windows. Horse brasses on the walls gave back reflections, as did the lovingly polished oak of a fine dresser.

She was examining a drawing of a horse race, flanked by a number of rosettes, when Heston returned.

"Was Flodden a jockey?" she asked. The connection of the oddly assorted couple with Heston had intrigued her.

"Yes." This short reply was not an invitation for further questioning, but Miranda persisted.

"What happened? Why is he...?"

"A cripple? There was an accident. He was riding a young horse in its first race. Something startled the creature...perhaps the shouting of the crowd...and it ran into the rails."

"And he was crushed?"

"No, he was thrown over the rail and into a heavy post on the other side. It was not thought that he would live."

"My lord, I know that you do not care to speak of it, but why you? Why did you help them? I could not help but notice their gratitude."

"Inquisitive!" He tugged at a straying curl. "It was my horse, you see. Flodden had ridden for me for years."

"And you set them up here?"

"What else could I do? His livelihood was gone, and the child was sick."

Miranda was silent. Many owners would not have

spared another thought for the injured man since he could be of no further use to them. Compassion was not a virtue which she had noticed much among the *ton*.

"And Mary?" she ventured.

"Their daughter is much improved since she came to live in Richmond. I have promised that she shall meet you later, if you do not object?"

"Of course not. I should like to meet her." She eyed Heston with new respect. Perhaps it was not so strange that she should be in love with him. Behind that hard exterior lay a warm heart. If only some of that warmth might flow in her direction.

She had emptied her glass without thinking, and he refilled it for her.

"Hungry?" he asked.

"I'm starving!" Miranda smiled up at him. "It must be the drive and the country air."

"I'm glad to hear it. Annie is a fine cook. She will be disappointed if we don't do justice to her efforts."

He spoke no more than the truth, and for the first time in weeks Miranda ate with a hearty appetite. She had expected the usual country fare of ham and beef and heavy meat puddings, and was surprised to be served with a feather-light omelette, followed by small strips of chicken breast in a tangy sauce. The salads were so fresh that they could only have come from the Floddens' garden that very morning.

She was lavish with her praise when Mrs Flodden appeared.

"I did not wish to overface you, miss. The day is so warm, but if his lordship is still hungry there is a saddle of mutton..."

Heston shook his head and laughed. "Annie, you would have me as fat as a flawn. I doubt if I could eat

another mouthful.'' There was a wicked twinkle in
his eyes.

"Not my fruit pie? Oh, sir, I made it specially, knowing how you like it, and the apples are our own, stored
from last year.''

"Well, if I must…'' he said with mock reluctance.
Miranda was undeceived.

"Lord Heston is joking, Mrs Flodden,'' she announced. "He tells me that your pies are famous. You
should punish him by refusing to let him taste them.''

"Oh, ma'am. I couldn't do that!'' Mrs Flodden was
shocked. "I'll fetch the pitcher of cream.''

She stood over him anxiously, waiting for his verdict.

"Delicious! Annie, you haven't lost your touch. I believe I might manage another morsel.'' In the end he
consumed a full half of the pie, much to the satisfaction
of his hostess.

"You have led me astray once more,'' he told her
with a grin. "Now I must walk for at least three hours
or I shall fall asleep.''

"Oh, sir, you can't be meaning to keep the young lady
out for all that time in the heat?''

"If she falls by the wayside, I shall sweep her into
my arms and bring her back to you, I promise.'' He saw
her worried frown. "Don't worry, Annie. We shall keep
to the shade of the trees down by the river. I think Miss
Gaysford will enjoy a stroll.''

Miranda was quick to assent. There was something
about this quiet place which had done much to restore
her peace of mind, and she felt at ease with these good
people.

Heston took her arm and led her through the inn and
down through the kitchen garden to a wicket gate. Beyond it a narrow path ran down towards the river.

He drew her arm through his and they strolled along in a companionable silence.

"Still cross with me because I brought you here?" he asked suddenly.

"No, I have enjoyed it very much. You were right. It is good to get away from the city."

"And your worries?"

Miranda did not answer him. How could she explain that the main cause of her apprehension was standing by her side.

She pointed to the swans. "May we not take a closer look at them? They have some cygnets."

"Feed them if you wish. Annie sent me out prepared." He produced a bag of broken bread from his coat pocket, and handed it to her. "Not too close though. They can be dangerous at this time of year."

Obediently she stood well back from the river bank and threw the bread into the water. It attracted the swans at once and they came towards her, their long, snake-like heads striking out towards the floating food. When it was gone they lost interest and swam away.

She turned to find that Heston was seated on the trunk of a fallen tree, regarding her intently. He patted the seat beside him.

"Come here," he said gently. "I want to talk to you."

She wanted to refuse, but somehow she could not. She hesitated, knowing that it was folly to be alone with him like this.

"I shall not eat you, my dear love, but if you will not come to me then I must come to you." He rose and walked towards her. Then he took her in his arms.

"Please don't!" she murmured.

"Why not, my darling? Don't you know how much I love you?"

His words brought her to her senses. She broke away abruptly.

"Haven't you punished me enough?" she cried in a broken voice. "On top of all else, must you pretend that you care for me?"

"You are sure that it is pretence?" He was so still that he might have been carved from stone.

"What else can it be? I admit that I was wrong, if that is what you want from me. I knew that you had no intention of offering for me, and I should not have pretended that I did."

"It was not a very serious pretence, my dear." His face was calm. "On the contrary, you gave me the impression that you wished to put me out of countenance."

"But you...but you..."

"I decided to call your bluff."

"Well, you certainly did so." Miranda's voice was bitter. "May we not end this farce here and now? I release you from your promise."

"But I have no desire to be released. Did I not make that plain?"

"Oh, no, you cannot mean it? How can you behave so ill? You know that I have not the least desire—"

"That I must beg leave to doubt." He bent his head and found her lips, and again the world was lost.

"Will you still tell me that you don't care for me?" he murmured. "Your body gives you the lie."

"You are mistaken!" Miranda struggled to free herself.

"Am I? I think not! I asked you once before to trust me. Is it so hard to do? Is there always to be this barrier between us?"

"I don't know what you mean."

"I think you do. This secret that you guard so closely? Must it never be revealed?"

"It is not mine alone to tell," she cried, goaded into flinging caution to the winds.

"Your sister again? Well, I had suspected it. I won't press you to reveal her confidence, but one day you will come to me in your own good time."

"You speak in riddles, sir. Now, if you please, I should like to return to London."

"I wonder why that should not surprise me?" His expression was imperturbable as he took her arm once more and led her towards the inn.

Miranda was desperate to get away, but she was not to be released so soon.

"I have promised to take you to see Mary," he announced. "I hope you will be kind to her."

Accompanied by Mrs Flodden, he led her through to a small private parlour at the far end of the inn.

At first she did not see the child who lay among a pile of cushions on a sofa by the window. Then she was aware of being inspected by a pair of bright blue eyes. The thin little face was a perfect replica of Flodden's own.

"Here is Miss Gaysford come to see you, Mary. She is very shy. Promise that you will not frighten her as you do me?" Heston sounded solemn.

"Sir, you are teasing me," a small voice cried merrily. "I don't frighten you."

"Indeed you do! Sometimes, when we have been playing spillikins, you looked so fierce that I was positively shaking in my boots."

A peal of laughter greeted this sally. Heston was clearly a favourite with the frail little girl.

Miranda guessed that she could not have been more

than eight or nine, although the traces of pain upon the child's face made her look older. She was desperately thin, with stick-like arms and legs, but her face was alive with intelligence.

Heston went across to sit beside her on the sofa.

"Well, what do you think of the lady who is to be my wife?" he said gravely.

Blue eyes and grey regarded Miranda so seriously that she began to smile.

"Mama told me that she was beautiful, and she is," the little girl announced. "She looks like the picture in my book."

"You mean the wicked witch?" Heston asked mildly.

"No, sir...I mean the fairy princess."

"I am relieved to hear it. I should not care to be married to a witch. She might put a spell on me."

"And turn you into a frog?"

"I shouldn't put it past her. It would be most inconvenient to be a frog, you know. I should have to hop about the garden and eat flies."

"Instead of Mrs Flodden's apple pies? You would not care for that, my lord," put in Miranda.

Miranda could not hide her amusement, especially when Mary nodded her agreement.

"He would not," she confirmed. "Mama says that Lord Heston is a splendid trencherman. I think it means that he eats a lot..."

"What a reputation!" Heston rose to his feet. "All these agreeable compliments will turn my head. Mary, we shall come to see you soon. If you do as the doctor says and eat up all your food, you may be well enough to come for a drive."

The child's eyes shone. "I will!" she cried. "Do you promise?"

"I give you my word on it. Now say your goodbyes to Miss Gaysford, for I must take her home."

A small, claw-like hand appeared from among the cushions and Miranda took it in her own.

"I hope we shall be friends," she said with a twinkle in her eyes. "Then you may teach me how to frighten his lordship."

"Both of you?" Heston threw his eyes to heaven in mock dismay. "I shall be a quivering jelly."

Mary was still laughing when they left her.

They had covered several miles of the journey back to London before she questioned him about the child.

"Is Mary very sick?" she asked.

"She was always delicate, but she is improving. There have been setbacks, naturally, but the spirit is there. It has pulled her through on many an occasion."

"She seems devoted to you."

"Purely due to my expertise at spillikins." Heston smiled down at her and her heart turned over. She turned her head, so that he should not see how her love for him betrayed her.

He drew the team to a halt in the shelter of some trees. Then a large hand reached out to cover her own.

"Can I have been mistaken? My love, we deal so well together, and in these last few days I have felt that you have changed. I think you do not dislike me as you did. In fact, I have begun to hope that you could learn to care for me."

Miranda did not answer him.

"You do not deny it?" he said eagerly.

She cast about wildly for some reply which would put an end to this dangerous conversation. Perhaps a half-truth would serve.

"I have misjudged you from the first," she replied in a low tone. "Perhaps we might be friends—"

"And that is to be all?"

Before she could protest he took her in his arms and kissed her soundly. Her mouth opened like a flower beneath his own, and he began to tease her with little flickering movements of his tongue. Her arms crept about his neck and she strained towards him, faint with longing for a fulfilment which she did not understand.

When he held her away his face was serious.

"Will you tell me now that you do not wish to marry me?" he asked.

"I can't!" Miranda did not recognise her own voice. The words had seemed to come from a stranger.

"You have not answered my question."

When she did not reply he sat in silence for a time. Then he turned to her again.

"Promise me this at least? Do nothing hasty for the moment. Next week I shall be in Portsmouth for some days. It will give you time to consider. On my return you may give me your answer."

When she began to speak, he stopped her.

"Don't worry, my dear. If you are still of the same mind I shall not press you further. You may put an end to our betrothal in any way you wish."

These were the words which she had once longed to hear, but the triumph felt like ashes in her mouth. There was nothing left to say, and indeed if she had tried to speak she must have burst into tears.

Heston picked up the reins and guided his team back on to the road. For the rest of the journey back to London both of them were silent, but in place of the easy camaraderie on the drive down to Richmond there was now an atmosphere of tension.

It was not until they reached their destination that Heston broke the awkward silence. He threw his reins to the groom, jumped down from the driving seat, and held out his arms to help Miranda from her perch.

"Cheer up!" he murmured as his lips brushed her ear. "Even friends are allowed to enjoy each other's company."

She responded with the faintest of smiles, and was in no mood to listen to Fanny's strictures after he had gone.

"What a trick to play on us! I am surprised that Aunt allowed you to go jauntering off with Heston on your own, and for so long…"

"Haven't you enjoyed your day?"

"No, I have not. We saw no one that we knew, and if there is one thing I detest it is a picnic. There were so many creepy-crawlies, and stinging insects too. I could not eat a bite."

"Then you must be very hungry…"

"Much you care when we might all have gone to Richmond."

"Lord Heston wished to speak to me alone."

"Are there not rooms enough in this house where you might be private with him without trailing out to Richmond on your own?"

Miranda did not reply.

"What had he to say?" her twin asked with a nervous laugh.

"He has offered to release me from my promise to him." Something in her face warned Fanny to proceed with caution.

"And did you agree?"

"I agreed to do as he requested."

"And that was?"

"To wait and to consider. I am to give him an answer when he returns from Portsmouth."

"Oh, you are a darling!" Fanny threw her arms about her sister's unresponsive form. "You did it for me, just as you promised."

"It must come to the same thing in the end. I cannot marry him..."

"Well, in my opinion he would make a most disagreeable husband, always looking down his nose, and making those strange remarks which no one can understand." She saw the pain in Miranda's eyes and stopped.

"Of course I do not know him as you do," she continued when her sister did not speak. "You seem to have seen something else in him, though what I can't imagine—"

"Leave it, Fanny!" Miranda begged in desperation.

"Very well," Her sister brightened. "You need not make a decision yet, you know. Anything may happen in the next two weeks..." Her face grew dreamy.

Miranda knew that she was thinking of Alexei Toumanov. Had he joined them on the infamous picnic, the stinging insects would have gone unnoticed. She could only be thankful that the handsome Russian was due to leave the capital so soon.

"I wonder that Harry Lakenham has not called upon us recently," she said. "You have not seen him?"

"We met him in the Park the other day," Fanny told her in casual tones. "He was with his friends, so we did not stop to speak."

"He seems to have taken his dismissal very well."

"It was you who told him that he must not try to see me."

"Not alone and in secret, but I did not say that he should avoid your company altogether."

"It cannot signify! I expect he feels as I do, that we were both mistaken in our hearts."

This cool dismissal of what was to have been the love affair of the century took Miranda's breath away. Angry words rose to her lips, but she suppressed them. The same thing had happened many times before, but on previous occasions no harm had been done. She struggled for composure.

"What a pity that you did not discover it before," she said quietly. "Much trouble might have been avoided."

"I can't help that, and I don't know why you should look so black at me. I thought you disapproved of Harry."

"I think him too young and foolish to be considering marriage."

"Well, then, you must be satisfied, and your precious Adam Heston will be delighted."

"Not if he thinks that you have formed an attachment for the Count…"

The colour rose to Fanny's cheeks. "What an idea! Pray why should he think that? Alexei has not spoken."

"Nor will he do so, Fanny."

"Are you so sure? He has been most particular in his attentions."

"He likes to flirt, as do most young men, but you can't believe that he is serious?"

"You think I am beneath his notice?" Anger sparkled in Fanny's eyes.

"Of course not, but I don't want you to be hurt. You should not refine too much upon his gallantries. They may be nothing more than the usual outrageous flattery which passes for conversation in the Polite World."

Fanny tossed her head. "Why should you be the only one to marry well? I have a fancy to be a Countess."

Miranda said no more. Further warnings would be useless. Her only hope that her twin would be saved from further folly lay in the fact that the Count would return to Russia within the next two weeks.

She was dismayed to find that he, together with his sister and her husband, were to be their fellow dinner-guests at Brook Street on the following evening. At Lady Heston's invitation Richard had also joined them.

He looked overawed at the prospect of visiting Lord Heston's home.

"How do I look?" he asked Miranda in an undertone. "I expect it will be all magnificence..."

"You are the epitome of elegance," she told him with a smile. She felt somewhat nervous herself, but her blonde silk gown, ornamented with cobweb-like blonde lace, was so becoming that it gave her confidence.

In the event, the evening was not the ordeal she had expected. Heston's major-domo, whilst perfectly correct in his manner, showed no trace of stiffness, and she guessed that he was an old retainer.

He announced their party to the group already gathered in the salon, and Heston came to greet them with all the easy address which was natural to him.

Miranda could not meet his eyes, but he took her hand and kissed it, and then saluted her upon the cheek.

"Friends?" he murmured.

She gave him a look of gratitude. She had dreaded a certain awkwardness after their last meeting.

His lordship appeared to have forgotten it. To her surprise it was the Count whose manner had changed. It was imperceptible to most of the party, and throughout the meal he joined in the conversation so merrily that he kept them laughing with his stories of life at the Russian court. Yet he made no effort later to monopolise Fanny for himself.

Miranda looked across at the Princess Chaliapine. She, too, was speaking with her usual vivacity, but it was impossible not to wonder if she had spoken to her brother, warning him not to raise hopes which could not be fulfilled.

She prayed that Fanny would not give herself away. Her twin was incapable of dissembling, and she was already looking dissatisfied to see the Count in conversation with the Alderman and Mrs Shere.

Miranda threw a speaking look at Richard, and he moved at once to Fanny's side.

Accompanied by Lady Heston, Miranda went to join them.

"This has been a delightful evening, your ladyship," Richard told his hostess warmly. "It was kind of you to include me."

"It was a pleasure, Mr Young. Now you three young people may advise me. I have a small gift for the Alderman. Do you think that he will like it?" She took up a small parcel from the table and unwrapped it to reveal a painting.

"How beautiful! It is one of my uncle's roses... He will be delighted!"

Miranda bent to examine the work more closely.

"Why, you have caught every detail," she murmured in wonder. "I had not realised that the petals were shaded so, and that the leaves are not all a solid green..."

Even Fanny was intrigued. "Ma'am, it is hard to believe that you have made the painting so quickly. Why, it is not more than a day or two since you took the flowers."

"That is experience, my dear, and a sad habit of ignoring all else in order to paint."

"How better could you spend your time, my dearest?" Heston had joined their little group. "We are all waiting for your *magnum opus.*"

"Now, Adam, I beg of you…" Lady Heston shook her head in reproach.

"Please tell us what it is, ma'am, if you do not object."

Richard was so clearly interested that her ladyship did not refuse.

"I am trying to record the flora and fauna in our part of Warwickshire," she admitted shyly. "It is a lengthy task."

"But well worth doing, Lady Heston. It will be a wonderful record for the future." Richard quite forgot his own diffidence as he began to tell her about the countryside in Yorkshire.

Heston took Miranda's arm. "We are *de trop,*" he told her with a smile. "If you ladies do not rescue me, I shall be forced to display my ignorance. Do you care for cards, or a game of billiards?"

"Billiards, my lord? I have never played, but I should like to try." Fanny's expression brightened in an instant.

"Then you shall do so." He led them through the hall and into a massive billiard-room, complete with baize-covered table and cues in racks upon the walls.

Fanny showed a surprising aptitude for the game.

"What fun it is!" she cried. "I had thought it only a game for gentlemen." She grew excited as her score increased, and her face was vivid with enjoyment. For the moment she had forgotten the Count's defection.

Miranda sighed with relief. "When do you go to Portsmouth?" she asked Heston.

"In a day or two. Alexei is to go ahead of the main party, to make sure that all is in readiness for the Tsar's suite." The penetrating eyes held amusement in their depths. "You have no need to worry, I assure you."

"No...no, of course not. It is just that..."

"You need say no more. I am not blind. Now will you not try your hand at this absorbing game? If you allow your sister to outshine you, she will be insufferable."

A smile took the sting out of his words and Fanny laughed at him as she relinquished her cue.

"You shall both try to beat me," she announced.

"Not I!" his lordship shuddered. "I have too much regard for the surface of this table."

"Lord Heston, you are joking!" Fanny reproached. "I suspect that you are an expert at this game."

"This...and others..." he murmured in Miranda's ear. "Now let me show you how to hold the cue."

He stood behind her, long arms stretched out, and his hands covering her own. "Don't rush at it," he advised. "Take it gently, and keep your eye upon the ball."

His nearness made Miranda feel faint with longing. She tried to pot the ball, and missed completely.

Fanny's laughter echoed round the room. "That is not the way," she cried. "Here, let me show you."

Miranda dropped the cue and turned, only to find herself still enclosed within his lordship's arms. Beneath the fine cambric of his shirt, she sensed the beating of his heart, and the pounding in her own breast threatened to overcome her.

Then Heston moved away. "We shall be missed," he said lightly. "Shall we join the others?"

They returned to the salon to find the Alderman lost

in admiration of his painting. ''I have just the place for it,'' he said with pride. ''I'll have it framed to match the gilding in the drawing-room. Then I shall see it every day.''

He was still gloating as they returned to Bloomsbury.

Chapter Fourteen

Fanny was unusually quiet on the following day. The reason was not far to seek, but Miranda did not question her.

"I thought Alexei seemed a little strange last night, did not you?" Fanny asked at last.

"He was pleasant, as he always is."

"Yes, but…well…he is used to be more loverly."

"You could not expect him to flirt openly in company."

"You mean in the company of his sister, I suppose?"

"Among others."

"No, it is she who does not like me. I knew it from the first. A Princess, indeed! Why, her husband is old enough to be her father."

"That is not our concern."

"Not yours, perhaps, but it is mine. She is so puffed up with family pride—"

"Oh, Fanny, that isn't true! I find her charming."

"That is because she doesn't try to interfere in your affairs." Fanny's laugh was angry. "It is to be hoped that she does not intend to join us for our visit to the Pantheon. Without her, Alexei is so different."

* * *

Her hopes were realised on the following evening, and Fanny was so delighted by the absence of the Princess that she failed to notice Alexei's continued reserve.

As always, his manners were delightful, but there was certainly a change in him.

It was obvious to Miranda. Alexei was his usual charming self, solicitous for their comfort and as entertaining as always, but he did not seek to engage Fanny in private conversation.

Surely her sister must realise that his interest in her went no further than the lightest of flirtations. A look at Fanny's expression convinced her otherwise. Her twin was gazing up at the Count with adoration in her eyes. She could not have made her feelings clearer if she had spoken them aloud.

"Out of the frying pan and into the fire?" Heston murmured wickedly. His words were for Miranda's ear alone, and she threw him a look of reproach.

"My sister is too susceptible," she admitted with an uneasy laugh.

"Unlike yourself?" There was something in his eyes which challenged her to deny it.

"We…we are very different, she and I," she said hastily.

"Indeed you are! It would be difficult to find two women less alike in temperament. I confess that your previous attachment to Harry Lakenham and his to you has often puzzled me."

His remark was so unexpected that it caught Miranda unawares. Her head went up and she looked at him in panic. Then she made a valiant effort to cover her confusion.

"Why should you find it strange, my lord? I explained my reasons well enough…"

"So you did! It was a splendid explanation, but I was thinking more of Harry..."

"I don't know why you should feel his wish to marry me outrageous."

"Not outrageous...just astonishing! Did he not quail at times?"

"That remark is unworthy of a gentleman, sir. You make me out to be some kind of dragon."

"Not a dragon, my love, although I have seen you breathing fire upon occasion." He looked down at her and she heard the laughter in his voice. "Now how shall I find the words to describe you when you are upon your high ropes...perhaps a pretty little hissing kitten, out to defy the world?"

"That is nonsense!" she said coldly. "Now, if you please, I should like to listen to the play."

"Of course. I, too, shall enjoy it. It is such a comfort to know that both your own undying passion and that of Lakenham is unlikely to survive into old age."

Miranda did not reply, although she herself had wondered why Harry no longer called upon them. After all, in the first hot throes of love he had been prepared to defy his grandfather. Yet that devotion had not survived an enforced separation. She realised that it was for the best, but it said much for the fickleness of a man's affection. Most probably they were all the same with their honeyed words at one moment, and indifference in the next. It was a lowering thought.

"Cheer up!" Heston teased. "I shall not change."

"No, I don't suppose you will," she snapped. "And that, my lord, is not a source of comfort to me!"

"Milling me down again?" His shoulders began to shake. "I shall advise my friends that they need not visit the great Jackson for lessons in the art of self-defence. They should come to you instead.''

Miranda gave him an unwilling smile. Such a notion was so ridiculous that it appealed to her sense of humour.

''That's better!'' he approved, and relapsed into silence until the interval. The one-act play which opened the evening's entertainment had not been received with much acclaim, but before the main performance could begin a buzz of excitement ran around the theatre.

Then the audience rose and began to clap and cheer. A woman had entered the opposite box, and now she came forward, bowing to the crowd.

Miranda knew at once that it was the Prince Regent's estranged wife, Caroline of Brunswick. Rumour had not lied, she decided. The Princess was heavily built, with rather coarse features. Her colouring was difficult to distinguish beneath the garish layers of paint and powder. Against the thick white coating blotches of scarlet rouge stood out in such startling contrast that they gave her the appearance of a clown.

The plunging neckline of her gown revealed a magnificent bosom, but it was cut even lower than those of the demi-reps who plied their trade on such occasions.

As Miranda watched the Princess threw back her head and laughed, displaying broken and discoloured teeth.

The vulgarity of her manner did not dismay the crowd. They cheered her to the echo.

''I did not know that the Princess was so popular,'' Mrs Shere announced.

''We are about to find out just how popular,'' Heston said with a significant glance at the adjoining box.

It was unfortunate that the Regent himself had chosen that particular moment to arrive at the theatre. He went unnoticed for a moment or two, and was forced to content himself with a back view of those of his fellow countrymen who had chosen to welcome the Princess Caroline. Then a murmur ran through the crowd. They turned and stood in silence as the heir to the throne took his seat.

The audience could not have made their opposition clearer, but the Prince's manner remained unchanged. He did not betray by the flicker of an eyelid that he was acquainted with the woman in the opposite box.

"Why, this is more exciting than the play," Fanny whispered to Miranda. "The Prince and his wife are looking through each other."

"I think it sad," Mrs Shere said quietly. "Sometimes men and women are ill suited to each other. They cannot be blamed for that."

"The blame is laid at the Prince's door," Heston told her. "He is considered to have treated both his wife and his daughter in a shabby way. The people will not stand for it. They have a love of justice, as you know."

"Perhaps they do not know the whole," Mrs Shere said kindly.

"You are generous, ma'am, and you are right. The Prince believes his wife to have an unfortunate influence on his daughter."

Mrs Shere was silent. She, like everyone else in the capital, had heard rumours that the Princess Charlotte had been actively encouraged by her mother into conduct which lacked propriety. On one occasion, Caroline of Brunswick had locked her into a bedroom with a handsome aide-de-camp, telling the couple to enjoy themselves.

"That will be ended when the Princess Charlotte is wed," Mrs Shere assured him.

"Let us hope so, ma'am, but she has just cried off from her engagement to the Prince of Orange, believing it to be a trick to get her out of the country."

"Oh, no, I don't believe it! Whatever his faults, the Regent has always loved his daughter." Mrs Shere spoke with conviction. From his early days, when the Prince was known and loved by all as the handsome Prince Florizel and the hope of the country, Mrs Shere had been his staunch supporter.

Heston smiled down at her. "Ma'am, the Prince stands in need of more friends like you," he said. "It is too easy to think the worst of him."

Miranda threw him a warm glance of approval. She was unsurprised to find him ready to defend his friend. Extravagant the Prince might be, changeable in his politics, easily swayed by the termagants who took his fancy, and emotional to a fault, but beneath the surface Heston had found a warm-hearted, cultivated man who believed in a civilised way of life, and would settle for nothing but the best in any field of the arts.

During the next interval she was able to study the Royal Party more closely. The Prince's appearance was as artificial as that of his wife. The paint and powder failed to disguise the fact that he had paled at the sight of her, and now looked morose.

Against the brilliant splendour of the satin coat and breeches which clothed his massive form, the dress of his Allies appeared simple and unostentatious. But it was for them that the cheering had begun again as they entered his box. The Regent had joined them in bowing to acknowledge the plaudits of the crowd, but there was a bitterness about his expression which Miranda could not fail to mark. He had suffered a public humiliation and she pitied him.

"Will the Princess Caroline be invited to attend the Proclamation of Peace with France tomorrow?" Mrs Shere enquired.

"No, ma'am. She does not attend official occasions." Heston frowned. "It is to be hoped that she won't invite herself and cause a disturbance."

"Shall you go with the Prince, my lord?" Miranda asked.

"No, I think not. You know my views upon this so-called peace, my dear. In my opinion it is but a temporary cessation of hostilities. We haven't crushed Napoleon yet."

He spoke in a low tone, for which Miranda was profoundly grateful. Mrs Shere had suffered enough as her eldest son had fought his way through the Peninsula with Wellington.

Miranda looked at the Prince again. "If you are right, will the Regent lead his troops in battle? I heard that he had always longed to do so."

"The King would never permit it."

"But why? His royal brothers hold the highest ranks in the army."

"That was one cause of the estrangement between Prince George and his father. He does not lack personal courage, but he was made to appear a coward through no fault of his own. It was in part a desire not to risk the life of the heir to the throne, but the main reason was the old king's dislike of his eldest son. Any request was met with a refusal as a matter of course."

"They are an unfortunate family," Miranda sighed.

"Indeed they are, but let us drop this depressing subject. Tomorrow I intend to leave for Portsmouth."

"So soon? The Review of the Fleet is a full five days away…"

"Would you keep me by your side?" he teased.

Miranda looked up to see a twinkle in his eyes.

"Your private arrangements are none of my concern, my lord..." She turned away, but not before the tell-tale colour had risen to her cheeks.

"Crushed again, and just as I was beginning to hope." He took her hand and raised it to his lips. "I intend to call upon Lord Rudyard," he told her. "He is not in the best of health, and as he lives near Midhurst, it seemed an excellent opportunity..."

"To report upon myself and Harry?" Miranda's tone was sharp.

"Why, no!" He looked at her in mock surprise. "I see no need for that."

"He is sure to ask." She felt uncomfortable.

"I don't intend to worry him with details of a matter which is now in the past. And Harry is behaving better than we might have hoped. I haven't seen him at the gaming tables, and to my knowledge he hasn't attempted any more balloon ascents."

Miranda could not take so sanguine a view of Harry as a reformed character. In the past few months she had come to know him well, and his absence from his usual haunts had worried her.

For a time she had suspected that he and Fanny might be meeting in secret, but since her sister had transferred her affections to Alexei Toumanov she had dismissed the idea. Fanny was transparent and, apart from the fact that she had had no opportunity to make furtive assignations, it was clear that she no longer had any wish to revive her former love affair.

"Will Count Toumanov go with you?" she asked.

Heston shook his head. "Tomorrow he is on duty. He will follow later."

Fanny looked across at her twin with a radiant smile. Without Heston by his side this would be an opportunity for Alexei to declare his love. She was in the highest of spirits for the rest of the evening.

Throughout the following day her air of suppressed excitement did not go unnoticed by the Alderman and his wife.

"What a child you are!" her aunt said fondly. "Such enthusiasm for our trip into the city! I hope it will be all that you expect, my dear."

They were not to be disappointed. As the family coach turned into the Strand, the crowd slowed them to a halt. The city was in gala mood and there was dancing in the streets. Every building was decked with flags and banners, and the fountains ran with wine.

"What a sight!" Tears sparkled in Mrs Shere's eyes as she turned to her husband. "May we not go into St Paul's Cathedral, my love? I should like to give thanks that our boy will now be safe..."

"Perhaps another day, my dear Emma. I think we should not leave the coach, or there is every likelihood of our being either separated or trampled underfoot."

The press of people was so great, and the shouting so loud, that the horses grew uneasy. The Alderman was quick to see the danger, and he ordered his coachman to turn for home. It was not easily accomplished, and it was late afternoon before they reached Bloomsbury again.

Mrs Shere sank into a chair. "What an exhausting day! I am glad to have seen the celebrations, but what a blessing it will be when all these foreigners leave the city..."

Miranda smiled at her. "You will like to have a quiet evening, ma'am, with perhaps a little music?"

"More than anything, my dear, if you are not too tired to play."

After their evening meal Miranda took her place at the spinet, signing to Fanny to turn the music for her. It soon became apparent that her sister's attention was elsewhere.

"Do pay attention, Fanny. You have missed the place three times."

Fanny's eyes were upon the clock, and her face grew longer as the hours ticked by.

"It is so late," she whispered. "He won't come now."

"Of course not!" Miranda did not pretend to misunderstand. "Tonight there is a dinner at Carlton House."

"A dinner at Carlton House, do you say?" The Alderman settled himself more comfortably in his chair. "The Prince will be hard put to beat the dinner we gave him at the Guildhall. Did I tell you that we had the first turtle soup of the season?"

"Many times," his wife assured him with a smile. "My dear, would you not be more comfortable in your bed instead of dozing in your chair? These girls must be tired to death."

It was a disconsolate Fanny who sought her bedchamber that evening.

"I quite thought that Alexei would have come tonight," she told Miranda.

"But I explained. The dinner will go on until the early hours."

"Yes, that must be it, but pray do not suggest that we go out tomorrow. He is sure to call..."

* * *

Her hopes were to be dashed. They had a number of visitors on the following day, but the Count was not among them.

"Do you think that he is ill?" she asked Miranda anxiously. "There must be a reason why he does not come to see us."

"We have no way of finding out." Miranda did not have the heart to voice her own interpretation of the reasons for the Count's absence. Fanny had been unable to hide her feelings for him, and he was too much of a gentleman to encourage her in a hopeless passion.

As the days passed Fanny grew more and more distraught. When Richard arrived she could not wait to question him.

"We have been worried about Count Toumanov," she said. "Have you heard that he is ill?"

"He was looking well when I saw him yesterday. He was on his way to Portsmouth."

This apparently innocuous remark brought a gasp from Fanny. She fled the room with her handkerchief to her eyes, and Miranda could only be thankful that she and Richard were the only witnesses of her distress.

His face fell. "Miranda, I know that you told me not to give up hope, but I can't believe that Fanny does not love the Count."

"Another infatuation!" Miranda told him calmly. "By next week he will be gone. Richard, if you are still of a mind to wed my foolish sister, I suggest that you seize the opportunity to offer for her. The love of a dear friend cannot but help to mend a broken heart."

"She won't look at me." His face was sad. "She thinks of me as a brother."

"Then you must change her mind." She gave him a

rueful look. "But who am I to advise you? I cannot manage my own affairs."

"How do you go on with Heston? Don't tell me if you don't wish it. I have no right to ask, but I should like to see you happy."

Miranda hesitated for a moment. "He says he loves me," she replied. "But I can't believe it."

"I believe it. I have thought so for some time, as I once told you."

"Even supposing it were true, I cannot marry him. In the first place, I should be forced to tell him of the way I have deceived him. What man could hear of it without disgust?"

"You are convinced that he has no suspicion of what has happened?"

"I am. I know well enough what his reaction would be." She shuddered. "I could not bear to hear what he would say…"

"Miranda, you misjudge him. He is one of the wisest men I know. His pride might be hurt, but he would soon forgive you."

"You sound like Aunt Emma. I know you mean to comfort me, but it is to late for that. He offered to release me from my promise to him…did Fanny tell you?"

"No, but I must hope that you didn't accept."

"I can do nothing else. When he returns from Portsmouth, I shall give him my decision."

"If he accepts it, he is not the man I think him." With those enigmatic words he prepared to take his leave.

"Will Fanny care to see the battle on the Serpentine?" he asked. "It is not until next week, but…"

"By then the Count will be gone. No doubt she will welcome the diversion." Miranda gave him her hand.

"What a staunch friend you are!" He bowed and left her.

Miranda went in search of Fanny, only to find her sister weeping in their room.

"How could Alexei do this to me?" her sister moaned. "He must have known how much I longed to see him."

"You certainly made it obvious. Fanny, I wish you will listen to me…"

"I won't! I won't! You don't understand! You have never cared for anyone as I care for him."

"Perhaps not!" Miranda lied. "But must you advertise it to the world? Richard was distressed to see you so upset."

"Richard understands. He is the only person in the world who does not criticise me."

"Then I am surprised that you are not kinder to him."

Fanny ignored this last remark. "When does the Court return from Porstmouth?" she asked. "There is so little time left to us. Perhaps Alexei does not know of my feelings for him."

"Then he must be blind. Fanny, I beg of you…please try for a little conduct. You lay yourself open to gossip."

Fanny was not attending. "That must be the reason. He thinks that I don't care for him. What a fool I have been! When he returns, I shall make my feelings clear."

"Oh, love, please don't! Think how mortifying it would be to discover that he does not feel the same."

Fanny glared at her. "Why should he not? The most mortifying thing to me is to discover that you are eaten up with jealousy. Do you want him for yourself?"

The gibe was unworthy of a reply and Miranda changed the subject.

"Richard has asked if you would like to see the mock

battle on the Serpentine next week. Shall you care to go? It is to be a re-creation of the battle of Trafalgar.''

''I suppose so. Anything would be preferable to this dreadful boredom. How dull we are without Alexei!''

Miranda held her tongue. She, too, was finding that life had lost much of its savour. It came as a surprise to realise just how much she had grown to enjoy her daily battle of wits with Adam Heston.

She missed the stimulation of his company, the laughter, the teasing, and above all the excitement when he held her in his arms.

She could not deny that she loved him with all her heart and she longed for the sight of his tall figure, the warmth of his smile, and his passionate caresses.

Without him the future would be bleak indeed. More than anything in the world she wanted to become his wife. It was cruel to think that she had found her love at last, only to be forced to give him up.

Yet their next meeting must be their last. The Review of the Fleet was to take place on the following day and then he would return from Portsmouth to seek her answer.

The thought of refusing him was agony, but she must be strong. To see him just once more was all she could hope for now. She looked so sad that Fanny was moved to question her.

''Are you ill?'' she asked. ''You don't look at all the thing.''

''I have the headache, that is all.''

''So have I,'' Fanny sighed. ''This waiting is enough to give anyone the megrims. I believe we should go shopping. That will cheer us up, and Aunt Emma will enjoy it.''

She hurried away to find their aunt and returned with

the news that the carriage would be at the door in half an hour.

Miranda as too preoccupied to take much interest in their expedition, though she did her best to hide her worries. Perhaps the Tsar and his retinue would sail back to Russia direct from Portsmouth after the Review. There had been some talk of it. That would prevent Fanny from carrying out her plan to tell Alexei of her love.

Three days later her hopes were dashed when the Count was shown into their drawing-room.

Chapter Fifteen

Fanny jumped up at once, oversetting her embroidery frame and scattering the brightly coloured silks across the carpet.

"At last!" she cried. "Oh, how I have missed you!"

Miranda was ready to sink with embarrassment at this open declaration and a glance at Mrs Shere told her that her feelings were shared. She tried to retrieve the situation.

"We have all missed your company, Count Toumanov. Is that not so, Aunt Emma?"

"Indeed it is! The Review went well, I hope?" Mrs Shere tried to hide her anger at Fanny's shocking lack of decorum.

"It was a great success, ma'am, but now, alas, I am come to take my leave of you." He did not look at Fanny as he spoke.

An audible gasp drew all eyes to her. Her colour rose and then receded, leaving her very pale.

"No, not yet!" she pleaded. "Oh, I cannot breathe! Sir, will you help me into the garden?"

"I will take you to your room." Mrs Shere rose to

her feet. "Count Toumanov, will you excuse us? My niece has not been well."

"I am sorry to hear it, and I must hope that Miss Gaysford will make a quick recovery..." He opened the door and stood aside as Mrs Shere thrust Fanny from the room.

An awkward silence followed their departure.

Then the Count walked over to the window. For some moments he was lost in thought.

"Have I been at fault?" he said at last. "I would not willingly give pain."

"The fault is not yours, sir." Miranda felt unable to discuss her sister further. It had been an appalling scene, and she wished to spare the young man further embarrassment.

"Adam did not return to London with you?" she asked.

"Forgive me, Miss Gaysford, I had quite forgot. I am charged with messages for you. Adam sends his duty to Alderman and Mrs Shere, and rather more than that to you, I fancy." He managed a faint smile. "He is gone to see his godfather."

"I thought he had intended to call upon Lord Rudyard on his way down to Portsmouth."

"He did so, and found the old man sadly pulled down. Adam was so worried that he decided to return."

"I see. Then we must expect him when we see him."

"That won't be too long, I imagine. He is anxious to return to you, as I'm sure you know." The Count pulled on his gloves. "This has not been the happiest of leave-takings, Miss Gaysford, and for that I must blame myself. I should not have come today."

"After all our happy times together? We should have taken it amiss if you had not called to say farewell."

Miranda hoped that her words would reassure him, but his face was troubled as he took his leave of her.

She was given no time to worry about it, for at that moment the door burst open and Ellen rushed into the room.

"Miss, will you come at once? Your sister is in strong hysterics, and Mrs Shere can do no good with her..."

Miranda hurried up the stairs. She could hear Fanny's screams from the first landing. Fanny was lying on her bed, laughing and crying by turns.

"Shall I send for the doctor?" Mrs Shere turned an anxious face towards her.

"Leave her with me." Miranda walked over to the bed and slapped her twin across the face. The laughing and screaming stopped as Fanny subsided into hiccuping sobs.

"My dear child, I had not the least idea that your sister had formed an attachment for the Count." For once Mrs Shere looked every year of her age.

"Infatuation, ma'am," Miranda told her crisply. "It has happened before."

"But Count Toumanov? Has he led her to believe...?"

"No, that is all in my sister's mind."

"Then I must wonder how your mama puts up with all this nonsense. I would suggest that she goes home, but your marriage is so close, and she must return for that."

"Aunt, if you will allow me, I will speak to her alone."

"Very well, my dear. You may succeed in bringing her to her senses where I could not." Her manner was unusually stern as she left the twins together.

Miranda walked over to the bed and looked at the weeping figure of her twin.

"You may stop that!" she said coldly. "It will not wear with me."

"How could it? You can have no idea of how I feel. Oh, how could he be so cold? I tried to see him alone, but he did not support me."

"Fanny, your behaviour was the outside of enough. That blatant attempt to persuade the Count into the garden! I thought I must have died of shame."

Fanny's sobs ceased. "That is all you care about," she accused. "I declare you are become as stuffy as Heston himself. You should deal well together."

"Don't try to change the subject. We are not discussing Heston. Surely you must realise now that Count Toumanov had no intention of offering for you?"

Fanny began to wail again. "I shall become a dried-up spinster," she declared. "Lakenham has deserted me, and now the Count. I hope you are satisfied."

"None of it was of my doing," Miranda declared with some asperity. "Now wash your face. You must apologise to Aunt Emma. She had almost decided to send you home."

"I should not care," her twin said in a sullen tone. "I am beginning to hate London. Nothing pleasant ever happens here." She turned her head away and buried her face in the pillow.

Miranda left her to her sulks.

By the evening of the following day she was growing worried. No food had passed he sister's lips, and Fanny replied to questions only in monosyllables.

"Perhaps we were too hard on her. You do not think

that she will fall into a decline?'' Mrs Shere was clearly anxious.

''No, I don't.'' Miranda gave her aunt a reassuring smile. ''I'll speak to her. She may be feeling better now.''

As she made her way upstairs she felt perplexed. It was difficult to know exactly what to do. Fanny might be genuinely ill, in which case they should summon the doctor without delay. On the other hand, this refusal to eat could be her way of punishing her sister and her aunt for the lectures which she had suffered.

She opened the door to the bedchamber as quietly as possible, in case her twin was sleeping. The blinds were drawn against the evening sunlight, but Fanny was sitting up in bed. She looked up startled as Miranda entered and pulled the bedcover up to her chin.

''Are you cold? Will you have a hot brick for your feet?''

''No!'' Fanny mumbled. Her guilty expression aroused Miranda's suspicions. She crossed over to the bed and threw back the coverlet to reveal a plate of cakes.

''I see! Ellen has been smuggling food to you. You have not been starving, have you?'' The contempt in her voice made her sister blush. She did not reply.

''How could you, Fanny? Aunt has been so worried and so have I.''

There was still no answer.

''You can't hide up here for ever,'' Miranda continued. ''You must come downstairs and speak to Aunt.''

''I won't! I'm tired of being scolded. I wish we had never come here...'' Fanny scowled at her.

''It's too late to think of that. We are here and you

must make the best of it. Now pray get dressed and do as I ask…''

"Not tonight. I'll come down in the morning. You may tell Aunt Emma that I feel a little better.''

Miranda felt dispirited as she returned to the salon, but her anger was mingled with relief. If Fanny might be persuaded into an apology, Mrs Shere would readily accept it. Count Toumanov was gone, so there could be no repetition of Fanny's ill behaviour as far as he was concerned.

''It think we have no further cause to worry, ma'am,'' she said. ''My sister is much recovered and will come down in the morning. She is distressed to think that she has worried you…''

''That she did!'' Mrs Shere replied with feeling. ''I cannot like the way that she goes on. If it were not for your wedding, I should send her home.''

''Ma'am, pray try to understand…she is so impressionable and she does not always consider…''

Mrs Shere gave Miranda a reluctant smile. ''You will always defend her, my dear girl, and I admire your loyalty, but I could wish that she were wed to some sensible man such as Mr Young. With her children about her she might settle down.''

''Aunt, I share your hopes, and so does Richard. He is devoted to her.''

''Heaven protect him!'' Mrs Shere threw her eyes to heaven. ''He cannot wish for a quiet life.''

''He knows her very well, Aunt Emma, and he does not mind her fits of temperament. When we were children he could always coax her out of them, and was happy to do so.''

''He must be a saint.''

''I have often thought much the same myself, but she

must be loved, you know, and he would give her all the love she needs.''

''Your twin is spoilt, my dear, but there, I shall say no more to distress you.''

''Or her?'' Miranda begged.

''I suppose not. My only comfort is the thought that you are to be wed so soon, and will no longer bear responsibility for her. When does Lord Heston return?''

''I'm not quite sure. He is staying with his godfather. The Count told me that Lord Rudyard is not well.''

''Doubtless reports about Harry Lakenham have reached him. I do not understand the young these days. It makes me wonder what the world is coming to.''

On this sombre note both ladies retired.

Fanny was on her best behaviour for the next few days. Her apologies were given and received with good grace. Then she exerted all her charm in an effort to restore Mrs Shere's kind opinion.

This was the calm before the storm, Miranda thought with a shudder. When Heston returned and she refused him, they would be plunged into further scenes involving herself.

And with each day that passed she missed him more. Even to endure his anger would be preferable to not seeing him at all. Perhaps if she threw herself upon his mercy he might forgive her? Then the memory of that harsh dark face rose before her eyes. No, he would not forgive deception followed by humiliation. It was alien to his nature, and an offence to any man of honour.

It was in no happy frame of mind that she joined the others in the carriage as they set off to see the mock battle on the Serpentine.

The Park was crowded, but Richard found a place for

them beside the water's edge. Fanny was in the highest of spirits, Count Toumanov apparently forgotten. She chattered gaily, begging to be told the names of all the miniature ships upon the lake.

"They are larger than I had expected...I thought they would be toys."

"Not if they are to hold the crews. It is all to be as realistic as possible, you know. The Prince has spared no expense." Richard was eager to explain. "He wished to mark the centenary of the House of Hanover in appropriate style. What better than a re-creation of the Battle of Trafalgar?"

Miranda looked about her. "I wonder if we should not move further back?" she said. "The crowd is pushing from behind and we are so close to the lake..."

"No, no!" Fanny clapped her hands. "We have a splendid view. I won't give up my place."

The Alderman had seen the danger. He took his wife's arm and moved back a pace or two, pushing the jostling mob aside. Other's took their place at once, and soon they were lost to sight.

Miranda heard him call to her to come away. Then his words were drowned in a cannonade of gunfire.

Startled, Fanny screamed and lost her footing as he turned. Then she plunged headlong into the lake.

A roar of laughter ran through the crowd as Richard waded after her.

"Oh, she will drown!" Miranda cried in anguish.

"No, ma'am, it ain't deep enough just here," the man beside her comforted. "See, the young man is only in the water up to his waist."

At that moment Fanny found her footing and flung her arms in a stranglehold about Richard's neck. It took him by surprise and they fell together into deeper water. The crowd grew silent.

"She will drown the pair of them," Miranda's companion murmured. He sat down and began to struggle out of his boots.

Miranda was frozen into silence as she watched the struggling pair. Then Richard brought both arms up through her sister's grip and broke it. He cupped one hand beneath her chin and forced her head back. Then he slipped behind her and began to tow her to the shore.

A circle formed about them as he lifted Fanny's unconscious figure up onto the bank. Then he turned her over and pressed upon her back. Streams of water flowed from her mouth and then her eyelids fluttered.

Alderman Shere was on his knees beside them. "Well done!" he said in a low voice. "Is she conscious?"

Richard nodded. "It is all my fault, sir. I should not have let her stand so close to the edge."

"You are not to blame. Let us take her home."

Miranda slipped an arm about her aunt's shoulders. The older woman was badly shaken, but with commendable restraint she refrained from any comment upon the accident.

It was only later, when Fanny had been taken to her room and the doctor summoned, that she began to cry.

"Now, Emma, don't give way," the Alderman admonished. "You ladies have held up well in spite of the shock, and there is no harm done." He looked across at Richard. "My dear sir, you showed great presence of mind, for which I thank you."

Clad in the Alderman's coat and breeches, which were too big for him, Richard was a comic figure, but no one smiled.

"She might have drowned!" He buried his face in his hands. "I shall never forgive myself."

"Nonsense!" Miranda told him briskly. "The lake is shallow. She might have walked out of it herself if she had not panicked."

"But she did, and she can't swim."

It took some time to comfort him, but reassured at last by the doctor's hopeful diagnosis he took his leave of them.

Fanny was unharmed, and the ducking had not resulted in an inflammation of the lungs as Mrs Shere had predicted. Once recovered from the shock she took full advantage of the near-tragedy, happy to be the centre of attention.

Richard was now her hero, though he disclaimed the honour.

"The lake was not deep, you know. We might have walked out if…"

"If I had not been so foolish?" Fanny smiled up at him. She was lying upon a sofa in the salon, dressed in one of her most becoming gowns. "Oh, Richard, you saved me from a watery grave. I never was so frightened in my life…"

"It is all over. You must forget it." He took her hand and held it in his own.

"How can I? What should I have done without you?"

He was spared the need to reply when Charlotte Fairfax was announced, and his gaze was rueful as he looked up at Miranda.

She smiled and shook her head. "There will be other opportunities," she assured him. "I believe you have slain the dragon."

After that, Charlotte was a frequent visitor, somewhat to Fanny's surprise.

"I thought her more your friend than mine," she said one day. "Yet she has asked if I will go to stay with her."

"An excellent plan!" Mrs Shere intervened. "It will give you a change of scene."

"But shall you wish to go?" Miranda asked. "It seems a little strange when she does not live above a mile away."

"Oh, I think so." Fanny dismissed the objection. "It will be only for a day or two, and Aunt is right. It will suit both of us. Charlotte is lonely, so she tells me..."

Miranda suspected that Fanny's main reason for agreeing to this plan was to avoid the stricter supervision which her aunt had threatened after the contretemps with Count Toumanov, but she made no comment.

When Fanny had gone, Mrs Shere did not mince her words.

"I cannot but be glad that you are separated for a time," she said. "Sometimes you look positively hagged, my love. Don't tell me that your sister is not a worry to you, for I won't believe it."

"She did not mean to fall into the lake," Miranda murmured.

"I was not referring to that, although the accident was due more to her own folly than to a lack of care upon the part of Mr Young."

"It may be no bad thing," Miranda chuckled. "He is now her hero."

"I know it. That was the only reason why I agreed to let her go to Charlotte. And Sir William Fairfax is a stern papa, you know. The girls will be carefully supervised."

Miranda grew thoughtful. Sir William's reputation as

a disciplinarian was well known. She doubted if Fanny would care to stay for long in such a household, but in the meantime it was a relief to be spared the need to fret about her.

In the next few days her life took on an almost dream-like quality. She wandered about the garden, helping the Alderman where she could, between intervals of playing on the spinet, much to her aunt's delight. Her book was long since finished, but she had managed to obtain a recently published copy of *Waverley,* which had taken the town by storm. It kept her occupied for many hours.

Even an invitation to take tea with Lady Heston did not trouble her as it might have done. The visit passed off without incident, and if she seemed preoccupied neither her aunt nor Lady Heston mentioned it.

Time seemed to have stopped. She was waiting in limbo as the dark cloud at the back of her mind grew ever larger. Heston must soon return and then...? Her face grew sombre. She dreaded the thought of that last interview with him, but it must be final. She would make sure of that.

"My dear, won't you take up your embroidery again? You have neglected it for so long, and it will help to pass the time," Mrs Shere said kindly. "His lordship cannot be long delayed, and then you will be happy once more."

"I beg your pardon, Aunt Emma. I did not mean to be so gloomy."

"Not gloomy, dearest, just a little sad. It is understandable when Lord Heston has been gone for all this time. I'm sure he would not wish you to give up all your pleasures. We might drive out, you know, or visit the shops in Bond Street..."

Miranda excused herself from the proposed expedition, and Mrs Shere did not argue.

"You fear that he might call when we are out? Very well, but I must go. I shall not be away for long."

Miranda settled herself at her embroidery frame, and began to look through the coloured silks. She threaded her needle, but it was only the striking of the clock which told her that she had not set a stitch for the past hour.

Lost in a reverie, she did not at first attend when the door opened.

"Lord Heston, ma'am," the servant announced.

Miranda looked up to find his lordship advancing towards her. Her smile of welcome vanished when she saw the expression on his face. His eyes were stony with contempt and his jaw was rigid. At that moment he looked capable of murder.

"Where is Fanny?" he said without preamble.

Miranda froze. "My lord, are you not mistaken?" she faltered. Then she heard an ugly laugh.

"Come, madam, let us have done with this charade. It has gone on for long enough."

Miranda made a last attempt to save herself. "I...I don't understand you."

He caught her wrist in an iron grip which made her wince and dragged her to her feet.

"Don't you? Will you deny that you have tricked me from the first? You shall not take me for a fool. Did you think it amusing to take your sister's place?"

Miranda knew that all was over. It would be useless to prevaricate further.

"How long have you known?" she asked in a low tone.

"Does that matter? It did not take long, I assure you.

You made a number of mistakes, although I did not need them to convince me. You and Harry Lakenham? It wasn't possible.''

''Not even for the money and the title?'' Miranda flared. He was entitled to be furious, but his icy disdain was not to be borne.

''Don't trifle with me! There is no time! I ask you again…where is your sister?''

''What concern is that of yours? If you must know, she is staying with Charlotte Fairfax…''

''Is she? You had best read this.'' He produced a letter from his pocket and thrust it into her hand.

Miranda opened it with shaking fingers. The characters seemed to dance across the page, blurring as she tried to make them out. They began to swim before her eyes.

''Here, let me!'' Heston said roughly. As he read the note to her, Miranda's worst fears were realised.

It was from Harry Lakenham, informing Heston that he had eloped. By the time the letter was received, he would be married.

Miranda swayed as the room seemed to spin about her. She sat down suddenly, feeling that her legs would no longer support her.

''I don't believe it!'' she whispered. ''Fanny would not…she could not…''

''On the contrary, I believe her capable of anything. Was this your idea?''

Miranda felt dumb with misery. She could not answer him.

''Don't play the innocent with me, my dear. It was a clever plan, I'll give you that. Were you to keep me occupied and throw me off the scent until Lakenham and your sister found a suitable opportunity to disappear?''

"No! I thought she had changed her mind in favour of Count Toumanov."

"Another clever ploy? It will not serve. Both you and she would know that Toumanov would never offer for her."

"I knew it, but she did not, and you yourself threw them together."

"I admit it. I have never trusted her. She was meeting Lakenham after you were supposedly betrothed to me. Don't trouble to deny it, for I have proof."

"Please listen to me," Miranda cried in despair. "Let me explain. I owe you that at least."

"Pray go on," he said in an ironic tone. "It should make an interesting story."

"It is the truth," she said brokenly. "When you first came here, Fanny would not see you. We thought that you had come to offer for her. I was simply to refuse you, and that was to be an end of it."

Heston said nothing, but his eyes never left her face.

"And then…and then you were so insulting that I lost my temper. I said more than I intended. You shall not blame Fanny for that. It was all my fault."

"I lost my temper, too," he admitted in a kinder tone. "I had no right to force you into a betrothal."

"I could not believe that you would go on with it. Each day I hoped that you would release me from my promise. I knew that you wished to punish me, but when everything went so far I could see no way of escape…"

"And did you wish to escape?" There was something in his voice which brought the colour to her cheeks.

She turned her head away. "I had to. I tried to cry off, if you recall, on the day we went to Richmond."

"I remember it well."

"Then why didn't you agree? By then you knew of the deception…"

"By then I had changed my mind."

Miranda did not speak, but a tiny flicker of hope stirred in her heart. She stifled it at once. It would be too cruel to raise expectations which could never be fulfilled.

"Have you nothing more to say to me?" Heston enquired softly.

"I can only apologise, my lord. What you must think of us…of me…I can't imagine."

"Then I must tell you some time."

Miranda looked up at that, and was surprised to see a twinkle in his eyes. She felt confused.

"I wanted to tell you the truth. I was ashamed to do so, especially when I thought about my aunt and uncle, and Lady Heston too. They were all so kind. Oh, sir, if only a scandal might be avoided…!"

"It might be possible." Before she could protest, he took her in his arms. "My love, you are a goose! Can it be that you don't know how much I love you?" He dropped a tender kiss upon her brow.

"But you can't! Not after the way…"

"After the way you have stolen my heart? I have deceived you too, you know, in pretending that I thought that you were Fanny. It is I who should beg for your forgiveness. Will you dash my hopes?"

Miranda found that she hadn't the least desire to release herself from his embrace. She buried her face in his shoulder.

"Why did you go on with it?" she asked in muffled tones.

"Well, you know, I hoped that you had learned to trust me enough to tell me the truth."

"I couldn't. I loved you so, and—" She could not go on as he caught her to him, and his mouth found hers. Miranda clung to him in ecstasy lost in the wonder of his love. Then the door opened.

"I thought I should find you here," said Fanny.

Chapter Sixteen

Two pairs of startled eyes regarded her, and then Miranda sat down suddenly.

"What are you doing here?" she asked in a faint voice.

"I live here, in case you had forgotten." Fanny was clearly in the grip of some powerful emotion. "You won't believe what I have to tell you." She threw herself upon the sofa in a dramatic attitude. "I have been tricked in the most shameful way."

"Who has tricked you?" Miranda feared the worst.

"Why, Charlotte and Harry Lakenham. It is the most deceitful thing. They have eloped!"

Her injured expression was too much for Miranda's composure, but she tried to keep her voice steady.

"Are you quite sure?"

"Of course I am. I suppose I may believe the evidence of my own eyes. We were shopping in the Emporium in Bond Street when I missed her. I looked about and then I saw her disappearing through the door at the back of the shop. When I followed, Harry was helping her into a closed carriage... I called to them, but they did not answer me."

"And then?"

"Well, I could not make it out. It seemed so strange of them to go for a drive without inviting me, and in a chaise with the blinds pulled down. I could not follow them, so I went back to Charlotte's home to see if they had returned, but they weren't there."

"Oh, Fanny, what a worry for you!"

"You may believe it! I never walked into such a turmoil in my life. Charlotte had left a note beside her bed, so there can be no doubt of the elopement. The worst of it is that Sir William blames me!"

"Astonishing!" Heston murmured. "What could have given him the idea that you would be party to such a plan, I wonder?"

Miranda threw him a reproachful look. "You knew nothing of it?"

"No, I did not. Charlotte may not think herself my friend in future. I shall not speak to her again. To steal off with Harry in that way…? It is beyond anything!"

"But you no longer care for him, I think?"

"No, I don't. He is a fribble. I have had a lucky escape, but that is not the point. I might have eloped with him myself…"

There seemed to be no immediate answer to this remark, but Fanny's expression tried Miranda sorely. Her sister resembled no one so much as a child who had been robbed of a favourite toy. She dared not look at Heston, but she guessed that his feelings were much the same as her own.

Fanny's glance was suspicious as she looked at the faces of her companions.

"You seem to find the situation amusing," she said sharply. "Had you not best go after them, my lord?"

"I think not, my dear Miss Gaysford. I believe I must

leave that task to Sir William Fairfax.'' Heston took Miranda's arm. ''Will you not take a turn about the garden with me, dearest, that is, if your sister will excuse us…?''

Fanny flounced out of the room, a thunderous expression on her face.

''Oh dear, I should not laugh,'' Miranda choked.

''Certainly not in here. Let me beg you to restrain yourself until we reach the summer-house…''

There Miranda laughed until she cried.

''What a wretch I am!'' she gasped as she wiped her streaming eyes. ''It is not kind to be so unfeeling, but Fanny looked so…so…''

''Injured?'' Heston's own shoulders were shaking. ''I thought I had best rescue you before you disgraced yourself in your sister's eyes.''

''She must be so hurt.''

''Not at all! Your beloved twin is mortified to find that she is not the central figure in this elopement. The injury is to her pride, and I have no doubt that Sir William Fairfax further injured it.''

''Fanny was right in one respect, my lord. This elopement will be a sad blow to Harry's grandfather, as well as to Charlotte's parents. Can you do nothing?''

''I wouldn't, even if I could. Sir William is a martinet, as Harry will discover to his cost. He may forget his previous ways. Sir William will have none of them.''

''Then you think it may be for the best?''

''I do. I can think of nothing better to bring Harry to his senses.''

''If they are already married…''

''Harry won't waste time. He is still under age and would fear pursuit. I imagine he would make for Doctors Commons with a licence in his pocket.''

"But Sir William may annul the match."

"I doubt it. Harry bears an ancient name, and he will soon be in possession of his fortune."

"But Lord Rudyard? Oh, dear, he is not well... The shock may be too much for him."

"He knows Sir William, and that will be enough for him."

"You seem so sure?"

"I am, my dearest one. Besides which, I am ready at this moment to consign Charlotte, Harry and even your sister to perdition. We have been parted for a full two weeks, and I have missed you so." He looked down at her with such a tender expression that her heart began to pound.

She lifted her face to his. "I felt the same," she said simply. "Without you, the days seemed endless..."

He bent his head and she surrendered her lips to his. With that kiss the world was lost to both of them. All the heartache of the past few weeks vanished in a rising tide of passion, and Miranda felt a joy which she had not known before. He loved her. Now she could be sure of it, and the knowledge sent her spirit soaring.

When he released her she was breathless. She rested her head against his shoulder and took his hand in hers, absently stroking his fingers.

"My lord..." she began.

"Adam," he corrected. "Or are we not yet well enough acquainted for you to give me my name?"

Miranda blushed as she saw the laughter in his eyes. She could not mistake his meaning. Her overwhelming delight in that kiss had been equal to his own.

"Adam...when did you first know? I mean, when did you decide that I was not the termagant you thought me?"

"It was difficult," he told her gravely. "Those dagger looks quite sunk me. They did serious damage to my self-esteem. At times I considered putting a period to my existence."

"I wish you will be serious," she reproached him. "I asked you a sensible question."

"There was nothing sensible about my feelings, I assure you. I think I must have loved you from the first time that we met."

"Oh, what a fib! You called me a doxy."

"Did I say that? You caught me off balance, my beloved. I had not expected to receive such a severe setdown, though I deserved it."

"You did indeed!" she scolded with a loving smile. "I may tell you that I have never disliked anyone so much. You were a perfect monster, and I wanted to crush you into very small pieces."

Adam began to nibble her ear. "What a fate! When did you change your mind?"

"I don't quite know," she told him in a serious tone. "As I grew to understand you better, I felt that I must have been mistaken in your character and your motives for behaving as you did."

"They were always dastardly," he assured her with a wicked grin. "You have no fear that I shall beat you daily, and lock you in your room for weeks?"

"No!" she said demurely. "I doubt if you would wish to lock me away."

"Minx! What a dance you will lead me!" The prospect did not appear to worry him, for he kissed her again until her head began to spin. "My dearest, I love everything about you, from the tip of your head to those charming little toes. How well I know that enchanting face! It is the mirror of your soul."

"Even when I am looking cross?"

"Especially when you are looking cross. Your chin goes up and your eyes begin to sparkle…"

"At least I do not arch my back and hiss, you will admit. You told me once that I looked like an angry kitten."

"Ah, you remembered that?"

"I think I remember every word you've ever spoken to me." She pressed her lips against his hand.

"Oh, dear, not all of them, I hope? Remember only that I love you more than life, my darling… Will you do that?"

Her answer was in her eyes. He held her to him and then they heard the sound of approaching footsteps.

Alderman Shere was hurrying down the path towards them.

"Ah, there you are, my dear. Your aunt is returned and wishes to speak to you." He bowed to Heston. "There is no immediate hurry, my lord."

"I will come at once." Miranda rose to her feet. "Will you join us, Uncle? We have something to say to you."

"Nothing is amiss, I hope?" He looked at their faces and was satisfied. "No, I see that there is not…but this is a bad business about Charlotte Fairfax."

He turned back to the house, leaving them to follow him.

"I shall have to tell them," Miranda said in a low voice. "I can't go on with this deception, but what on earth am I to say?"

"Will you leave it to me?" Adam slipped an arm about her waist and hugged her. "Don't worry, my dearest. I promise you that all will be well. You must learn to rely on my support, you know."

Miranda threw him a speaking look of gratitude. It was a comfort to think that she need no longer carry her burdens alone.

They found Mrs Shere alone in the salon and she was looking stern.

"My lord, you will forgive me for speaking out in front of you, but I must know. My dear, did your sister play any part in helping Charlotte to elope? She denies it, but there is no speaking to her…"

"No, ma'am, she did not. Fanny was as shocked as we were ourselves."

"Fanny? But you are Fanny. It was Miranda who went to stay with Charlotte…"

"No, ma'am." Adam sat down beside her and took her hands. "We must beg your forgiveness, Mrs Shere, and yours too, my dear sir. When I first came to you, I asked if I might pay my addresses to Miss Gaysford. I should have asked for Miss Miranda Gaysford. It was she who had my heart. The fault is mine. It was a foolish mistake, but I had thought Miranda the elder of the two."

"But, Lord Heston, you should have spoken when you found out your mistake. We should have understood…"

"You are too kind, ma'am, but I felt an utter fool. My pride was at stake. It is a sad failing in me, I fear. The trouble was that I did not at first realise…fond though I was, I did not know your nieces well."

"Perfectly understandable." The Alderman laughed aloud. "Emma, have I not always wondered how Lord Heston knew one twin from the other?"

Mrs Shere was not so easily satisfied. "The girls are not in the least alike in temperament," she said doubtfully. "I confess that it was a puzzle to me to learn that my sister relied so heavily upon Miranda when I found her such a scatterbrain..."

"That was Fanny, ma'am. I feel a perfect wretch. I should have thrown myself upon your mercy long ago."

He was smiling as he spoke and Mrs Shere could not resist his charm. He had always been a favourite with her.

"I should give you a cruel scolding, and Miranda too," she said with mock severity.

"And I should deserve it, ma'am." He bent his head and looked so meek that Mrs Shere began to smile.

"Pray do not add play-acting to your other misdeeds, my lord... Just tell me one thing. Are you convinced that the lady by your side is indeed Miranda?"

"I'm certain of it, ma'am. Aren't you?" He stretched out a hand and drew Miranda to his side.

"Yes, I am, and I wish you happy, sir. You will not find a better wife."

Miranda threw her arms about her aunt and kissed her. Then she went to hug her uncle.

"May I tell Fanny that you know the truth?" she asked.

Mrs Shere reached out for the bell-pull and sent her servant to summon Fanny to the drawing-room.

She entered, looking subdued and in the expectation of another scolding, but Miranda set her mind at rest.

When Heston's apparent folly was explained to her, she looked at him with awe. Then she began to laugh.

Mrs Shere took her to task at once. "This is no laughing matter, Fanny. I am surprised that you should find it so amusing. Pray do not try to convince me that you knew nothing of it."

"No, ma'am, but you see... I was trying to protect Lord Heston's reputation."

"Lord Heston has no need of your protection. He would do nothing dishonourable."

It was clear that Adam was now to be absolved of all blame for his part in the charade.

"Don't look so smug!" Miranda hissed at him. "We have still to face your mother."

"She knows all about it, my love. I had to tell her. She was so worried about you."

"Deceiver!" Miranda threw him a fulminating glance. She might have said more but at that moment Richard was announced.

He seemed unsurprised to discover that a change had taken place and that he might now address his love by her own name.

The conversation now centred upon the arrangements for Miranda's wedding, and for the first time she was able to take part in the discussion with a happy heart.

"And your honeymoon, my lord. Where will you go for that?" Mrs Shere asked.

"Paris, I think, if Miranda agrees." Adam looked a question at her, but before she could reply Fanny intervened.

"Famous!" she cried. "I shall enjoy that above anything…"

Miranda stared at her in stupefaction. Beside her, she sensed that Adam was about to speak, but before he could do so Richard walked over to her sister and took her hand.

"You cannot go with Miranda," he said gently.

"Why not? It is quite the thing, you know, for a bride to have a friend or a relative with her for companionship."

Adam stirred again, but Miranda stilled him with a hand upon his arm.

"I thought you might prefer to go there as a bride yourself, Fanny." Richard stood quite still, but his face was alight with hope.

"How can I? I have no husband."

"You might have, if you will take me?"

He had Fanny's attention then. She stared at him.

"You can't mean it! Are you making me an offer?"

"Hand and heart, dear Fanny. Will you disappoint me?"

Fanny looked about her. The Alderman and Mrs Shere were speechless with astonishment but Adam and her twin were smiling. It was a most public declaration, and she was certainly the focus of all eyes.

"I'd like to marry you," she announced. "But, Richard, I always wanted to elope..."

"Then, of course, we shall elope, but there are arrangements to be made. Your aunt and uncle will wish to know where we are going."

"Is that usual?" she asked doubtfully. "I thought it was always meant to be a secret?"

"Not always!" Richard's face was grave. "I thought we might elope to Yorkshire, and go to Paris later. Then your mother and my father will be able to attend the ceremony..."

Beside her, Miranda felt Adam's shoulders begin to shake. "Hush!" she whispered. "Will you spoil everything?"

"I couldn't if I tried," he moaned in anguish.

Miranda dug her elbow into his ribs. Thankfully, Fanny had not noticed his paroxysms. She bestowed an enchanting smile upon her suitor and allowed him to clasp her in his arms.

Over her head Richard sought Miranda's eyes. His own held a curious mixture of love and rueful amusement but she nodded, happy to think that he had won his heart's desire. Life with Fanny would not be easy, but he loved her dearly and he knew her well. She need have no fears for her sister's future happiness.

"I am about to collapse," Adam whispered in a voice intended only for Miranda's ears. "In a moment I shall disgrace myself…"

He was rewarded with a stern look.

"Don't torture me," he begged. "I rescued you. Won't you do the same for me?"

Her own composure was sorely tried, but she made her excuses after offering the happy pair her good wishes for their future life together. Then she allowed Adam to lead her back into the garden.

This time they did not reach the summer-house. Adam clung to one of the supports of the pergola, unable to speak.

"My lord, I do not take this kindly," she told him with quivering lips. "Richard meant well…"

"I know it," he choked out at last. "The man is braver than Wellington himself. It was the elopement that was too much for me."

"You have a sadly frivolous side to your nature, sir."

"No, you are mistaken. I am the dullest dog in all the world. It did not occur to me to offer you an elopement, although you must have wished it."

"You are behaving very ill, my lord." Her own voice was not quite under her control. "If you go on like this, I shall begin to doubt your sanity."

"Only mine?" The look he gave her destroyed the last vestiges of her self-control, and her peals of laughter rang around the garden.

"Pray don't go on!" she gasped at last. "I feel quite weak…"

"Not weak enough to invite a companion to join us on our honeymoon journey, I hope?"

Miranda studied her fingers. "I had considered it," she announced.

"Really? You do not feel that I shall provide enough companionship for you, both day and night?"

"I don't know," she murmured wickedly.

"I think we had best continue this conversation in the privacy of the summer-house, my love..." He slipped an arm about her waist and led her along the path. Once inside the little wooden building he gripped her shoulders and looked down, still laughing, into her eyes. Then he shook her gently.

"Exasperating creature!" he said fondly. "Haven't I been punished enough? Must you continue to tease me?"

"Why, sir, I can't think what you mean."

"Can't you? Then I had best show you." He sat down and drew her on to his knee.

"Now, fair maiden," he uttered in melodramatic tones. "I have you in my power. To struggle will avail you nothing." He twirled an imaginary moustache.

Miranda found that she had no desire to struggle. Instead she slid her arms about his neck.

"You are behaving very foolishly," she whispered.

"I expect to behave foolishly for the rest of my life, my darling." He pressed his lips into the hollow of her throat. "Shall you mind?"

"I think I shall like it very much." She kissed his cheek, aware only that his lips were teasing as they travelled upwards. Then his mouth found hers, and all else was forgotten in the wonder of his love.

* * * * *

Gifford's Lady
by
Claire Thornton

Claire Thornton grew up in Sussex. It is a family legend that her ancestors in the county were involved in smuggling. She was a shy little girl, and she was fascinated by the idea that she might be distantly related to bold and daring adventurers of the past – who were probably not shy! When she grew up she studied history at York University, and discovered that smugglers were often brutal men whose main ambition was to make money. This was disappointing, but she still feels justified in believing in – and writing about – the romantic and noble heroes of earlier ages. Claire Thornton has also written under the name of Alice Thornton.

To Sally –
For naming Gifford's ship

Chapter One

The knife was slippery with blood and sweat. Gifford switched it to his left hand and rubbed his right palm against his breeches. He crouched in the shadows and listened. Above him the huge sails of the privateer blotted out the starlight. The darkness was Gifford's only ally—but it forced him to rely on his hearing and sense of touch as he crept undetected through the enemy ship.

There were at least three men on the quarterdeck. He'd seen the glow of the binnacle lantern a few moments ago. Now he could hear their voices intermittently drifting forwards to him on the night air. He couldn't distinguish their words, but one man laughed.

Gifford pressed his lips together. Let the fellow enjoy the joke while he still could. Soon the boot would be on the other foot.

There was a man dead in the cabin that had been Gifford's prison cell. Another one dead in the shadows close to the cabin door. From the little Gifford had overheard from the privateer crew, he believed his own men were prisoners in the hold. He had to find them, release them—and arm them.

He crept along the gangway towards the fo'c's'le. Every sense was alert. Had he been captain of this vessel he'd have had at least six lookouts spaced around the ship to scan the horizon. He didn't want to stumble into one in the darkness. But the lookouts would be watching for danger from the sea—not from behind them on their own ship.

The smell of pipe smoke was his only warning that a privateer crewman stood barely three feet away. Gifford froze. His right hand tightened convulsively—then relaxed into a normal grip on the knife handle.

Before this night he had killed only in the heat of battle, when the enemy was armed and facing him...

The pipe-smoking seaman gazed contemplatively out towards the Caribbean Sea. Gifford slipped behind him, his bare feet silent on the wooden deck. He made it to the hatch and down to the next deck without being detected. A few seconds later the lookouts were hailed from the quarterdeck. Gifford tensed like a panther about to strike. Had his escape been discovered?

No. They were simply the normal hails. None of the lookouts had anything to report. Gifford released an unsteady breath, and gave thanks he'd slipped undetected past the pipe-smoking lookout.

Two men armed with muskets guarded the prisoners. Gifford's men had been crowded together into the airless hold. He wondered how many had already died of suffocation. Anger at the unnecessary cruelty fuelled his ruthless determination to destroy the privateers.

Both guards had their back to him, and Gifford paused for a few seconds, letting his vision adjust to the lantern light. He had a brace of pistols stuck through his belt, but they would do him no good here. The sound of a shot would bring all his enemies down upon him.

He also had two knives. He altered his grip on the first knife, focussed his attention on the guard's back—and threw the dagger. The throw was hard, fast, and accurate. The man slumped forward with a soft grunt. The other guard froze with disbelief as his friend toppled silently over. He started to turn towards Gifford, automatically raising his musket. Gifford threw his second knife...

* * *

He woke suddenly. His heart pounding. His limbs paralysed with fear.

The dark room was full of unfamiliar shapes and shadows. The night air hot and oppressively muggy. His naked body wet with sweat.

For two seconds Gifford remained enslaved to the nightmare. Then he leapt from the bed, seizing up his dirk as he did so—and roared his defiance at the demons who haunted his sleep.

He'd barely registered that there was carpet beneath his feet—not the wooden deck of the privateer—when the door was flung open.

Anthony stood on the threshold, holding a multibranched candelabrum in one hand, a book in the other. His dark skin glistened in the candlelight but, unlike Gifford, he was naked only to the waist.

'What the *devil's* happening?' he demanded.

The August night was so hot and still that Abigail had given up all attempt to sleep. She'd opened her curtains and her window and pulled her chair as close to the casement as possible. She was clad only in a thin muslin nightgown, and she felt very daring letting the night air caress her nearly naked body. If some of the more prudish Bath gossips knew what she was doing, they'd be scandalised by her behaviour. But she'd doused all the candles before opening her curtains, and her room was two floors above street level. It was hardly likely anyone would notice her at one thirty in the morning.

She fanned herself gently, relaxed and comfortable in her chair.

The next instant a ferocious shout split the night. Abigail's blood froze. For a few seconds she was transfixed with shock. Then her heart started to pound with fear and excitement. She leant forward, trying to locate the source of the cry.

A room in the house opposite suddenly lit up. She

blinked and jerked backwards at the unexpected brightness, then gasped as she saw two men facing each other—one holding a candelabrum aloft, the other with a knife in his outstretched hand. Abigail half rose in her chair. She was certain she was about to see murder committed.

Frantic thoughts hurtled through her mind. Should she call out in the hope of distracting them? Or summon help? Who could help her at this hour? She peered down into the street below, but there was no one there.

She heard one of the men speak, and immediately returned her attention to the room opposite. She saw that the man with the dagger had let his hand fall to his side.

She let out a shaky breath. Perhaps the moment of danger had passed. But she couldn't take her eyes off the frightening scene. She gripped the windowsill and strained to hear what they said to each other. The other window was also open to its widest extent and the men's voices carried on the still night air.

'What the *devil's* happening?' It was the man with the candelabrum who spoke. He sounded startled, but not afraid.

'A dream. Just a damned dream.' The man with the knife sounded so disgusted with himself that, despite her alarm, Abigail involuntarily smiled.

He turned to lay the knife down. His action further reassured Abigail. He obviously wasn't planning to commit murder any time soon. Now she had an opportunity to fully register what she'd already subconsciously noticed.

The uneven play of candlelight obscured some portions of his anatomy in shadows and threw other parts into bright relief; but Abigail could see quite clearly that he wasn't wearing a stitch of clothing.

He was entirely naked! And as well formed as a Greek god. She'd seen the strength and tension in his whole body when he'd first confronted his light-bearing friend. He'd eased into a more relaxed stance, but his broad-shouldered

frame still emanated virile power. Candlelight delineated
the sculptural planes of his hard, muscular body.

He was beautiful. Abigail had never seen a completely
naked man before. She couldn't tear her eyes away from
him. It didn't even occur to her that she should.

'Remember the wager?' The man with the candelabrum
spoke again. Abigail reluctantly turned her attention to him.
He was also a well-made man. He had black skin, but he
talked to the white man as an equal. He had a pleasant,
well-modulated voice, which currently held a hint of
amusement.

'A month in Bath with no adventures—I know.' The
white man lifted his arm to run his fingers through his hair.
Abigail was fascinated by the fall of light on his shifting
muscles. The hard ridges of his stomach were so unlike her
own soft flesh. She unthinkingly stroked her thigh as she
wondered how different his body would feel if she touched
it. He was very pleasing to look at. *Very* pleasing.

'Yes. But, Giff—that means no adventures in your sleep
either.'

'A man has no control over his dreams!' the man called
Giff retorted. 'I'll not lose my wager over a dream. Besides,
I'm not the one haunting the house with a candlestick and
a book at…whatever ungodly hour this is. I lay down to
sleep. I did sleep.'

It seemed to Abigail that his words contained a challenge.

'I was too hot to sleep,' the other man said mildly.

'Hah!' said the man called Giff. 'Well, now I'm awake
I'll share your light. I'm hungry. There must be decent ra-
tions somewhere in the bowels of this house.'

'You might want to dress first?' his friend suggested,
when it looked as if Giff intended to set out on his mission
straight away. 'Encountering Mrs Chesney in your current
state might come perilously close to having an adventure.'

'Nonsense,' said Giff briskly. 'A scandal is not the same
as an adventure. However, in deference to your finer feelings…'

He turned away from the light towards the window. Abigail could no longer see him clearly, but it suddenly occurred to her they were separated only by the width of the street below. With the light behind him—perhaps he could see her?

He stood very still, looking across at her window. She held herself motionless, horrified that her unintentional eavesdropping had been discovered. She knew he could see her silhouette as she leant against the windowsill, but she prayed he couldn't see her features—or anything that might subsequently allow him to identify her.

The tense moment lengthened. Then, very calmly but smartly, he saluted her.

'What the hell...?' Anthony demanded, following Gifford on to the landing.

Gifford closed his bedroom door, then pulled on the breeches he had collected on the way out.

'We must find out who has the house opposite,' he said tautly. 'And, in particular, who occupies the room directly across from mine.'

'Someone saw you?' Anthony stared at him, then started to laugh.

Some of the tension ebbed out of Gifford's body and he grinned ruefully. 'No doubt a prudish old dowager, scandalised because I don't wear a nightcap,' he said.

'Are you sure it was a woman?'

'Yes. This is at the worst a scandal,' Gifford reminded Anthony firmly. 'If you hear rumours circulating the Pump Room about a naked madman with a dagger, you'll know where they originated. But it is definitely *not* an adventure.'

'What I most admire about you, Giff—I believe it's an admiration shared by many flag officers—is your slippery ability to reinterpret plain English to suit your own intentions,' Anthony observed. 'I wonder who the lady was?'

'So do I,' said Gifford. 'I hope she does justice to the drama of the moment when she spreads the tale.'

* * *

Abigail closed her curtains with trembling hands. Without even the meagre circulation of air the open drapes had facilitated, her room rapidly became stifling. It was far too hot to be so embarrassed, but her whole body burned with mortification.

She fanned herself briskly and resisted the urge to hide under her bedclothes. She'd found out a long time ago that, however much she might long for the floor to swallow her up, hiding never did anything to relieve emotional or mental distress. And hiding under the bedclothes in this heat would only make her ill.

She'd simply have to brazen the situation out. Very few people visited Bath in August unless they were genuinely sick. Both of the gentlemen she'd seen opposite had looked to be in the peak of physical condition—Abigail took guilty pleasure in remembering how fit they'd been—so perhaps they'd leave soon.

No. They were here for a month. A month in Bath without an adventure. That's what they'd said.

She wondered what kind of adventures they'd had in the past. Dangerous ones, if 'Giff's' response to his nightmare was any indication.

She was impressed and a little scared by his fierce reaction to his bad dream. On the rare occasions when she had nightmares she lay very still and waited for her fears to recede and rational thought to return. She was far too timid to leap out of bed and confront her monsters the way he had.

She wondered what it was like to be so brave. She wondered who they were.

If the visitors followed Bath custom they would have their names and place of abode entered into the Pump Room book. It was Miss Wyndham's pleasure that Abigail should check the Pump Room book every day to see if there were any interesting arrivals. So tomorrow morning Abigail might have the answer to her question.

But Abigail wasn't sure if men who wandered around

their lodgings naked, or semi-naked, and kept daggers by
their bedside, would be familiar with Bath customs.

There was always the *Bath Chronicle*, which listed new
arrivals every week. Failing that, there was Mrs Chesney,
the owner of the house opposite. Abigail was surprised she
hadn't already heard all about the new visitors from her
neighbour. During the Season Mrs Chesney hired out the
different floors of her house to visitors. Sometimes a family
would even lease the entire house, with Mrs Chesney acting
as their housekeeper. But Mrs Chesney had not had any
visitors the last time she'd spoken to Abigail, nor had she
mentioned the imminent arrival of any. But then, the last
time they'd met, Mrs Chesney had been so full of her
daughter's recent confinement and the arrival of her new
grandchild she hadn't had a thought to spare for anything
else.

It wasn't usual for bachelors to take lodgings, they normally stayed at one of the hotels. Perhaps the two men had
brought their families with them? For some reason Abigail
didn't care for that idea.

She knew all her speculations were utterly pointless.
Within the next twenty-four hours she was bound to find
out more about the men than she could possibly wish to
know. But the brief scene she'd witnessed was certainly the
most intriguing, exciting thing she'd ever seen in her hith-
erto exceptionally staid life.

When Gifford returned to his room he checked the window opposite. The curtains were firmly drawn. It was too
much to hope his female eavesdropper would provide him
with reciprocal entertainment.

He grinned briefly at the notion. But he wasn't comfortable with what she'd seen. A fool beset by nightmares who
faced down invisible phantoms with a dirk. Hardly the actions of a true hero.

He closed his own curtains. The heat was unpleasant, but he'd capered enough for the entertainment of his neighbours.

'Ah, Miss Summers! The very person!'

Abigail was inspecting the Pump Room book when Admiral Pullen accosted her. She turned towards him with a smile. The admiral had retired to Bath eighteen months earlier and they'd quickly become friends. Abigail always enjoyed talking to him. He told her fascinating stories about worlds she'd never seen.

'Good morning, Ad…mir…al…' Her voice faded away as she realised he wasn't alone.

Two men stood beside him, watching her with polite interest.

Her heart skittered into a more rapid beat. One of the men was black. The other…

Was dangerous.

He wore a patch over his left eye. A scar extended down his left cheek and up across his forehead into his hairline. A streak of white hair marked the path of the healed wound across his scalp. The rest of his hair was jet black.

His face was tanned from long exposure to the sun. His good eye was a startlingly brilliant blue. His features were strongly defined and unquestionably aristocratic. His face would have been handsome before he was injured. His appearance was still commanding. But he also looked…lethal.

Even though he stood quite still an aura of raw power surrounded him. He was conventionally dressed in a well-tailored blue coat and a neatly tied cravat, but those indicators of civilisation couldn't disguise the underlying wildness of his nature. His stance was relaxed yet alert, and his bearing supremely self-confident.

He was several inches taller than the admiral, and a whole head taller than Abigail. She felt dwarfed by his height and the breadth of his shoulders—and nervously excited by the cool challenge in his gaze.

She saw at once that he knew the impact he'd made upon

her. No doubt he was accustomed to women swooning over him. She drew in a careful, shallow breath, aware he was watching her as closely as she watched him. She prayed he couldn't hear the frantic beating of her heart.

The first time she'd seen him he'd been entirely naked. Did he know that? She swallowed nervously. Had he recognised her as surely as she'd recognised him?

She had no doubt the admiral's companions were the same two men she'd seen last night. Two men: one black, one white, travelling to Bath as friends. A man who woke from a nightmare to snatch up a dagger…

She hadn't seen his face clearly enough to notice his scars, but she was certain this was the same man who'd saluted her at the window.

She felt a moment of sheer panic. Convinced he knew her secret as certainly as she knew his. No wonder he looked so arrogantly amused. Eavesdroppers traditionally fare badly when discovered.

'I know the poor devil looks rather piratical these days, but he was the best young officer I ever served with.'

Abigail belatedly realised the admiral had just finished introducing her to his companions.

'I'm so sorry.' She struggled to compose herself. 'I was m-memorising the new arrivals for Miss Wyndham when you spoke to me. You took me by surprise. A little by surprise,' she amended hastily, not wanting the admiral to think he'd upset her. 'How do you do, gentlemen?'

She held out her right hand, proud it wasn't trembling. Proud also of her command over her voice. To her own amazement, she'd sounded relatively calm. Her heart still thundered in her ears.

'Miss Summers has been kindness itself since I moved to Bath,' Admiral Pullen declared. 'I would have been lost without her advice, and lonely without her friendship.'

'Oh, no!' Abigail protested, at the same moment the piratical gentleman shook her hand. 'Oh, my,' she added involuntarily. The first time she'd seen him he'd been holding a dagger in the same hand which now held hers.

He gripped it with just the right amount of pressure, as if he were so confident of his own strength that he felt no need to draw attention to it by unnecessarily exaggerated gentleness. His touch was very stimulating. She felt acutely conscious of her own body as she remembered how he'd looked without his clothes.

She'd been sitting in the dark, she thought desperately. He couldn't be certain she was his unintentional eaves-dropper. If only she could keep her wits about her he might never be sure.

'I trust my appearance doesn't alarm you, Miss Sum-mers,' he said bluntly. 'It may be more suited to the quar-terdeck than the Pump Room.'

She recognised his voice. She liked his voice. It was deep and a little gravelly. In keeping with his distinctive person-ality. She heard it not just with her ears but her whole body.

'Oh, n-no, sir! Not your *appearance*...!' she stammered. 'Or rather...I was daydreaming, and when the admiral spoke to me, I j-just naturally assumed he was alone. So your *presence* surprised me. That's all. I d-do assure you.' She nodded emphatically, then burned with embarrassment. She wanted to appear serene—not flustered and inappro-priately forceful.

'Well, you have some interesting arrivals to tell Miss Wyndham about today!' Admiral Pullen declared. 'Miss Wyndham is a fine old lady, but sadly no longer strong enough to leave her house,' he explained to the two men. 'Miss Summers here is her companion. I tell Miss Wynd-ham she is fortunate to have such a loyal and caring friend.'

Abigail's cheeks burned even more fiercely at this forth-right praise. 'Miss Wyndham has always been very kind to me,' she said breathlessly. 'Will you be staying long in Bath?' she asked, dividing her question between the visi-tors. She wished she'd paid attention when the admiral had introduced them. She still didn't know their names.

'A month,' said the black man. She recognised his voice as well. He was as well dressed as his friend. His manner was quietly self-assured.

'But you both look so *healthy*!' she exclaimed, unable to forget her first impression of both men. It took no effort at all to recall the lean, muscular body concealed by the pirate's blue coat.

Both men laughed and her own clothes suddenly felt too tight for her to breathe.

'Oh, forgive me!' she burst out. 'You've come to see the *admiral*, of course! Not drink the waters.'

'Strong as a bull, this young fellow!' Admiral Pullen clapped his piratical friend on the back. It was clearly a hearty buffet, but the pirate didn't budge an inch, proving the accuracy of the admiral's claim. 'A fine figure of a man. He's survived everything the French could throw at him— and more besides! Hill's the same, I don't doubt—though I never had the privilege of sailing with him.'

Hill?

Abigail wished desperately she'd paid attention to the introductions. She glanced involuntarily at the black man, an unconscious query in her eyes, and he nodded imperceptibly, as if answering her unspoken question. He didn't look as dangerous as the pirate, but he was definitely amused by the situation.

'When you wrote to tell me you were coming to Bath, I immediately thought of Mrs Chesney,' said the admiral to the pirate, though from the way he smiled at Abigail it was obvious he still considered her to be part of the conversation. 'I was commissioned to find suitable quarters for these two gentlemen,' he explained to her in an aside. 'They have made a foolish wager with each other over whether it is possible to spend a month in Bath without having an adventure! Can you believe such a thing! But I digress. When I received my commission I knew the perfect billet! They have leased Mrs Chesney's house. Miss Wyndham and Miss Summers have the house immediately opposite! Miss

Summers has been kindness itself to me. I knew she would be equally welcoming to you!' he concluded triumphantly to the pirate.

Abigail wanted to die. She wanted to fall through the floor and vanish from human society forever. Her eyes flew to the pirate's face. She saw he was looking at her searchingly, his interest in her obviously intensified by Admiral Pullen's revelation.

'Well...well...well...' she stuttered, remembering what she'd seen—and what he knew she'd seen...

'I hardly like to impose on Miss Summers,' said the pirate, drily courteous.

'Not at all, not at all,' the admiral assured him. 'Miss Summers has a taste for stories of the sea. A fair exchange is no imposition. And you have scores of adventurous tales to tell. Miss Summers will show you around the Pump Room this morning. And on your next meeting you will tell her of your hi-jinks when I sent you off in command of your first prize. A gentle promenade around the Room will suit you both.'

They'd been given an unmistakable order.

'Aye, aye, sir,' said the pirate, surprising Abigail with his easy acquiescence. He seemed amused rather than affronted by the admiral's high-handedness. 'Miss Summers.' He offered her his arm. 'It's twenty years or more since I was last in Bath,' he said conversationally as they strolled away from the others. 'And hardly at an age to appreciate its more sophisticated attractions. But—'

'It was me!' Abigail interrupted hastily. 'You know it was me. I didn't mean to s-spy on you, but I was just so *hot*!' Though not as hot as she felt now! She was sure there was a furnace raging beneath the Pump Room floor! 'And then you shouted and I thought someone was going to be *murdered*! And I was trying to work out what to do next...I *truly* didn't mean to spy on you. I will *always* keep my curtains closed in future. I am so very sorry.'

They'd stopped walking as she made her confession.

Now she stared up at him in an agony of anticipation over what he might say to her.

'And I wasn't paying attention when the admiral told me your name,' she added, deciding to make a clean breast of all her failings. 'So I don't even know who you *are*. I was so very *startled*, you see.'

'Gifford Raven,' he said.

He'd looked rather startled himself when she'd begun her confession, then uncomfortable, and finally amused.

His smile changed his whole aspect. The danger Abigail had sensed in him was still a tangible part of his personality, but it was balanced by the kindness she now saw in his expression.

She sighed, feeling weak with relief. He didn't seem either offended or angry with her. No doubt it had been a very minor incident for someone who was used to having dangerous adventures. 'I'm afraid Bath can be a very boring place,' she said, following up on her thoughts. 'Particularly in the summer. I'm sure it will answer your purpose perfectly.'

'My purpose?' He gently encouraged her to start walking again.

'Not to have an adventure,' she said. 'Oh!' She suddenly realised she'd now admitted not just to seeing him, but also overhearing his conversation with his friend. 'Oh, dear!' She pressed her hands against her fiery cheeks. 'I w-wish the floor would open up!' she muttered. 'I am *so* mortified. I assure you, sir, I am not usually so—'

'What a very handsome clock,' said Raven smoothly. 'Do you know anything of its history?'

Abigail took a deep breath and managed to gather up some of her tattered composure. He probably thought she was a complete ninny. She was surprised he was so patient with her.

She pulled a fan out of her reticule and opened it with trembling hands. She avoided Raven's gaze as she fanned herself briskly. She was grateful for the cooling breeze over

her crimson cheeks. Her whole body was on fire. Even
though it was still only mid-morning, the Pump Room was
already uncomfortably warm. It was going to be another
sweltering August day.

She turned back to the longcase clock, determined to
prove to Raven that she wasn't entirely lacking in address.

'It is a fine clock, isn't it?' she agreed. 'I think…that is,
I believe it was made by Thomas Tompion. He gave it to
the city in…oh, in 1709, I think,' she recited from memory.
'And this is a statue of Beau Nash. From the days when
Bath was a truly fashionable place.'

She finally dared to risk a wary glance at Raven.

'Perhaps you would do me the kindness of forgetting
your first sighting of me,' he said.

'Kindness?' She was surprised.

'My conduct was hardly appropriate for my surroundings,' he pointed out stiffly.

Beneath his calm demeanour Abigail thought she detected a hint of discomfort, possibly even self-disgust. She
had been so caught up in her own feelings of mortification
she hadn't given much thought to how he might feel about
the situation. Perhaps he was as embarrassed as she was at
being caught in such an unusual situation. He was the one
who'd suffered the nightmare.

'I thought you were very brave,' she said, instinctively
responding to his unspoken mood rather than his actual
words.

'Brave!' He looked dumbfounded by her assertion.

'When I have a nightmare I'm too frightened to move,'
she explained. 'I'd never be brave enough to jump up and
fight back.'

Raven stared at her so long she was afraid she'd offended
him.

'I didn't m-mean to be impertinent,' she assured him anxiously. 'We will never talk of this again.'

In the silence that followed her words she cast around
rather desperately for another topic of conversation. It sud-

denly occurred to her that there was no need for her to feel embarrassed at knowing Raven had come to Bath to avoid adventure. Admiral Pullen had told her the self-same thing only a few minutes ago.

'Are you—are you *prone* to having adventures?' she asked courageously, hoping Raven would not consider her question impertinent.

He laughed, some of the tension easing from his body.

'I'd like to deny the charge. Unfortunately it was my own lack of self-restraint that provoked Anthony's ridiculous wager,' he admitted. 'Only days after returning to England from our last voyage, the mailcoach Anthony and I were travelling was held up by highwaymen—'

'You didn't kill them!' Abigail exclaimed in horror, remembering the deadly knife she'd seen him brandish.

'No, I did not!' Raven said forcefully. 'Good God! What a flattering opinion you have of me. Surely it would be more conventional to enquire after *my* safety and that of the other passengers—rather than the fate of highway robbers!'

'Well, well, well...' Abigail stammered, dismayed that she had ruffled Raven's temper.

'They are now awaiting transportation,' Raven said stiffly after a few seconds of awful silence. 'But Anthony was most amused that I couldn't even reach London without an adventure overtaking me. So I am now obliged to spend the next month proving that I can be as sedate as a becalmed merchantman.'

'Oh. I see.' Abigail looked at him warily. It seemed to her that he was not as insulted by her earlier comment as she had first feared.

'I would be happy to tell you anything I know about Bath,' she said, remembering the admiral's request to her. 'I'm sure you understand my duties to Miss Wyndham must always take priority—and I think Admiral Pullen exaggerates my helpfulness to him. If I can be of any assistance...but please don't feel obliged...'

'When the admiral gives an order, he expects it to be obeyed.' Raven smiled slightly. 'And as a stranger to Bath I'm certainly in need of friends here. I'd be honoured if you would consider me your friend.'

Abigail fanned herself diligently. 'The admiral is a very kind man,' she said. 'Oh, sir. You didn't tell me...I'm sure the admiral did so. Your rank? He'll notice if I get it wrong—it would be most embarrassing. Even more embarrassing,' she corrected herself.

'Yes, he's having enough fun at our expense as it is,' Raven agreed, surprising her. 'I was beginning to feel a little like his prize pig at one point. "Strong as a bull" indeed!'

Abigail was startled into laughter by his unexpected comment. There was no venom in Raven's tone, simply good-humoured exasperation.

'He introduced me to you as Captain Sir Gifford Raven. My cousin is Mr Anthony Hill.'

'Cousin?' Abigail was startled into an unwary question.

Gifford tensed as he looked down at her. But he saw only puzzlement in her eyes. She did not seem shocked by his statement, nor did he detect in her the repulsively prurient curiosity about his family he'd sometimes encountered. She simply appeared bewildered—and now perhaps a little embarrassed by her question.

For once in his life Gifford was disposed to offer a fuller explanation for his relationship to Anthony.

'My uncle was Anthony's father,' he said coolly. He felt under no obligation to tell her that his uncle had never married Anthony's mother, nor that both of Anthony's parents had died when his cousin was a baby. Gifford's father had raised Anthony along with his own sons.

'Oh?' Abigail glanced at Anthony again, then back up at Gifford. Then she smiled at him. He was surprised at how relieved he was by her easy acceptance of his relationship to Anthony. He was usually indifferent to other people's opinions.

'I'm honoured to meet you both,' she said. 'Will
you…that is, I'm sure Mr Hill knows it was me at the
window. I wouldn't want him to think…'

'I'll explain to him,' Gifford assured her.

'Thank you. It has been so *very* hot recently,' she said
feelingly.

Her face was flushed and, despite her best efforts to appear composed, Gifford could see she was still very agitated.

He wasn't feeling particularly calm himself, though he'd
done his damnedest to hide his discomfort. This was the
woman who'd seen him make such a fool of himself last
night. She must think he belonged in Bedlam! No wonder
she'd been so flustered when the admiral had forced his
company upon her.

She must have recognised him immediately. Gifford
knew his appearance was distinctive, and Anthony had been
brandishing that damned candelabrum right in his face.

She was a pretty woman, though by no means outstand-
ingly beautiful. He'd had only a few moments to appreciate
her clear, creamy complexion before her face had become
hot and shiny with embarrassment.

He couldn't see her hair. It was hidden beneath her plain
straw bonnet, but he could see her eyes. They were a soft
jade green, except for small gold stars which circled her
pupils, like tiny sunflowers—and they revealed exactly
what she was feeling. Shock. Embarrassment. Puzzlement.
Compassion…

Her eyes were dangerous, he thought. *She* was dangerous. She'd noticed that he was embarrassed by his own
stupid weakness and she'd tried to comfort him with praise!

He grew hot at the notion she considered him in need of
such reassurance.

She was of average height for a woman, but that meant
she barely reached his shoulder. She had to tilt her head
back to look at him. It should have made her seem vulnerable, but her clear gaze left Gifford feeling that he was the

one who'd been exposed. She wore a modest gown made of some kind of pale green material, decorated by an overall pattern of sprigs a slightly darker shade of green. Gifford didn't like green, and though he didn't know much about female fashion, he thought Abigail's clothes were plain to the point of being dowdy. But she had a trim figure, and her breasts were pleasingly full beneath her demure bodice.

Gifford rather wished that she had been the one who'd been careless with a bright light and open curtains. He wondered what she had been wearing when she sat at the window. Very little, he guessed, and immediately imagined her in a transparently thin muslin nightgown.

He cleared his throat as he realised the direction of his thoughts were hardly appropriate to the situation. He noticed that Abigail carried a furled parasol as well as her reticule in one hand, and that she continued to fan herself energetically with the other.

'Does the heat bother you?' he asked, remembering the fierce Caribbean sun under which he'd so recently sailed. He suspected it might have been the oppressive warmth of the previous night that had provoked his nightmare.

'N-noo,' said Abigail slowly. 'Not usually. That is, I would enjoy it more if I was staying in the country, but even in town I prefer summer to winter. Sydney Gardens are very pleasant. Sometimes during the summer they hold concerts with fireworks and illuminations.'

'Do you attend?' By mutual, but unspoken agreement, they began to stroll back towards Admiral Pullen and Anthony.

'Miss Wyndham seldom feels strong enough to leave the house,' said Abigail. 'But Admiral Pullen kindly took me to a concert last summer. It was beautiful!' Her face lit up with remembered pleasure. 'He said perhaps he might take me to another one this year if Miss Wyndham can spare me. Please do excuse me,' she added as they rejoined the others. 'I've been gone so long. Miss Wyndham will be expecting me.' She smiled at them all with genuine friendliness. 'I'm so pleased to meet you, Mr Hill. Captain. Good-bye, Admiral.'

'A very fine girl,' said Admiral Pullen as the three men watched her hasten away. 'Always cheerful and kind-hearted. Practical too. An excellent housekeeper by all accounts. Miss Wyndham gives her a free hand to run the household. Well, let's get out of this mausoleum and find something civilised to drink.'

'You don't favour the water?' Gifford said, falling into step beside the admiral.

'No. Only time I drank it I was bilious for two days.'

'But you still brought us to the Pump Room?' Gifford remarked off-handedly.

'Of course. Best place to meet people. Hear the latest news…'

Gifford exchanged a brief glance with Anthony. He was damn nearly sure the admiral had brought them to the Pump Room for the sole purpose of meeting Miss Abigail Summers.

Pullen had hastened them along the streets, one eye on his pocket watch, as if he were late for a meeting with the Board of Admiralty. Once inside the Pump Room he'd marched straight up to Abigail without a single deviation. Gifford wasn't surprised the poor woman had been startled into incoherence by the admiral's abrupt salutation. Then Pullen proceeded to puff off their respective virtues to each other with a stunning lack of subtlety. And he'd arranged for Gifford to lease the house immediately opposite to Abigail!

When Gifford had decided to accept Anthony's wager he'd also decided that, rather than staying in a hotel, he would prefer the greater privacy afforded by hiring a house. The mere thought that his nightmares might lead him to make a fool of himself in public had made him shudder. It was ironic that his own house in Bath hadn't been available to him. But neither Gifford nor his brother had lived in England for years, and his uncle, who took care of Gifford's business affairs, had leased the house to the large family of a distant maternal relative. Gifford had no personal knowledge of those particular relatives. He intended to make a formal call upon them, but he had no intention of imposing upon them—or of living in their pockets. Instead, he had asked Admiral Pullen to seek out suitable quarters for him in Bath.

It had never occurred to him that in doing so he had provided the admiral with a perfect opportunity to do some matchmaking. Did Pullen really think Gifford's wager with Anthony was no more than a ruse to enable him to search for a wife? Or had the admiral simply decided it was time his protégé wed, and taken advantage of Gifford's arrival to select Miss Abigail Summers for the questionable honour of becoming his lady?

Gifford could only hope Abigail had been so flustered she hadn't noticed the admiral's broad hints. He most definitely wasn't looking for a wife—no matter how amiable or good at housekeeping the lady might prove to be.

He was in Bath solely to prove he was capable of doing nothing more adventurous than stroll down to the Pump Room every morning for a month without kicking over the traces from the predictable boredom.

But he privately acknowledged to himself his stay in Bath would also give him a chance to consider his future. Would he go to sea again? Or was it time to take up his position as head of the Raven family with all the responsibilities that entailed?

'Perhaps it will be harder for you to avoid an adventure in Bath than I'd anticipated.' Anthony's low-voiced comment interrupted Gifford's thoughts. 'The next month might turn out to be quite entertaining.'

Gifford frowned at his cousin's obvious amusement. 'I see no reason for you to assume that,' he said coldly.

Chapter Two

Abigail walked home slowly, partly because of the heat, but mainly because she needed time to compose herself. Miss Wyndham would be especially interested to hear about such fascinating new arrivals. Abigail couldn't suppress the information, but she did want to present it in such a way that she didn't call any undue attention to herself. It was essential she didn't blush or look self-conscious. Miss Wyndham had a lively interest in romance, and she would tease Abigail good-humouredly if she believed she was smitten with Gifford Raven.

But when she arrived at the house, she discovered Miss Wyndham had a much more important visitor.

'Abigail! You've been gone so long! Charles has come to stay!' Miss Wyndham exclaimed, the moment Abigail entered the drawing room.

'Miss Abigail, how do you do?' Charles Johnson rose from his chair to greet her. 'You look as charming as always.'

'Thank you, sir. I hope you're well?' Abigail allowed him to kiss her hand, but retrieved it as quickly as possible.

'In fine form, Miss Abigail,' he declared. 'And all the better for seeing my favourite aunt and her lovely companion.'

'I'm your only aunt!' Miss Wyndham protested, her eyes

bright with pleasure. She was in better spirits than Abigail had seen her for weeks.

'Very true. But you could be my only aunt *and* an old harridan I never venture near from one year's end to the next. Or—you could be my own, gracious and charming aunt whose society I long for whenever we are apart.' Charles swept an extravagant bow towards her.

'What a rascal!' Miss Wyndham was flattered and delighted by his fulsome compliment. 'I didn't expect to see you until the autumn. When you wrote, you mentioned you'd be spending the summer in Brighton. I'm so glad to see you. So thoughtful. Isn't he thoughtful?' she appealed to Abigail. 'To choose to spend time with a tired old woman when he could be cutting a dash with his friends.'

'Very considerate,' Abigail agreed drily. It seemed to her there was an undercurrent of anxious hopefulness in Miss Wyndham's voice, as if the old lady didn't quite believe her own words, but very much wished they were true.

Charles Johnson was in his mid-twenties. He always dressed in the height of fashion, and he boasted that he moved in the most elegant circles. He had expensive tastes, but his only source of income was the heavily mortgaged estate he'd inherited from his father several years earlier. Though he referred to Miss Wyndham as his aunt, she was in fact his great-aunt. Miss Wyndham's younger sister had been his grandmother, but he hadn't made Miss Wyndham's acquaintance until after the deaths of his parents and grandparents a few years previously. He was Miss Wyndham's sole surviving relative.

Abigail managed the household accounts. After every visit by Charles Johnson she was forced to budget very frugally for the rest of the quarter. She'd tried, tactfully, to suggest to Miss Wyndham that Charles was a grown man, capable of supporting himself, but Miss Wyndham had brushed her reservations aside. Abigail suspected that, deep down, Miss Wyndham was afraid that Charles was taking advantage of her, but it distressed the old lady to think her only relative might have no genuine regard for her. Miss Wyndham preferred to believe that her great-nephew's visits were motivated by thoughtfulness rather than financial necessity.

It wasn't Abigail's place to disillusion her employer, especially when she had no evidence for her suspicions except for Johnson's willingness—if not eagerness—to accept his great-aunt's generous gifts of money.

On this occasion, his unexpected arrival did have one beneficial effect. Miss Wyndham was so entranced by the London and Brighton society gossip he regaled her with she entirely forgot to ask Abigail if there had been any other newcomers to Bath that day.

Gifford strolled into his room. He shrugged out of his coat and tossed it on to the bed, then went immediately to open the curtains and the window. The bedchamber was appallingly stuffy. It was only just past nine o'clock. He was unlikely to scandalise Miss Summers with his actions at this early hour.

He and Anthony had spent the day with Admiral Pullen. The admiral and Gifford had reminisced about the past, and they'd all told stories of their individual adventures since they'd last met—though Gifford's account had been heavily edited. He'd expected Pullen to continue with his clumsy matchmaking efforts. He'd been ready to deflect any unwelcome encouragement to pursue Abigail Summers—but the admiral had barely mentioned her during the rest of the day. Quite contrarily, Gifford had ended up frustrated by his lack of information about her. He didn't *want* the woman—but he was curious about her.

It belatedly occurred to him that, although she'd been agonisingly embarrassed, she hadn't seemed shocked by what she'd seen. Her discomfort appeared to have been caused simply by the fact that she'd inadvertently spied on him. Apparently his actions hadn't scandalised or even greatly alarmed her. She'd made no arch references to his nudity. She hadn't simpered knowingly at him.

His pride was sore because she'd seen him act so stupidly, but he couldn't help being impressed that she hadn't succumbed to missish theatrics. On the other hand, he cautioned himself, it wouldn't do to feel unnecessarily positive towards the woman Admiral Pullen had apparently selected to be his bride. Gifford naturally resisted all efforts to push him towards matrimony. He decided that Abigail's absence of maidenly delicacy was probably a reflection of her practical, housekeeper's soul. No doubt she had been more worried about bloodstains on Mrs Chesney's carpet than the fate of his possible victim.

Having settled with himself that Abigail's unquestionable fondness for beeswax polish and fuller's earth rendered her completely unattractive to him, Gifford looked across at her window.

To his surprise, she *was* in her room and, like him, she had left her curtains open. His hands stilled momentarily in the process of undoing his cravat. Then he stepped to one side and watched her from behind the partial concealment of the curtain.

It was hardly the act of a gentleman, but what was sauce for the goose...

Abigail was very busy doing something, but at first he couldn't quite make out what. It was only when she gave up on the attempt that he realised she'd been trying to wedge a chair under the door handle. He frowned, and drew back a little as she turned halfway towards the window to set the chair aside. Then she stood in the middle of the room, her hands on her waist, and gazed around at the rest of the furniture.

Her pose drew attention to curves which were normally disguised by the long lines of her high-waisted dress. She had a very trim waist, and the fall of her skirt indicated her hips might be pleasingly rounded beneath her modest gown. From where Gifford was standing Miss Summers was desirably slim in certain places and provocatively curvaceous in others. He wished very much she was wearing only her nightgown to carry out her peculiar activities or, better yet, nothing at all. That would only be fair, Gifford decided, since she'd already seen him make a fool of himself in a state of complete undress.

The mental image of Abigail wearing no clothes had a surprisingly powerful physical effect upon him. Gifford frowned and conjured instead a housewifely picture of her scouring the floor with fuller's earth and sand. It was a mundane activity which should have dampened his arousal—unfortunately he couldn't get his fantasy Abigail to put her clothes back on while she scrubbed the floor.

In the meantime, the real Abigail advanced briskly on a small chest of drawers. Gifford watched in amazement as she tried to push it along the wall. It was obviously too heavy for her because, after a few moments of unavailing effort, she stopped pushing and turned round. She half-leant, half-sat on the chest as she rested, and tipped back her head to draw in several deep, cooling breaths. Gifford's muscles tensed, partly from an instinctive desire to help her—but mainly because of the distracting way her posture drew attention to her full breasts. After a few moments she turned her back to him and removed all the drawers from the chest. When she'd finished, she tried to move the carcase again. This time she succeeded. She wedged it across the door, then replaced all the drawers and dusted her hands together in an obvious gesture of satisfaction.

Gifford hastily hid behind the curtain. It was far too warm for so much exertion and, as he'd expected, Abigail walked over to her window to cool down.

What the devil was she up to? Surely she wasn't protecting herself from him? If that was the case, she would have been better off closing the curtains than barricading the door. Gifford absently stripped off his cravat as he pondered the problem, then unfastened and removed his collar with an enormous sense of relief. He'd spent years living and fighting in restrictive uniforms. It was always a pleasure to discard unnecessary garments.

He believed Abigail was a practical woman. She'd displayed resourcefulness in removing the drawers to make the furniture easier to handle. It had taken quite an effort for her to move the chest of drawers. She must believe she had good cause for her unusual actions.

Gifford frowned. He didn't like the idea that Abigail felt the need to lock herself into her room at night. Apart from anything else, it wasn't safe. If there was a fire—having lived half his life at sea, Gifford was acutely sensitive to the dangers of fire—Abigail would be trapped.

He stared into the shadows of his unlit room as he considered the situation. There was little he could do tonight, but tomorrow he would search for some answers. Perhaps he would start with Admiral Pullen. He didn't think it would take much to prompt the man into talking about his favourite Miss Summers. Gifford's only problem would be to avoid giving the impression that he had any kind of *romantic* interest in Abigail—but it wouldn't be the first time he'd played verbal chess with a flag officer.

Abigail took one last breath of the evening air before she reluctantly closed her curtains. She had no idea what time Captain Raven would retire to bed—though not as early as this, she was sure—but she didn't want any repetition of the previous night's awkwardness. It was better to be stiflingly hot than give the impression she was either vulgarly curious or shockingly immodest.

A large moth blundered around her room, banging against walls and ceiling before it finally flew too close to the candle. She sighed. She was now a prisoner in her own room until morning.

Miss Wyndham's rooms were on the first floor. She rarely ventured either upstairs or down, and most of the time Abigail had the entire second floor to herself. But when Charles came to visit he also had a room on the sec-

ond floor. His manner towards her made Abigail feel uncomfortable. When Miss Wyndham was present he was always punctilious in his attentions to Abigail—though never
to such an extent that his great-aunt might feel jealous. But
when he and Abigail were alone there was a subtle change
in his behaviour. It was clear he regarded her as his inferior.
Her feelings were of no more consequence to him than
those of a housemaid. Once on the stairs he had pressed
himself a little too close to her…

Abigail's skin crawled at the idea of him touching her
more intimately. She hoped she was being over-cautious,
but she knew she would be the one who would pay the
price—in more ways than one—if her suspicions were ever
proved correct. It would be her word against Charles's. The
poor companion versus the handsome, favoured young relative. It would be easy for him to claim she'd made brazen
advances on him—and difficult if not impossible for her to
prove otherwise.

It was a pity the key to her bedroom had gone missing
shortly after Charles's last visit. She felt ridiculously melodramatic, blocking her door with the chest of drawers, but
she hadn't been able to wedge the chair satisfactorily under
the handle. She laughed a little ruefully at herself. She was
acting like a heroine from a Gothic novel. But if she lost
her good name, and the security of her position with Miss
Wyndham, she would have nothing.

She sat on the edge of her bed and fanned herself. There
was no chance she'd sleep well tonight. She was too hot,
and her mind was too full. She glanced towards the closed
curtains. She wondered what Captain Raven was doing.
Would he sleep peacefully—or would he have another
nightmare?

She remembered his naked body, illuminated by the candlelight. She'd been startled, scared, excited, and ultimately
embarrassed by her unconventional interactions with
Raven. But he'd never made her skin crawl.

* * *

'Miss Summers. Good morning!'

Abigail looked up, surprised by the interruption. She'd been sure she wouldn't be disturbed.

She had left Miss Wyndham and Charles at home, engaged in a session of mutual flattery. They'd had no need of her presence. Miss Wyndham was unlikely to be interested in other visitors to Bath today, so Abigail had chosen not to visit the Pump Room. Instead she'd retreated to her favourite lending library.

'C-Captain Raven,' she stammered. He towered over her. With his piratical eye-patch and tangible aura of danger, he seemed quite out of place among the calf-bound volumes. 'I had no idea you are fond of reading,' she said breathlessly.

'Very. May I?' He gestured gracefully to the vacant space next to her on the bench.

'Please sit down,' she said. Her mouth was dry with nervousness. But she was also excited by the unexpected encounter. No one could accuse her of soliciting another meeting with him, so she had no reason to feel awkward or self-conscious. Perhaps she might even be able to enjoy her conversation with him today. He was certainly the most *interesting* man she'd ever met.

'Thank you.' He sat down beside her.

His legs were so long, she thought distractedly. He was so tall and uncompromisingly male. He made the space around him shrink, yet at the same time he introduced an indefinable air of wildness into the room. She could sense distant horizons and unfamiliar hazards.

She was too nervous to look into his face. Instead her gaze was drawn to his hands. They were well-shaped, strong and tanned.

As she watched, he reached across and took the book she'd been reading out of her nerveless grasp.

It didn't occur to her to protest. She was held in thrall by his self-assurance and her memories. He'd held a dagger in the hand that now held her book. She had a vivid picture of him poised naked in the dramatic candlelight. He didn't belong in these sedate surroundings. He belonged on the open seas, battling the elements with all the fierce strength at his disposal.

'Did you ever sail in a hurricane?' she asked, without thinking.

'Twice,' he replied. 'Once as a midshipman. Our masts went by the board on that occasion.' He grimaced at the memory. 'We nearly broached. We were lucky to survive. And once when I was captain of the *Unicorn.*'

By now Abigail had lifted her gaze to his face. She was intrigued by the brevity of the second half of his reply.

'You didn't lose your masts when you were captain,' she deduced.

'No.' Raven smiled slightly. 'But that was more by good luck than any particular skill on my part. You are familiar with nautical terms, Miss Summers?' he changed the subject.

'A little. Admiral Pullen tells me stories.'

'Ah, yes, so he said.' Raven nodded. 'Now.' He glanced down at the book in his hand. 'What were you reading when I arrived that caused you to frown so direfully?'

'I wasn't frowning!' Abigail exclaimed, instinctively trying to retrieve the book.

'With respect, Miss Summers, you were frowning,' Raven replied, holding the book out of her reach.

Abigail's stomach fluttered nervously. It almost seemed as if he was flirting with her, but she found that very hard to credit. Most gentlemen under the age of fifty hardly seemed to be aware of her existence.

She folded her hands in her lap. She was determined not to let Raven provoke her into an undignified tussle for the book.

'Little boys tease their sisters by stealing their toys,' she said primly. 'It's not the conduct I'd expect of a distinguished naval officer.'

'I don't have any sisters,' said Raven immediately. 'So I

must have missed that period of my boyhood. I'm compensating for it now.'

Abigail's breath caught. His rakish grin was devastatingly attractive. No man should have such a powerful weapon at his disposal. It inspired a woman to indulge him when, if she was wise, she ought to be keeping him at a safe distance.

'Are you claiming you've entered your second childhood?' she enquired lightly. 'If that's the case, I must tell Mrs Chesney to withhold all the adult pleasures you no doubt enjoy. Port after your dinner, perhaps? A game of cards? Or a wager on your ability to survive a month without having an adventure?' she added daringly.

She reached once more for her book, but Raven caught her hand in his and compelled it gently downwards. He didn't need to use force. Abigail was so startled to feel his hand on hers she let him do as he pleased. In fact, she enjoyed the sensation.

'I hate port,' he said, 'and I seldom gamble. It was Anthony's wager that brought us to Bath. When I gamble…' he hesitated for a moment '…it's not on the turn of a card.'

Something in the tone of his voice chilled Abigail, undermining her self-preserving attempt to seem flippant. His voice reminded her of the nightmares that harried his sleep. She almost didn't notice that he kept his hand on hers as he scanned the page of her book.

Almost.

She liked the feel of his strong fingers wrapped around hers. It was a remarkably stimulating experience. She felt it throughout her whole body. She liked sitting so close to him and she liked him touching her. Her heart beat faster with excitement and nervousness.

But she had no desire to be the target of gossip. Nor did she wish to give Raven the wrong impression of her. She blushed, and withdrew her hand from his. She glanced surreptitiously around the lending library, hoping no one had noticed that unprecedented intimacy.

'I think I have it.' Raven sounded pleased with himself.
She wondered if he'd even noticed that she'd removed her
hand. Touching her obviously held no particular significance for him. 'Your indignation is either on behalf of a
gentleman of your acquaintance who is thirty-five,' he declared, 'or of a lady who is twenty-seven. "A woman of
seven-and-twenty can never hope to feel or inspire affection
again,"' he quoted from the volume he was holding. 'I dare
say it would be indelicate to ask you how old you are?' He
raised his eyebrow at her.

Abigail glared at him. 'You have absolutely no reason to
suppose I was frowning because of s-something I'd read!'
she pointed out. 'I might have been thinking of something
else entirely.'

'If it will ease your anxieties, I'll freely confess to being
thirty-five in December,' Raven said helpfully. 'At which
point it appears—at least according to Miss Marianne—that
I will be condemned to wear flannel waistcoats and suffer
from rheumatism and...' he lifted the book and checked the
offending passage again "...and every species of ailment
that can afflict the old and the feeble,"' he quoted. 'Perhaps
you're right, I am about to topple over into my second
childhood.'

'You are not!' Abigail exclaimed. There was nothing either childlike or decrepit about Raven's muscular form. But
when he cocked her an amused glance, Abigail wished she
hadn't been quite so emphatic in her denial. 'Senility may
afflict the mind while the body remains hale,' she observed,
trying to retrieve her position.

'What a cheering thought for a fine August morning!'
Raven returned the book to her. 'The admiral did not see
you in the Pump Room this morning,' he remarked casually.

'Oh, no. Was he looking for me particularly?' Abigail
asked worriedly. 'I know I often speak to him there. But
since *you're* in Bath—' She broke off, afraid she'd made it
obvious she'd been avoiding him. 'Miss Wyndham's

nephew is visiting her,' she hurried on. 'And no other new
arrival is half as interesting to her. I didn't think I needed
to look at the Pump Room book this morning.'

'I see,' said Raven. 'You were free to indulge your own
interests.'

'Exactly.' Abigail was relieved by his quick understanding. 'Though I should be getting back. Miss Wyndham
might miss me if I'm absent too long.'

'Allow me to escort you,' Raven offered, standing at the
same time.

'There's really no need,' she protested, a little flustered
at the idea. 'I wouldn't want to inconvenience you.'

'No inconvenience,' he assured her, his lips curving into
that heart-stoppingly attractive smile. 'On the contrary. It
would be far more inconvenient if I were obliged to dodge
about behind you in an effort to avoid your notice. We are
heading in the same direction, after all. Does Miss Wyndham's nephew plan to make a long stay in Bath?' he asked,
as they left the lending library.

'I don't know.' Abigail twirled her furled parasol indecisively. Despite her better judgement she was pleased
Raven would escort her home. But now she was distracted
by an unfamiliar dilemma. She wasn't used to walking with
someone else. She had the dreadful suspicion she might
poke Captain Raven's one good eye out if she put up her
parasol now.

'An interesting implement,' Raven commented, watching
her action. 'We have an awning over the quarterdeck to
protect us from the sun. Is it broken?' he added, when she
didn't open it. 'Let me see. I have a very useful ability to
mend broken things.'

'It's not broken,' said Abigail, frowning worriedly. 'I was
just afraid of unwarily prodding you with it. You are so
much taller than I am.'

'True. I'll hold it for you.' He took it from her before
she could protest.

'Don't you feel any sense of unease walking through

Bath carrying a pink parasol?' she asked interestedly, after they'd covered several yards in silence.

'No. Do you think I should?'

'Well…'

There was something very incongruous about the sight of the piratical and very masculine Raven carrying such a feminine article. She wondered how he'd lost his eye. She'd had so much else to think about at their first meeting that she'd barely thought about his eye-patch. Now she felt curious, and a little sick, as she tried to imagine the injury which had left him so scarred.

'What are you thinking of now?' he asked suddenly.

'Nothing. Nothing.' She shook her head.

'It distressed you,' he said, a little harshly. 'Does it distress you to walk with me?'

'Of course not!' She looked at him in amazement. 'Why should it?'

Raven didn't answer. It was a couple of minutes before he spoke again. 'Have you been Miss Wyndham's companion for long?' he asked.

'Nine years,' she replied.

'It is…a rather restricted life,' he said carefully.

Abigail laughed. 'Most people's lives are,' she pointed out. 'When you're on board ship—and perhaps even when you aren't—are you not bound by the Articles of War? Admiral Pullen has told me all about them. I live by different conventions but, unlike you, I won't be court-martialled and perhaps hanged if I make a mistake.'

'What happens if you make a mistake?' Raven asked.

'I stammer and go very red,' said Abigail lightly. She sensed a deeper layer of meaning beneath his question, but she wasn't sure if he was thinking of his own life or hers.

'You didn't make a mistake,' he said, understanding her reference to her embarrassment of the previous day and bluntly responding to it. 'You are not culpable in any way because you were hot and decided to sit at your open window in the dark.'

They stopped walking in a moment of unspoken, mutual agreement. Abigail looked up at him. He was holding the parasol entirely over her, as he had done from the moment he'd taken it from her. The sun was shining full on his face. She could clearly see the scar on his cheek and forehead, the streak of white hair among the black, and his forbidding eye-patch. The first time she'd seen him she'd been afraid he was about to commit murder. The second time she'd seen him she'd sensed he was dangerous. She was still aware of the stormy wildness only just concealed by a thin layer of civilisation. But she also saw scars which went much deeper than the obvious physical injury he had suffered.

'It was a splinter,' he said, answering at least one of her unvoiced questions.

'A splinter?' Abigail confusedly imagined the small splinters she occasionally ran into her fingers.

He smiled slightly, understanding her bewilderment. 'When a round shot hits a ship it throws up huge splinters of wood or metal,' he explained. 'The splinter which blinded me was nearly six feet long—so I'm told. I never saw it coming. It was only a glancing blow. If it hadn't been…'

'Oh, my God,' she whispered, appalled at the image he'd just conjured for her. 'Is that why…? Is that what you were dreaming about?'

'No.' He pressed his lips together, as if he regretted having said so much. She could feel the coiled tension in his lean body, as if it was only by an extreme effort of will that he didn't stride away from her.

Abigail wished she'd been more tactful. She cast around for a way to change the subject. 'Are you hungry?' she asked, noticing they were standing outside a pastry shop. 'I have a sudden f-fancy for gooseberry pie,' she rattled on, hardly aware of what she was saying. 'If they have one, I'll take it home for Miss Wyndham and her nephew.'

'If they have gooseberry pies we will buy two,' said

Raven, holding open the door for her. 'One for you to give
to Miss Wyndham and her nephew, and one for you to keep
for yourself.'

By the time they reached their respective front doors,
Gifford had established that Charles Johnson had arrived
the *previous* morning. So there seemed little doubt that Abigail's furniture-moving activities of last night had been
prompted by his arrival. Gifford asked her several casual
questions about the man, but all her responses were conventionally bland. Whatever her own doubts, she wouldn't
criticise her employer's great-nephew to a relative stranger.

Gifford respected her loyalty, but he was frustrated by
the situation.

'Does Mr Johnson intend to make a long stay in Bath?'
he enquired.

'He didn't say,' Abigail replied. 'I imagine a few days.
Mr Johnson has many friends all over the country. I'm sure
they will be eager to enjoy his company again soon.'

'We must hope he doesn't keep them waiting long,' said
Gifford drily, detecting the slightly acid note in Abigail's
voice.

Her eyes flew to his face. He saw surprise and then a
hint of guilty self-consciousness in her gaze.

'Thank you for escorting me home,' she said, after a few
moments' silence. 'I hope you don't find your visit to Bath
too boring.'

Gifford smiled. 'Contrary to popular belief, the life of the
captain of one of His Majesty's ships is largely composed
of boredom,' he said.

'Oh, but surely…'

'I may give the orders, Miss Summers, but, having done
so, I've usually nothing else to do but maintain an air of
untroubled serenity,' he explained. 'It would be bad for my
lieutenants' confidence—not to mention their morale—if I
interfered unnecessarily in the way they carry out their orders.'

'Oh, dear,' said Abigail. 'How exhausting. But excellent training for a month in Bath,' she added brightly.

Gifford grinned. Despite himself he enjoyed talking to the dowdily practical Miss Summers. She had an unexpectedly lively sense of humour—and a rare sensitivity to his changeable moods.

'Well, goodbye, Captain.' Abigail turned to face him, holding out her hands as she did so. 'Thank you for carrying my parcels.'

'It was my pleasure,' Gifford said gallantly. He returned Abigail's parasol and her purchases from the pastry shop. It was only when she'd entered the house and the door had closed behind her that he realised he was still holding the three volumes of her book along with the pie she'd prompted him to buy.

He took a couple of steps after her, then stopped. If he kept the books he'd have an excuse to seek her company in future. He could even act the part of a true lover and return the novel one volume at a time. Admiral Pullen would expect no less of him. He laughed at the notion, then frowned at the direction of his thoughts. He had no intention of becoming Abigail's lover. It would be unfair of him to raise expectations within her he could not fulfil.

Chapter Three

'Anyone interesting?' Gifford asked, leaning over Abigail's shoulder as she leant over the Pump Room book.

She spun round to face him, one hand instinctively pressed against the base of her throat.

'Heavens! You s-startled me!' she gasped.

Gifford was acutely conscious of the rapid rise and fall of her breasts, visible proof that he really had taken her by surprise. She was wearing a dress of pale primrose yellow. The gown was suitably demure—except for an unexpectedly provocative bow tied beneath her bosom. The long ribbon streamers struck Gifford as positively flirtatious.

With an effort he lifted his gaze to focus his attention more appropriately on her face. Her cheeks were flushed. He wondered uncomfortably if she'd guessed what he'd been thinking. He didn't want her to think of him as a leering scoundrel.

Despite his absolute determination to avoid any kind of romantic entanglement with Abigail, he hadn't been able to resist seeking her out in the Pump Room. Bath was a lamentably predictable place for a man used to the unpredictable routine of a naval officer in wartime. At sea, weeks of routine boredom could suddenly be interrupted by incidents of explosive violence. In Bath, Abigail was the only

source of interesting unpredictability Gifford had so far encountered.

'My apologies.' He stepped back and bowed gracefully.
'Indulge me with a calming stroll around the room.' He
offered her his arm.

She looked at him warily. 'You don't need to be indulged,' she said. 'I'm the one who nearly jumped out of
my skin.'

'Then a gentle promenade will help settle you back into
it,' Gifford suggested.

Abigail raised her eyebrows at him. He could see the
amused scepticism in her expressive green eyes. He waited.
After a few seconds she fell into step beside him, though
she didn't take his arm.

'You've returned to your daily duty, I see,' he observed.
'Has Mr Johnson left already?'

'No. But Miss Wyndham would hate it if I missed a new
arrival of consequence,' Abigail said, then bit her lip.

'What did she say about me?' Gifford asked curiously.

Abigail blushed, and looked embarrassed.

'You haven't told her!' Gifford said in amazement. 'Anthony and I are in the book. Mrs Chesney even told me this
morning we're mentioned in the *Bath Chronicle*. Miss
Wyndham's idea of consequence must be very exacting,'
he continued, unable to resist teasing Abigail.

'I'm saving you for a rainy day.' She'd regained her composure. Now it was her turn to cast a teasing glance at
Gifford.

'I beg your pardon?'

'I mean, Miss Wyndham will be disappointed when
Charles leaves,' Abigail explained. 'That will be the perfect
moment to divert her with the story of—'

'What?' he interrupted, more harshly than he'd intended.
He had visions of Abigail entertaining the old beldame with
a description of his nightmare.

'Of your presentation to me in this very room by Admiral
Pullen,' said Abigail steadily. 'He is *very* proud of you,

Captain. And once Miss Wyndham hears of your arrival she will insist the admiral brings you to call upon her.'

Gifford glanced away, cursing himself for his overreaction. They circled the Pump Room in awkward silence, then both started speaking at the same time.

'Have you—?'

'I read—'

And both deferred to the other.

'I was only going to ask if you've visited Sydney Gardens yet,' Abigail said, when Gifford insisted she speak first.

'Yesterday afternoon.'

It was two days since he'd met Abigail in the lending library. She hadn't visited the Pump Room the previous morning. He was careful not to mention he'd noticed her absence. He didn't want to give the impression he'd deliberately sought her company. He liked talking to Abigail, and he thoroughly enjoyed picturing the shapely body he suspected her modest gowns concealed—but he was absolutely certain that he wasn't in the market for a wife.

It was a common saying amongst his fellow officers that when a man married he was lost to the navy. Gifford was slowly coming to terms with the realisation that, as head of his family, he had certain domestic responsibilities—but he still wasn't ready to accept he might never go to sea again.

'They're very pretty, aren't they? The gardens?' Abigail prompted, when he stared at her blankly.

'Yes. I read your book,' he said abruptly.

'My book?' She looked bewildered.

'The one you were reading in the lending library. *Sense and Sensibility*. I forgot to give it back to you the other day.'

'Really?' She looked up at him in surprise. 'Whatever for? I mean, why did you read it? I'm sorry.' She lowered her eyes briefly. 'I j-just wouldn't have thought you'd enjoy such a story.'

'It was…educational,' Gifford replied.

He wondered why she was embarrassed at asking such a natural question. He would have asked the same thing in her position. The honest answer was that it had been a way to avoid his nightmares—but he didn't intend to tell her that.

He looked down at the brim of her straw bonnet. He still hadn't seen her hair. When he'd watched her move the chest of drawers she'd been wearing a cap. Today when she lifted her face all he could see was the ruffles of her cap peeking out beneath the edge of her bonnet.

She was covered up and buttoned up. He preferred the yellow dress to her green one, but she was still a picture of conventional propriety. He hated her bonnet. His fingers twitched with the urge to take if off—and then encourage her to shake out her hair in the breeze.

But there was no breeze in the Pump Room. Instead he could see motes of dust floating lazily in the beams of light from the huge windows. The room was a monument to desiccated respectability. Suddenly he was desperate to feel a brisk ocean wind against his face.

'Educational?' Abigail reminded him. 'The book, sir?'

Gifford dragged his attention back to his companion. She was watching him patiently—and perhaps a little quizzically.

'It was,' he said, remembering the mixture of claustrophobia and frustration he'd felt when he read it. 'I'd never considered such a mode of living before,' he continued slowly. 'The boredom I spoke of—we have our petty grievances in the navy—but the trivial pointlessness of the lives that book describes! How can such an existence be tolerable?' He couldn't quite keep the horror out of his voice.

Abigail looked at him thoughtfully as she tried to understand his point.

'I haven't read it yet,' she reminded him. 'But what is it you particularly objected to?'

Gifford took a deep breath and thrust his hand through his hair, thinking about her question.

'It was a woman's world,' he said at last. 'The men had no substance. Two of them were entirely dependent on the whims of their elderly female relatives—like Charles Johnson, I suppose.' He frowned. 'Even the men we were meant to view favourably were indecisive, ineffective—'

'You think the author was too harsh towards your sex?' Abigail asked.

'No, no.' Gifford started walking again. He was too restless to stand still. 'I said it was a woman's world. What I meant...was that we were shown the world through a woman's eyes. If that's what it's like to be a female, I can only thank God I was born a man.'

Abigail blinked at his fervent declaration. 'What's wrong with being a woman?'

'You have no choice. No genuine freedom of action. You must wait modestly to see if a man favours you. And if his conduct confuses you, you must appear unconscious and pretend indifference. Unendurable!'

Abigail laughed.

Gifford glared at her. He hadn't read a novel since he was fifteen years old. The characters and their situation had made a powerful impression on him, partly because of his own horror of becoming trapped into domesticity. He realised too late that a more sophisticated reader might find his fierce emotional response risible.

He straightened his spine, unconsciously summoning a haughty demeanour to hide his discomfort. He knew exactly what he was about on the quarterdeck of the *Unicorn*—but it seemed the moribund respectability of Bath contained hazards he hadn't foreseen.

'I'm sorry.' Abigail laid her hand apologetically on his arm. 'But you sounded so outraged! This can hardly be new information to you. You said yourself you'll be thirty-five in December.'

Gifford looked down at her hand, still resting on his blue coat sleeve. She had reached out to him so naturally. He'd made her laugh, but she wasn't mocking him. His tense muscles relaxed into a lesser state of readiness.

'I haven't spent more than a couple of months on shore at a stretch since I was sixteen,' he said stiffly. 'I have never given this matter any thought before.'

He might not have thought about it now if he hadn't watched Abigail barricade herself into her bedchamber. She'd deliberately turned herself into a prisoner in her own room for the night. The implications of her action—that she clearly didn't feel safe in her home, yet she also didn't feel able to challenge the situation—appalled him. It reflected the relative helplessness of the female characters in the book he'd just read. And left him acutely aware of how little control Abigail had over the circumstances of her life.

Gifford still had nightmares about his time as a prisoner on board the privateer. He wanted to ask Abigail how she could endure such powerlessness with such a good-humoured grace. But that wasn't an option. He wasn't supposed to show any particular interest in her.

'I'm sure you have similar restraints on your behaviour at sea,' Abigail said. 'Don't you have to pretend indifference if a senior officer abuses you or blames you for something that wasn't your fault?'

'Yes.' Gifford frowned. 'Don't you ever feel the urge to take your bonnet off and feel the breeze through your hair?'

'Frequently,' said Abigail, taking him by surprise with her straightforward response.

'But if you did, it would cause a scandal?'

'It might excite comment,' Abigail acknowledged. She looked at him curiously. 'Why are you so unusually... animated...on this issue?'

Gifford exhaled carefully. 'I'm not *unusually* animated,' he corrected her. 'You haven't known me long enough to be familiar with my *usual* manner. Would you be satisfied with a man worth two thousand pounds a year—or are you aiming higher?' He reverted to one of the themes in the book he'd just read.

'I'm not aiming at all!' Abigail exclaimed, removing her hand from his arm and stepping back. 'Good heavens, sir!'

'Why not?' Gifford asked bluntly. 'Surely running your own household would be better than running pointless errands to see who's new in town?'

Abigail opened her mouth, then closed it again.

'Miss Wyndham's claims upon me have certain boundaries,' she said at last, obviously picking her words with care. 'She is very kind, very generous to me. But if I was unhappy with my situation I could leave. I could seek an alternative position. That option is not so readily available in marriage. Besides, I have no fortune. I am not young. And I'm no great beauty. I haven't read much of your disturbing book.' She smiled at him, a definitely teasing gleam in her eyes. 'But I do remember that one of the characters claimed someone in my situation could only be desirable for my nursing or my housekeeping skills. If I'm going to be a housekeeper, I'd rather get paid for my labours.'

Gifford stared at her. It occurred to him that, beneath her demure exterior, Miss Summers had some decidedly independent opinions of her own.

'Do you like being a woman?' he asked. 'Wouldn't you rather be a man?'

'That's a very arrogant question!' Abigail exclaimed. 'If women's lot is so undesirable, then surely it's men who have made it so? Why should I want to become one?'

Gifford frowned. '"The meek shall inherit the earth"? You claim the moral high ground of being the weaker party?'

'This is a very odd conversation!' Abigail declared. 'I'm sure there are many gentlemen who believe women are devious and manipulative and have no sense of honour at all. That we aren't, in fact, weak, because we slyly influence events in our favour.'

'You're not sly,' said Gifford. He was quite sure on that point.

'I lack sufficient address. It's a defect in me,' Abigail said, straight-faced.

'You don't believe that!' Gifford abruptly realised she was teasing him. He squared his shoulders. With the exception of Anthony, it was a long time since anyone had teased him. The position of captain was inevitably isolated, and Gifford had left the easy familiarity and joking of the wardroom behind him years ago.

His visit to Bath was turning into quite an adventure— though not in the way Anthony had meant.

Abigail glanced at the clock. 'I've stayed too long,' she said. Gifford thought he caught a hint of reluctance in her voice, but he couldn't be sure.

'I'll walk back with you.'

Abigail didn't protest at his suggestion. 'Is Mr Hill enjoying his visit to Bath?' she enquired, as they turned towards the entrance.

'I think so. He has been on several sketching expeditions around the local countryside. But he seems to be deriving most enjoyment from encouraging Admiral Pullen to tell him about some of my more misjudged youthful exploits,' Gifford said ruefully.

'Did you serve with the admiral long?' Abigail enquired.

'For several years, on two different ships,' Gifford replied. 'As fourth lieutenant and later, on a different ship, as first lieutenant. He specifically asked for me to serve with him. I learnt more from him than any other officer.'

'He's a very kind man,' said Abigail.

'In appropriate circumstances,' Gifford replied.

He thought of the men who had died because of the orders Pullen had given during his long career. He thought of the men who had died as a result of his own orders. Such losses were an inevitable part of warfare—but Gifford never forgot the price that other men had paid for his decisions.

He abruptly realised Abigail had stopped beside a trio of three older ladies, and forced himself to pay attention to her introductions.

* * *

Abigail had been hoping to avoid the need to introduce
Raven to anyone but, as soon as she saw Mrs Lavenham
and her friends, she knew that wouldn't be possible. She
made the best of the situation, keeping her tone light and
relatively impersonal.

'It is *such* a pleasure to meet you, Sir Gifford,' Mrs Lavenham exclaimed. 'We have read all about your daring
exploits in the *Gazette*.'

'Will you be going to sea again soon?' Mrs Hendon enquired.

'Have you known Miss Summers long?' Miss Clarke
asked.

'My son, Edward, is a lieutenant in the navy,' said Mrs
Hendon.

'The two of you seem to be very well acquainted,' Miss
Clarke said archly. 'I'm sure you must have known each
other some time.'

'He's in daily expectation of being commissioned in a
seventy-four,' said Mrs Hendon. 'He wrote requesting a position several weeks ago.'

Abigail risked a quick glance at Raven, then had to bite
her lip to stop herself from laughing aloud at his wooden
expression. It appeared the gallant captain was more at
home piloting his ship through a hurricane than dealing
with so much feminine effusion.

'Captain Raven is an old friend of Admiral Pullen,' she
explained. 'The admiral asked me to introduce him to
Bath.'

'Admiral Pullen is a charming gentleman,' said Mrs Lavenham majestically. 'I believe you served with him, Captain?'

'Yes, I did,' Raven said briefly.

'But Edward's greatest ambition would be to serve with
you, Sir Gifford,' said Mrs Hendon eagerly. 'He has often
told me how much he admires you. Are you going to sea
again soon, Captain?'

'Not immediately,' said Raven.

'Then you'll be spending some time in Bath?' Miss Clarke's bright eyes flashed curiously between Abigail and Raven.

'Several weeks,' said Raven non-committally.

'But there are so few *public* attractions here at this Season,' Miss Clarke protested. 'For a man such as yourself, in the very prime of life. But perhaps…' she smiled, throwing a meaningful glance at Abigail '…there are *private* attractions to hold you here.'

'I will ask my husband to call upon you, Sir Gifford,' Mrs Lavenham announced. 'We would be honoured by your presence at an informal dinner party we are holding on Friday.'

'I'm obliged,' said Raven curtly.

Abigail's heart beat fast with anxiety. She was mortified by Miss Clarke's vulgar insinuations, but she also sensed Raven's growing impatience with the three women. She'd never seen him lose his temper, but he might easily be provoked into saying something she'd regret—since she would be the one who would later have to listen to the ladies' voluble opinion of him.

'I believe you are due to meet the admiral and your cousin very shortly,' she said, looking enquiringly at Raven.

To her relief he picked up her cue without a blink.

'Indeed I am,' he exclaimed, with uncharacteristic heartiness. 'Ladies, my apologies for leaving you so precipitately, but I hate to be late for an appointment. Miss Summers, may I escort you part of the way?'

Abigail was torn. She didn't want to be left in the clutches of three of the worst gossips in Bath. On the other hand, if she left with Raven she would give them even more to talk about.

'Thank you, Captain.' She smiled a polite dismissal. 'But I know you don't want to keep the admiral waiting, and I'm afraid I simply can't walk very fast in this heat. Please give my compliments to the admiral and Mr Hill.'

'Of course.' He bowed to all four women and strode out of the Pump Room.

'What abrupt manners,' said Mrs Lavenham disparagingly. 'The man may be a hero at sea, but he lacks polish when speaking to ladies.'

'He has a very fine figure,' said Miss Clarke, her gaze lingering on his disappearing back. 'He would look quite spectacular in uniform. And his eye-patch! So deliciously shocking. I could hardly catch my breath when he turned his commanding gaze upon me.'

'Edward has been on half-pay for months,' said Mrs Hendon despairingly. 'Has the Captain not said *anything* to you about returning to sea, Miss Summers?'

All three women turned and fixed their attention on Abigail.

'No, he hasn't,' she said calmly, wondering if this was how it felt to face a firing squad.

'Well, he was certainly very forceful when he was speaking to you earlier,' said Miss Clarke, her inquisitive smile setting Abigail's teeth on edge. 'The two of you seemed quite in a world of your own.'

'Bladud,' said Abigail, fixing on the first unexceptional fact about Bath that came to her mind. 'I was telling him about the legend of Bladud.'

'Who's Bladud?' asked Mrs Hendon. Her interests were entirely contemporary and revolved around the careers of her three sons.

'A leper.' Miss Clarke looked at Abigail in horror. 'You told Sir Gifford about a leper?'

'He was also the son of a king,' said Mrs Lavenham austerely. 'And the founder of our city. Had the waters not cured Bladud, we would not be standing here today. No doubt Sir Gifford's travels have given him an interest in curiosities and antiquities.'

'He seems to be a very well-informed man,' said Abigail cautiously, wary of making too large a claim on Raven's behalf.

'He's a very odd sort of man to speak so urgently about an ancient legend,' said Miss Clarke suspiciously. 'I'm sure you are teasing us, Miss Summers. And what a coincidence—that he should take lodgings directly across the street from you.'

'Isn't it?' said Abigail. 'Please excuse me, ladies. Miss Wyndham will be expecting me.'

'I understand her nephew is visiting,' said Mrs Lavenham. 'A great comfort to her, I'm sure.'

'Yes, indeed,' said Abigail, smiling brightly. 'Goodbye, ladies.'

She hurried out of the Pump Room and didn't even begin to relax until she was halfway up Union Street.

She hoped that Raven had been too overwhelmed by the onslaught of questions and comments to notice Miss Clarke's hateful insinuations. Of all the people they could have encountered, Miss Clarke and Mrs Hendon were two of the most mortifying—Miss Clarke with her vulgar hints and observations, Mrs Hendon with her undignified scramble to find patrons for her sons.

Abigail walked so fast in her agitation that she was out of breath. It was too hot to hurry, so she compelled herself to slow down.

Raven would be in Bath for a few weeks. They were bound to meet on occasion. But Abigail had only to be calm and natural in her dealings with him and she would have no reason to reproach herself.

It was true that Raven was a very attractive man, and very stimulating company, but Abigail had spoken to Mrs Chesney only that morning. The landlady had been full of news about her exciting guests. Abigail now knew that Raven was not just an extremely successful naval officer, he'd also inherited a baronetcy and owned property in several counties. In short, the man was not only a hero—he was also the wealthiest, most eligible bachelor Abigail had ever met.

It would be intolerable if either Raven or the Bath gossips thought she was setting her cap at him.

She did wonder about the strange conversation she'd had with him earlier. It seemed so peculiar that a man in his position, with all the diversions available to him, should even have chosen to read her book—let alone give it as much thought as he clearly had done.

She remembered the first night she'd seen him, when he'd leapt from his bed to confront his nightmares armed only with a dagger. She knew nothing about Raven's naval career. Despite his obvious affection for Raven, Admiral Pullen had never mentioned him before his arrival in Bath. And Abigail had no relatives or close acquaintances in the navy, so she didn't bother to read the *Gazette*.

What adventure had given him those nightmares? Perhaps if she knew that, she would understand the man a little better.

Anthony was sitting in the twilight, beside the open window, when Gifford walked into the drawing room.

'What the devil—?' He broke off as he realised Anthony was listening to pianoforte music, drifting across the street from the house opposite.

'A hawker interrupted a fine sonata a little while ago,' said Anthony softly. 'But fortunately the traffic has been light this evening.'

'Who?' Gifford crossed to the window and looked out. The drawing room was on the first floor. The windows of the room immediately opposite were open, though the curtains were disobligingly closed.

'That'll be Miss Summers,' said Mrs Chesney comfortably, coming into the drawing room behind Gifford. 'I've brought you some supper, sir. I know how hungry you gentlemen get, and I don't want you raiding my larder again. I'll light the candles.'

'No, I'll do it later,' said Gifford quickly. 'Miss Summers is the musician, you say?'

'Oh, yes,' said Mrs Chesney. 'She plays to Miss Wyndham for hours at a time some days. When Admiral Pullen visits, she plays sea shanties for him. Is there anything else I can do for you, gentlemen?'

'No. Thank you,' Gifford replied, aware that Anthony was getting restive at the interruption to his evening's entertainment.

Anthony truly appreciated music. When he went to a concert or the opera he went to listen to the performance—not to socialise with his friends. Gifford enjoyed music, but he lacked Anthony's ability to concentrate on a lengthy piece. After ten or fifteen minutes he'd grow restless, eager to be up and doing again.

'A true test of your patience,' Anthony murmured a little while later, during a brief silence between the first and second movements of a piece. 'To sit in the dark with nothing to do but eat and listen to Mozart.'

'I could eat elsewhere,' Gifford replied. 'Is she good?' he asked abruptly. His ears told him that she was, but he didn't trust his expertise in this field.

'Yes,' said Anthony simply. 'There's an occasional technical hesitancy which would be out of place in the concert hall—but her interpretation of the music is exceptional.'

Anthony's praise pleased Gifford, which he considered ridiculous. He had no proprietary interest in Miss Summers. It was a matter of indifference to him whether she played like an angel or with all the sensitivity of a crow.

From his experience that morning, Bath seemed to be full of vultures, beady-eyed crones who picked and harried anyone unfortunate enough to enter their territory. He'd been only too glad to escape their clutches, though he'd felt guilty at leaving Abigail alone with them. But she'd seemed capable of looking after herself, and he had given her the opportunity to leave with him. It wasn't his fault she'd chosen to stay with the vultures.

He closed his eyes and listened to her play. He'd never

thought of her as a musician—but her performance was full of fire and tender subtlety. He tried to imagine her emotions as she brought the music to life, and for once his attention didn't wander after the first few minutes.

Chapter Four

Gifford jerked awake to the sound of a woman's scream.

It took him three seconds to place himself. Not in the captain's cabin on the *Unicorn*. Not a prisoner on board the privateer. He was in Bath.

Abigail.

He leapt from his bed, instinctively diving for the window. There was nothing to see. Abigail's curtains were drawn and no sound came from her room.

Gifford wrenched open his bedroom door and raced downstairs. A few moments later he was across the street and pounding on the front door of Miss Wyndham's house opposite.

After beating ferociously against the wooden panelling, he stepped back, impatiently scanning the dark house front to see if there was any way he could climb up to the second-floor window.

His feet were bare, he wore nothing but a pair of breeches. Since he couldn't tolerate the airless heat of his room with the curtains drawn, he'd taken to sleeping in the minimum of clothing—to make absolutely sure he never offended Abigail's modesty in future.

'Miss Summers! Miss Summers!' He heard a woman's muffled voice crying and shouting from inside the house.

Then he heard a crash and a thump and another scream.

He hammered on the front door again, then backed off with the intention of breaking it in. He was aware that Anthony had appeared beside him, but he didn't take the time to acknowledge him. He could always count on Anthony for support.

The door opened and he pushed inside. He noted the sketchily dressed footman in passing, but knew Anthony could deal with him if necessary.

'Abigail?' he roared, taking the stairs three at a time. *'Abigail?'*

Apart from the footman's candle, it was dark in the hall and the stairwell. Gifford had to guess the layout of the house. He was on his way up to the second floor when he heard Abigail's voice coming from a room on the first floor.

He spun on the ball of his foot and sprang like a panther down the five feet or more back to the first floor landing.

'Abigail?'

'I'm here.'

He followed the sound of her voice. When he turned the corner of the landing he saw an open door with light flooding out.

He strode inside—and stopped dead.

There were several lanterns placed around the room. He paused for several heartbeats as his eyes adjusted to the light and his mind adjusted to the unexpected sight confronting him. He'd pictured scenes of rape, but he was the only man present until Anthony and the footman came to peer over his shoulder.

They were in Miss Wyndham's bedroom.

There was a woman he'd never seen before, standing to one side, wringing her hands and weeping. There was the old woman on the bed, partially concealed from his gaze by the bed drapes. And there was Abigail.

She was standing next to the bed. She was dressed only in her white muslin nightgown. Her hair fell in rich abandon around her shoulders. In the lantern light it shimmered in a multitude of shades of auburn and red.

Gifford had time to notice how the light shone through the thin muslin, silhouetting her lush body, before she turned towards him and he saw the shocked expression on her face.

She lifted her hands in front of her, almost as if she was in prayer, as she raised her eyes to his.

'She's dead,' she whispered disbelievingly. 'Miss Wyndham's dead.'

'Let me see.' Gifford quickly recovered from his surprise. He went forward, gently moving Abigail aside with his hands on her shoulders, and looked down at the old woman.

She was indeed old, he realised, as he lightly touched the papery skin, then checked for a pulse he was already sure he wouldn't find. For some reason he'd assumed that Miss Wyndham was a middle-aged invalid, but the woman on the bed was well past her three score years and ten. He wondered exactly how old she had been.

'Yes, she's dead,' he said gently, confirming what Abigail and the maid already knew.

Life had stopped making sense to Abigail from the moment she heard Bessie scream. It hadn't occurred to her that anything had happened to Miss Wyndham, she was afraid her suspicions about Charles Johnson had proved true and he'd chosen another victim.

She'd been struggling in the dark to move the chest of drawers from her bedroom door when she'd heard the insistent banging from downstairs. The hammering had confused and alarmed her even more, but before she'd had time to think, Bessie had come knocking and crying at her door. In her efforts to move the chest of drawers Abigail had pulled it right over. It had crashed forward, only just missing her toes.

With Bessie's help she'd pushed the door wide enough to squeeze out and had gone straight to Miss Wyndham's room. She'd barely noticed Raven's second assault on the front door, she'd been too shocked by Miss Wyndham's death. But when she'd heard him call her name she'd realised who it was.

His presence in the house made no sense to her, but Abigail was too glad to see him to question it.

For a moment she covered her face with her hands. There were orders she must give, but she couldn't think clearly enough to know what they were. She wasn't even sure if she'd be able to speak without breaking down.

For nine years Abigail's life had been spent abiding by Miss Wyndham's preferences. The old woman had been frail, but perfectly sharp-witted—and there had been little obvious alteration in her condition for years. It was hard to believe she was dead. Abigail had loved her. She felt as if she'd lost an elderly relative, not an employer.

When she looked up, she saw that every member of the household, including the cook, the footman and the two housemaids, were crowding around Miss Wyndham's open door, murmuring to each other in shocked whispers. With the death of their employer they would all shortly be without a home or a job.

Abigail drew in a deep, unsteady breath. But before she'd had time either to voice reassurances or to formulate orders, Raven took command.

He did so with such natural authority that no one questioned his right to take charge. He sent Anthony on one errand, the footman on another. The footman took a little while to understand his instructions, but Raven repeated them patiently until the manservant was clear what he was to do. Then Raven ordered the cook to make tea for everyone and sent both housemaids to help her.

Bessie, Miss Wyndham's personal maid, was determined to remain with her mistress, and Raven didn't overrule her wishes.

Even in the midst of her distress, Abigail was impressed. Raven had respected the feelings of shock and confusion that threatened to overwhelm the household, but he'd given everyone something to do and started the gradual process of coming to terms with this new state of affairs.

He picked up one of the lanterns and ushered her gently out of Miss Wyndham's bedroom. There were always lanterns left burning in Miss Wyndham's room at night because the old lady had refused to sleep in the dark. They would not need so many candles in future, Abigail thought distractedly, then realised how foolish she was being. Without Miss Wyndham, the household would cease to exist.

'This way.' She recollected herself sufficiently to lead Raven into the front drawing room.

He lit a few more candles from the candle in the lantern and turned to look at her. She realised for the first time he wasn't wearing his eye-patch, but there was nothing particularly disgusting about his old injury. His eyelid covered an empty socket.

The intelligence and authority in his remaining eye more than compensated for his loss.

She also registered that he wasn't wearing a shirt. She'd already seen him completely naked from a distance, but it was somewhat more overwhelming to see him semi-naked when he was only a few feet away. Now she could see the curls of black hair upon his chest. His skin was smooth and firm. His torso was covered in a sheen of perspiration, and the candlelight emphasised the clean definition of his muscles. She could smell his tangy, virile scent.

He resonated with potent energy. He was more alive than anyone Abigail had ever seen. She almost forgot why he was there. Her fingers flexed with the desire to touch him, to discover if he felt as good as he looked.

'Miss Summers,' he said gruffly. 'You should sit down.'

'Oh, yes.' She blinked, then sat in the nearest chair, and gazed around the room. Everything looked so familiar yet the colours were all wrong. Too harsh and acidic. Nothing looked truly real.

'I played for her this evening,' she said blankly, as her eyes settled on the pianoforte. 'Only a few hours ago. There is so much I must do, but I can't think.' She lifted her hands and buried them in her hair, bewildered by the situation.

Raven snatched a breath and turned abruptly away from her. His hasty movement caught her attention. Her eyes fell and she noticed his feet were bare.

'Oh, my,' she murmured. *'Oh!'* She suddenly remembered her feet were also bare, and that her attire was almost as revealing as Raven's.

She was horrified. She glanced around desperately and noticed one of Miss Wyndham's Indian shawls cast over the back of the sofa. She darted forward, seized it, and threw it around her shoulders, carefully covering the whole of her upper body.

She looked up and met Raven's aware gaze. She held her breath. Neither of them spoke, yet there seemed to be layers of meaning in their exchange of glances. Her heart fluttered in her throat.

He smiled crookedly, and asked the question that hadn't yet occurred to her.

'Where's Johnson?'

'I don't...I don't know.' She looked around the room in puzzlement, almost as if she expected Miss Wyndham's nephew to appear from the shadows. 'He was here when I went to bed. He must—surely he must have heard all the commotion?'

'One would have thought so,' said Raven drily. 'Unless he's deaf?'

'I'm sure he isn't... Mrs Chesney!' Abigail said in amazement.

'Miss Summers, I'm sorry to hear your news.' Raven's landlady came briskly into the room. 'Mr Hill fetched me straightaway. Very sensible, sir,' she added, nodding at Raven.

'Oh...he shouldn't have troubled you!' Abigail exclaimed. She'd been so distracted she hadn't paid attention to the content of Raven's instructions to his cousin. 'Thank you for coming. But I'm so sorry you've been disturbed.'

'I was disturbed already by the way the captain slammed out of my house, then thundered on your door,' Mrs Chesney said, with cheerful practicality. 'Enough to wake the dead it was—begging your pardon, my dear.'

For the first time it occurred to Abigail that Raven's presence was quite unaccountable.

'Why…?' She stared at him. 'How did you know?'

'I didn't know Miss Wyndham was dead,' he said briefly. 'But I heard a woman scream. I thought it was you—'

'It was Bessie, when she found her,' Abigail said. 'Poor Bessie, it was such a shock. You came to rescue us!' A smile lit up her face at the idea.

Raven flushed. 'Hardly,' he said tersely. 'I have an ingrained habit of investigating unexplained disturbances… that's all.'

'Yes, sir,' said Mrs Chesney. 'I'm sure we're very grateful. But now you know Miss Summers is not under attack from the French, be good enough to put some clothes on! This is a respectable lady's drawing room. I'll take care of Miss Summers.'

Abigail blinked. Mrs Chesney had spoken to Raven in pretty much the same tone she reserved for her youngest nephew. Abigail's gaze flew to Raven's face to see how he responded to this cavalier treatment. To her surprise, he took his dismissal in good part.

'Thank you, ma'am,' he said. 'I knew I could rely on you.'

Four days after Miss Wyndham's death, Abigail escaped from the demands of the bereaved household to walk in Sydney Gardens. It was the first time since Bessie had screamed that she'd had more than a few minutes to herself for quiet contemplation.

Charles Johnson had returned to the house the following morning with no explanation for his absence. Abigail had already sent for Miss Wyndham's lawyer, Mr Tidewell, and it was Mr Tidewell who'd informed Charles of his great-aunt's death.

Charles had looked momentarily surprised—then unmistakably delighted by the news. He'd tried to hide his gratification beneath a suitably mournful demeanour, but there had been no doubt that his only real interest was in discovering when he would learn the full extent of his inheritance.

Mr Tidewell had been polite, but firm. Miss Wyndham had been his client, not Mr Johnson, and it was her wishes which the lawyer intended to carry out. Miss Wyndham's will was to be read after her funeral. Charles had tried to persuade Mr Tidewell to take a more flexible attitude to his duties, but the lawyer had been stolidly determined. Eventually a dissatisfied Charles had gone to stay with friends outside Bath until his presence was required as chief mourner. Abigail had been glad to see him go.

The servants were understandably worried about their future. One of the housemaids had already found another position. The other one had declared she was shortly to be married. Bessie and the cook were torn between their genuine grief for the mistress they'd served loyally for more than twenty years, and their fear they were too old to find another place. The footman was handsome—Miss Wyndham had always had a weakness for good-looking men—but slow-witted. Abigail felt responsible for all of them—and worried about her own prospects. She hoped Miss Wyndham had made provision for Bessie and the cook but, unlike Charles Johnson, Abigail had no great expectations for herself.

She paused in the welcome shade of a large willow tree. It was late afternoon and the gardens provided a tranquil balm for her anxious spirits. Golden sunlight filtered through the trailing willow fronds. The slender leaves shimmered and whispered in a gentle breeze. The limpid green shadows beneath the tree produced an illusion of coolness, but the weather remained extremely hot.

Abigail turned her face gratefully towards the slight

breeze. Her mourning dress was outmoded and too warm for the season, but with her future so uncertain she was reluctant to make any unnecessary purchases. She hoped Miss Wyndham would understand.

She'd first worn the dress for her father nine years ago. Sir Peter had died in the chilly late autumn, and left behind an even colder atmosphere in the only home Abigail had known. Abigail's mother had died when she was thirteen years old. Sir Peter had remarried a year later. His second wife had treated Abigail with formal correctness, tinged with triumph when she'd produced the son and heir Sir Peter craved.

Sir Peter had left Abigail three hundred pounds in his will and the earnest hope that her young brother would always treat her with generosity and affection. Since the little boy had barely learned to speak by the time of his father's death, that hope was rather optimistic.

It had become clear to Abigail that, if she remained at the Grange, she would always be the poor relation, her presence tolerated because she could be treated like an unpaid servant. So she'd chosen to find a position where, as she'd told Raven, she would at least be paid for running other people's errands.

Lady Summers had protested at Abigail's decision. She was worried that it might reflect badly upon her and, since Abigail was still a minor, her stepmother's wishes might have prevailed. But Abigail had had the support of one of Sir Peter's oldest friends. It was Sir Peter's friend who'd arranged for Abigail to become Miss Wyndham's companion. Had he still been alive, Abigail knew she could have called upon him for help, but the kind old gentleman had died years ago.

She played idly with a flexible willow wand as she considered her situation. She still had her three hundred pounds. Her father's friend had ensured she'd received it on her twenty-first birthday and she'd never spent it. She'd even added to it. Miss Wyndham hadn't paid her much, but

Abigail had been very careful with her money, and interest had added to her capital. For a wild moment she wondered if she should invest it all in a London Season. Or perhaps, less ambitiously, in a Season at another watering place.

She couldn't stay in Bath. Everyone here knew her as Miss Wyndham's poor companion. But, if she went further afield…Harrogate perhaps, or…

But she'd need a sponsor. A lady of unimpeachable reputation who could introduce her into society and act as her chaperon. Abigail knew no one who could fill that role for her. And once she'd spent her money she'd have nothing. Gentlemen were notorious for preferring brides whose charms were bolstered by a comfortable fortune.

Abigail sighed. The picture of herself dancing at Almack's or visiting the theatre was enticing, but she knew it was no more than an idle dream. Her small capital was her only security in the world. If she couldn't find work, or if she ever became too sick or old to work, it was all that would save her from destitution. Most of the time, Abigail tried not to look too far ahead. She took all the reasonable precautions she could to protect her future, then she focussed on finding as much pleasure in the present as possible. When she did look ahead the vision of a lonely, impoverished old age chilled her blood and gave her sleepless nights. The future was a black void she feared and had little control over.

She shivered, in spite of the August sunshine, and brought her attention back to her current precarious situation.

She liked children and she had most of the skills required of a young lady. Miss Wyndham had always encouraged her to practise her music and her sketching. Her embroidery was adequate. At eighteen she'd lacked the confidence to become a governess, but perhaps she'd acquired the necessary authority with age?

She saw a movement from the corner of her eye and turned to see Raven striding towards her. She hadn't seen

him since the night of Miss Wyndham's death, though both
Mrs Chesney and Admiral Pullen had been in regular attendance.

She felt a ripple of pleasurable excitement, modified by
a certain amount of self-conscious shyness. In the midst of
all her other concerns, she hadn't been able to banish the
memory of Raven standing before her barefoot and bare-
chested. When he'd heard Bessie scream he'd dashed to the
rescue without even waiting to dress! The knowledge
thrilled her. He was strong, dangerous...and kind.

He might look like a pirate, but his genuine consideration
for others was beyond doubt. Abigail took comfort from the
knowledge. It gave her the courage she needed to broach a
very important matter with him.

'Miss Summers.' He halted in front of her and took the
hand she instinctively offered. 'How are you?'

'I'm...' She hesitated. The words 'very well' hovered on
her tongue, yet they weren't true, and this man would know
it. 'How are you?' she asked, ducking his question.

'In rude health.' He studied her keenly, his grip on her
fingers tightening. 'I gather Johnson left Bath till the day
of the funeral,' he said abruptly.

'That's right.' Abigail couldn't keep the relief out of her
voice.

'Mrs Chesney tells me you've been cleaning the house
from top to bottom,' said Raven.

'Miss Wyndham leased it,' said Abigail. 'It seems only
right that we should return it to the owner in good order.'

Raven still held her hand in his. She liked it when he
touched her. The physical contact was both reassuring and
thrilling. It would be nice to suppose he found it equally
enjoyable to touch her—but she thought it was more likely
he'd simply forgotten he was holding her hand.

'I'd suggest we stroll on,' said Raven, 'but you don't
have your parasol, and the sun is still quite strong.'

'Frivolous pink,' said Abigail wryly. 'I didn't think it

would be quite the thing. But we could easily keep to the shady paths.'

Raven drew her hand through his arm and they began to walk slowly through the gardens.

'This is not an easy time for you,' he said. 'I know you've had Mrs Chesney and the admiral to call upon, and I'm sure they've served you well—but if there is anything I can do, please—'

Abigail stopped dead. Raven had given her the perfect opening and she had to take it, before she lost her nerve.

'Yes,' she said baldly. 'Captain…Sir Gifford…' She turned to look anxiously up at him. Her blunt statement had surprised him. He searched her face with an intently narrowed gaze.

He was so tall. Abigail realised afresh what a commanding personality he possessed. Her mouth went dry as she considered how presumptuous her request might seem to him. She swallowed and took a deep breath.

'Sir…I'm afraid…that is, I hope you won't think I'm trying to take…take advantage of your kindness to me…' she said in a strangled voice.

'Please, Miss Summers, tell me what it is you want,' he said gently.

'I…well…' Abigail pressed her hands against her overheated cheeks. 'This is very awkward…'

Raven waited while she composed herself. To her relief he didn't seem impatient.

'I'm sorry,' she said at last, laughing uncomfortably. 'I did not know this would be so hard. Mrs Chesney has told me—I don't want you to think we've gossiped about you—but Mrs Chesney has told me that you have several estates?' She looked at him warily. She was encouraged by the fact that he didn't seem offended by her revelation.

'That is so,' he agreed.

'You must employ dozens of individuals—in different capacities,' she said tentatively.

'Hundreds, I imagine,' said Raven. 'I'm not closely acquainted with the day-to-day management of the property.'

'You aren't?' Abigail was startled. 'Oh, of course. You've been at sea,' she added, relieved at this obvious explanation for what she would otherwise have been inclined to consider a dereliction of his duty.

'I'm sure I wouldn't escape your censure if I didn't have that excuse,' Raven murmured, a touch of humour in his voice.

'Censure? Oh, no! Though I do feel a landlord has a responsibility to his tenants...b-but all this is neither here nor there!' Abigail exclaimed, flustered. 'You have distracted me!'

'From henceforth I'll be quiet,' Raven promised. 'Though may I just point out we're standing in the sun. Perhaps we should haul off into the shade before you continue.'

'Of course.' Abigail's skirts swished as she turned smartly about and marched into the shade of the next tree. She was trying to throw herself on Raven's mercy and he was making fun of her! Indignation overcame her natural nervousness. She would not allow him to make a game of her delicacy.

'Sir,' she said briskly. 'I'm seeking places for a cook, a lady's maid and a footman. It seemed to me that you might either have such positions available upon your own estates, or you might know of another employer who is trying to fill such posts.'

'You're trying to find new employment for Miss Wyndham's staff?' Raven exclaimed.

'Yes, sir.' Abigail took advantage of his startled silence to press her case. 'Mrs Thorpe is an excellent cook. Her roasts and soups are particularly good. Her eggs *au miroir* was one of Miss Wyndham's favourite dishes. She is also adept with jellies, trifles and syllabubs.' Mrs Thorpe's Achilles' heel was her pastry, but Abigail decided not to tell Raven about that. 'And, as I mentioned first, her roasts are substantial and excellently dressed,' Abigail emphasised.

Mrs Chesney had told her that Raven was a hearty trencherman, who preferred plain, wholesome fare to fancy sweets.

'Now, Bessie Yapton,' she continued, not sure whether Raven's silence was a good or a bad omen. At least he was doing her the courtesy to listen carefully to her petition. 'Miss Wyndham's maid. I know you probably don't have a place for a lady's maid, sir, but you may have an older female relative who is seeking someone suitable?' She looked at him enquiringly.

'Older?' Raven prompted her, fascination in his gaze.

'Not necessarily,' said Abigail hastily. 'Bessie knows her trade well. But Miss Wyndham was not at the forefront of fashion for some years, so Bessie is not totally familiar with the latest modes...styles of hairdressing, for example. But she kept Miss Wyndham's clothes in perfect condition. Her needlework is very fine. For mending, you understand,' Abigail hastened to assure him. 'I don't mean she gives herself airs with a tambour frame when her mistress needs her. She is hard-working, honest and loyal.' Abigail hesitated a moment, frowning. 'Did I mention that Mrs Thorpe is also hard-working, honest and loyal?' she asked.

'I believe that was implicit in your testimonial,' Raven said gravely.

'Good!' Abigail took a deep breath. 'Now Joshua,' she said resolutely. 'The footman. He is not *very* sharp-witted, but he is good-natured and hard-working. Miss Wyndham gave him a splendid livery. He's so proud of it and he's always taken very good care of it. I don't think he would be suitable for a position of *responsibility*, but he would be a very impressive addition to any large hallway you might have in any of your houses. With a big sweeping staircase. I always thought Joshua was wasted in our little house. He's also very patient and gentle. He used to carry Miss Wyndham between her bedroom and drawing room every day.

She always enjoyed that.' Abigail sighed. 'I didn't realise how comfortable our life was until now it's gone,' she said sadly. Then she smiled hopefully at Raven. 'Do you think you may be able to help?'

'To find places for a cook, a lady's maid and a footman?' he said. 'I have no idea, but I will certainly enquire. The man in the best position to help you is my uncle, Malcolm Anderson. He has managed all my family's affairs for years, first on behalf of my father, and now for me. I'll ask him.'

'Thank you so much!' Abigail exclaimed. 'I hate to impose on you like this, but you're the only person I know who might be able to help. Admiral Pullen is very kind, but he lives in lodgings. He doesn't need a cook, and he wouldn't know what to do with a lady's maid or a footman!'

'Surely it's Mr Johnson's responsibility to take care of his aunt's staff,' Raven said drily.

'Oh.' Abigail stared at him blankly. The idea had never occurred to her. 'Oh…yes…I suppose so. But I d-don't think…that is, it is obviously easier for me to deal with the matter because I know them all so much better than he does,' she said, recovering her poise.

'What about you?' Raven asked.

'Me?' Abigail squeaked, alarmed by the question. 'Oh, no, sir! I assure you. You mustn't think I w-want you to do anything for m-me! No, indeed.' She smoothed down her black skirts in an agitated gesture and started to walk off through the gardens.

She'd dreaded the possibility Raven might think she was asking help for herself. Miss Clarke's horrible insinuations that she was throwing her cap at Raven still rang in her ears. As if she would do such a thing! The mere suggestion was mortifying. If he hadn't been such a handsome, attractive man, she could have laughed off the notion without a second thought. But, of course he was handsome and attractive, and it was absolutely essential he should understand she wanted no favours from him—that she had no inappropriate expectations of *any* kind.

Raven's long legs easily kept up with her hurried pace. He let her continue at her breakneck speed for a little while, then he put his hand on her arm, obliging her to slow down.

'It's too warm for so much exertion, he said apologetically.

'It is m-most important,' said Abigail breathlessly, swinging round to face him. 'You should understand that I d-do not *at all* wish you to…to be of pecuniary or…or employable…employ…find me a job!' she finished, inelegantly but unambiguously. 'No, *indeed*!'

'I'm sorry I insulted you,' Raven said stiffly.

Abigail heaved in a deep breath. She was very hot and very agitated. 'You did not,' she said. 'Of course you d-didn't. I did not mean to offend you, either. Perhaps I am a *little* sensitive on the subject. But I assure you—I am perfectly capable of fending for myself.'

'I know you are,' said Raven. 'May I ask—if you won't consider it an impertinence—how you intend to do so?'

Abigail winced at his pointed phraseology. 'Oh, please, don't be angry with me!' she begged, impulsively laying her hand on his arm. 'I'm sure you understand. Mrs Thorpe and Bessie, they are quite…quite mature. They are afraid it may be hard to find another place. They are not old!' she added hastily. 'But not in their first youth either. And Joshua—he needs someone to speak for him. But I—'

'Don't,' Raven finished for her, as she struggled to find a less antagonistic way of repeating what she'd already said.

'Sometimes, perhaps I do,' she said honestly. 'But in this situation…' She realised she was still clutching Raven's sleeve and quickly withdrew her hand. 'Oh, dear.' She'd creased the blue cloth and she tried to smooth it with quick, nervous gestures. Then she realised that stroking Raven's arm was totally improper and snatched her hand away.

'I'm sorry. I didn't mean… A g-governess.' She switched topics desperately. 'I like children. I think they like me…that is, Mrs Chesney's grandchildren like me,' she said conscientiously. 'I have taught two of them their letters. And I have many…that is, *some* of the necessary accomplishments of a young lady. I play…I play…I play the pianoforte a little.' She blushed, uncomfortable at singing her own praises. 'I can sketch…a little. In short, I think I would suit a genteel family with not too many ambitions for their daughters. I c-cannot speak French or Italian,' she concluded, rather defiantly.

Raven's lips twitched and he glanced away across the gardens. When he looked back at Abigail his expression was perfectly sober.

'You wish to become a governess?' he said gravely.

'I think it might be a rewarding occupation,' she said cautiously. 'Of course, I don't have much experience. But I believe…I hope Mr Tidewell will provide me with a reference. If you know of anyone looking for a governess, of course I would…but that did not seem very likely to me. And you are not in a position to recommend me,' she continued more confidently. 'You do not *know* if I have the accomplishments I've just claimed. And even if you did—it would seem very odd if you sponsored me. I don't want to hurt your feelings, but I don't think a gentleman's recommendations would help my cause.'

'A cogent point,' said Raven. 'But what will you do—where will you live—while you are looking for a suitable position?'

Abigail hesitated. 'Mrs Chesney…the very first night when you sent for her—she asked me to stay with her until I can find a suitable place. In her part of the house, of course,' Abigail assured him earnestly. 'I wouldn't be in your way at all. In fact, you won't even know I'm there,' she finished optimistically.

'That would be a pity,' said Raven.

'Oh.' Abigail blushed. 'I don't mean to be tiresome,' she said a few seconds later. 'But would you…do you suppose you could ask Mr Anderson about Bessie and the others soon? They are so worried.'

'Yes, I will,' he assured her.

'Thank you.' Abigail sighed with relief and then smiled radiantly at him. 'It's such a weight off my mind,' she said. 'I know you cannot promise anything, but at least I've *asked*.'

Malcolm Anderson was already ensconced in the drawing room when Gifford returned from his walk in Sydney Gardens with Abigail.

'Good God!' he exclaimed. 'I didn't expect you for another two days.'

'I'm yours to command,' Anderson replied, in his dry Scottish accent. 'I have but to receive your summons and I fly to your side. Actually, I was on the point of leaving London for Oxfordshire when I received your letter, but one should always curry favour where one can.'

Gifford grinned and shook his uncle's hand. Malcolm Anderson had managed the Raven family affairs for nearly twenty years. Malcolm's older sister had married Gifford's father and, since Malcolm was a younger brother with no prospects of his own, he had rapidly shifted his loyalty to his sister's new family.

He'd worked hard to protect and extend the interests of the Raven family, but he'd also done well on his own account. Gifford suspected Anderson would resist any attempt to relieve him of some or all of his responsibilities. If Gifford did stay in England it was a situation which would need to be handled with some delicacy.

But that was for the future. In the meantime, it was Miss Wyndham's bereaved staff who needed to be handled with delicacy.

'We need a place for a cook, a lady's maid and a footman,' he said to his uncle, and proceeded to tell him what he'd heard about them from Abigail.

'You summoned me to Bath for this?' Anderson enquired, when Gifford had finished.

'No,' Gifford admitted. 'Somewhat foolishly, it hadn't occurred to me that Miss Summers would be so concerned with the servants. It was her situation I thought you might be able to help with.'

'Really?' Anderson leant forward, his shrewd eyes sharp with curiosity. 'Why?'

'She is not without friends in Bath,' said Gifford, remembering the admiral and Mrs Chesney. 'But unfortunately they lack resources. You, on the other hand, have an infinite number of resources available to you, and a very creative way of making the best use of them.'

Anderson grinned. 'You have a fine knack of evading the question, lad. What do you have in mind for your Miss Summers?'

'She's taken a notion to be a governess,' said Gifford. 'But she's adamant she doesn't want any assistance for herself—only for the rest of the household. So you might as well start with them. We'll call upon them tomorrow morning and you can arrange everything.'

Anderson laughed. 'I could make some suggestions now,' he said. 'You could convey them directly to Miss Summers if you wish. I'm sure she'd be very impressed with you.'

Gifford threw his uncle a sideways look. 'I'm not trying to impress her,' he said edgily. 'Besides, this place is a hotbed of scandal. I've done my best over the past few days to avoid giving the gossips any more ammunition. We'll tell Miss Summers you came to see me about family business and I took the opportunity to mention her worries about the staff.'

'As you wish.' Anderson's eyebrows lifted almost to his hairline, but he didn't comment any further on his nephew's behaviour.

Chapter Five

'What's he doing here?' Charles demanded belligerently, gesturing towards Admiral Pullen.

'Admiral Pullen is one of the executors,' said Mr Tidewell calmly. 'Miss Wyndham wished that he should be present.'

'And them?' Charles waved towards the servants sitting uncomfortably around the seldom-used mahogany table.

Mr Tidewell had decided the dining room was the most convenient place in which to reveal the contents of Miss Wyndham's will.

'They are also present at Miss Wyndham's request,' Mr Tidewell replied. 'If you will be patient a little longer, sir, I'm sure all your questions will be answered.'

Despite her nervousness, Abigail had to suppress a quick smile. Mr Tidewell's dislike of Miss Wyndham's great-nephew was evident, though he concealed it beneath professional courtesy.

Abigail expected nothing for herself, except perhaps a small token of gratitude, but she did hope that Miss Wyndham had remembered Bessie Yapton and Mrs Thorpe, though the matter was less pressing than it had been a few days before. Mr Malcolm Anderson, Raven's uncle, had already offered places to both women and to Joshua. Bessie and Mrs Thorpe would be leaving to take up new positions on Raven's Oxfordshire estate the very next day. And Joshua had been offered a place at the town house in Berkeley Square.

Abigail was so happy for them, and so relieved she no longer had to worry about their future.

Mr Anderson had also asked if there was anything he could do to help *her*. His manner had been so disinterestedly kind yet also practical that she'd found it surprisingly easy to confide her plans to him. When she'd blushingly said that she thought she had many of the skills necessary to be a governess he'd asked her to show him examples of her embroidery and painting. Then he'd asked her to play upon the pianoforte. She'd even shown him the household accounts she'd kept for Miss Wyndham, to demonstrate her facility for practical mathematics.

Mr Anderson had complimented her briefly, but sincerely, upon her accomplishments, and said he would make enquiries on her behalf. Abigail sensed he was a man of his word. She didn't plan to depend upon his services, but she did feel less anxious about her future after speaking with him.

'If everyone is ready?' Mr Tidewell glanced around the dining room. 'Thank you.'

To Abigail's relief, Miss Wyndham had left forty pounds each to Bessie and Mrs Thorpe. She'd also bequeathed some of her clothes to the two women. They had the option of selling the garments, or of keeping them for their own use.

A few moments later, Abigail was dumbfounded to discover that she was to receive Miss Wyndham's finest gowns. Dresses of silk and satin more costly than anything Abigail had ever worn before. Silk and cashmere shawls. Three pelisses. Two riding habits.

Abigail was speechless with shock as Mr Tidewell's precise voice described in careful detail each of the garments Miss Wyndham had left to her. *Riding habits?* Abigail had never known Miss Wyndham to ride in the whole time she'd been her companion. But now Abigail was the over-whelmed owner of one riding habit of peacock blue, and another of burgundy red. And so many other fine clothes...

She pressed her fingers against her trembling lips and glanced around the table at her companions. She saw that both Bessie and the cook were nodding with satisfaction.

'Good,' said Bessie. 'We talked about which would be the best gowns for you,' she told a bemused Abigail. 'Miss Wyndham and me. They were very old-fashioned, of course, but I've already made most of them over into the current mode for you. Miss Wyndham enjoyed that. We looked at all the latest fashion plates. And she liked to make suggestions for the alterations...' Bessie's voice failed and her eyes filled with tears.

Mrs Thorpe patted her hand comfortingly.

Abigail's throat grew tight with emotion. The idea that Miss Wyndham and her lady's maid had taken so much trouble on her behalf was almost unbearably poignant.

'Can we get on!' Charles demanded impatiently.

Miss Wyndham had left Joshua ten pounds and his splen-did footman's livery. She also spoke kindly of his diligence and honesty.

Charles Johnson drummed his fingers on the dining room table and muttered with dissatisfaction. Mr Tidewell peered at him over the top of document he held in his hand, then continued reading at the same measured pace.

'To Miss Abigail Summers I bequeath my pianoforte...'

Abigail's mouth dropped open. She'd expected a token. Perhaps a small ornament or personal item. But she'd al-ready received all the finest of Miss Wyndham's clothes. And now the pianoforte...

Abigail knew the instrument was one of the only two pieces of furniture which Miss Wyndham had actually owned. All the other pieces had been leased with the house.

'To my nephew Charles Johnson, I leave my bed...'

Mr Tidewell read the closing sentences of Miss Wynd-

ham's will, and then laid it upon the dining room table and
folded his hands on top of it.

'Go on, man! Go on!' Charles snarled.

'There is no more,' said Mr Tidewell placidly.

'What the hell are you talking about?' Charles plunged
forward and snatched a corner of the will, dragging it out
from beneath Mr Tidewell's hands.

Abigail heard the sound of tearing, then Charles rapidly
scanned the maltreated document.

He swore viciously as he reached the end, balled it up in
his hands and hurled it at Mr Tidewell.

'Is this some kind of lawyer's joke!' He shouted.
'Where's the real will?'

Admiral Pullen was on his feet, standing between Mr
Tidewell and Charles Johnson, though the lawyer seemed
undisturbed by Johnson's outburst.

Abigail clenched her hands in her lap. Her heart hammered with alarm at the ugly scene. This was what she'd
been afraid of from the moment they'd entered the dining
room.

She hadn't anticipated Miss Wyndham's generosity to
her, because she'd known how little the old woman had to
leave—but she had anticipated Charles Johnson's rage
when he discovered how little he would inherit.

'This is Miss Wyndham's will,' said Mr Tidewell flatly.

'Dammit, man, what about this house? Her fortune. She's
been living on its interest for years!'

'She had no capital,' said Mr Tidewell. His voice was
dry and precise. Only the angry glint in his eyes revealed
how much he disliked his late client's young relative. 'She
received no interest. She was the recipient of an annuity,
paid to her quarterly. With her death, the annuity also dies.
She leased this house and all the furniture in it—with the
exception of the pianoforte and her bed. This document is
a true expression of her wishes.'

He carefully opened out the crushed will and smoothed
it very deliberately against the table top.

'What about her jewels?' Charles flung at him. 'My grandmother often mentioned her jewels. Answer that, vulture!'

'Vulture?' Bessie started up in outrage. 'Aye, she had jewels. Once. They're all gone now. Unforeseen expenses, she told me, when I asked her where they were. She sold them to cover *unforeseen expenses.'*

'What unforeseen expenses?' Charles braced his knuckles on the table top and leant forward menacingly.

Bessie mirrored his pose, leaning forward with her palms resting on the table. Their faces were barely a foot apart.

'You!' she cried, all her hatred of him throbbing in her voice. 'She sold them to give you the money you came a-begging for. There's nothing left for you to take. You already sucked her dry!'

'You doxy!' Charles swayed back, then lifted his hand to strike her.

Joshua knocked him down. Charles crashed into a chair, then sprawled, dazed on the floor for several seconds.

'Well done, man!' Admiral Pullen exclaimed.

Joshua flushed. He rubbed his grazed knuckles and looked anxiously at Abigail for confirmation that he'd done the right thing.

'Thank you,' she said, as calmly as she could. 'That was very chivalrous of you. Very gentlemanly,' she added, when she saw that he didn't know what she meant. She managed to smile, so that he would know for sure she wasn't cross with him.

'He didn't ought to have talked to Bessie like that,' said Joshua. He scowled and lifted his fists into a fighting stance as Charles stumbled to his feet.

'I believe Mr Johnson's business here is now concluded,' said Mr Tidewell. 'You will no doubt wish to make arrangements for the removal of the bed, sir...'

'I don't want the damn bed!' Charles spat. 'What good is that to me?'

His necktie was ruined. He clutched his hand against the

side of his jaw, where Joshua had hit him. His narrowed eyes blazed with spite. He looked vicious—like a cornered rat.

He frightened Abigail more now than he ever had before.

'Get out of here!' Admiral Pullen thundered. 'Joshua! Put him out!'

'Yes, sir!' Joshua grabbed Charles' arm and hustled him out of the dining room.

Joshua might not be needle-witted, but Miss Wyndham had initially hired him at least partly because of his splendid physique. He was several inches taller than Charles and, on the evidence so far, his fighting reflexes seemed to be considerably faster.

Abigail realised she'd been holding her breath. She released it in a long, very unsteady breath. Her ribs ached with tension. Her heart still pounded with the horror of the past few minutes. She drew in several slow breaths in an attempt to calm herself.

'Miss Summers?' Admiral Pullen came around the table to take her hand. 'Do you feel faint?' he enquired solicitously. 'I'm sorry you had to witness such an ugly scene.'

Abigail swallowed and made a determined effort to appear composed. On her other side, Bessie was panting with anger and indignation.

'I've bin wanting to speak me mind for years!' she exclaimed excitably. 'Vulture, indeed! Hah! Who was the real vulture, hey?' She burst into tears.

Mrs Thorpe patted her shoulder and made soothing noises.

'I believe you spoke for us all, Miss Yapton,' Mr Tidewell observed. 'This is a sad time for all of us—Miss Wyndham will be sorely missed—but the one fortunate consequence is that none of us will need to have any further dealings with Mr Johnson.'

'Perhaps…' Abigail's voice trembled. She consciously relaxed her shoulders and tried again. 'Perhaps we should all retire to the drawing room,' she suggested. 'Miss Wynd-

ham never used this room. It seems more fitting we
should…should offer a toast to her upstairs. Mrs Thorpe,
do you think you could find something suitable for the occasion?'

'Yes, miss,' the cook agreed eagerly. 'Miss Wyndham
had me set aside a fine brandy for this very occasion. She
didn't want long faces… I was just waiting for *him*—' her
jerky nod indicated the recently departed Charles '—to
leave before I brought it out. If you'll all go upstairs, I'll
be there in a trice.'

'She left me her dresses—such exquisite dresses—Bessie
showed them all to me,' Abigail said, still awed by the
magnificence of what she'd seen. 'And her pianoforte. I
never imagined…she was so *generous*.'

She was sitting in Mrs Chesney's drawing room, in the
soothing company of Admiral Pullen, Mr Anderson and Mr
Hill, and the rather less soothing presence of Gifford Raven.

After they'd all toasted Miss Wyndham with the fine
brandy Mrs Thorpe had produced, the admiral had decided
that what Abigail really needed was a calming cup of tea
well away from the scene of the recent débâcle.

'You were her loyal companion for nine years,' Pullen
said stoutly. 'Of course she treated you generously.'

'The dresses are already made over,' Abigail said wonderingly. 'Just think of them both—Bessie and Miss Wyndham—taking such trouble.'

'You've certainly repaid Bessie's trouble,' said Malcolm
Anderson. 'And before you knew the part she'd played in
your inheritance. She seems well satisfied with the position
I offered her.'

'Joshua would make a fine prizefighter!' said Admiral
Pullen. 'I had no idea the fellow was so fast. No flourishing,
or signalling his attentions.' He demonstrated with a quick
jab of his right fist. 'Splendid!'

'Joshua is *not* going to be a prizefighter,' Abigail retorted hotly. 'He's going to be a footman in Berkeley Square?' She glanced questioningly at Anderson for confirmation.

'That's right,' he said. 'Although, I'm wondering…' His eyes narrowed thoughtfully. 'By your account of this afternoon's events, his loyalty to you and to the rest of Miss Wyndham's household is very strong. I'm wondering if it might serve better to send him to Oxfordshire with the two women.'

'He is more comfortable with people he knows,' Abigail agreed. 'But…do you need a footman in Oxfordshire?' she asked worriedly. 'I did not intend…that is, he is not to be a burden upon you. But he does need a *little* guidance.'

'I'd say he deserves a pension for life—just for knocking Johnson down!' Raven said unexpectedly.

'Hear, hear. Couldn't agree more!' the admiral agreed enthusiastically. 'Now. Where are you planning to wear those splendid gowns, Miss Summers? A Season in London at the very least, I hope.'

'Oh, no!' Abigail protested instinctively.

She was overwhelmed by Miss Wyndham's generosity, but neither the clothes nor the pianoforte altered her fundamental situation. She was already trying to come to terms with the knowledge she would have to sell her inheritance. She would keep a few of the dresses, she couldn't bear to part with them, but when the lease expired on the house she would have nowhere to keep the pianoforte.

'Wouldn't you enjoy a London Season?' Raven asked brusquely.

'Oh…well, yes…I think I m-might,' Abigail replied, flustered both by the question and his unusually terse manner.

All through the conversation she'd been intensely aware of Raven's listening presence. She tried not to look too conscious, or glance too often in his direction. These men were all his friends. She wasn't nervous when she met any of them individually, but it was very agitating to find herself surrounded by them—and with Raven himself in the same room. She was afraid they might notice something different in her manner when she spoke to him. And she was afraid *he* might think she was trespassing on his goodwill, or…or…taking advantage…if she addressed him too familiarly.

'Of course you would,' said the admiral. 'It's high time you danced the night away and broke a few hearts into the bargain!'

Abigail blushed and took care not to look in Raven's direction. In her secret dreams he was the man she wanted to dance with—but she'd die of embarrassment if any of the men present guessed that.

'I can't dance!' she exclaimed, saying the first thing that came into her head. 'I never had the opportunity to learn.'

'I can,' said Anthony cheerfully. 'Country dances. The minuet…quadrille…cotillion…the waltz. I perform them all with grace and precision. I'll teach you.'

'That's very kind of you.' Abigail gazed at him helplessly. 'I do appreciate your offer, but I really don't think…'

'You will need a sponsor,' said Malcolm Anderson briskly. 'I know two or three ladies who would be suitable and might be agreeable to introducing you to the *ton*.'

'Splendid!' said Admiral Pullen, rubbing his hands together with satisfaction. 'Anderson will find you a chaperon. Hill will teach you to dance. You have the gowns already. What else must be arranged for your first Season?'

Abigail pressed her hands against her cheeks. Her head was spinning with all these suggestions which sounded staggeringly like foregone conclusions as far as her companions were concerned.

'I haven't anywhere to put the pianoforte,' she whispered, plucking one coherent thought out of all the dreams, hopes, and sharp-splintered doubts which whirled around in her mind.

'Bring it here,' Pullen said. 'Mrs Chesney will look after it for you.'

'I thought I will have to sell it,' she replied, her confusion

evident in her muddled tenses. 'I don't want to,' she added
quickly. 'It's a beautiful instrument. I love to play it. But...I
have nowhere to put it.'

'Mrs Chesney will look after it,' the admiral repeated
impatiently. 'We must decide what you are to do for the
rest of the summer. You should begin your dancing lessons
straight away. Can you dance?' he shot the question at
Raven.

'Not with Anthony's degree of expertise,' Raven replied.

'You can have lessons as well, then,' the admiral decided.

'Please...!' Abigail threw up her hands, palms outward.
'Please. I do appreciate everything...everything... But I
can't have a London Season!'

The silence following her declaration sounded very loud
to her. All the men stared at her. She drew in a careful
breath and tried to speak calmly.

'It is very kind of you all to plan such wonderful things
for me,' she said unsteadily, 'but it's really not...not *possible*. Please don't think me ungrateful, but it wouldn't... I
don't... In short, gentleman, I am not a suitable candidate
for such an enterprise,' she said desperately. 'A lady whose
dowry consists of one pianoforte does not have many prospects in the Marriage Mart—I think that's what you all have
in mind, isn't it?' She glanced around at their startled faces,
though she avoided Raven's eye. 'And I could never mis-
represent myself as something I'm not.'

'But you might still enjoy yourself,' said Anthony, and
smiled at her. 'After nine years of loyal service, I think you
are entitled to a holiday, Miss Summers.'

Abigail let her hands fall into her lap. She was confused,
agitated and suddenly exhausted after all the excitements of
the day.

'All this can be discussed at a later time,' said Raven,
standing up. 'Miss Summers has had no chance to rest since
Miss Wyndham died. I will escort you home, ma'am.'

'Oh.' Abigail was disconcerted by his abrupt statement,

but she didn't argue with him. 'Thank you.' She took the hand he offered her and let him draw her to her feet. 'I do thank you, gentlemen, all of you, for your kind suggestions. But I really don't think they are practical.'

'Would you like to take a little walk?' Raven asked, when he and Abigail had gained the relative privacy of the pavement.

'I…yes. If it's not an inconvenience to you,' Abigail said breathlessly.

'Not at all,' said Raven.

They walked slowly down the steep street for several minutes before either spoke.

Abigail's thoughts were still in a turmoil. The idea of a Season in London—of dancing with Raven—was so enticing. So different from the future she'd planned for herself. One moment she thought perhaps it was a dream that *could* come true—the next she knew it was an impossibility.

Would Raven dance with her? She sneaked a quick glance at him from the corner of her eye. Deep down she knew the most seductive aspect of going to London was the chance it might offer of extending her friendship with Raven.

She'd known from the first meeting that he intended to spend only a month in Bath. Even if she accepted Mrs Chesney's kind invitation, they would be living under the same roof only briefly. Raven would be gone within the next few weeks.

But if she went to London…

Was it worth sacrificing the security of her future for a few nights of dancing and glamour now?

'Why don't you wish to go to London?' Raven asked, breaking into her musings.

'Oh, I do!' she exclaimed, before she could stop herself. 'I…that is, I've never been to London.' She tried to sound more composed.

'Never?' Raven stopped walking, clearly startled by her unthinking revelation.

'No.' She looked up at him. 'I was born in a small village near Gloucester. Then I went to live with Miss Wyndham in a small house a few miles north of Bath. Then about five years ago Miss Wyndham decided to move into Bath itself. She was still able to visit the Pump Room when we first arrived. Sometimes we went to the Assemblies. But after the first year she wasn't strong enough to go out anymore.'

'You've barely travelled fifty miles from your birth-place!' Raven said wonderingly. 'How can you tolerate—?' He broke off. 'I beg your pardon,' he said. 'Not everyone has a desire to travel incessantly.'

'I would like to travel,' said Abigail. 'Admiral Pullen has told me so many stories…he promised me that *you* would tell me tales about faraway lands,' she reminded Raven brightly. 'I hope you will before you leave Bath.'

'Before I leave Bath?' Raven focussed on only one part of what she'd said.

'You are only here for a month,' she said. 'And you've already been here…some time.' She didn't want to reveal she'd been counting off the days till his departure.

'Ah, yes. That is so,' Raven agreed.

They took several measured steps in an electric silence.

'Why do you feel unable to go to London?' Raven demanded. 'I've never known Malcolm's assurances to lack substance. If he says he can find you a patroness, be sure he can.'

'I *am* sure! But only consider, sir. I have no fortune. Well, I have a little,' she corrected conscientiously. 'I have three hundred pounds from my father, and I've added to it a little by savings and interest. But if I have a Season in London, it will all be gone—'

'No, it won't!' Raven protested. 'You have Miss Wyndham's dresses. There may be a few other trifling expenses— but hardly enough to eat into your capital.'

Abigail smiled tremulously at his fierce assertion. He was

arguing in favour of her going to London, but it didn't seem as if he had a personal interest in her visit. He sounded much more like Mr Anderson and the admiral, who had both obviously intended her to display herself to her best advantage in the London Marriage Mart. They'd even settled it amongst themselves that she was to have dancing lessons from Mr Hill!

She didn't know whether to be grateful or mortified by their clumsy efforts to arrange her future.

'I see no reason why you should leave Bath yet,' Raven declared. 'You can accept Mrs Chesney's invitation to stay with her—and I'm sure she'll be pleased to look after your pianoforte. Anthony can teach you the cotillion and the waltz and…what have you.' Raven's knowledge of fashionable dances was somewhat less extensive than his cousin's. 'So when Malcolm has arranged things in London you'll be fully prepared. This will be the first Season I have ever spent in London,' he added casually.

'The *first*…?' Abigail exclaimed, as surprised by his revelation as he had earlier been by hers.

'I've visited London briefly during the Season,' Raven said. 'I've certainly attended balls and routs. I've even danced at Almack's—though I'm afraid I didn't appreciate the honour as much as I perhaps should—but I've never spent more than a couple of weeks at a time in such activity. And I've often gone years between balls.'

'Then you'll have to ask Mr Hill to teach *you* to dance,' Abigail dared to tease him.

'Only if you'll go to London,' he said.

Abigail gasped. She couldn't believe she'd heard him correctly. Was he suggesting he wanted to extend their friendship beyond these few weeks in Bath?

'I don't think many other ladies would be brave enough to dance with such an unsightly fellow,' Raven said.

Shock held Abigail rigid for two seconds. Then his comment knocked every other thought out of her head. She swung to face him.

'You are *not* unsightly! How can you *think* such a thing?'

'I see myself every morning when I shave,' Raven said tightly. 'I know what I look like.'

'You don't know anything!' Abigail's voice shook with anger. 'You are a s-stupid man!'

She spun away from him and marched off down the street. When Raven caught up with her she stopped so suddenly he nearly outpaced her. She prodded him in the chest.

'How can you think such a thing? You should be ashamed to say such a thing!'

She strode off again, leaving him no time to respond.

'Abigail…! Miss Summers…' Raven hurried after her, for once in his life completely at a loss for words.

It had never occurred to him that Abigail might be capable of displaying such anger. Or that she might *ever* be angry with him. He'd only made a simple statement of fact.

Her blazing green eyes rocketed every coherent thought out of his head. He'd heard her passionate nature translated into her music—but now he was experiencing its strength at first hand. He wanted to seize her and kiss her. He wanted to shout back that she had no business to abuse him. He didn't permit *anyone* to call him stupid.

'I beg your pardon,' said Abigail, looking straight ahead, but slowing to a more reasonable pace. 'I should not have insulted you. But you should not have said such a ridiculous thing.'

'I don't consider it ridiculous,' Gifford said tautly. 'I'm scarred across half my face. I have only one eye. Do you have any idea how hard it is to judge distances when you have only one eye? How often I miss my stroke?'

'Now you are confusing the practical consequences of your injury with other people's reactions to it,' Abigail said. 'Because *you* are frustrated by the limitations it imposes on you, doesn't mean the rest of us share your bitter feelings towards it.'

'I am not bitter!' Gifford's voice rose with rage and indignation. 'I was lucky to survive.'

Abigail stopped and turned to face him. 'You said a woman would have to be brave to dance with you. Those are not the words of a man who is at ease with his appearance.'

'It's not my lack of ease I was worried about.' Gifford suddenly realised their heated conversation was attracting the attention of other people taking a quiet promenade in the warmth of the early evening. He forced himself to lower his voice. 'It was the shock of other people suddenly confronted by it I was considering,' he said in a fierce undertone. 'What is acceptable on a man-of-war is not necessarily equally acceptable in a lady's drawing room.'

'If a lady should turn you out of her drawing room for having been injured in the fight to *preserve* her drawing room, then she doesn't deserve to *have* a drawing room!' Abigail said categorically.

'So my scar does not disturb you?' said Gifford.

Abigail pressed her lips together and didn't deign to reply.

Gifford suddenly remembered the night of Miss Wyndham's death, when he had raced to Abigail's rescue without even considering whether he was wearing his eye-patch. Abigail had been confronted by him at his most gruesome, and she hadn't flinched at all. Of course, she'd already been in shock, but she might still have shown a little discomfort if she'd been prone to do so.

The lady's maid and the cook had been shocked by Miss Wyndham's death, but they'd also been upset by his scar. He'd seen how both women had first stared at it in horrified fascination and then carefully averted their gaze from his empty eye socket. He'd noticed a similar dreadful fascination with his eye-patch in at least one of the gossiping women Abigail had introduced him to in the Pump Room. He'd been indifferent to whether he shocked the gossiping women—he was even capable of playing up to their expectations of his piratical nature. But he wasn't indifferent to Abigail's opinion of him.

'I am not bitter,' he said. 'It was the fortune of war.'

'V-very philosophical.'

She was still angry with him. Gifford discovered he very much wanted Abigail to stop being angry with him. Unfortunately he had absolutely no experience in coaxing the people around him into a better mood. A captain who tried to placate his men was a captain heading for disaster, in Gifford's opinion. He'd never courted popularity. Consistency and equal treatment for everyone was a far better recipe for success.

'Perhaps we should turn around,' he said. 'We've walked quite a distance.'

'As you wish.' Abigail smartly about-faced and began to head back the way they'd come.

'You must be aware that not everyone has your indifference to…physical irregularities,' said Gifford carefully.

Abigail sighed, and fished in her reticule. She extricated her fan.

'I know,' she admitted. 'It is so *very* hot, even this late in the day,' she complained, fanning herself briskly.

Gifford wasn't surprised she was overheated. The weather was unpleasantly humid and, even to his inexperienced eye, Abigail's gown seemed too heavy for the season.

'Perhaps there might be a cooler dress amongst those Miss Wyndham has left you,' he suggested.

Abigail shot him an unreadable look and he wondered if he'd said the wrong thing. It seemed a perfectly sensible comment to him.

'She might have had a black parasol,' he added, remembering what Abigail had said about the unsuitability of her pink one. 'Did she leave you any parasols?'

Abigail started to laugh.

'What is it?' Gifford was first surprised and then bewildered by Abigail's inexplicable merriment.

She hid her face behind her fan and simply laughed.

'I don't see what's so amusing,' Gifford said stiffly. 'What is so funny? It was a very practical question.'

'I'm sorry.' Abigail retrieved her handkerchief and wiped her eyes. Then she fanned her hot pink cheeks. Gifford wished he could tear off her hideous black bonnet. She couldn't be comfortable in it. But no doubt he would shock everyone if he did that—Abigail included. He liked the way her eyes sparkled with warmth. He smiled himself in response to her vitality.

'I was just thinking about…about…the kindness all you gentlemen have shown me,' Abigail said unsteadily.

'You find kindness a cause for laughter?' Gifford couldn't understand it. How could she find kindness a source of humour when she'd been so cross with him for disparaging his own appearance—something he had every right to do, now he came to think of it. It was his face.

'No, no. I didn't mean that. It's just that you are all so…so practical and logical about what I need to do to have a London Season,' Abigail explained. 'I can't say exactly why it's funny. But only imagine if I came on board your ship, and started ordering you to 'luff your helm' or something similar. All the words might be correct, but what I said and the context I said them in might provoke you to laughter.'

'Our ideas seem naïve to you?' said Raven. He remembered the world described in the novel he'd read and thought perhaps she was right. The subtle gradations of gossip, intrigue and insult had appalled him.

He'd always taken care to avoid the machinations of the Marriage Mart. He knew, without conceit, that he was one of the glittering prizes ambitious mothers tried to snare for their daughters. He also knew that his scar had not made any appreciable difference in his desirability to those mamas. It was his family's wealth which attracted their attention—not his personal attributes.

But his position and prolonged absences had rendered him relatively immune to all the manoeuvring. He ignored everyone but the few people he genuinely respected and whose company he enjoyed. He wanted Abigail to go to London for selfish reasons. He wanted to spend more time with her, but he wasn't ready to take the irretrievable step of committing himself to her.

It was only when he tried to imagine the situation from Abigail's point of view that he realised her position would be very different. She would be obliged to pander to the prejudices of fashionable society. She would have to take care not to offend anyone, nor to do anything which would draw criticism upon herself—and she would be in direct competition with all those other hopeful débutantes. Kittenish young females with the well-developed claws of fully grown cats. Gifford shuddered. He'd rather be thrown into a pool of sharks than expose himself to such hazards.

'Perhaps you would prefer not to be exposed to the hurly-burly of the Season,' he suggested tentatively.

Abigail stared at him. 'I'm twenty-seven, not eighty-seven,' she replied. 'I think I can withstand a certain amount of hurly-burly.'

'You've probably had more practice dealing with pinch-faced matrons,' said Gifford, thinking of the trio of harridans who'd interrogated him in the Pump Room.

'If you have such a jaundiced opinion of the Season, why stay in London at all?' Abigail enquired.

'I haven't decided if I'm staying or not yet,' said Gifford unwarily.

'Oh.' Abigail fanned herself industriously and took care not to meet his eye.

Gifford cursed his hasty tongue. His successful career was based on his ability to keep a cool head. He'd made a point of never revealing any more than was absolutely necessary of his intentions to either friend or foe. Unfortunately his discretion deserted him around Abigail. Would she realise he only meant to go to London if she did?

'Have you decided?' he asked.

Abigail lifted her gaze to his face, then quickly looked

away. 'I will need to find employment until then,' she said. 'I cannot impose upon Mrs Chesney.'

Gifford bit back his instinctive offer to help. Abigail's unselfconscious revelation of her three-hundred-pound inheritance had emphasised both the differences and the similarities between them. Admiral Pullen had told him that Abigail's father had been a baronet. Gifford hadn't bothered to look up the title, but it was entirely possible that Abigail's pedigree was more impressive than his. Gifford owed his own consequence to his family's wealth and extensive property, not to the relatively recently acquired baronetcy.

He frowned. He wouldn't say anything to Abigail yet—but he would consider the matter. Possibly discuss it with Malcolm. There must be something they could think of for Abigail to do for which they could pay her a reasonable wage. And without her feeling as if she was the object of their charity.

'Then you will go to London?' he said, suddenly realising her reply had sounded like a tacit agreement.

'I think I may,' she said cautiously. And smiled at him.

Chapter Six

Abigail took one last tour around the house which had been her home for the past five years. Bessie, Mrs Thorpe and Joshua had all left for Oxfordshire. The pianoforte had already been moved to Mrs Chesney's.

Mrs Chesney occupied the ground floor rooms in her house. She had given over her sitting room for Abigail's use. The room was somewhat cramped with a narrow bed and the pianoforte squashed in together with the existing furniture, but Abigail was grateful she had a place to sleep.

She paused in what had been Miss Wyndham's drawing room. Apart from the absence of the pianoforte it looked unchanged—yet also subtly different. It was tidier than Abigail had ever seen it. The small personal belongings which gave a house a sense of homeliness were missing. Abigail swallowed back tears. She had been quite contented with her previous life. Miss Wyndham had been kind to her, and to a large extent her duties had comprised of doing things which gave her pleasure.

Abigail loved her music, and often Miss Wyndham had encouraged her to play for hours. When she wasn't playing for Miss Wyndham she'd read to her, or painted pictures for the old lady to admire—and criticise where necessary. Miss Wyndham had been a well-informed critic. Abigail's most onerous duty had been to manage the household accounts. She'd rarely been called upon to perform intimate chores for her employer, because Bessie had been responsible for Miss Wyndham's personal care.

Abigail had never questioned what was expected of her, Miss Wyndham was the only employer she'd ever known. And though Abigail had been reasonably content, she had also often been lonely, and even frustrated by the limitations of her life. Sometimes it had been hard to fully appreciate her good fortune. But now she realised she was unlikely to find another such indulgent employer. Miss Wyndham had spoiled her.

But the future was not necessarily gloomy. Her pulse quickened as she contemplated the various possibilities. It might even be quite…interesting.

Abigail took one last look around the drawing room, then closed the door on it forever. She ran lightly downstairs. There was no real reason for her to check the dining room again, they'd never used it. But she saw that the door was open, and went towards it.

Charles Johnson stepped out.

Abigail's heart thudded up into her throat.

In one horrified instant she noticed the ugly bruise discolouring his jaw. The vicious glint in his eyes. His unkempt appearance.

Charles still wore the customary attire of a dandy—but his chin was darkened with stubble. His neckcloth was askew, and the sour smell of stale wine clung to him.

He scowled at her, his lips curling back from his teeth with hatred. The disgusting image of a gutter rat dressed as a gentleman flashed into her mind.

For a few seconds she was paralysed with disbelief. Then she dived towards the front door.

He seized her from behind. His arms locked around her, clamping her elbows to her sides in a suffocating hold. Hot, sour breath dampened her cheek. He panted against her ear and she cringed away from the revolting intimacy, trying to kick backwards.

Charles cursed obscenely and tightened his painful grip upon her.

'If you don't stop fighting, I'll give you to Sampson,' he hissed viciously.

Abigail lifted her head and found herself staring at a thickset man with lank, straw-coloured hair. She'd never seen him before, but he grinned at her. She saw he would be happy to hurt her.

She went still. Cold with terror.

Charles released her but she didn't move. Sampson was less than a foot away from her.

'Come into the dining room, Abigail?' Charles invited her. His voice dripped with vile unction.

He stepped back and threw her a mocking bow.

She glanced at Sampson. He stood between her and the front door. She was trapped.

She walked into the dining room and briefly debated whether it was better to put the width of the table between herself and her tormenters—or whether she should stay close to the door.

She moved to the end of the room, but she didn't seek refuge behind the long table.

She watched Charles and Sampson. Her heart raced. She felt sick. She was aware only of the two men and every obstacle blocking her route to the door.

Charles laughed at her.

'Abigail at bay!' he sneered. 'All your airs and graces won't save you now, bitch! You turned the old harpy against me. *You!*'

Abigail stared at him. The civilised veneer Charles had always presented to his aunt had been scoured away. Fear suffocated her. Threatened to devour her.

'No smug set-downs?' Charles mocked her. 'No slippery, disdainful evasions?'

'Why are you here?' she asked. Her voice was pitched too high, but she was amazed she could speak at all.

'To collect my dues!' he snarled.

'The bed?' Abigail didn't understand what he meant. Was he going to contest her right to the clothes and the pianoforte?

'*No!* You bitch!' Charles lunged at her. Rammed her against the wall. Drove the breath from her lungs.

She gasped. Wheezed. Struggled for air. And inhaled the sickening wine fumes Charles breathed into her face. She twisted her head to the side. Charles cursed.

'The jewels. Aunt Fanny's jewels.' He dragged her forward a few inches—then slammed her back into the wall. Her head jolted backwards, then rebounded off the hard surface.

It hurt. Her eyes filled with tears of shock and pain. But the thick coils of her hair beneath her muslin cap absorbed some of the impact.

'Where are they?' he snarled. 'Where've you hidden them.'

'I don't…I don't have them!' Abigail gasped.

'Where are they?' He moved his hand from her shoulder to her throat. Caressing it obscenely. 'Who has them?'

'*No one!*' With a huge surge of effort Abigail flung him off.

Charles hadn't expected her to retaliate. He staggered backwards, almost tripping over a chair. Abigail stumbled behind the minimal protection of the table. Sobbing for breath.

Charles cursed and lurched after her.

She ran and pitched up against the far wall. She thrust away from it, intent on reaching the door.

Sampson blocked her. She saw the flash of his teeth as he grinned at her.

She stood sobbing for breath, her terrified gaze darting between the two men. Charles advanced on her down the length of the room. His smile was the most unpleasant thing she'd ever seen.

'What happened to the jewels, Abigail?' he purred. 'It was a plot between you and the lawyer, wasn't it?'

'She *s-sold* them.' Abigail backed away from both men until she found her shoulders jammed into the corner.

She'd never seen Miss Wyndham's jewels. Hadn't even been aware of their existence until Charles had demanded them at the reading of the will. All she could do was repeat what Bessie had said then.

'Every time…every time *you* visited—we lived on soup and bread and butter for *weeks* after. You've already *had* whatever they were worth!'

Charles stared at her. She stared back. She couldn't tell what he was thinking. Too late she realised she should have pretended she *did* have the jewels. Or at least knew where they were. Any excuse to get out of this room—away from her captors.

'So…' Charles exhaled on a long hiss of frustration. 'The maid was right. But there's another way to screw money out of the old bitch's leavings.'

He moved away from Abigail and gestured towards the table. She risked a brief glance away from him. There was a bottle on the table. Two glasses of wine already poured. One had been half drunk. The other was still full.

'Shall we drink a toast to my old aunt?' he asked ironically, taking up the half full glass. 'Her *deceit*?'

Abigail mutely shook her head, her lips pressed tightly together.

'Don't you know it's rude to turn a gentleman down?' Charles mocked her. He reached towards the full glass.

'We're wasting time,' the servant interrupted edgily. 'She don't need to drink the wine. A drugged doxy can be more trouble than she's worth sometimes. Just tell her I'll shoot her if she don't come peaceable.'

Drugged? Abigail's eyes flew to Sampson. He was levelling a pistol at her. He grinned at her.

'You c-can't t-take me anywhere!' Her voice was a strangled scream.

Charles laughed. 'Who's to stop us?' he asked rhetorically. 'A few old scolds? Or that old woman of a lawyer?

Pullen's a blustering old fool. Even that clod of a footman isn't around to stop us. Accept it, Abigail. You've got no one. No one and nothing. Now move.'

Sampson opened the front door and she saw a carriage waiting in the street. Sampson hustled her into it. Charles followed them. A few moments later the carriage rumbled over the cobblestones, carrying Abigail away from Bath.

Gifford had spent the afternoon riding with Anthony and Malcolm Anderson. In recent years it had been a rare occurrence for him to spend time with his uncle. Both men knew that their relationship would have to undergo changes if Gifford stayed in England, but neither of them were in a hurry to address the subject. Anderson planned to go to Oxfordshire the following day. Perhaps by the time they met again, Gifford would have made a few decisions about his future.

He walked into the drawing room, feeling a pleasant buzz of anticipation. Today Abigail was coming to live in the same house with him. It was true she had a room in Mrs Chesney's quarters, but Gifford was hoping she could be tempted to dine upstairs with them.

Mrs Chesney brought in a tea tray.

'Perhaps Miss Summers would like to join us?' Malcolm Anderson suggested to the landlady, sparing Gifford the trouble.

'She's not here, sir,' said Mrs Chesney apologetically.

'Not here?' Gifford swung round to look at her. 'I thought she moved in today.'

'She did, Captain.' Mrs Chesney set the tray down on a table. 'Nice and snug in my sitting room, she'll be. But she wanted to take one last look at the old house. See everything was set to rights before she handed over the keys.' Then Mrs Chesney frowned, glancing at the clock on the mantelpiece. 'She's been gone longer than I expected. Maybe…'

'I'll go and find her.' Gifford didn't like the thought of Abigail sitting alone in the empty house.

Just as he opened Mrs Chesney's front door he heard screeching from the house opposite.

'Ezra! *Ezra!*'

Gifford raced across the road and pounded on the door. Almost instantly it flew open, and a maid tumbled out into his arms.

'He's dying!' she sobbed. 'He's dying! He's dying! He's dying!'

'Where?'

'*Here!*' The hysterical girl grabbed his sleeve and hauled him into the house. 'Quick! Quick!'

Gifford followed her swiftly into the dining room. He immediately saw a man lying huddled on the floor between the dining table and several chairs. Gifford tossed the chairs aside and knelt beside the collapsed man.

He was unconscious, but when Gifford bent over him he discovered the fellow was breathing loudly. He also smelt wine. He shook the man, but it had no effect.

'Quiet!' he ordered the maid. 'Come here, girl!'

She gulped and shuddered, her eyes huge with fear.

'Come here,' Gifford repeated more gently. 'Come.' He held out his hand to her. 'If you're quiet, you can hear he's still breathing,' he told her.

'Ezra?' She sniffed and fell on her knees beside the unconscious man. She leant over him until her ear was almost against his mouth, her hand resting on his chest. 'Ezra? *Ezra?*' She shook him more roughly than Gifford had done. 'Why won't he wake up?' She lifted her panicky gaze to Gifford's face.

'He's drunk.' Gifford had taken time to look around the room. He'd noticed the wine bottle on the table. There was a half-empty glass on the table. And a broken glass lying beside the fallen man.

Anthony, Malcolm Anderson and Mrs Chesney crowded

into the dining room, peering around each other's shoulders
to see what was happening.

'Taking advantage!' Mrs Chesney said scathingly. 'What
are you doing here, Polly Smith? You've no business—'

'He's *not* drunk!' the maid interrupted excitedly. 'One
glass of wine—and he fell off the chair! He's *poisoned*.
He's poisoned, sir!' She fixed her desperate gaze on Gifford.

'Where's Miss Summers?' he demanded.

'She's not here. Sir…*Ezra!*'

'His pulse is strong,' Gifford said curtly. 'Feel. You see,
his heart is beating strongly.'

'Oh, sir.' Tears poured down Polly's blotched cheeks and
she clutched Ezra's wrist against her breasts. 'Are you sure
he's not poisoned?'

Gifford picked up the largest piece of the broken wine
glass and sniffed carefully at the wine dregs. He was impatient for information about Abigail, but he knew the panicky maid would answer his questions more coherently if
she was reassured about her young man.

'I think he's drugged,' he said. 'He'll wake with a thick
head, I dare say. Now—*where is Miss Summers?*'

'I don't know. I think she was here. Ezra and me, we
was upstairs—but we wasn't noticing much—'

'What *did* you notice?' Gifford cut across her embarrassed excuses. He could guess what kind of an opportunity
the apparently empty house had represented to the couple.

'We was about to come down, but we heard voices. So
we went back to the attic,' Polly snuffled. 'Ezra saw a carriage through the window. When it was gone…later…we
come down…'

'Which direction was the carriage facing?'

'I don't…I don't know,' Polly stammered. 'Ezra saw it.
He didn't t-tell…'

'Mrs Chesney!' Gifford snapped over his shoulder.
'Question the neighbours. I want to know if anyone else
saw the carriage. Which way it went. Anything else they

noticed about it. Malcolm! Go with her. Did you recognise the voices?' He turned his attention back to Polly.

'N-no. Ezra was ahead of me. He just pushed me back up the stairs.'

'How long ago?'

'I d-don't know.' Polly scrubbed her cuff against her tear-stained cheek. Her anxious attention was divided between Gifford and the unconscious Ezra.

'What did you do when you came down?'

'I showed Ezra all the fine rooms. I wanted to show him the dining room. We saw the wine. No one...no one was here. Ezra said it was a pity to waste it. It weren't *stealing*, sir.'

'No. You won't be accused of stealing,' Gifford said curtly. 'Stay with your Ezra. If he becomes worse, call me. But I think he'll sleep it off.'

He stood up and walked into the hallway with Anthony.

'Johnson?' Anthony asked sharply.

'Who else? Dammit!' Gifford's hands curled into frustrated fists. 'Pullen said his estate was mortgaged to the hilt. He didn't tell me where it was.'

Gifford strode out of the house, Anthony at his side. Gifford headed straight for the landlady who was talking to someone from a nearby house. Gifford noted in passing that Mrs Chesney and Anderson were talking to different neighbours. He was grimly pleased with their initiative.

'Ma'am, do you know where Johnson's estate is?' he demanded, interrupting her conversation with a startled housemaid.

'No, sir. N-oo.' She thought about it a few moments. 'I'm sorry, sir.' She looked pale and anxious.

'Fetch Pullen,' Gifford barked at Anthony. 'And the lawyer. One of them will know.'

'Sarah here saw the carriage,' said Mrs Chesney.

Gifford questioned her. The housemaid had seen Abigail climb into the carriage, and she knew which direction it had travelled along the street, but she was vague about the time.

'It's *him*, sir!' Mrs Chesney wrung her hands together, staring up at Gifford in horror. 'Why's he *taken* her?' Frightened tears started in the landlady's eyes. 'Sir, what'll we do?'

Gifford gazed straight ahead for a few seconds. A deadly stillness had possessed him from the moment he'd realised Abigail had indeed been taken by Charles Johnson. At his core he was filled with fear for Abigail—and a murderous rage directed at Johnson. But years of fierce discipline locked into place.

He focussed on Mrs Chesney. He'd met several of her male relatives that morning when the younger ones had moved Abigail's pianoforte. Her brother kept a shop only five minutes walk away.

'Go see your brother,' he said curtly. 'Tell him what's happened. Ask him to send his sons to check for sightings of the carriage on every route out of Bath. I want to know for *sure* which way it's heading.'

'Yes, sir.' She set off at a jog trot, despite the afternoon heat, obviously relieved that she had something constructive to do.

'London?' Malcolm appeared beside Gifford.

'Perhaps.' Gifford's lack of local information frustrated him. So did his complete ignorance of Charles Johnson's character. To his knowledge he'd never even laid eyes on the man—let alone spoken to him. He couldn't predict with any degree of certainty what Johnson intended to do with Abigail.

'Ransom?' Malcolm suggested, as they walked back towards Mrs Chesney's house. 'You to pay for her safe return? Only a fool would think we'd let him get away with it. But a desperate man with massive debts...'

'Possibly.' Gifford frowned. 'But I've never met him. And Johnson spent so little time in Bath over the past week I doubt he's heard any gossip linking me to Abigail. Nothing to suggest I'd pay a large sum for her return.'

Malcolm's sombre expression briefly lightened. 'Giff,

you could receive a demand to rescue a complete stranger and you'd leap into the breach! Anyone who knows anything about you—' He broke off as his nephew scowled. 'By the same token, anyone who knows about you would know you'll never let this go unpunished,' he continued quietly.

Gifford acknowledged Malcolm's words with a brief nod. 'Horses,' he said crisply. 'I want them here, ready saddled. Four at least.'

Gifford only knew for sure that he would take Anthony with him, but one of the local men might prove a useful guide.

Malcolm nodded acknowledgement and hurried back to the livery stable they'd already used once that day.

Gifford stood still for several seconds, assessing the decisions he'd made and the decisions he had yet to make. He tried not to think of Abigail in Johnson's power. She'd stepped into the carriage without assistance. Did that mean that Johnson hadn't drugged her as Ezra had been accidentally drugged? Or had it simply not taken effect yet?

Gifford ruthlessly put aside such speculations. His priority was to find and rescue Abigail. He'd once told her that the life of a ship's captain could be very boring. But it also required the kind of self-discipline which enabled him to stand still in the midst of feverish activity, waiting for absolutely the right moment to commit himself to a course of action.

'Put this on!' Charles threw a dress at Abigail.

She let it fall across her lap, then slide onto the floor in a flurry of white muslin. She stared at him impassively.

'Put it on, damn you!' he snarled.

Abigail folded her hands in her lap. She didn't want him to see how frightened she was.

He'd brought her to an inn not far from Bath. When the carriage had rattled over the cobblestones into the court-

yard, she'd assumed he simply intended to change horses.
Instead, he'd ordered her out of the coach.

She'd stepped down, her hopes rising that she might have
a chance to escape. But Charles had forced his arm through
hers and grabbed her hand. Then he'd bent her arm up, and
clamped her elbow against his side, compelling her to walk
where he chose. Sampson had been an attentive presence
on her other side.

She'd briefly had time to notice that it wasn't a regular
coaching inn before she'd been forced inside. Lounging
male servants had openly leered at her in the courtyard.
Inside she'd been assaulted by a miasma of unpleasant
odours—some more familiar to her than others. She'd recognised the smell of stale wine and beer. Lingering tobacco
smoke. A nauseating taint of rotten eggs. Other smells she
couldn't identify.

She sat on a grimy chair in a tawdry room and stared at
Charles. Her fear had coalesced into an unrelenting, para-
lysing sense of dread. It lay like a stone beneath her ribs,
threatening to suffocate her every time she tried to take a
breath.

For an instant she almost wished she had drunk the
drugged wine. At least she'd have had some relief from this
soul-destroying terror.

Images of Raven flickered in and out of her thoughts.
Her heart cried out to him. If he was here he would save
her.

But he wasn't here.

He had no way of knowing where she was. Or what was
happening to her.

A vivid picture of the way she'd first seen him suddenly
filled her mind. It was so clear her dingy surroundings
briefly faded away. He'd leapt from his bed to confront his
nightmares. Naked. Armed only with a knife…

She locked on to the memory. She'd always known, even
without asking, that his enemies had not always been phantoms. Once they'd had the flesh-and-blood power to wound

him. And she knew he'd confronted them just as boldly when they were real.

She hugged the memory to her. Drew courage from it. If Raven could face his enemies with courage, then so could she.

'Put the dress on!' Charles's voice rose dangerously. He pointed a pistol at her. Abigail didn't know if it was the same weapon Sampson had held, or whether it was a different one.

'Now?' she whispered.

'Yes, now.'

Another wave of fear surged over Abigail. She'd never undressed in front of a man. She'd never even undressed before a woman since her childhood. She'd never had a maid of her own.

'I'll do it for you.' Charles advanced on her, eagerness blazing in his eyes.

'*No!*' Abigail sprang to her feet. The sudden movement made her head spin. She blinked back dizziness, then started to unbutton her bodice with stiff, unresponsive fingers.

'Hurry up!' Charles watched her lasciviously.

Abigail's mourning dress was formed in two sections. She turned away from Charles and slowly pushed the bodice off her shoulders and down her arms. Then her movements suddenly became feverish as she realised the quicker she stripped out of her own clothes and put on the new dress the safer she'd feel.

'Take off your corset!'

'*What?*' Abigail twisted her head to stare at him over her hunched shoulder.

'Take off your corset. And turn round so that I can see.'

Abigail's body shrank with horror at his demand. She turned around and saw that, in his eagerness to look at her, he'd allowed his pistol hand to drop a few inches. It wasn't much, but perhaps she could take advantage of his distraction.

She let the muslin gown fall on to the floor and began to unfasten the front lacing of her corset. She listened to Charles's heavy breathing, disgust coiling through her shaking body, and from the corner of her eye watched the pistol drop a little lower.

'Good.' Charles stepped nearer. With the muzzle of his pistol he circled her nipple through the sheer fabric of her chemise.

Abigail's breath stopped. She was too numb with horror to protest, hypnotised by the dull grey metal which caressed her so obscenely.

Charles felt the weight of her other breast with his free hand.

The loathsome feel of his flesh against hers jolted Abigail out of her appalled trance.

She spun away from him. Stumbling over the clothes on the floor, she fell against the bed, grabbing the bedpost and whirling around it. She clutched it desperately as she stared, panting at Charles.

He laughed.

'If I'd known how much sport you'd offer, I'd have indulged myself years ago!' he exclaimed. 'Of course, that would have queered my chances with the old bitch. And now...' He sighed theatrically. 'Sometimes a man has to put business before pleasure.'

He picked up the white gown and threw it onto the bed.

'Put it on,' he ordered.

Chapter Seven

'I understand that it is something like a revival of Sir Francis Dashwood's Hellfire Club.'

Mr Tidewell's precise voice echoed in Gifford's memory as he brought his horse to a halt at a bend in the road, a hundred yards from the entrance to the Blue Buck Inn. He was accompanied by Anthony and Mrs Chesney's youngest nephew, Ned, a strapping nineteen-year-old.

The Blue Buck was located between Bath and Bristol, but it wasn't on the main thoroughfare. Ned had led them through a complicated route of local roads which would have defeated a stranger to the region. The inn was only a few miles from Bristol, but it stood in an isolated, desolate piece of countryside—although it was doing good business tonight. Gifford could hear a low drone of voices and the occasional burst of laughter coming from the courtyard.

He glanced behind him, checking they were alone on the road. Then he dismounted. His companions followed suit and they all led their horses into the concealing shadows of a small stand of trees. It was not much later than nine thirty, but dark clouds obscured the stars.

Gifford briefly recalled the last time he'd been forced to prowl after his enemy through dark and unfamiliar surroundings. He pushed the memory aside. Abigail was his only consideration tonight.

Answers to their enquiries along the route indicated Charles Johnson had indeed brought Abigail in this direction. But had he taken her to the Blue Buck?

Mr Tidewell and Admiral Pullen had both heard whispers about the debauched and even blasphemous activities that took place in the disreputable inn, but neither of them knew its exact location. Ned had never been inside the Blue Buck, but he ran regular errands into Bristol for his father. He knew where the inn was located. And he'd heard rumours about it on the streets of Bristol that hadn't reached the older generation in Bath.

'It used to be a common flash-house,' said Ned in a low voice. 'Landlord bought stolen goods—so I heard. Never caught, though. But everyone knew 'twas full of thieves and whores. Now it's a fancy gentlemen's club. Strange kind of gentlemen, to my mind. Rubbing shoulders with such vermin.'

'Yes,' said Gifford grimly. The things some gentlemen would do for entertainment had stopped surprising him years ago. 'Do you know its layout?'

'No, sir.'

'Very well. Stay with the horses,' Gifford commanded, and gestured to Anthony.

It was years since Gifford had pitted his wits against his father's gamekeeper, and Anthony's field craft had always been better than his. He was happy to follow his cousin's lead as they circled silently through the shadowy fields that surrounded the inn.

'Only clear way in and out is through the courtyard,' said Anthony at last. 'We could take to the fields if we have to—but with Miss Summers along it's not a good option. Better to carry it off with a high hand. Judging by the specimens we've seen entering, you should fit in. A likely recruit for the Devil if ever I saw one.'

Gifford grinned wolfishly. 'And you're a damn Obeah

man who can kill with a curse,' he retorted. 'Lot of connections to the trade in Bristol. They'll know how scared
the planters are of slave superstitions.'

'Just don't ask me to demonstrate,' Anthony retorted.
'You know a great deal more about that than I do!'

Anthony's mother had been a runaway slave, his father
had been the older brother of Gifford's father. His parents
had been killed in a carriage accident when he was a baby.
If they'd been married, Anthony would have inherited the
Raven lands and title which had now devolved to Gifford.
Gifford's father, Sir Edward Raven, had reared his brother's
bastard with his own sons. Anthony knew how much he
owed to Sir Edward's integrity and deep humanity. He was
as close to Gifford as if they really were brothers. But even
with Gifford he was sensitive to casual references to his
mother's people.

Gifford, sure of who he was and where he came from,
had never hesitated to learn about the various cultures and
peoples he had encountered during his naval career. Anthony hadn't left England until he'd finally sailed with Gifford in the *Unicorn* frigate. He'd acted as an unofficial artist, recording the scenes he'd witnessed in quick sketches
and, later, on larger oil canvasses. He'd enjoyed life on
board ship, but he'd found their brief run ashore in the West
Indies a disturbing experience. His feelings about his own
antecedents were complicated and still unresolved. But he
knew one thing for sure—even to help rescue Abigail he
wouldn't impersonate a West Indian slave.

'The Blue Buck may or may not host some kind of
devil's club,' said Gifford grimly, as they rejoined Ned.
'Most likely it's just a drinking and gambling den. But it's
busy tonight and, according to Tidewell, it's still a licenced
alehouse. Let's ride in and call for a tankard of ale. Ned,
you can hold the horses for a shilling. Try to look less
upright and more hangdog. And don't let anyone distract
you from your post.'

* * *

Gifford's party was stopped at the entrance to the inn yard by a thick-set, stubble-chinned man leaning casually on a thick wooden staff, taller than he was.

'Evening, gentlemen,' he greeted them, his eyes flicking intently from Gifford to Anthony. 'Strangers, aren't you?'

'Anchored yesterday,' Gifford said. 'Only in port a few days. But we heard there was rare entertainment to be had at the Blue Buck.'

'You're seafaring men, friend?'

'Aye. And thirsty!' Gifford said belligerently. 'What's the problem, *friend*? Our rhino not good enough for you?'

Anthony watched the gatekeeper, and listened as his cousin transformed himself into a swaggering sailor. Gifford had coarsened his voice and manner by a few degrees. The subtle changes blurred his social station, without committing him to any particular role.

What the gatekeeper saw when he looked at Gifford might well depend on what he expected to see. A pirate playing at being a gentleman—or a gentleman playing at being a pirate. Either was likely to be acceptable in a thieves' den turned into a rake-hellish gentlemen's club.

'Sailors are always welcome at the Blue Buck,' said the gatekeeper, bowing without taking his eyes off Gifford. 'Are your friends also sailors?'

'My mate, Job,' said Gifford jerking his head at Anthony. 'And our Ned. Are you plannin' to keep us talking all night, *friend*? I've got a powerful thirst.'

He altered his stance. The threat was a subtle one. It could be ignored without loss of face if the gatekeeper decided to let them in—but it also sent the unmistakeable message that Gifford wouldn't back down without a fight.

If there was some kind of Hellfire Club centred around the inn, it seemed to Anthony that membership would certainly depend on more than a gatekeeper's nod. But if it was no more than an alehouse for thieves and whores, Gifford's money should be as good as the next pirate's.

Black clouds lay over the landscape like an oppressive shroud. The hot, humid night increased the tension coiling around the small group at the entrance to the inn yard. Anthony could sense Gifford's roiling anger. Gifford was edgy and dangerous as the Devil tonight. His scowling impatience at the gatekeeper's slow response threatened to boil over into violence.

Anthony kept his face impassive but he was alert to the gatekeeper's smallest movement. To his immense relief the man backed down. A few seconds later they walked into the Blue Buck's yard.

Gifford exhaled carefully, trying to rid himself of some of his tension, as he scanned his surroundings. Lanterns hanging at intervals from the first-floor gallery illuminated the cobblestoned courtyard. Deep shadows hid recessed spaces beneath the gallery the lantern light couldn't reach. The dark clouds trapped the oppressive heat of the August night close to the ground. Dirty straw stuck to the soles of Gifford's boots. The inn yard smelled of horses and unwashed men crowded too close together.

Gifford forced his emotions back under his full control. He was walking a fine line. His anger at Charles Johnson burned in his gut like hot lava. He'd used his rage to his advantage when he'd intimidated the gatekeeper—but he knew he was dangerously close to genuine violence. Cold logic would serve Abigail better.

A quick assessment of the men crowding the inn yard told him that many of them undoubtedly possessed equally hair-trigger tempers. They were an odd assortment, though Gifford had little doubt he was surrounded by the scum, not the cream, of society. Two gentlemen in well-tailored riding coats and glossy boots stood a few feet away from him. Both men looked as if they'd be at home in Gentleman Jackson's boxing saloon. Near them was a villainously scarred fellow in a dirty coat and scuffed, down-at-heel boots. But his eyes were watchful and he moved with insolent self-confidence. When he turned to speak to his neighbour Gifford briefly saw the pistol he carried beneath his coat. Gifford had no doubt that most of the men here were armed, some less obviously than others. Both of the well-tailored gentlemen carried sword sticks.

The atmosphere was tense and filled with expectation. Men talked or joked with their friends—but they were waiting. When one of the inn doors opened, eager eyes looked towards it. When a tapman emerged carrying drinks into the yard, the waiting men lost interest. All the men were drinking. Occasionally voices were raised in brief arguments. It was a volatile assembly. A murderous brawl over an accidentally spilled drink was only an unwary gesture away.

The inn door opened again. Two men emerged first, one of them holding the end of a rope in his hand.

Scalding fury seared through Gifford, reducing every rational thought to ashes. For four seconds he was deaf and blind to everything but his own rage. Then he heard Anthony's low growl, and sensed rather than saw his cousin's instinctive movement forward. Behind them he heard Ned's shocked intake of breath, then his muttered curse.

'*Stand!*' Gifford's low-voiced order was the most compelling he'd ever given.

'Giff…?'

'*Still!*'

Three men against the fifty-odd crowding the inn yard didn't have a chance.

'What're we gonna do?' Ned's desperate question was covered by the whistles and obscene comments of the men around them.

'Wait.' Gifford's gaze never left the small party walking across the cobblestones to the empty farm cart drawn up beneath three gallery lanterns.

One man held the end of a rope in his hand. The other end had been tied into a noose. The noose was around Abigail's neck.

Abigail followed Charles across the dirty cobbles. She heard the catcalls but she neither looked at the men who shouted at her, nor flinched from the sound of their voices. Her dignity wasn't much, but it was all she had left. She couldn't stop the tears of fear and humiliation which ran silently down her cheeks, but she was determined not to break down.

When Charles had first told her what he intended, she'd had a wild hope that she might be able to appeal to the men's chivalrous instincts. As soon as she'd stepped into the yard that hope had died. She didn't understand the import of all the lewd suggestions hurled at her—but she understood that her comfort was no one's concern.

Rough wooden steps had been placed at the back of the cart. Abigail ignored Charles's mockingly outstretched hand and climbed up unaided. She turned towards her hateful audience. The faces confronting her were blurred and featureless. She could barely see through her tears, but she lifted her chin proudly, as if the rough hemp noose wasn't chafing her neck. As if it wasn't there at all.

The impulse to hug her arms protectively around herself was overwhelming, but she held her hands stiffly by her side. She'd never before appeared in public without her corset. She'd never worn such an immodestly low-cut gown, even in the privacy of her own bedchamber. Not since she was a child had she gone outside without wearing a hat or a bonnet, but now her unpinned hair tumbled in disarray all around her shoulders.

She listened as Charles Johnson briefly explained the auction to his leering audience.

Wife sales were commonplace, he declared. All the men present had come across such things. A low murmur of agreement followed his words. But tonight, Charles announced triumphantly, he had something much rarer to offer. Untouched purity—sold to the highest bidder.

Despite her best intentions Abigail folded her arms protectively across her breasts.

The first man made his bid. A second man raised it. Abigail's heart hammered with fear. Her throat was so tight she couldn't swallow—she could barely breathe. She couldn't see the men bidding on her, but their voices were hateful. She blinked to clear her tears, but more tears flooded her eyes, blinding her just as surely as if she had a cloth across her face.

A third man bid for her. His voice was clipped. Hard-edged. Familiar?

Another bid. The familiar voice raised it.

Abigail blinked furiously, then lifted a trembling hand to her eyes.

Gifford.

Her legs gave way. Just before she hit the floor of the cart Sampson grabbed her from behind and hauled her up to her feet.

She panted, desperate for air in her fear-cramped lungs. Her eyes locked on Gifford's face. She was hardly aware that Sampson still held her.

Gifford's gaze met hers. He gave no indication that he recognised her. His expression was as chillingly brutal as his voice when he bid for her a third time.

Abigail's attention was caught by a movement beside Gifford.

Anthony. When he saw that she was looking at him he nodded almost imperceptibly, but he didn't smile. His eyes flickered to Charles, acting as auctioneer, then back to her face.

Abigail looked beyond Gifford and saw Ned. She frowned in confusion. Ned had no business in a place like this. Ned was a fine young man…who looked grimly angry.

Abigail finally noticed Sampson's grip on her arms and jerked out of his grasp. He chuckled, but let her go.

The bidding went high. Charles's voice became increasingly excited. Abigail had time to collect her wits and pay some attention to what was happening.

Was Gifford here to rescue her? It seemed to her that he should be—but why was he bidding for her? Why didn't he simply denounce Charles for the abductor that he was, and—?

For the first time she noticed how many men were present in the yard. They were shudderingly disgusting—and they all looked as barbarous as Charles and Sampson at their worst. Even the men not bidding for her were enjoying her degradation. Perhaps it was all one to them. A public hanging. A cock-fight. The sale of a woman…

Not one man in the yard would be willing to let this spectacle come to a premature conclusion.

She could smell their rancid bodies. The stench nearly made her throw up. She swallowed her bile. Stood as straight as she could. And waited.

Gifford knew the moment Abigail saw him. His stomach clenched as he saw her fall. It took all his ruthless self-control not to launch himself at the man who laid cruel hands upon her.

He didn't think it would matter if Abigail revealed that she knew him. As long as she didn't cry out his name. He'd been counting on the fact that Charles Johnson had never met him to preserve his anonymity. Johnson might or might not have an interest in naval affairs. But if he had heard or read about some of Gifford's recent exploits he might well be suspicious of his motives for attending the auction. Gifford didn't want to be thrown out of the Blue Buck yard. If possible, he wanted to rescue Abigail without exposing her to violence.

The violence would come later, when Abigail was safe.

Gifford was bidding against one of the well-tailored gentlemen he'd noticed earlier. Whenever the fellow made a bid he lifted his sword stick towards Johnson. Gifford controlled a desire to ram it down his throat. He also took careful note of the man's appearance. For future reference.

Gifford raised the bidding again. Sword stick turned to stare at him, his expression hostile. Gifford recognised that he'd made an enemy. His lips curled in a smile that resembled a tiger's snarl.

Abigail clung to the side of the cart and prayed.

And then the auction was over. The man with the cane who'd been bidding against Gifford fell silent. Gifford shouldered his way through the crowd towards her, Anthony a couple of paces behind his cousin.

Abigail felt a rush of relief so overwhelming she nearly fell a second time. She clutched the side of the cart, fighting off her light-headedness. She *wouldn't* faint in front of this crowd.

Then she realised Anthony's attention was not on her, nor even on Gifford. He was watching the men on either side of Gifford. Then she knew with frightening clarity that, although the auction was over, they still weren't safe.

But Gifford was taller than most of the men around him. And he looked more disreputable than any of them. A dangerous pirate no sane man would willingly cross, she thought hopefully. She was so used to his eye patch and his scar she was almost comforted by the sight of them, but that was hardly likely to be how he affected most people.

She could feel his simmering rage even when he was still several feet away from her. See it in the tension in his jaw, his burning ice-blue eye—and in the fluid movement of his fierce predator's body as he leapt up into the cart. Fear washed over her. Not for herself, but that she might see men die tonight.

She locked her hands together and tried to maintain her composure as she turned to face Gifford.

His gaze contained barely a hint of recognition as it brushed across her. But he took the time to loosen the noose around her neck. Then lift it over her head. His touch was gentle, but she felt his fingers tremble against her skin, and knew it was rage, not fear, that he struggled to control.

Charles edged behind Sampson. Sampson grinned. Abigail hated Sampson's grin, but in a jumble of confused thoughts it briefly occurred to her that it was his master's fear which amused him.

'An exceptional bargain.' Gifford's left hand stroked

lightly over Abigail's hair, then slipped beneath the heavy mass to caress her neck. 'Do you have many such?' he asked, his predator's smile curving his lips.

Abigail shivered, and refolded her arms across her chest, her hands gripping her opposite elbows. In a tiny, calm corner of her mind, she knew his gesture was intended to convey different meanings to her and to the rest of his audience.

Reassurance for her. Ownership to anyone inclined to dispute his claim on her. But there was nothing reassuring about the dangerous emotions radiating from Gifford's powerful body. She was scared, excited, stimulated by his touch. But she wasn't reassured.

'Not—not often.' Charles stumbled over the words. 'Are you...*interested* in such...bargains?'

He licked his lips, and Abigail saw he was calculating the possibility that he might have found a new source of income.

'Assuredly,' said Gifford. He smiled.

Abigail looked at him and shuddered. She was dimly aware that the men in the yard were silent. Held in thrall by the force of Gifford's lethal personality and his quiet-voiced conversation with Charles.

Everyone wanted to know what he would say next. What he would *do* next. They were watching him, not Anthony or Ned.

Thunder growled somewhere in the distance. The hot summer's night lay dark and oppressive over the isolated inn.

Charles jerked his eyes away from Gifford, like a rabbit trying to free himself from the hypnotic gaze of a snake.

'Perhaps...perhaps you would like to discuss future...arrangements in more privacy,' he suggested, gesturing vaguely towards the inn.

'I don't think so.' Gifford reached into his pocket with his left hand, withdrawing his card case. His movement was so unobtrusively fluid, yet so swift that Sampson didn't start to react to it until Gifford's card case was already in his hand.

He flicked it open with one finger, then thumbed up and extracted a card. He did it so dextrously he didn't call attention to the fact that he used only one hand.

'My card.' He presented it to Charles and in the same continuous movement swept up Abigail and tossed her over the side of the cart into Anthony's arms.

Gifford vaulted to the ground, then into the saddle of the horse Ned had led quietly through the crowd—and a second later Abigail was once more in his arms.

'Call upon me for settlement!' Gifford shouted. He hauled the horse around on its haunches and spurred straight through the scattering crowd of men—heading for the gate.

Abigail's world spun crazily before her eyes. One minute she was standing next to Gifford, the next she was flying through the air. Her breath flew out of her lungs. She jolted against Anthony's chest, then before she even had time to feel shocked she was airborne once more.

Later she would remember and be amazed by the strength and precision both men possessed to execute such a feat successfully. At the time she was only aware of a flurry of confusing, terrifying sensations.

She heard shouts. The thunder of shod hooves over cobblestones. Pistol shots.

Gifford was first to the gate when a man leapt in front of them. Abigail briefly saw him waving a long pole while Gifford lifted his right hand. A pistol fired so close Abigail screamed. The horse shied away from the shot and Gifford swore, his voice a savage growl in Abigail's ear. She felt the iron-hard tension in his whole body as he fought to control the horse with his legs and his left hand.

His left arm was all that held her safely in front of him and she started to slide over the pommel. His right arm clamped against her, but she couldn't hold on to him because her arms were pinned to her sides. She was afraid if she tried to free them he'd lose his grip on her completely.

Then they were through the gate. Abigail heard one final shot, then Anthony and Ned were close on their heels.

Gifford kept up the same hard pace for the first quarter of a mile, back down the road they'd already travelled earlier that evening. But it was too dark to race at breakneck speed along the rutted roads.

He called an order to the others, then slowed to a walk before they finally halted and turned to listen for pursuit.

Abigail took the opportunity to rearrange herself in his arms. It wasn't that she didn't trust him, but she hated the slithery, jolty feeling she might end up in the ditch at every pounding stride.

'W-where's your gun?' she asked, suddenly realising his right palm was pressed against her stomach and there was no sign of the weapon he'd fired at the gatekeeper.

'I dropped it.' A hint of surprised laughter underpinned his brief reply. 'It was either you or the pistol at that moment.'

'Good.' She wrapped her arms tightly around him. She was trembling so violently she couldn't stop her teeth chattering. 'I d-don't w-want to be d-dropped.'

'I won't drop you.' His voice gentled and he pressed his cheek briefly against her hair. 'Anyone hurt?' he asked the others tersely. 'Lead us out of here, Ned.'

Abigail hid her face in his coat. Deep shudders racked her body. Her arms locked convulsively around him. She felt cold despite the humid warmth of the night.

For several miles she was barely aware of her surroundings. She didn't know that both Ned and Anthony directed anxious, low-voiced enquiries to her. She didn't say anything to anyone. She clung to Gifford and found comfort in the strong arms which encircled her almost as tightly as she held him.

He wouldn't drop her. He'd promised.

Chapter Eight

Gifford held Abigail close and battled with the fury which coursed through his body. His anger hadn't abated just because he had her safely in his arms. If anything, it had magnified. He wanted to go back and tear Charles Johnson apart. He knew he should say something to comfort Abigail, reassure her that nothing would harm her now. But the only words which sprang to his lips were vengeful curses.

For several miles he trusted to Ned to find the route ahead and Anthony to watch for pursuit behind. He'd maintained his icy self-control throughout the auction. But now rage clouded his mind and his senses. His tense muscles burned with the self-restraint he'd imposed upon himself since he'd learned of Abigail's capture. He needed the release of action, more violent, cathartic action than the brief skirmish in the inn yard.

But the only action he could allow himself was to ride through the night to safety. He clenched his teeth until his jaw ached, but he said nothing and did nothing to alarm Abigail.

She trembled and panted in his arms. Her body vibrated against his, reminding him of the soft, vulnerable fear of a wild bird. But there was nothing soft about the death grip she had around his neck. It was uncomfortable to the point of painful, but it was a pain he welcomed.

Her distress stoked his anger—but her fierce embrace was strangely soothing. He liked how she clung to him, as if he was the only sanctuary she needed. Of course, that was an illusion. As soon as he got her back to Bath, she would turn to the comfort of old, familiar friends like Mrs Chesney.

But *he* was the one she'd turned to first. She'd not bothered even to ask how he'd found her. She'd simply put her arms around him and told him not to drop her.

He liked that.

He liked that in the most traumatic experience of her life she'd trusted him without a single question. He liked that even after the degradation of the auction—even though he'd *bought* her—she was willing to let him hold her close to him.

He suddenly worried that he might be holding her too tightly. He loosened his embrace slightly. Immediately she pressed herself closer to him.

'Don't let go!' Her whisper was panicky.

'I won't.' His voice sounded husky and he cleared his throat before continuing. 'I didn't want to hurt you—holding you too tight.'

'Oh.' She sighed. Her trembling eased and he felt her relax against him. 'You're not hurting. It's nice. Safe.'

She moved her head, pushing up a mass of curls which caressed his cheek and filled his mouth when he opened it to speak. He blew the curls out of the way and felt her shivering response. He lifted his chin and she snuggled more comfortably against his shoulder.

'No sign they're following,' said Anthony softly. 'Are we heading back to Bath now?'

'*No!*' Abigail roused abruptly in Gifford's arms, startling him. '*Please!* I don't want…' Her voice broke and she turned her face towards him. He felt her breath warm against his neck, and then the dampness of tears on his skin.

'Abby? You'll be safe in Bath.'

She shook her head. 'No. *Please*...I'm sorry...' She swallowed and pressed against him.

Her distress hurt him. He didn't know what to say to reassure her. His right hand closed to a fist in the thin muslin of her gown. He hated the dress, not because it didn't suit her, but because it had revealed to the lascivious mob all the feminine charms he'd spent days dreaming about.

In this dress, standing beneath the lanterns, there had been no mistaking the full swell of Abigail's breasts. Her nipples had pressed against the sheer muslin of the bodice. Her hair had fallen in a riot of Titian curls around her shoulders, a temptation no man could resist.

The only previous occasion when Gifford had seen her uncovered hair had been the night Miss Wyndham had died. And as soon as Abigail had realised how improperly she was dressed she'd wrapped herself in a shawl.

Tonight...

Gifford carefully opened his hand and smoothed the thin muslin against her back.

He wasn't used to worrying about other people's opinions. He lived according to his own code. There were very few men whose judgement mattered to him. He had no time for scandal or gossip. He'd meant to take Abigail straight back to Bath because he thought she'd feel safer in familiar surroundings with familiar people.

But perhaps not.

He usually tried to block out memories of his time as a captive on the privateer ship—but now he let them surface. He remembered the bitter sense of defilement he'd felt as a prisoner. His shame that he'd ever been captured—even though he'd been wounded and unconscious when his first lieutenant had surrendered the ship. He had escaped from—killed—his own guards, then crept through the privateer ship to release his men. Together with his crew he had gained control of the enemy ship and eventually recaptured his frigate, the *Unicorn*. He'd ultimately turned defeat into a resounding victory.

But the shame and horror of waking a prisoner on board the privateer ship had never left him.

He knew why Abigail couldn't face her old friends so soon after the terrible thing that had been done to her. She was ashamed.

'Ned.' He raised his voice. 'Do you know an honest inn nearby? Where the innkeeper is discreet?'

'To change the horses, sir?'

'To take a couple of rooms.'

'Rooms?' Ned rode in silence for a while. 'Yes, sir,' he said at last. ''Bout three miles away. I'll take you there.'

'Thank you.'

'Good idea,' said Anthony. A breeze had picked up as they were riding. The heavy cloud cover was breaking up, allowing starlight to brighten their path. When Gifford glanced at his cousin he saw the flash of a smile. It occurred to him that Anthony might have been ahead of him on this matter.

Anthony had also been a prisoner of the privateers. He had his own share of nightmares from that time. And in some respects he might understand how Abigail felt better than Gifford did. Gifford was grateful for his cousin's intervention.

Abigail stirred in his arms.

'Thank you,' she murmured. 'I'm sorry to be a nuisance. But...I've never spent a single night at Mrs Chesney's before. For this to be the first time...I couldn't...I'm sorry. But...thank you.'

Gifford's arms tightened. 'You're not a nuisance. Never.'

Abigail rested against Gifford. She wished they could go on riding through the night forever. Through the dark. Unseen.

Her arms ached from holding on to him so tightly. She marginally relaxed her grip, knowing he would never let her fall. She didn't want to think about the future—or the recent past. She didn't want to think at all.

She was glad they were going to an inn. She couldn't bear the thought of exposing herself to Mrs Chesney in her current state. The landlady was kind-hearted and practical—but she would be so shocked if she saw Abigail. So... scandalised.

Abigail knew Mrs Chesney would be scandalised by what had happened to her, because *she* was scandalised.

So deeply ashamed of what had happened to her she didn't know if she'd ever be able to show herself in daylight again. Ever be able to talk to anyone who'd known her before this night.

She moaned softly at the thought.

'Abby? What's wrong?'

She shook her head at Gifford's worried question, and hid her face against him.

He held her firmly with his left arm and stroked her hair gently with his right hand.

'Everything will be all right,' he said softly. 'Everything will be fine.'

Tears forced their way beneath her closed eyelids, scalding her cheeks. She didn't see how anything could ever be all right again.

She was dimly aware when they arrived at the inn Ned had selected. She felt the cessation of motion and heard voices as Anthony and Ned spoke to the innkeeper. But she didn't react until Gifford adjusted his hold on her and leant to one side.

'No!' She panicked, clinging tightly to him.

'I'm just passing you down to Anthony,' he reassured her.

'Oh. I'm sorry.' She forced herself to open her eyes and allowed the men to make the transfer. She heard Anthony give a soft grunt as he accepted her weight and she flinched, embarrassed and self-conscious at her situation. For some reason such intimacy was acceptable with Gifford, but not with any other man.

'I really can walk,' she mumbled. 'Please put me down.' She struggled a little, and heard his quick intake of breath.

'Steady!' His voice was low and strained. 'Giff'll never forgive me if I drop you. Just rest a little longer. Please, ma'am.'

The discomfort in his voice jolted Abigail into a fuller awareness of her companions. She'd been lost in her own misery, but now she noticed how Anthony held most of her weight in his right arm, and how his left arm trembled under the strain.

In a flash she remembered how he'd caught her and then thrown her up to Gifford at the Blue Buck. There had been nothing wrong with Anthony then. But there was something wrong with him now.

'Put me down at once!' Anxiety about him pushed her other concerns into the background and gave emphasis to her command.

'I've got you.' Gifford reclaimed her and strode after the innkeeper, into a small parlour.

Abigail twisted her head to see if Anthony was following. 'Anthony, come with us. Make him come!' she told Gifford imperatively.

Anthony gave a long-suffering sigh and followed them into the parlour.

Gifford lowered Abigail into a chair and turned to look at his cousin. In the candlelight it was easy to see the blood-stained handkerchief Anthony had tied around his upper arm while they were riding.

'You damn fool!' Gifford snapped. 'I asked if you were hurt.'

'It's hardly significant.' Anthony sounded amused. 'I was winged going through the gate. That's all.'

Abigail didn't know a thing about bullet wounds, but the thought that Anthony had been wounded for her sake propelled her into action.

She pushed herself to her feet, and stood swaying slightly for a few seconds. She was horribly light-headed, but she was determined to make herself useful. To exert her own free will on this matter at least. By the time she was ready to take an active part in the proceedings, Gifford had already issued orders to the innkeeper to fetch warm water and clean clothes. Abigail helped him to take off Anthony's coat.

'There is no need for all this fuss,' Anthony protested.

'I think you should sit down,' Abigail said.

'And there's no need for you to witness this,' Anthony replied almost crossly.

'I'm not squeamish.' She frowned at his bloody sleeve.

Unlike Gifford, Abigail's father hadn't been a rich man. He'd been actively involved in farming his land. On several occasions as a child, Abigail had helped her mother tend injured farm workers, but most of those wounds had been caused by sharp-bladed farming tools. And once a man had crushed his hand. She'd never seen a shot wound before.

'I wish I had my scissors,' she said, reluctant to tear Anthony's sleeve and perhaps hurt him.

'Here.' Gifford offered her a knife.

'Thank you.' Abigail took it, hesitating briefly as she felt the weight of the dagger in her hand. Then she took a deep breath and carefully slit Anthony's sleeve to his shoulder.

Over her head the two men exchanged glances. Anthony nodded slightly, and Gifford stood back, allowing Abigail to continue with her ministrations. It hadn't escaped his notice that, the moment she'd realised his cousin was hurt, she'd snapped out of her lethargy.

He allowed her to wash Anthony's wound without interfering, though his own fingers itched to take over the task. He'd seen his share of injuries. But Abigail was careful. She frowned with concentration as she knelt in front of Anthony, gently cleaning away the dried blood from his arm.

Gifford divided his attention between his cousin and Abigail. He saw how she showed no embarrassment over her own appearance in her worry about Anthony. Her eyes were

red-rimmed and bloodshot. Dried tears stained her cheeks.
Her rich auburn hair cascaded over her shoulders. She
didn't seem to notice she was still wearing the scandalous
white gown, though Gifford had great difficulty *not* noticing.

He shrugged out of his coat, intending to give it to her
at the first opportunity. Sooner or later she would remember
how she was dressed, and he wanted to spare her any unnecessary distress at her situation.

At last Abigail sat back on her heels, biting her lip. She
looked at the wound, still bleeding sluggishly, then up at
Gifford.

'I don't know what to do next,' she confessed. 'I don't
think the bullet is still in his arm. I *think* it went straight
through. But I've never seen anyone get shot before. It's
not like when Clem put a fork through his foot.'

'Who's Clem?' Anthony asked through gritted teeth, as
Gifford moved forward to investigate his wound more
closely.

'One of the farm workers. Before I went to live with Miss
Wyndham.' Abigail leaned over Gifford's shoulder to see
what he was doing.

'You're in my light,' he said gently.

'Oh, I'm sorry.' She stepped back.

'Why don't you put on my coat?' he suggested, his attention fixed on Anthony's arm.

'Oh…oh, thank you.' She slipped her arms into the
sleeves, embarrassed that she'd forgotten her state of virtual
undress. But Anthony's injury had been more important. It
was amazing how much better she felt simply because she'd
been able to help take care of Anthony.

'I'm so sorry you got hurt because of me,' she said, sitting on a chair next to him. 'Thank you for rescuing me.
Thank you *both* for rescuing me. I don't know what…' Her
voice faltered as she thought of what might have happened
to her if they hadn't turned up at the Blue Buck. 'Where's

Ned?' she asked a few moments later, looking around the parlour.

'Tending the horses,' said Gifford.

'I must thank him too,' said Abigail. She lifted a hand to push her hair back from her face. Gifford's coat was far too big for her. Only the tips of her fingers extended beyond his sleeves. She perched on the edge of her chair, a sense of total unreality stealing over her.

She couldn't possibly be sitting in a strange parlour in the middle of the night, wearing Gifford's coat and watching him bandage Anthony's wound. She looked around the room. Her eyes focussed on the back of a dining chair. Without being aware of what she was doing, her eyes began to trace the pattern carved into the wood—over and over again.

She jerked her head away, irritated with herself. And noticed now ugly the carpet was. She frowned.

'This is all very odd,' she announced, bewildered.

'Abby?' Gifford crouched in front of her, a steadying hand gripping her shoulder, as he peered into her face.

'I think I'm not q-quite myself,' she whispered. 'The carpet's very ugly, isn't it?'

'Yes.' Gifford stroked her hair with his other hand.

'You haven't looked at it.' She frowned at him.

He smiled at her. 'I have confidence in your good taste,' he said.

'Oh.' Abigail blinked. 'Is the bullet still in Anthony's arm?'

'No.'

'That's good. It would hurt if you had to dig it out.' Her thoughts disintegrated in a kaleidoscope of splintered images. She narrowed her eyes, trying to pull the picture together again. 'He would have to bite on a piece of wood,' she said suddenly. 'He might get splinters in his mouth.'

'Abby, you need to sleep,' Gifford said.

Abigail blinked again, accepting the truth of his comment. Then she jerked awake again. 'Don't leave me alone!' She clutched his wrist desperately. 'Please, don't leave me alone!'

'I won't leave you alone,' he promised.

Chapter Nine

'Captain Sir Gifford Raven.' A mocking voice pierced Gifford's pain-filled consciousness.

Gifford opened his good eye but couldn't see anything. Fear consumed him. Ever since he'd lost his left eye he'd dreaded the prospect of total blindness.

Then he realised his eyes were covered by cloth. His wrists and ankles were bound. He wasn't blind, but he was totally at the mercy of the mocking voice.

A prisoner.

He moved his head and sickening pain jolted through him. He clenched his jaw. Resisting the nausea that flooded him. Memory took longer to return.

The *Unicorn* had been sailing in company with another British frigate when they had encountered two enemy privateers. Two thirty-six-gun frigates should have been a match for the privateers. Why was he lying bound and blindfolded on an enemy ship?

He knew he wasn't on board the *Unicorn*. The smells, the sounds, even the motion of the ship through the water were all wrong for him to be on board his own frigate.

'A lucky knock on your head—for us,' said the mocking voice. 'Your master was killed by the same flying debris which only knocked you unconscious. But your officers seem to have thought you were hit by a sniper. So much blood. Very distressing for them.'

Gifford's mouth was dry and tasted foul.

'Is this how you always treat your prisoners?' he asked harshly. 'Where are my men?'

'In the hold.'

Gifford's lips curled in a silent snarl. Mocking voice clearly didn't believe in the honourable treatment of a defeated enemy. In all his years at sea Gifford had never once treated a captured enemy officer with so little respect.

'Who are you?' he growled.

'Captain Paul Olivier,' mocking voice replied. 'A sweet victory you've given me, Sir Gifford. One fine frigate. One hundred and ninety-three prisoners. Five slaves. And, of course, the honour of defeating such a renowned officer as yourself.'

Gifford's anger chilled. England had been at war with America for over a year. There were many American privateers preying upon English merchantmen in the Caribbean. But from everything Gifford had heard so far, it seemed clear that Olivier was little better than a pirate. He probably did possess the letters of marque which gave his ship the status of an American privateer, authorising him to fight enemy ships. But in Olivier's case the letters of marque were no more than a cover for acts of unauthorised piracy. It was unlikely that his government would condone his conduct if it ever came to light.

Five slaves?

There had been four black seamen on board the *Unicorn*. And Anthony.

'Your cousin is a well-educated fellow,' said Olivier.

Gifford felt the blade of a knife glide lightly down his body from his shoulder to his groin. He tensed but didn't flinch even a hair's breadth.

'He'll fetch a good price. He's now my brother's prisoner. On the other privateer? You do remember you were attacked by *two* ships, Sir Gifford?'

'I remember,' Raven said grittily.

'Good. Because your cousin and half your crew are now prisoners on board my brother's ship,' said Olivier. 'One false move from you—and they will all be killed.'

Gifford felt the cold knife blade against his skin, then the rope around his wrists fell away.

Abigail woke in the grey light of morning. Her sleep had been disturbed, her dreams confusing. Her body ached. She was too hot. But nameless fear chilled her soul. She opened her eyes and stared at an unfamiliar wall.

Her confusion increased. And her fear intensified as she realised she wasn't alone in the room—or even in the bed. Behind her she could hear someone else, their breathing harsh and agitated.

Memories of her kidnapping and the nightmarish auction crashed in upon her. She pulled her knees up into her chest and screwed her eyes tight shut. Trying to block out the horrifying images.

Who was behind her in the bed?

Her throat locked with fear. She recalled Charles caressing her breast with the barrel of his pistol. An obscene memory.

And Gifford. Buying her. Riding out of the Blue Buck with her. Shooting at the gatekeeper.

She uncurled her body, her movements stiff and a little jerky. Whoever was in bed with her cursed in a low, vicious voice. Her heart thudded with fright. She pushed herself forward and fell out of the bed, landing on her hands and knees. The fall jarred her tense body, but she gripped the edge of the bed and peered cautiously over the top of the mattress.

Gifford was lying on the other side of the bed. Abigail had been sleeping beneath a sheet—the night was too hot for any further covering. Gifford was lying on top of the sheet. He was saying something. At first she thought he was speaking to her. She was nervous about talking to him for the first time in such circumstances. Then she realised he was talking to himself.

He was in the throes of a nightmare.

He wore only his breeches and shirt, which was open nearly to the waist. His torso glistened with sweat. And he was having a nightmare.

Abigail rose unsteadily to her feet, staring at him in dismay. She didn't know what to do. Would he wake up and threaten her with a dagger? Shout at her? Hurt her in the mistaken belief she was his enemy?

She looked helplessly around the room. Where was Anthony? Should she try to find him? Then she remembered Anthony had been wounded.

She swallowed. Bit her lip. And climbed back on to the bed.

Gifford's good eye flew open. He stared at her.

She stared back. Her heart thudded so loudly she could hardly think. She supposed he'd sensed the movement of the mattress. But why hadn't he woken up when she'd fallen *out* of the bed?

She knelt beside him and tentatively stretched out her hand towards him. She was still half-afraid he might confuse her for an enemy, and she wanted to reassure him as quickly as possible.

'It's me,' she whispered. Very bravely she laid her hand flat against his shoulder and felt him jerk in response. 'We're safe,' she said, and then gazed at him helplessly. It didn't seem like a very intelligent thing to say, but she couldn't think of anything better.

Gifford continued to stare at her, his hawklike expression unreadable.

'You rescued me,' she reminded him.

His shoulder was hot, hard, and slick with sweat beneath her hand. She stroked him a little bit, trying to keep her touch firm and reassuring, as if she were trying to gentle a dangerous animal. Which she supposed he was.

She had a dim notion that you shouldn't let a dangerous

animal know you're scared of it. Or make it feel cornered.
The muscles beneath her palm were rigid with tension. Perhaps he didn't want to be reassured.

Very slowly and carefully she withdrew her hand and
then folded both hands together in her lap. She smiled hopefully at him.

'It's morning,' she said. 'Are you hungry?'

Gifford stared at her for a further heart-stoppingly potent
thirty seconds. Then he jack-knifed off the bed, and stood
with his back to her.

Abigail jerked away in surprise. She pressed one hand
against her breast bone, in an effort to contain the wild
jumping of her heart, and stared at his broad back.

As her shock receded, she saw the rigid set of his body,
the way he held his clenched fists so stiffly at his sides, and
guessed how difficult his awakening had been for him. She
was sure he hated that she'd witnessed the first nightmare
he'd had in Bath. Now she'd seen another one.

The tension in the room was thick, almost suffocating.
Abigail had no experience to guide her in such a situation.
Only instinct.

She was powerfully aware of Gifford's virile masculinity.
All the social conventions which usually masked the most
potent differences between male and female had been
stripped away.

Gifford was unshaven. His feet were bare. His sweat-
soaked shirt clung to the muscular contours of his back. His
shoulders were unbelievably wide. Her hand still tingled
from the feel of his hard muscles beneath her palm.

Abigail tipped her head to one side as she wondered what
to do, and felt her unconfined hair brush across the nape of
her neck. She looked down and saw that she was still wearing the same white gown in which she'd been sold. The
ribbon that fastened the neckline had come undone, and the
bodice now dipped almost to her nipples. She gasped, and
snatched up the sheet to hide herself.

Gifford turned around at her unwary utterance. He looked

down at her, at the sheet she clutched against her breasts, and a faint, almost mocking smile curved his lips. His gaze rose and locked with hers.

The tension between them increased. Abigail's body vibrated with awareness of Gifford. She stopped breathing. Stopped thinking. Her eyes widened and her lips parted.

Gifford swore and spun away from her.

Abigail's hands trembled. She felt dizzy, but finally remembered to breathe. She didn't know what to do, or to say. She felt utterly exposed, in some ways more exposed than she had done when the men leered at her in the inn yard. They'd only seen her scantily clad body, but it seemed as if Gifford had just looked straight into her confused, excited soul.

'I have to know.' Gifford's voice was harsher than she'd ever before heard it. 'What did Johnson do to you?'

He asked the question—but he didn't look at her as he said it.

'Do?' Abigail's grip on the sheet tightened. 'He sold me!' Her own voice sounded strident in her ears.

'What…else?'

She stared at Gifford. Her throat closed up. Her eyes filled with tears as she remembered her terror and humiliation at Charles Johnson's hands. She couldn't describe that to anyone.

Gifford whirled around, took one long stride to the bedside and seized Abigail's upper arms. He lifted her until they were face to face.

'What did he do to you?'

Gifford's scarred features, dark with anger and torment, misted before Abigail's eyes. He was so full of rage and savage emotion. He frightened her. Words clogged in her throat and she turned her face away from him.

'Dear God!' He lowered her gently on to the bed and sat down beside her. *'I'm sorry!'* he whispered thickly. 'God, I'm sorry! Abby.'

Abigail swayed uncertainly, then leant against his side,

resting her head on his shoulder. A few seconds later his arms closed around her.

'I didn't mean to upset you,' he murmured against her hair. 'I promised myself I wouldn't—dammit!' He broke off, cursing both Johnson and himself.

Abigail didn't want Gifford to be angry. She wanted him to be calm and quiet and hold her.

She pushed him away and looked up at him.

'Why are you angry with yourself?' she demanded, swiping her tears away with the back of her hand.

'I should never have let him take you!' Gifford ground out.

'You knew what he meant to do?' Abigail was stunned.

'Of course not! How the hell…? But I shouldn't have let him take you.'

'Now you're God!' Abigail leapt to her feet, her own temper suddenly spiralling out of control. 'Why are *you* so angry? *You're* not the one he sold! *I am!* It's *me* he frightened and humiliated and u-used…'

She started to sob with a mixture of shame and fury.

'Abigail…?'

'Don't touch me!' She pushed him away with so much force he stumbled back, lost his balance, and sat down suddenly on the edge of the bed.

'I don't *want* you to be angry with him and me and you!' she said wildly. 'It's *horrible*! I h-hate it! It *hurts*!'

'You want me to let him get away with it?'

'*No!* But I d-don't want to think about it now. I don't want to *think* about it! I want to be *myself* again. I w-want to wear my own clothes…and put my hair up…and wear my cap…and…and…be *me* again!' Her lips trembled as she whispered the last few words.

Gifford stood up. It occurred to her that he was moving unusually slowly. Warily. It didn't make any sense. Gifford never moved warily. He moved with the assurance of the great predator he was. Then she realised he was wary of *her.* The idea was so ludicrous she burst into slightly hysterical laughter.

'Abigail? Abby? Don't.' He pulled her up against his chest. One arm circled her waist. His other hand stroked her hair. 'Abby, don't.' He sounded distracted and anxious.

Abigail let him support her weight. She didn't want to think or argue. She just wanted to be quiet. His body was a hard, secure haven for hers. She sighed, and allowed herself to enjoy his soothing caresses. She liked the little tingles than ran up and down her spine when he stroked her hair. It was very pleasant to have such…direct…experience of the contrasts between his strength and her softness.

She closed her eyes and relaxed.

Gifford was rapidly discovering that torture could take many forms. His experiences with the privateers had taught him more about powerlessness, fear, and the desire for vengeance than he'd ever wanted to know. He'd relived many of those emotions when Abigail had been abducted and he'd been forced to buy her.

And then he had woken from his nightmare to find her sitting next to him. Her hair rumpled from sleep, her dress so unselfconsciously disarrayed she might have been less tempting totally naked. He'd been aroused by the sight of her. He'd hated the fact she'd seen him have another nightmare. He was tormented by fears of what else Johnson might have done to her. He was furious with himself for desiring her so soon after her ordeal.

He was also angry with her—which made him even angrier at himself. Abigail had done nothing wrong, but he found himself wishing she hadn't gone back to make one last check on Miss Wyndham's house, hadn't put herself, however innocently, in a position where Johnson could hurt her.

And now she rested quietly in his arms, her anger as well as his apparently forgotten. Her soft, rounded breasts pressed against his chest. They both wore so little clothing that he was acutely conscious of her voluptuous contours. The slick heat of their bodies. This was torture of another kind. Abigail was only seeking comfort, but Gifford's body hardened with arousal. He continued to stroke her hair in gentle caresses, but he ached to sweep his hand down her back, over the enticing swell of her hips. He wanted to tip her head back and kiss her. He wanted to press her against his pelvis, let her feel his excitement. He wanted to strip off her dress and his breeches and bury himself in her.

The bed was only a foot away, and only her sheer muslin gown and his sense of honour protected her from his lust.

Abigail stirred slightly in his arms. 'He didn't do anything,' she said quietly.

'Do?' Gifford had momentarily forgotten Charles Johnson as he fought the more immediate battle with his desires.

'He took me from the house. He said no one would notice or care. Sampson pointed a pistol at me.' She shuddered at the memory.

'Sampson?' Gifford fought to keep his voice calm.

'His servant. He was in the cart with us.'

'I remember.' With a severe effort, Gifford managed to stay still and continue stroking Abigail's hair in the same soothing rhythm.

'Then he took me to that place.' Abigail's shoulders twitched. 'He made me p-put on this dress,' she whispered. 'Then he…then he put the…put the rope round my neck and took me outside. To the cart. You saw everything after…after that.'

Gifford's arms burned with the need to punch something—some*one*. He waited until he could trust his voice. Then he said, 'Is that…did he…did anything else happen?'

He felt Abigail draw in a deep, unsteady breath.

'No. He said…he said…he couldn't sell damaged goods.'

Gifford's relief was so immense it knocked all the strength from his limbs. He held on to Abigail, taking as much comfort from her warm, pliant body as he hoped she found in his embrace. His worst fear—that Abigail had been raped—had been laid to rest.

He remembered Johnson's introductory speech, before he'd opened the bidding on Abigail. Johnson had indeed boasted about her untouched purity, but Gifford had listened with self-imposed detachment. He'd known he couldn't let his emotions blind him to what he needed to do to rescue her.

'He had no right to sell me!' Under any other circumstances Abigail's indignation might have been comic, as she pushed away from Gifford to frown up at him. 'He said men sell their wives all the time, and he was perfectly entitled to sell me—since I belonged to his aunt, and his aunt hadn't left him anything else worth selling. *Do* men sell their wives? It's very, very wrong.'

'I've heard of occasions,' Gifford admitted. 'When the people involved can't afford the legal formalities of divorce. Malcolm wrote to me about such a case a few years ago. A blacksmith from a village near one of our estates sold his wife to a man from another village. I don't remember the details.'

'And everyone thinks it is so splendid to be married,' said Abigail tartly. 'I wouldn't want to be married to any man who was at that…that *place* last night. I expect most of *them* were married.'

'Probably.' Gifford let his arms drop to his sides as Abigail moved away from him. To his relief her mood seemed to have improved. She almost sounded her usual self. 'But last night was different, Abigail.'

'I know that!' she exclaimed, rubbing her palms against her upper arms.

'I just meant…in the case of the blacksmith and his wife—they'd already arranged the sale with the other man beforehand,' Gifford explained. 'The public sale was just to make sure all the local people knew what had happened—so they wouldn't go on dunning the blacksmith for her debts. She wasn't put up for auction…'

His voice faded away as he realised his explanation would hardly be of much comfort to Abigail.

'I don't *have* any debts,' she said caustically. 'You're confusing me with Charles.'

Gifford opened his mouth, then closed it again. In the circumstances, silence seemed the best course of action.

'I'll see if I can find us something to eat,' he said practically. 'And a brush and comb,' he added, remembering her desire to put up her hair.

When he'd gone, Abigail slumped onto the edge of the bed. She was grateful for the brief respite from Gifford's volatile temper.

His rage at Charles Johnson had been a tangible entity, sucking all the air out of the small room. It had been painful to tell Gifford what had happened to her, and she had missed out some of her more disturbing memories—she knew she would never be able to tell anyone about the muzzle of Charles's pistol stroking her breast. But she'd forced herself to find the words to reassure Gifford.

In the rational light of morning she knew that nothing irreversibly bad *had* happened to her. It would be hard to go on with her life from here, but not really much harder than it would have been before Charles had kidnapped her. She was sure to find a way to manage. But Gifford's fury had frightened her.

There was a pitcher of water and a bowl on a stand. The water had been there all night, but it was cool and refreshing against Abigail's face and neck. She washed as well as she could, though she was too nervous to remove the white gown completely. The dress was very damp when she'd finished, and concealed even less than before.

Abigail had heard that dampened petticoats were fashionable, but when she looked down at the muslin clinging to her breasts, she could only conclude that London was a very scandalous place indeed—or that she'd somehow misunderstood the gossip.

She couldn't possibly let Gifford see her like this.

She cast desperately around the room, and then in sudden inspiration pulled the top sheet off the bed. She wrapped it around her, trying as best she could to imitate the pictures of Roman togas that she had occasionally seen.

The result was a far cry from conventional respectability, but at least she was modestly covered.

Gifford soused his head and torso under the outside pump. Several small children, an ostler and an old man stood in a comfortable circle around him and watched. A maid and the innkeeper's wife watched from behind the parlour curtains.

At last he straightened up and scrubbed himself dry with the towel the innkeeper had given him.

'Are you a pirate?' asked one of the children.

'No.'

'Oh.' They all looked disappointed.

'Do you *want* me to be a pirate?' Gifford asked, puzzled.

'We thought you might have treasure.' Another child scuffed his toe along the ground.

'From the Spanish Main?' Gifford grinned, entertained by the brief diversion.

'In a chest.'

'Buried. Uncle Jeremiah told us about pirates burying treasure.'

The children looked at him solemnly. The ostler looked blank. The old man squinted at him suspiciously.

Gifford shook his head like a great dog. His black hair stuck up on end and drops of water flew everywhere. The children squealed and jumped back.

'No buried treasure,' he said. 'I'm not a pirate. I catch the pirates.'

'Oh?' The children looked hopeful. 'What do you do with their treasure?'

Gifford laughed and dug his hand into the pocket of his breeches. He flipped a coin in turn to each of his audience.

He noted with amusement that the children all managed to catch their coins. The ostler fumbled his unexpected reward for gawking. The old man prudently tested his coin between his teeth.

Gifford strode towards the door, giving the maid and the innkeeper's wife just enough time to hide behind the curtain before he entered the building. He saw the curtains flutter, but he was damned if he was going to reward *everyone* who watched his morning ablutions.

It was a small inn with only two bedchambers. Anthony was in one, and Abigail and Gifford had shared the other. Its main business was to provide a meeting and drinking place for the local people, but Ned had claimed the innkeeper was respectable. Gifford had no reason to doubt that, and he was grateful it wasn't a busy posting inn. Abigail's reputation was now his first consideration.

He'd sent Ned with a letter to Malcolm Anderson in Bath. He'd given Malcolm certain instructions and also asked him to reassure Mrs Chesney—and prevent the landlady from rushing straight to Abigail's rescue.

Gifford had belatedly realised he hadn't given any thought to scandal when he'd set out to rescue Abigail. By now Bath was probably humming with gossip about her abduction. He would let Abigail make her own choice, but he was strongly of the opinion it would be better for him to take her straight to London. At least until the Bath tabbies had something new to gossip about.

He borrowed a shirt from the innkeeper, which wasn't really wide enough for his broad shoulders, and checked on Anthony.

His cousin looked tired, and admitted he'd had a restless night, but there was no sign of fever or infection.

'How is Miss Summers?' Anthony asked.

'She seems very…resilient.' Gifford frowned, selecting his words carefully. 'He only sold her. He didn't do anything more…personal.'

'He must be desperate,' said Anthony. 'How could he

imagine he'd get away with such a thing? She's hardly—'
He broke off.

'He thought no one would notice—or care,' Gifford said
grittily, remembering what Abigail had told him. 'She was
just his aunt's poor companion. If we hadn't been there—
you and I...'

'Pullen would have done something. Tidewell, too. And
Mrs Chesney and her army of relatives. Miss Summers has
a lot of friends.'

'Yes, she has,' said Gifford. 'They would have gone after
her—but they would have been too late. We were only just
in time. Only just in time,' he repeated grimly.

'But now Miss Summers is safe, we have all the time in
the world to find Johnson,' said Anthony flatly.

Gifford looked at him, and knew that his cousin was no
more likely to forgive Charles Johnson for what he'd done
to Abigail than Gifford was.

Chapter Ten

There was only one straight-backed chair in the room. Abigail sat on it, waiting for Gifford. After a few minutes it was clear why he'd decided to sleep beside her. The chair was hideously uncomfortable, and rocked on uneven legs whenever she made an unwary movement. But she didn't want to sit on the bed, it was too suggestive.

No one had come near her since he'd left. She'd been half-expectant, half-fearful a maid would come. Perhaps Gifford had given orders that she wasn't to be disturbed. She wanted him to come back. She couldn't walk around the inn wearing her makeshift toga, and she didn't know what was happening. She felt very vulnerable. She also felt hungry.

But even though she was impatient for his return, her heart jumped with nervous excitement when she heard his voice at the door.

'Come—come in,' she stammered.

'Breakfast,' he announced, bringing in a heavily laden tray.

'I am…I am a little hungry,' Abigail said.

She noticed immediately that his hair was damp, and that he was wearing a coarse linen shirt which wasn't quite big enough for him.

'Good.' He put the tray down on a roughly hewn dresser.

All the furniture in the room was well cared for, but not well crafted.

'How is Anthony…Mr Hill?' Abigail asked anxiously.

'Tired. Probably a little weak—though he'd deny that!' Gifford replied, smiling. 'But otherwise he's doing well.'

'I'm so glad. It would be terrible if he was badly hurt because of me.'

'Not because of you,' Gifford retorted. 'Unless you fired the pistol.'

He rearranged the furniture so he could sit on the bed near Abigail with the tray between them.

She carefully extended a hand from beneath her toga-sheet to accept a plate of bread and butter and cheese from him.

'I've sent Ned to Bath to fetch your clothes,' said Gifford. 'I did think of asking if any of the women here have a dress you could wear. But I thought you might not be quite comfortable with that. If you wish me to do so…?'

'No! No!' Abigail said hastily. The idea of revealing to a stranger that she had nothing appropriate to wear was unthinkable. 'What—what have you told them—about me?' she asked more hesitantly. 'Here, at the inn. And—and…did you send a message to Bath with Ned?'

'I told the landlord that you're my wife. That we were attacked by highwaymen—when Anthony was shot. And that you were so frightened by the incident that you need to recover quietly in your room,' Gifford replied. 'I sent a letter to Malcolm with Ned. May I pour you some tea?'

'Yes, thank you,' Abigail said, awkwardly adjusting her sheet. She wasn't finding it easy to eat and manouevre her plate one-handed and was afraid if she didn't hold on to the sheet with her other hand her carefully constructed toga would come adrift. 'I can't think how the Romans conquered an Empire!' she said in exasperation.

Gifford's lips twitched. 'Perhaps they didn't wear togas *all* the time?' he suggested. 'Let me take your plate. Now, you take the teacup—leave me the saucer.'

'What did you say to Mr Anderson?' Abigail asked, when she'd taken several soothing sips of tea.

'That you are safe and well, and that I will send a further message as soon as you've decided what you want to do.'

'*I've* decided? I have to go back to Bath. Don't I?' Abigail stared at him in bewilderment.

'You weren't keen to do so last night,' Gifford reminded her.

'I wasn't thinking clearly last night,' Abigail replied, biting her lip. 'Not even as far as this morning. I suppose I was hoping for a miracle. I'm glad you sent for my clothes. I couldn't go back to Bath dressed like this. But...there isn't anywhere else I *can* go.'

'You were planning to go to London,' said Gifford. 'We could go straight there—by easy stages.'

'London?' Abigail blinked at him. 'I don't *know* anyone in London!' she exclaimed. 'Mr Anderson said he would speak to someone—Lady...Lady...I don't remember her name. He surely can't have done so yet. And even if he *has*, I couldn't...I *couldn't* go to her now...'

'I have a house in London,' said Gifford.

'*Your* house? But that's...that's...' Words failed Abigail. She stared at Gifford, wild speculations tumbling through her mind. 'You *bought* me!' she exclaimed, unwarily voicing her thoughts. 'I'd forgotten. You *bought* me!'

'Dammit all to hell!' Gifford leapt to his feet, nearly upsetting the tea tray as he thrust away from the bed.

The crockery clattered. Abigail spilled tea on her sheet. She watched with trepidation as Gifford strode angrily about the room. One minute he'd been as serene as she could have wished—the next he was acting like a furious bull about to charge someone.

'I did not *buy* you!' he snarled at her, from the other side of the room.

'Yes, you did.' She didn't know what streak of perversity prompted her to contradict him, but she was determined not to let him intimidate her. 'I was there. You bought me for—' She broke off, trying to remember her final price. 'I was *really* expensive!' she exclaimed in amazement. 'I'd forgotten. I was really, extremely *expensive!*'

Gifford glared at her. 'Don't get too excited about it,' he growled. 'I don't intend to pay the bastard.'

'Oh, no! Of course not! But that other man—the nasty-looking one with the stick—he was willing to pay a great deal of money for me too. Only not as much as you.'

'Don't let it go to your head!' Gifford scowled, striding back to loom over her. Her chair wobbled on its uneven legs as she instinctively leant away from him. 'You wouldn't have liked it if he'd bought you. Believe me, Abigail!'

Abigail swallowed. 'I *know* that,' she said unsteadily. 'I *know* that. But I'm t-trying to be positive about all this. No one ever showed any interest in me at all before. Just…just because I'm grateful the nasty man *didn't* buy me—doesn't mean I can't be a little…a little *encouraged* that someone was willing to pay anything for me at all.'

'More likely he couldn't stand to be outbid by *me*,' Gifford retaliated arrogantly.

Abigail threw the rest of her tea at him.

'Oh, my goodness!' She dropped the cup and pressed her fingers to her lips, staring at him in consternation.

Gifford stared at her in amazement, then looked down at his borrowed shirt. A scatter of tea leaves stuck to the coarse linen, and milky tea dripped to the floor.

'I'm so sorry!' Abigail whispered, horrified at herself.

Gifford started to laugh. 'I deserved it for being so conceited,' he replied, tension oozing out of his powerful body. He sat down on the bed again. 'My brother and sister-in-law are currently living in the London house,' he explained. 'I thought you could stay with them for a while. Honor is expecting to be confined in…November, I think.' He frowned. 'We might need to make other arrangements before then, but for the time being it seems an excellent solution.'

'Oh.' Somewhat contrarily, Abigail felt quite put out by Gifford's apparent lack of interest in his purchase. 'So you only bid for me from disinterested gallantry?' she said, then immediately blushed and wondered what had happened to her sense of decorum.

Her embarrassment wasn't eased by the long, slow look Gifford gave her. His gaze tracked down over her sheet-swathed form, her naked forearm and her bare toes which were all he could see of her. Then his gaze lifted to her eyes, before dropping a little lower to focus on her lips. 'I wouldn't say that,' he drawled.

He moved until he was sitting on the edge of the bed, then he reached out and hooked a hand behind her head. The steady pressure of his hand against her nape compelled her to lean towards him. The wobbly chair jolted her an inch or two closer. Gifford leant towards her. Their lips touched.

Abigail gasped.

His mouth was warm, firm, and gentle on hers. Her lips parted in surprise. He caressed them softly with his mouth. His hand was buried in her thick hair, but he didn't touch her anywhere else.

Her fingers and toes curled up in response to the first real kiss she'd ever received. She closed her eyes and trustingly surrendered to the experience—and to Gifford. She felt warm all over, but this fire burned from the inside outwards.

It started deep within her. Warm embers of pleasure burst into flames of excited desire. Fiery excitement coursed through her body with increasing urgency until it reached her very fingertips. Almost of their own volition, her hands opened and sought to touch Gifford. She reached blindly but surely for his strong shoulders, and gripped convulsively when she found them.

Gifford broke the kiss. He groaned softly and lifted his head away from her.

Abigail opened her eyes, gazing at him in bereft confusion. Without realising what she did, her arousal swollen lips pouted as she leaned further towards him to renew the kiss. Her hands still clutched his shoulders. She could feel the bunching tension in his solid muscles.

He took one of her hands in his and turned it over, softly kissing the inside of her forearm, then worked his way upwards with exquisitely sensual caresses towards the tender skin of her inner elbow.

Abigail sighed with pure pleasure. Her bones turned to jelly. She swayed towards him, ready to melt all over him if he'd only let her.

'Abby!' he groaned. He muttered under his breath, then pushed her upright. The chair rocked back on its wonky legs. The sheet had fallen around her waist. Her nipples jutted against the thin muslin gown.

Gifford groaned again. The woman apparently had no sense of self-preservation where he was concerned. First she'd knelt on the bed, watching him rouse from sleep when she was barely dressed. It had taken all his self-control not to strip her out of that poor apology of a gown, and make hot, sweet love to her. Then she'd provoked him with her naïve, *ridiculous* question. Disinterested gallantry, for God's sake! The woman had behaved as if she thought he was some kind of damned eunuch! He'd kissed her entirely against his better judgement. Now that she'd filled him with throbbing, savage desire for her—and while he was belatedly *trying* to act like a gentleman—she displayed herself to him like a sacrificial virgin.

Which was exactly what she was.

Gifford's sudden insight brought him up short, as if he'd just been doused with a bucket of icy well water.

Abigail had no defences against him because, until yesterday, she'd never needed to protect herself from a man. Even after everything that had happened to her, she could still be innocently pleased that men had bid for her, because she couldn't fully imagine what might have happened to her once she was sold.

He had to take her to London and give her the opportunity to meet other men. Decent, caring men who could give her the compliments and consideration she'd never before received. It was a crime that she'd received so little of the admiration most young women took for granted—that she therefore had so little power to discriminate between good and bad attention from a man.

Yes, he decided, he would take her to London. That was the right thing to do. But his hasty decision immediately began to weigh in his gut like a round shot. He didn't want other men to flirt with her or flatter her. He didn't want any other man to see her like this, her cheeks and breasts flushed with arousal. Her eyes dilated with excitement, her lips swollen from kisses. Her nipples…

He stood, grinding out a curse, and stalked to the other side of the room.

'Cover yourself!' he ordered.

Abigail wrapped the sheet around her with shaking hands. Her soft green eyes were huge as she followed his progress around the bedchamber. She looked so uncertain— so unsure of herself. He suppressed another oath. This was true torture.

'Perhaps you should go away if you're just going to prowl about!' Abigail said, hurt as well as indignation in her voice. 'When Ned arrives with my clothes I'll go back to Bath. You won't have to bother with me any more.'

'When Ned arrives, we're going to London!' Gifford said categorically.

'You said I could decide where I go!' Abigail protested.

'I changed my mind. You don't have any idea what's best for you!' Gifford wrenched open the door and slammed it behind him.

Denied the chance to reply, Abigail stared after him in astonishment, which quickly turned to furious indignation. She let the sheet fall unheeded the floor as she sprang to her feet. Who the *devil* did Gifford Raven think he was?

She was halfway to the door when she remembered she really wasn't dressed for a public confrontation with him.

She turned aside, seething with impatience and irritation. It was intolerable that she was a virtual prisoner in this room while Gifford was free to roam where he chose.

There was a small orchard behind the inn. Anthony had refused to spend any more time in bed. It was hot and stuffy in his bedchamber, and in any case he wasn't sick. So he sat in the shade of an apple tree and talked to a distracted and bad-tempered Gifford.

'Johnson will never turn up to collect payment from me,' Gifford announced. 'Not if he has any wits at all. We'll have to hunt him down.'

'Of course.' Anthony leant his head back against his chair and watched Gifford pace up and down under the trees.

Gifford was once more bare-chested as he waited for Ned to arrive from Bath with his clothes. The landlord's tea-stained shirt had been too small for him. He'd put up with the discomfort for a little while, then ripped it off with an exasperated curse.

Every now and then as Gifford paced through the trees he had to duck to avoid a low branch. The minor impediment didn't slow his progress. Gifford had spent most of his adult life at sea living in uncomfortably cramped conditions. When he'd first boarded the *Unicorn* Anthony had repeatedly banged his head until he'd learned the knack of ducking or holding it to one side when he moved about below decks. Gifford adapted relatively easily to changes in his physical surroundings—but his powerful emotions sometimes prompted him to behave like a caged tiger when he wasn't able to take immediate action.

'I'm taking Abigail to stay with Cole and Honor,' Gifford announced.

'Is that what she wants?' Anthony enquired.

'She isn't experienced enough to know what she wants!' Gifford snapped. 'Until a few days ago she was surrounded by a gaggle of old women.'

'And Joshua,' said Anthony mildly.

'Who?' Gifford whirled round and pinned his cousin with a diamond hard stare.

'The dim-witted but loyal footman,' Anthony reminded him. 'He knocked Johnson down at the will-reading. If he'd still been in Bath to protect Miss Summers, she would probably never have needed rescuing.'

'Dammit!' Gifford slammed his fist into his open palm. 'You're right. We shouldn't have sent him away. She obviously needs a maid and a footman, and we just sent them both into Oxfordshire.'

'For God's sake!' Anthony snapped. 'Will you stop acting like you're meant to be some kind of omniscient, omnipotent saviour to the rest of creation! It's damned arrogant, and damned insulting to the rest of us to boot.'

Gifford's broad, muscular chest rose and fell with each fierce breath he took. His large body tensed with coiled, dangerous energy. Sunlight glinted on his white-streaked black hair. His scar and eye-patch seemed out of place in the quiet country orchard. He fought a battle with himself while Anthony watched and waited. At last he pressed his lips together and turned his head away. He ran his fingers through his hair until it stuck up from his scalp in black spikes.

'It wasn't your fault,' said Anthony quietly. 'Not what happened yesterday. And not what happened on the *Unicorn*. It was not your fault that you were knocked unconscious by a piece of shrapnel. You're lucky—*we're* lucky—you're still alive. It was not your fault that when he thought you were dead, Captain Radner turned tail and left the *Unicorn* to face both enemy ships alone. And it was not your fault that Lieutenant Pemberton panicked and surrendered to the privateers.'

'Pemberton's loss of nerve was my fault,' said Gifford coldly. 'If I train my officers so badly that when I'm out of action they go to pieces—I am responsible.'

'But Pemberton was not your choice as first lieutenant,

and you didn't train him,' Anthony countered. 'He was forced on to you at Kingston by Admiral Evans because he owed the man's father a huge tailor's bill, for God's sake! Giff—even you can't turn an admiral's lapdog into a fighting man in three weeks!'

'I shouldn't have let Evans foist him on to me after Winters was promoted,' Gifford muttered. 'Fenton was more than ready for the responsibility of being first lieutenant.'

'And Lieutenant Fenton helped you retake the *Unicorn*,' Anthony reminded him. 'And he *did* become your first lieutenant after Pemberton's death. And perhaps Pemberton wouldn't have lost his nerve if Captain Radner, for whom you had *no* responsibility at all—he was senior to you, on the captains' list, dammit!—hadn't fled from the battle. The man was court-martialled for cowardice!'

At some point during the argument Anthony had hauled himself to his feet and now he stood virtually nose-to-nose with Gifford.

'And I still think there was a good chance Pemberton might have rallied after the first shock of seeing you fall if Radner hadn't let us all down so catastrophically,' Anthony continued, his voice quieter, but no less intense. 'It was like having the legs knocked from under us—the breath knocked out of our lungs—to see him sail away from us, Giff! Unbelievable. Just simply unbelievable.'

'Then I'm doing Pemberton an injustice,' Gifford said bleakly.

'Perhaps.' Anthony sighed. 'I don't know, Giff. I don't know the finer points of seamanship well enough to know whether another commander would have been able to claw his way out of the hole Radner had left us in. Fenton said once you could do things with the *Unicorn* he wouldn't have believed possible if he hadn't seen it with his own eyes. So perhaps you're judging the whole affair—something you didn't see with your own eyes, let me remind you—according to standards which are just too impossibly high.'

Gifford looked at Anthony for silence for several intense moments. 'For God's sake, sit down before you fall down,' he said harshly, and turned away.

Anthony sighed, and eased himself carefully back into his chair. This argument had been brewing ever since they'd been reunited after Gifford had recaptured the *Unicorn*. Anthony understood some of Gifford's mental anguish. He understood that, from the moment a captain read out his commission to his crew, he became responsible for every man, beast and inanimate object on the ship—and for every order that his junior officers gave. If, for example, one of Gifford's lieutenants had ever made a mistake which allowed the *Unicorn* to run aground—it would have been Gifford who would have been court-martialled for the loss of his ship.

It made no difference to Gifford that he had been unconscious when his first lieutenant surrendered his ship and crew to the privateers. He still held himself ultimately responsible for what had happened.

But Anthony thought that perhaps, if Gifford's officers had surrendered to a more honourable enemy—and if the surrender hadn't been forced upon them by an act of gross cowardice by another British captain—Gifford might have felt less bitter about the whole affair.

Gifford turned his back on Anthony. His cousin's forthright comments had angered him. They'd also left him feeling shaken and painfully exposed. He knew his response to the *Unicorn*'s capture wasn't entirely rational. Every time he tried to think about what had happened, he shied away from the memories. The nightmares were bad enough. Deliberately choosing to relive those days was profoundly disturbing. He'd never felt so helpless in his life. He'd never before comprehended the hellish torment of being utterly powerless—and he never wanted to experience it again.

Captain Radner's betrayal of the *Unicorn* was impossible for Gifford to understand or to forgive, an affront to everything Gifford believed in, and a blemish on the navy he had served half his life. Upon his return to England, Radner had been court-martialled under the Articles of War. The intervention of influential friends had enabled him to escape the severest penalty for his actions, but he was a ruined man. His act of cowardice had also led to the destruction of Lieutenant Pemberton.

Anthony had exaggerated when he'd claimed Pemberton had owed his advancement to the debts Admiral Evans owed to the lieutenant's father, but it was certainly true that the lieutenant had been one of the admiral's protégés. He'd had limited experience on board a frigate before he'd been appointed Gifford's first lieutenant, and he'd had only three weeks in his new position before he'd been forced to make life-or-death decisions about the fate of the *Unicorn* and her crew.

Gifford's hands fisted at his sides. The game of 'what if' was a useless waste of time. But what if Pemberton had had a little longer to gain confidence in handling the *Unicorn*? Could he have outmanoeuvred the two privateers and sailed to safety?

What if…? What if…?

Gifford was well aware that, to most observers, the *Unicorn*'s capture represented no more than a minor, temporary reversal of fortune. He'd retaken his frigate, and ultimately captured both privateers as his prizes. A personal and professional triumph. To Gifford, it had been gained at too high a price.

He gazed unseeingly at the daisy-studded grass, listened distantly to the drone of a bumblebee, and tried to forget about the *Unicorn*. He had more pressing concerns. He was going to take Abigail to London and introduce her to fashionable society. Or, at least, he was going to arrange for her to be introduced to the *ton*. He was under no illusions about how poorly he fitted into that world.

The damsel was no doubt delighted to see St George when she needed him to slay her dragon, but she wouldn't want to dance with him at the grand ball the following night. She'd favour a man with more address and fewer battle scars.

'Well, I'll be damned!' Anthony exclaimed suddenly, getting slowly to his feet. 'What have you done to upset Miss Summers? She looks as if she's about to start breathing fire.'

Gifford raised his head to discover Abigail was striding through the orchard towards him. He blinked, and checked her attire more carefully.

'Good heavens!' he said in disbelief, when she came to a halt in front of him. 'The Romans have been trounced. Boadicea rules victorious.'

Abigail planted her hands on her hips and lifted her chin defiantly. She'd torn up the bedsheet and turned it into a flowing white tunic, fastened with knots over each shoulder. She'd braided additional strips of linen into a long chord, which was loosely tied around her trim waist. Her rich auburn hair fell all around her shoulders in shining waves. At some point she'd found the time to make use of the brush Gifford had put on the breakfast tray for her and forgotten to mention, but she'd made no effort to pin her hair up.

In her simple white tunic, with the morning sunlight shining on her cascading curls, she looked absolutely magnificent. She certainly managed to stun every coherent thought out of Gifford's dazed mind.

'Who the devil do you think you are, Gifford Raven?' she demanded fiercely. 'Telling me I'm not fit to make up my own mind?'

'Is walking around in public like some kind of barbarian priestess supposed to convince me that you *are* of sound mind?' Gifford retaliated, unsticking his tongue from the roof of his mouth.

The way she squared her shoulders to confront him pushed her breasts forward against the linen folds. She was modestly covered, but he had no difficulty remembering what lay beneath the draped cloth. He was standing right out in the open, but he felt as if his back was trapped against a wall.

'I am not a barbarian! I'm a practical Roman!' she declared. 'If the Romans had torn up their togas they might not have lost their empire!'

'You may have a valid point there,' Anthony observed, sounding interested. 'It is a fact that togas increased in size during the later centuries of the empire.'

Abigail's mouth dropped open in surprise. 'They did?' Then a triumphant smile lit up her face. 'You see!' she told Gifford with great satisfaction, before hurrying over to Anthony.

'Anthony...Mr Hill. Please sit down again,' she said anxiously.

'Please call me Anthony.' He subsided into his chair.

'Does it hurt?' Abigail asked, kneeling on the grass beside him. 'I'm so sorry you were wounded. May I do anything for you?'

Gifford clamped his jaw together to prevent himself uttering the instinctive protest that rose to his lips. He intended to take Abigail to London to introduce her to decent, honourable men. He wanted her to learn to be more discriminating in her judgements of other people...other men. He knew better than anyone that his cousin was decent and honourable—and was therefore a good man for Abigail to spend time with—but Gifford hated it when she ignored him in favour of Anthony.

'No, no, there's no pain,' Anthony assured her. 'A little stiffness. Nothing to worry about. Giff was overzealous when he tied me up in this sling. It really isn't necessary.'

'If he thinks your arm should be in a sling, I'm sure he's right,' Abigail said firmly.

Her unhesitating confidence in him gratified Gifford, but he was less happy about her subsequent words.

'He must know all about that kind of thing by now,' she continued. 'Gunshots and such things. But he doesn't know *anything* about what's best for me.'

She pushed herself back to her feet and turned to confront Gifford.

'You have no business ordering me what to do!' she said fiercely. 'You may have bought me, but you haven't paid for me—and you certainly don't own me.'

'I know damn well I don't own you!' Gifford glowered down at her.

'You're acting like it. Thinking you can keep me a prisoner in that horrible little room because I haven't got any clothes to wear!' Abigail took a couple of paces towards him and pointed an accusing finger at his bare chest. 'And why are you parading around half-naked like a common prizefighter? What happened to your shirt?'

'You threw tea at it! Besides, it was too small.'

'Your own shirt.' Abigail put her hands back on her hips and frowned at him impatiently.

'It wasn't fit to be worn after sleeping in it all night.'

'Well, wash it! In this heat it will dry in a trice. Go and get it!' Abigail pointed one hand imperiously towards the inn. 'I'll wash it. Good heavens! You're enough to try the patience of a saint!'

'You will not wash my shirt!' Gifford said categorically.

'I don't see how you can accuse me of being a barbarian when you're parading around like…like…'

'That's twice you've accused me of parading.' Gifford bent his head until his nose was almost touching hers. 'I *never* parade. And I did not accuse you of being a barbarian.'

'You said I looked like Boadicea!'

'You look like a damn witch!'

'Witches wear black!'

'Dressed in white—ready to be burnt at the stake for tempting innocent men to their doom.'

'Oh.' Abigail's lips parted in a soft exclamation of surprise.

Gifford's face was so close to hers he could see the gold rays that circled the pupils of her green eyes. Tiny sunflowers that expanded as her pupils dilated in response to her change of mood. If he lowered his head a few more inches he could kiss her. He saw her shifting awareness in her eyes, then she leant closer to him, lifting herself on her toes. He responded to the inexorable pull towards her—then jerked back as if he'd been burnt.

In an unguarded moment he saw her lips pout and her eyebrows draw together with disappointment. Then her expression cleared and she looked at him severely.

'You are evading the issue,' she said. 'You cannot hope to convince people we're respectable if you...walk... around half-naked. It's not civilised. Put the landlord's shirt back on until Ned gets here.'

'I am not civilised. And whatever plans you may have for the future you are not—and never will be—*my* governess. Don't imagine you can rule me.'

Gifford held her gaze for several unnerving seconds, before spinning on his heel and striding away through the apple trees.

'Well, goodness,' said Abigail, glancing at Anthony with some embarrassment. 'He is very temperamental, isn't he?'

Anthony laughed. It seemed to Abigail that he had been greatly amused by the whole interlude. 'You're more than a match for him, Miss Summers,' he assured her.

'Please call me Abigail,' she said. Then she gasped with indignant realisation. 'He just marched off without even discussing my plans. He thinks he can tell me what to do without a by-your-leave. And insult me into the bargain!'

'I think it might be more accurate to say that he ran away,' said Anthony, grinning. 'As opposed to marching off,' he explained, when she looked at him askance. 'Which would erroneously imply that he had some kind of clear objective in mind when he left.'

Abigail blinked. 'I thought he was going to put on a shirt,' she said, surprised.

Anthony threw back his head and laughed.

Chapter Eleven

Gifford scowled as he wrung out his shirt. He'd commandeered a bucket from a servant, and washed his own shirt in water from the pump.

His peculiar actions had naturally attracted another audience. This time it was augmented by several of the inn's regular customers. They'd turned up to quench their midday thirst after a hot morning's labour—and discovered a rake-hellish pirate doing his own laundry at the yard pump.

Gifford twisted his wet shirt viciously, wishing it was Charles Johnson's neck between his big hands, and cast a forbidding look at the curious bystanders. All the men took several hasty steps backwards. The children didn't budge.

'Are you goin' to hunt the highwayman now?' one of them asked.

'What highwayman?' Gifford untwisted his tortured shirt.

'The one who shot yer friend,' said the child. 'And stole yer lady's clothes.'

'Stole…?' Gifford held his shirt by its shoulders and snapped it briskly downwards. It made a sound like a cracking whip. The most nervous of the men took another step backwards. 'Who told you he stole her clothes?'

'She did,' said the child. 'I asked why she was wearin' a sheet. Are you going to kill him when you catch him?'

'Yes,' said Gifford.

* * *

Abigail sat with Anthony in the orchard. She could feel the grass beneath her bare feet. It was an unfamiliar but very pleasant sensation. Now she was no longer fired up by the first flush of outraged indignation, she was rather shocked at her temerity in leaving her room so unconventionally dressed. She wasn't entirely comfortable with the situation, but now she'd braved the wider world, she wasn't ready to scurry back into her hidey-hole just yet.

Anthony was a pleasant and unalarming companion. He didn't talk about her ordeal. Instead he entertained her with funny stories from his and Gifford's boyhood.

'You're as bad as each other!' Abigail exclaimed at one point. 'The poor gamekeeper! The pair of you must have sent him grey!'

'Don't forget Cole,' said Anthony lazily. 'Gifford's younger brother. He got into his share of scrapes too.'

'I don't know anything about him,' said Abigail. 'Gifford...Captain Raven said I should stay with his brother and his wife. But...I don't even *know* them!' Her voice lifted a little, revealing her discomfort at being forced to stay with unknown and possibly unwilling hosts. 'I c-can't just inflict myself on them.'

'Strictly speaking, they're inflicting themselves on Giff,' Anthony said calmly. 'Or they would be if he hadn't insisted they stay in London so Honor can be close to her mother. The house in Berkeley Square belongs to Giff. If you go there, you'll be his guest, not Cole's—but Honor's presence will make things more comfortable for you.'

'Respectable,' said Abigail, her voice a little hollow.

'Yes. Abigail...' Anthony paused, choosing his words carefully. 'No one wants you to do anything you're not comfortable with,' he said at last. 'Least of all Giff, no matter how much he might rant and rave. But you have a lot of friends—more, perhaps, than you realise. Old friends like Admiral Pullen, Mrs Chesney—all of Mrs Chesney's formidable family. Even Mr Tidewell arrived at the double when he heard you were in trouble.'

'Mr Tidewell?' Abigail repeated in amazement. She'd always liked Miss Wyndham's lawyer, but it hadn't occurred to her he'd had any hand in her rescue.

'Very fierce on the need to rescue you, he was,' said Anthony, smiling slightly. 'So was the admiral. If Giff hadn't put his foot down, they'd have been riding along with us to your rescue.'

'Oh, no!' Abigail instinctively pressed her hand against the base of her throat. It would have been dreadful if those two respectable, middle-aged gentlemen had seen her humiliation, but it comforted her to know they'd cared so much about her fate. 'They might have been hurt,' she said. 'I don't think they could have managed all that leaping and jumping that you and Gifford…Captain Raven…did. You were so brave and strong.'

'I just followed Giff's orders.' Anthony shifted his legs uncomfortably. 'As I was saying, you have many old friends—and also newer friends. Like Malcolm Anderson…and me…and Giff, of course. You are not alone. You don't need to be afraid about the future.'

Abigail's eyes filled with tears at his blunt assurance. It meant so much to her, but she didn't know how to thank him—or even if he wanted her thanks. By the time she'd collected herself enough to speak, he'd risen to his feet.

'I'm hungry,' he said gruffly. 'Giff will keep you company for a while.'

She looked up and through misty eyes saw Gifford striding towards her. She was so shaken by Anthony's words, and by her sudden excited nervousness when she saw Gifford approaching, that she didn't immediately notice anything odd about his appearance.

She brushed her fingers across her eyes and looked up at him as he closed the distance between them.

'What's the matter?' he demanded, looming over her. 'Why are you crying?'

'I'm not crying.' She gave him a watery smile. 'Your shirt's all wet!' she exclaimed an instant later. His shirt tails hung halfway down his thighs. The damp linen clung to the muscular contours of his upper body.

'You told me to wash it.' He continued to stand over her, his hands on his lean hips.

'*You* washed it?'

'There's a pump in the yard,' he said pugnaciously. 'I believe I'm as competent to wash my own shirt as the next person—as you.'

'I don't suppose you've ever washed anything before in your life!' Abigail retorted. 'I've never seen such a creased-up rag. What did you do to it?'

'It's clean and I'm wearing it!' he growled. 'What more do you want?'

'Nothing,' she said hastily. She couldn't resist touching the fine crumpled linen. He'd squeezed a myriad knife-edged creases into it so fiercely she wondered if it would ever iron flat. But she knew he was rich enough not to care.

She almost thought she could see the damp fabric steaming in the combined heat of his body and the sun. She smoothed the linen over the hard ridges of his stomach. His muscles jerked and grew even harder beneath her palm. She caught her lower lip between her teeth, excited and fascinated by the feel of his virile body.

Gifford's large hand shackled her wrist.

'When we go to London, you are not to stroke every man you meet!' he said harshly.

'*What?*' Abigail tried to jerk her arm away from him, but he held her firmly—though not so tightly he hurt her. 'You oaf! Let me go! I wasn't stroking you. I was wondering whether the creases would ever iron out!' she said tartly.

'Well, don't let your obsession with smooth linen prompt you to stroke any other men!' Gifford said disagreeably. 'Even I know that's not the conduct expected of a young lady embarking upon her first Season.'

Abigail hit his stomach with her free hand. It wasn't a very hard blow. She was still sitting on the chair in front of him, which limited her freedom of movement and, in any case, she was too soft-hearted to put any real weight behind the punch.

Gifford grunted softly and grabbed her wrist before she could hit him again.

'That wouldn't have stopped a kitten!' he said scornfully. 'If you're going to hit a man—put some power behind it. It's no damn good if you just annoy him.'

'I didn't want to hurt you!'

'You can't hurt me, you ninny!' Gifford released her. He planted his feet astride and put both hands on his hips as he looked down his nose at her. 'Not like that.'

'You want me to hit you where I can hurt you!' His arrogant pose as he stood over her was so infuriating that Abigail was tempted to do just that.

'You have no idea—' Gifford began, then broke off to intercept a well-aimed blow to his groin. 'Dammit, woman!' he snarled through gritted teeth. 'Have you got no decorum?'

'I was extremely decorous for twenty-seven years,' Abigail declared hotly. 'It's not my fault that my careful plans to go *on* living a decorous life have been ruined. And if you didn't want me to retaliate, you shouldn't have loomed over me b-boasting about your invincibility.'

Gifford flung her wrists out of his hands and spun away from her.

'I have *never* claimed to be invincible,' he said in a low voice which throbbed with anger, and another emotion which Abigail couldn't identify.

She folded her trembling hands in her lap. For some reason she was finding it increasingly difficult to have a calm, rational conversation with Gifford. She didn't understand why he was so upset at being called invincible. He was the most powerful, ruthlessly competent, unconquerable man she'd ever met.

She looked up to see the landlord approaching them, and wasn't sure whether to be relieved or sorry at the interruption.

Abigail sat in the dark on the wobble-legged chair. Gifford had curtly told her she would be safe to spend the night alone. She hadn't argued with him. Of course she was safe. He was only a few yards away, and all the danger was over.

But without Gifford's forceful, overwhelming presence to distract her, she was plagued by memories of her brief captivity. She wrapped her arms around herself and shuddered as she recalled how Charles Johnson had spoken to her. How he'd breathed on her. The way he forced her to undress in front of him and stroked her with his pistol.

She hated him. She'd never believed it would be possible for her to hate another human being as much as she hated Charles Johnson. She tried not to think about him. Hate was not an emotion she enjoyed feeling. It spoiled her peace of mind and served no useful purpose.

She felt oppressively hot and uncomfortable. Gifford had forced open the small window in the bedchamber the previous evening. It was open now, but it didn't provide much relief from the humid night. Abigail was wearing her green sprigged gown. Her black mourning dress was still at the Blue Buck.

It was reassuring to wear her own familiar clothes again, but Abigail had to admit she'd been physically more comfortable in her makeshift linen tunic. Her damp skin prickled within the confines of her corset. The heat pressed down upon her. It felt difficult to breathe. She shifted her weight on the chair and it rocked forward. She stood and picked up her fan from the dresser. Then she went to lean against the wall next to the window.

She could hear thunder rumbling in the distance. She saw a brief flash of lightning. Thunder growled a little closer. She unfurled her fan, remembering how she'd sat at her window the first night she'd seen Gifford.

So much had happened since then. She grieved for Miss Wyndham. She was still shocked by what had happened with Charles Johnson. But she also felt more alive—and in some ways happier—than she had at any time since her mother's death.

Gifford had held her in his arms. He'd kissed her. As she remembered, she closed her eyes and rested her head against the wall. She touched her lips wonderingly with her fingertips. No one had ever kissed her before. Dowdy, penniless Abigail Summers. No one had ever flirted with her before—not that she could recall. But gallant, daring, magnificent Gifford Raven had kissed her.

She smiled against her fingers. Perhaps he would kiss her again. She hoped he would kiss her again. Put his arms around her and let her explore his virile body. His hard musculature fascinated her. She loved touching him.

A flash of lightning nearly blinded her. Thunder crashed almost immediately afterwards. A few seconds later it started to rain. Almost at once a cooler breeze stroked Abigail's face. She put down her fan and gripped the windowsill, delighted by the occasional large raindrops which splashed on her skin. The clean, refreshing smell of parched earth as it accepted the rain pervaded the small bedchamber.

Lightning lit up the landscape. Thunder responded. For a few minutes the storm crashed noisily overhead. At last it moved on, and only the steadily falling rain disturbed the peace of the night.

Abigail extended her arm out of the window. The summer rain was warm, but it was cooler than her overheated skin. It felt wonderful. Her body was still too hot and uncomfortable within her corset. She wished she could feel the raindrops rolling down her neck and between her breasts. The desire to experience that sensation became as compelling as the desire to drink when she was very thirsty.

She stood undecided for a few seconds, but she would probably never get another opportunity to indulge such a fantasy. No one would know if she went outside. She slipped out of her room and down the stairs, unbolted the door and went out into the pouring rain. She stood in the yard for a moment or two, then realised someone might see her from one of the windows. It was one thing to do something a little peculiar if no one else knew, but she didn't want to be discovered in the midst of fulfilling her whim.

She navigated carefully across the yard until she found the edge of the orchard. The trees were dark and slightly ominous shapes ahead of her. She shivered in momentary apprehension, and glanced back at the solid security of the inn. She wouldn't go any further.

She unpinned her cap and shook out her hair. She loved the feel of the cool rain on her scalp. She lifted her face to the sky and unfastened the top two buttons of her high-necked bodice. The rain beating against her body felt cleansing and invigorating, washing away the lingering sensation that she had been defiled by her abduction and auction.

Then two hands closed on her shoulders from behind. Shock slammed through her. She opened her mouth to scream.

'Abigail?' Gifford growled in her ear. 'What the *hell* are you doing?'

Her legs sagged with relief. She slumped against him. He grabbed her before she could fall on the muddy ground. A moment later her relief turned to anger. She twisted round and gave him a big shove.

'Will you stop making me *jump*?' she shouted at him. 'Haven't you got any sense?'

'*Sense?* Where's the sense of standing out here in the rain?' Gifford demanded incredulously. 'What's wrong with you?'

'Nothing's wrong with me. I'm perfectly well.'

'Don't be ridiculous. No sane person goes out in a thunderstorm.' Gifford seized her upper arm and dragged her towards him. 'I'm taking you inside.'

'Stop it!' Abigail pushed him away. Rain plastered her

hair to her head. Water ran into her mouth when she opened it to speak. 'Stop giving me orders and telling me what to do!'

'Someone has to. Even a halfwit has the sense to come in out of the rain.'

'I'm sorry you have such a poor opinion of my under-standing. Go away.' In the darkness, Abigail saw Gifford make another move towards her. She stepped hastily aside. 'And don't just pick me up and haul me off like a sack of corn.'

'What are you *doing* out here?' Gifford said through clenched teeth.

'It's none of your business.' Abigail turned her back on him.

'Are you meeting someone?' Gifford's broad chest pressed intimidatingly against her shoulders, crowding into her.

The sky above was dark. The sound of the rain, as it drummed on the cobblestones to one side of them and the trees to the other, isolated them from the rest of the world.

'Meeting…?' Abigail could hardly believe what she'd just heard. She whipped round to face him. Her waterlogged skirts banged against his legs. 'That's a witless question if ever I heard one,' she said scornfully. 'Of course not.'

She felt the expansion of Gifford's chest as he drew in a deep, frustrated breath. 'Then what *are* you doing out here?' He sounded at the end of his patience. 'Abby?' He took hold of her upper arms.

It seemed natural to Abigail to rest her palms against his chest. It didn't take any time for her to notice he wasn't wearing a shirt. Of course he wasn't wearing a shirt. It was the middle of the night, when any sensible man would be asleep—and Gifford Raven prowled around half-naked.

'How did you know I was out here?' she asked.

Rain drenched both of them. It sluiced over Gifford's wide shoulders, over his chest and over Abigail's hands. Rivulets of water coursed down her angled forearms and

dripped from her elbows onto her already soaking skirts.
Water filled her eyes and her ears.

'Of course I knew where you were,' Gifford said irritably. 'I heard you open your door and come downstairs.
When you came outside I thought you must be sleepwalking! Perhaps dreaming... No one in their right mind—'

'We've already established I'm only fit for Bedlam!' Abigail interrupted crossly. 'Why weren't you asleep? I
thought no one would notice if I came outside.'

'You don't seriously believe I would leave you unguarded in a public inn?' Gifford sounded incensed. 'After
everything that has happened?'

'You said I was s-safe in my room alone.'

'You were. I was watching.' Gifford's hands moved from
her arms to rest on her upper back. He pulled her a little
closer to him.

'I didn't know.' Abigail filled with warm wonder at the
knowledge Gifford had been actively guarding her. 'I
didn't... Thank you.' She lifted a hand to his rain-wet
cheek. 'I should have known you'd take care of me.' She
put both arms around his neck and lent against him confid-
ingly.

Gifford cleared his throat. 'So what *are* you doing out
here?' he asked hoarsely.

'I was hot,' she said simply. 'And the rain looked so cool
and inviting. I thought no one would know. I can't put my
head under the pump the way you can.'

'How do you know about that?'

'The children told me.' Abigail's fingers explored the
nape of his neck. 'You are very tall,' she murmured.

'Damned inconvenient at sea,' Gifford growled. 'This is
one of your benighted witch tricks, isn't it?'

Abigail laughed softly, feeling a surge of warmth that
owed nothing to the hot, hard body pressed against hers. It
was an emotion akin to affection, but something deeper and
more tender. Gifford shouted at her, insulted her, and ordered her about with no thought for her sensibilities. But

he'd guarded her repose, followed her out into the rain—and now he was holding her with care and gentleness.

She slipped the fingers of both hands through the rain-soaked hair at the back of his head, lifting it from his scalp. A warning sound rumbled deep in his chest.

'No one ever suggested I could bewitch them before,' she said breathlessly, intoxicated by the effect she appeared to be having on him. 'It's very k-kind of you to—'

'Dammit! I'm not kind at all,' Gifford said savagely.

He bent his head and fiercely claimed her mouth with his. In the darkness Abigail closed her eyes. She could hear nothing but the rain falling all around them. Her awareness was dominated by her sense of touch and her sense of taste.

Gifford's kiss was flavoured by summer rain—and the faint tang of salt. His mouth was cool when it first touched hers, but his tongue burned against her lips. His kiss was hot and demanding. One hand slid down her back to her waist, and then lower to curve around her bottom, moulding her soaking dress against her body. The heat of his hand scorched through the cold wet muslin, warming her body where no man had ever touched her before. Pleasure pulsed through her. She wriggled against his hand, because it felt so good. He pressed her hard against him. Suddenly they were clamped together from breast to thigh.

Abigail gasped—then gave a small moan of excited discovery. She felt stunned—dizzy—with all the wonderful new sensations bombarding her. The contrast of the cool rain falling on her back with Gifford's scalding, urgently exploring hands. Her soft breasts pressed against the hard wall of his chest—the solid length of his thighs...

His kisses were hot and fierce. His tongue stroked boldly against her soft lips then confidently invaded her mouth. He tasted wild and dangerous. Abigail lifted herself on to her toes, wrapping her arms tightly around his neck as she pushed eagerly up to meet his passion.

Gifford groaned. He lowered his head to press his open

mouth against the side of her neck. His hands kneaded her buttocks and rocked her against his pelvis.

Excitement soared through Abigail. She couldn't distinguish one overwhelming sensation from another. Gifford's passion was hot, hard and undeniable. Her legs trembled. Her body throbbed in places she hadn't known it was possible to throb. She moaned helplessly, and rested her forehead against Gifford's shoulder, as he kissed her beneath her ear.

Rain fell all around them. Concealing them like a curtain and a blanket in one. It was getting colder, but Abigail burned with arousal.

Gifford went utterly still. He rasped something against her rain-slick skin. Abigail was too passion-dazed to understand what he said.

'W-what?' she gasped. 'What happened?'

'Nothing happened.' An instant later Gifford swept her up in his arms and started to carry her back towards the inn.

'Are we going in now?' Abigail put her arms around his neck and stretched up to kiss his rigid jaw.

'Yes.'

'All right.' She pressed another kiss against his jaw.

Gifford gritted his teeth. Her breath was warm against his cheek. Her body was soft and yielding against his. Desire for her raged through him like an insatiable beast. He was determined to protect her from the consequences of her own innocence, but his mind was clouded by the fumes of his passion. His driving need to satisfy his hard, insistent arousal.

He reached the doorway and paused, tipping his head back to the sky. Rain fell in long straight spears out of the darkness, temporarily blinding him, but doing little to cool his ardour.

He took Abigail inside. He ordered her to bolt the door and pick up the lantern he'd left beside it. He hadn't taken the lantern out into the storm. The light would have interfered with his night vision and might well have been extinguished by the rain.

'We're dripping on the floor,' Abigail whispered.

'You should have thought of that before,' Gifford retorted.

He carried her up to her bedchamber. He set her down in the middle of the floor, closed the door, took the lantern out of her hand and placed it on the dresser.

They looked at each other. Abigail's wet hair appeared as black as Gifford's as it hung in ribbons around her shoulders. The green muslin dress clung to every curve. Gifford could see her nipples jutting against her bodice. Water dripped steadily from her hem to create a circular puddle around her. Drops of rain ran down her face, shimmered on her eyelashes and her lips. He wanted to taste her all over again.

Abigail gazed at him. She looked at his face, then lowered her eyes to look at his torso. She took a couple of steps closer to him to touch the rain drops which glistened on the black curls which lightly dusted his chest. Her hesitant touch was exquisite torture in his state of total arousal. Her lips parted slightly with fascinated, breathless anticipation. Her gaze dropped lower. His waterlogged breeches did little to hide his erection. It was her turn to stand completely still.

Gifford's breath locked in his throat. His heart hammered against his ribs. Very, very slowly, Abigail laid her splayed hand flat in the centre of his chest. She leant forward and kissed him, quite close to his nipple.

He groaned, his self-restraint destroyed. He seized the open sides of her bodice and ripped it down. Material tore, buttons bounced and rolled on the floor. Abigail's eyes widened in surprise, but she didn't protest. She let him push the gown over her shoulders and down her hips to the floor. He put his hands on her waist and lifted her away from the pile of soggy material. She was left standing in her front-lacing, boneless corset and chemise. Her corset strings were soaking wet and resisted his impatient fingers. He muttered a curse and pulled a sheathed knife from the waistband of his breeches.

Abigail's lips parted with mild shock as the knife blade gleamed in the lantern light. Gifford cut delicately through the corset strings, re-sheathed the knife and laid it safely on the dresser. The front of her corset hung loosely open. Abigail hadn't moved an inch when Gifford turned back to look at her. The rain, falling on the cobblestones below the open window provided the musical accompaniment for the suspense-filled moment.

'You're so damn beautiful,' Gifford said huskily.

'I...am?' Abigail whispered.

She didn't see him move, but suddenly he was towering over her. He touched his hands lightly, almost hesitantly to her sides. There was nothing between them but her flimsy chemise. She quivered with nervous, eager anticipation. He lifted his hands, slipping them beneath her loosely hanging corset. His palms grazed the outer curves of her breasts. For several seconds he remained perfectly still. Her breasts rubbed tantalisingly against his hands in rhythm with her quickened breathing.

Her gaze locked with his. She caught her lower lip between her teeth. Tension coiled deep within her. Her breasts throbbed with unfulfilled need. She moved from side to side, instinctively pushing herself against his unmoving hands. He responded, cupping her breasts in his large, warm palms, circling her erect nipples with the side of his thumbs.

A soft cry escaped her lips. She could feel the effect of his caresses deep in her core. Her body clenched and ached in unfulfilled yearning. She reached out to him, holding on to his upper arms to anchor herself in the physical, emotional maelstrom he deliberately created within her. His biceps bunched beneath her clutching fingers. He bent his head to kiss the upper swell of her breast. She cupped her hands behind his head. His breath against her damp skin was warm and intimate. His lips caressed her, the tip of his tongue teased her. She moaned. Her body turned to liquid fire. She ached, quivered, then pushed herself restlessly against him.

He slid a supportive arm around her waist as he rid her of the corset. Her rain-soaked chemise stuck to her skin. He tipped her against his chest so that he could reach around her to grip the chemise between his two hands. Abigail felt the hard muscles surrounding her bunch and flex as he ripped the flimsy garment apart. He stepped back, peeling the almost transparent material away from her breasts—and then she was naked.

She experienced a flicker of uncertainty. Of shyness. Her hands fluttered to her breasts, but he gently caught her wrists and drew her close to him. His damp chest hair teased her pert nipples. He put her hands on his shoulders and bent his head to claim her lips. He kissed her gently until she lost her hesitancy and pressed up against him. She kissed him back, claiming his mouth as eagerly as he claimed hers. Instantly he deepened the kiss. His hands moved urgently down her body to hold her hips hard against him. His wet breeches felt rough against the bare skin of her thighs. His erection pressed insistently against her stomach.

When he'd kissed her in the yard, Abigail had been assailed by so many different sensations she hadn't been specifically conscious of his arousal. Now she was acutely aware of how his body reacted to hers.

He felt so big and hard. Such a powerful, virile man. He was so strong. So much larger than her in every way. A flicker of apprehension slipped into her mind. She knew nothing. Gifford knew everything. What they were doing must be completely familiar to him—yet it was so unfamiliar to her. What if he hurt her? What if she failed to please him?

He moved down her body and his mouth closed around her nipple. He sucked hard on it, then nipped and tugged at it with his teeth. Abigail cried out. Her nervous doubts burnt to nothing as her level of arousal became even more intense. He manoeuvred her towards the bed, kissing and touching her every inch of the way. He tore back the covers, picked her up and deposited her in the middle of the mattress.

She sprawled on the cool linen, naked but for her stockings. She was so hazed by impatient desire she'd lost any sense of shyness. She watched openly as he stripped off his breeches. His lean, muscular body resonated with barely contained virile energy. His arousal jutted proudly as he turned towards her. Her mouth went dry. She licked her lips with nervous anticipation as he joined her on the bed.

His firm skin was warm where he touched her. And though they'd never been in exactly this situation before, the feel of his hard body close to hers was not unfamiliar. She put her hand on his shoulder, welcoming his weight as he bent over to kiss her. His lips teased her mouth, while his fingers teased her nipple.

She moaned with pleasure and rolled a little towards him. Without conscious thought on her part, her leg bent so that she could rest her inner thigh against him. He muttered something. It sounded almost like a groaning laugh. He lifted his head to look down into her eyes.

'This is nicer lying down,' she breathed, too overwhelmed by her feelings to censor her words.

'It is?' Gifford stroked his hand lazily down her side to her hip, then returned to cup her breast. He bent to flick her nipple with his tongue. 'Why?'

'Because…be-cause…ohhh…' She sighed and arched up towards him as his tongue continued to play with her nipple.

'Abby?' he prompted her, lifting his head. His hand slid down to her hip once more, then onto her thigh. He pulled her closer to him.

'Because it doesn't m-matter if my legs melt!' she gasped.

Gifford groaned and moved lower. He kissed her ribs

beneath her breasts, then his lips caressed her belly. His hand rested on her knee, then his fingers began to stroke up her inner thigh.

Abigail panted, melted and burned with new delight. His hand moved higher. She tensed, automatically closing her knees together. He kissed the soft skin of her stomach, both distracting and frustrating her. She moved restlessly beneath him. He was filling her with need, but it wasn't her stomach that most craved his touch.

His hand moved higher, tangled with her dark auburn curls. Abigail held her breath. She was on the edge of a precipice. She wanted to scream at him. She wanted to plead with him, she wanted...

He stroked her. Parted her. Her hips jerked beneath his hand. Her breath jolted out of her lungs on a ragged moan. This was *not* what she'd expected. In a distant corner of her mind she was amazed at her brazen loss of modesty. She'd expected something less...less *intimate* than this. More—more...

Her thoughts splintered, her legs dissolved as he caressed her hot, swollen flesh. Then tension returned to her muscles and she began to rock against his hand as the urgency of her need increased. He inserted a finger inside her and she stilled, startled by the invasion.

He was inside her, but...

Even in her state of dazed arousal, Abigail was confused. She put her hand on his side, and discovered his body fairly vibrated with the rigid tension in his powerful muscles. He jerked and swore when she moved her hand up over his chest.

He didn't sound angry. More as if he was fighting a battle with himself. With the effect that *she* was having on him. Abigail liked that idea. She was thrilled that she could have such a strong impact on him. Especially since he was doing something to her which she definitely hadn't been prepared for.

His finger was still inside her. His thumb rested on the

mound of her curls. It was very intimate and strange—and not particularly satisfying in her current state. Or, at least, he was arousing needs he wasn't fulfilling, which was very frustrating.

Her hand explored his chest. She found his nipple and teased it, wondering if it would feel as good to him as it did to her.

'Dammit!'

An instant later she was flat on her back and Gifford was poised above her. Even in the shadows thrown by the lantern light she could see the dark tension in his face, the blazing fire in his blue eye. His thighs were between hers. His arms braced on either side of her body.

Well, good. According to her limited education on the subject, this was how he was supposed to do it. She put her arms around him. Her heart beat up into her throat with excitement and some nervousness as she waited for him to make his next move. She felt the hard, blunt tip of his erection nudge her hot, swollen flesh. His chest heaved. He shuddered and was still again. Abigail's gaze locked with his, looking for answers in his face. Looking for completion.

He pushed inside her, paused—and thrust deep.

Abigail gasped. She clutched his back convulsively. He filled her. Hurt her, momentarily, until her body began to adjust to his. He was face to face with her, looking at her, as he had done so many times before—but not when his expression was fierce with arousal. And not when his body was so deeply embedded in hers.

His muscles shook with tension. His body was hot and slick with sweat, even though cool rain still fell outside the open window.

He closed his eye and bent his head, hiding his face from her. Abigail's confusion grew. Obviously her education on this subject had been totally inadequate. Perhaps it was like dancing. There was a set of pre-ordained steps you were supposed to follow. It seemed very unfair that no one had told her what she was supposed to do next. Perhaps they'd thought she'd never need to know.

'Horses move more,' she said, in a slightly disgruntled tone. 'I thought—'

Gifford's large body started to shake uncontrollably. He rocked over her. Gasping, groaning and half-laughing. His weight settled more heavily on her. He was still hard within her, but he trembled, choked, struggled for self-control.

'You're l-laughing at m-me!' Abigail was mortified, close to tears.

'No, I'm not.' He kissed her neck, his mouth hot and hungry against her skin. Then he lifted his head to look down at her face, flushed now with embarrassment as well as desire.

'I was trying not to hurt you,' he said gruffly.

'Oh. I'm sorry,' Abigail said in a small voice. 'You should have explained. I thought it was my turn to do something. You bow. I curtsy. But I don't know what—'

He cut off her words with a hot, demanding kiss.

'So...I'm not hurting you?' he said hoarsely, a little while later.

'No.'

'Good.' He pulled gently out of her.

'Oh!' Abigail's thighs tightened against his hips. 'Ohhhh!' she sighed with satisfaction as he pushed back into her.

At first his strokes were slow and careful. He watched her intently. She closed her eyes, holding tightly to him as she surrendered to the inexorably building tension within her. Her body throbbed and tingled all the way to her toes. Her pulse raced. Her breath came in ragged gasps. His power filled her. Consumed her. Sent her spinning into a vortex of ecstasy.

She moaned and shuddered, her body jerking spasmodically with the strength of her exquisite release. Gifford's completion quickly followed hers. She felt the pulsing intensity of his climax as he pumped his body ever more urgently into hers—till at last he shuddered and groaned and let his weight subside on top of her.

Chapter Twelve

Abigail returned slowly to the world. Gifford's hot, heavy body pressed her into the mattress. He was still inside her, but now he was completely relaxed.

At last he stirred, lifting himself away from her. He pulled a sheet over them, then slipped an arm around her. She snuggled against him, her head resting on his shoulder. For a while neither of them spoke. Abigail savoured the moment. She had never known Gifford to be so peaceful or relaxed. She listened to the soothing sound of the rain and let her mind drift.

'Horses *move more*?' said Gifford suddenly, a disbelieving note in his voice.

It took a few seconds for Abigail to comprehend what he'd said—and why. She stiffened with embarrassment.

'Just what do you know about horses in this… ah…context?' he asked in astonishment.

Abigail cringed and rolled away from him, but when she reached the edge of the bed she realised she was stark naked. She lay rigid with mortification, unwilling to get up and expose herself to him. Her whole body was on fire with self-consciousness. It was bad enough that she'd lost all self-restraint in Gifford's arms—why on earth had she allowed herself to become so indifferent to propriety that she'd *said* such a shocking thing?

'Abby?' Gifford's arm circled her waist from behind.

She jerked and pressed her face into the pillow, covering her exposed cheek with her hand. She wanted to hide from him.

'Abby?' He fitted his long body around hers, spoon fashion, and nuzzled her neck. His kiss was leisurely, warm and relaxed. His teeth tugged gently at her earlobe. Her body still glowed with the aftermath of their lovemaking. Despite her embarrassment she couldn't help responding to the tenderness of his caresses.

At last she sighed, and leant back against his chest.

'You're laughing at me,' she mumbled, still hiding her face with her hand.

'No, I'm not.' He stroked her stomach in slow, languid circles, then moved his hand upwards to cup her full breast. He weighed it gently, lifting it slightly against the pull of gravity. His thumb played idly with her nipple.

Abigail began to melt. It was hard to remain embarrassed when he was making her feel so good.

'I just want to hear more about this stallion you compared me to so unfavourably,' he murmured provocatively.

'You…!' Indignation burned away the last remnants of her mortification. Abigail tried to flounce over on to her other side to face him. Unfortunately she was so close to the edge of the bed she nearly fell out.

Gifford grabbed her and moved them both nearer to the middle of the mattress.

'Get off me!' Abigail tried to push his hands away. 'You haven't got any finesse!'

'If I had less,' he began, grinning, 'perhaps I'd have fared better in comparison with—'

Abigail launched herself at him. She pushed him on to his back and half-sprawled across his body as she clamped both her hands over his mouth.

'Be quiet!' she said crossly.

He shook with laughter beneath her and his arms closed around her, holding her prisoner. She heaved in a deep, frustrated breath. It was quite difficult to concentrate when she was so acutely conscious of the way her breasts were squashed up against the hard muscles of his chest. Not to mention the distracting sensation of other parts of his body against her inner thigh.

She repositioned herself gingerly and glared at him through narrowed eyes.

'You aren't going to laugh—or say anything improper— if I take my hands away, are you?' she said warningly.

She felt him grin against her palm. She sighed. She should have known better than to expect any quarter from him.

She removed her hands anyway, and laid her head on his chest. Looking down at him made her neck ache. His words were extremely aggravating, but the way he touched her told a different story. His tender caresses made her forget— or at least push to the back of her mind—the significance of what they'd just done. She would worry about the consequences later.

He pushed her damp hair back from her face, then lazily stroked his hand down her body, over the curve of her bottom and along her outer thigh. She was still wearing her stockings, though they'd sagged below her knees since she'd first put them on. He hooked a hand behind her bent leg and dragged it possessively up his body. Then he slipped his fingers inside the top of her stocking. His possessiveness and the casual intimacy of his gesture made her quiver responsively.

'Tell me about this stallion,' he persisted, a smile in his voice.

Abigail sighed. He obviously wasn't going to be diverted from the subject. 'My father kept two horses,' she explained. 'They were carriage horses, I suppose, but mostly he used them on the farm. Two mares. And he wanted to breed from them. He borrowed Mr Woodford's stallion. Mr Woodford was one of our neighbours. I happened to be going for a walk...' Her voice faded away.

Gifford chuckled. 'So your education in this area is entirely based on the amorous activities of your neighbour's stallion?' he said. As he spoke he massaged her back in slow, seductive circles.

'Miss Wyndham was very interesting, too,' Abigail replied drowsily.

'Miss Wyndham?' His hand momentarily stilled against her back in his surprise. Abigail wriggled, in an unspoken demand that he continue to stroke her.

He resumed his gentle massage. 'What did Miss Wyndham tell you?' he asked, intrigued.

'She said it was a very pleasant experience to share a bed with a man,' said Abigail. 'A well-formed man. Miss Wyndham was always partial to a handsome man.' She moved against Gifford, stroking his hard pectoral muscle in a languid gesture which stirred his blood. 'Miss Wyndham would have been very impressed by *you*,' she murmured.

'Indeed?' Gifford said warily. His perspective on Miss Wyndham was undergoing a radical amendment. 'I thought she was a very respectable old lady.'

'Oh, she was,' Abigail assured him. She lifted her head to look down at him. Even in the flickering light of the candle he could see the mischievous expression on her face. 'But when she was younger, she wasn't respectable at all. She was…well, I mustn't tell you *whose* mistress she was, she made me promise to be discreet—but he was very wealthy and very indulgent. He died over thirty years ago, but he left instructions that Miss Wyndham was always to receive an annuity from his estate until the end of her life. His heir very honourably fulfilled his father's wishes.'

'Good God!' said Gifford. 'So she was respectable for the last thirty years only?'

'Yes. But she said that was long enough for the scandal to be dead and buried when she finally returned to Bath,' said Abigail. 'She could remember Beau Nash.' There was a note of awe in her voice. 'Back in the 1740s. She could tell wonderful stories.'

'But in that case, why the devil did Johnson have such expectations of her?' Gifford demanded. This new information made it clear that Miss Wyndham had always lived on the favour of rich men. If Abigail had known it, why hadn't the woman's own nephew?

Abigail's warm, relaxed body stiffened abruptly. Gifford silently cursed his unwary tongue. He hadn't meant to remind her of her ordeal. His question had been prompted by uncomplicated curiosity. His black rage against Charles Johnson was temporarily in abeyance. It was almost impossible for him to feel anything but slow-burning desire when Abigail was in his arms.

'I don't think he knew,' she said, a note of tension in her voice. 'Charles was…is…only twenty-six. For all of his life she *was* respectable. Her sister—his grandmother—didn't approve of Miss Wyndham. It seems she expressed her disapproval by not talking about Miss Wyndham—rather than publicly condemning her. Charles's parents both died several years ago. So when he finally met Miss Wyndham he believed her to be what she appeared to be—a respectable old gentlewoman in very comfortable circumstances.'

'So she trusted you with the truth, but not her greatnephew?' Gifford said. He stroked his large hands reassuringly up and down the soft warm skin of Abigail's back.

He loved the way she moved responsively to his touch, even when her attention seemed to be entirely focussed on their conversation. She was as naturally sensuous as a cat. Just thinking about the way he'd found her standing in the rain, with her top buttons undone and her head thrown back to feel the water on her skin made his body harden with renewed desire. Right now he wasn't willing to think beyond the end of the night—or even the edge of the bed. There would be consequences for what he'd done—but he'd spent his adult life dealing with consequences. Tonight, while the rain fell and Abigail nestled in his arms, he would take a holiday from responsibility.

'She wanted Charles to think well of her,' Abigail said,

distracting Gifford from his increasing arousal by the outrageous nature of her statement. 'But I'm not quite sure she
trusted him,' she added, over the top of Gifford's scornful
exclamation at her previous comment.

'If she didn't trust him, why was she so pleased to see
him?' Gifford demanded. 'According to what you said,
when he arrived in Bath—'

'I know. I know.' Abigail frowned, biting her lip. 'She
was pleased to see him,' she said. 'He was charming and
attentive. She wanted to think well of him—and have him
think well of her—because he was her only relative. I think
it hurt her that her sister disowned her so completely. I think
Miss Wyndham *wanted* to trust Charles—but deep down
she wasn't really sure that she could.'

'*Were* there any jewels?' Gifford asked, remembering
Johnson's main grievance had been the absence of expensive jewellery.

'I think there probably were. Men do give their mis-
tresses jewellery, don't they? But I never saw any. Bessie
said she sold them—to pay for "unforeseen expenses".'

'Charles Johnson,' said Gifford grimly.

'Don't think about him now,' Abigail begged. She circled
her fingertips beguiling over his chest, playing teasingly
with the dark hair she found there. 'I didn't tell Miss Wyndham about you,' she said musingly. 'I'm sorry you never
met her. But I was afraid—if she knew you were in the
habit of sleeping naked—she might have wanted to
exchange bedchambers with me.'

'*What?*' Gifford half-rose from the bed in shocked disbelief at Abigail's demure statement. 'You little vixen!' He
rolled her on to her back and pinned her down with his
large body. 'The woman was old enough to be my grandmother!'

'I know. But she still appreciated what she called "a fine
specimen of manhood",' Abigail replied. As she spoke she
delicately investigated the muscles along Gifford's side
with her fingertips.

'And she taught you how to appreciate one too?' Gifford said tautly. His body tensed with arousal beneath her sensuous exploration.

'Yes. But it turned out there were large gaps in the things she told me,' Abigail said breathlessly.

'Perhaps I could help you with those…gaps,' Gifford said, moving suggestively against her.

'You…already did!' Abigail gasped. 'Oh, my goodness!'

'And she left you all her clothes,' Gifford said, suddenly struck by the significance of that. The mistress of a wealthy man had no doubt dressed not only to impress, but to draw attention to her feminine charms. The image of Abigail in a seductive silk gown was irresistible. 'You must wear one of her dresses tomorrow,' he said hoarsely. 'In the evening.'

Abigail froze. Gifford's large body was still poised above her. His virile strength surrounded her. His erection pressed demandingly against her stomach. She had only to move a little to accommodate him, and she knew he would soon be inside her.

But he'd just called forth her own secret, never to be admitted to anyone, belief about Miss Wyndham's generous bequest. Abigail was sure Miss Wyndham had left her the exquisite gowns to help her attract the attention of a rich protector. Such finery would be of little use to a respectable governess or companion. An elegant appearance would hardly be sufficient to counterbalance her lack of fortune for a man in search of a wife, but a man looking for a compliant mistress might well appreciate Miss Wyndham's taste in clothes.

Gifford had not said one loving word to her since she'd surrendered herself to him so completely. He'd teased her about the coupling of horses, and questioned her about Miss Wyndham and Charles Johnson—but he hadn't said a single thing about the two of them. Or what the future held for them now.

Abigail closed her eyes. Shame rolled over her in suffocating waves. Her own feelings for Gifford were so strong she'd foolishly assumed his feelings for her were just as compelling. Now she realised she'd mistaken male lust for a tenderer emotion. After all, he had *bought* her from Charles Johnson. No wonder he felt he was entitled to enjoy the pleasure of his purchase.

Abigail was fascinated by what she privately thought of as Miss Wyndham's mistress gowns. She wanted to wear them, to have the opportunity of looking pretty and seductive instead of dowdy and old-maidish. But she wasn't going to settle for being Gifford's mistress—even if he had rescued her from Charles's grotesque plans for her. What had been good enough for Miss Wyndham was *not* going to be good enough for Abigail.

Gifford's very male, rampantly aroused body was still poised above her. She could feel the tautness in his muscles, the urgency of his desire. Despite her intellectual determination to resist him her body responded to his. Instinctively, almost against her will, her legs began to open for him. Her hands still held him tight. She wanted him to give her all the exquisite pleasure she'd already found once in his arms tonight.

But it was wrong.

'No,' she whispered desperately.

'What?'

'No!' she repeated fiercely. Somehow she found the strength and resolution to put her hands flat against his chest and thrust him away.

He rolled on to his side next to her. She could feel him tremble as he fought to control the demands of his powerfully aroused body.

'What's wrong?' His voice sounded strained. Gritty. 'Did I hurt you earlier?' A second later his hand curved gently over her hip and downwards across her stomach. 'Are you sore?'

'Don't touch me!' Abigail pushed his hand away. What should have been a considerate question seemed to her to be motivated by simple practicality. She knew that a reasonable man—in most respects Gifford was a reasonable man—would make a point of breaking in a new horse gently. No doubt he would also take pains to break in his new mistress gently.

'What's the matter?' he demanded, brusque and impatient.

Abigail resisted the desire to turn onto her side and curl up into a protective ball. It was her fault she'd unintentionally misled Gifford about her expectations. Now she had to deal with the matter with as much dignity as possible. Her throat was so tight it was difficult to speak, but at last she managed to do so.

'I would like you to get out of my bed,' she said jerkily. 'If you please.'

'I don't please.' Gifford sounded angry. 'Not until you tell me why.'

'I'm not obliged to offer you an explanation.' She clutched the edge of the sheet in desperate fists.

'It's a bit late to plead offended modesty!' he rasped.

'I'm not pleading anything!' Abigail retorted. 'I told...I *asked* you to get out of my bed.'

'You pleaded earlier!' Gifford shot back, physical frustration and emotional confusion overcoming his discretion. 'When you wanted me to move like that damn stallion you compared me to.'

'How could you! How *could* you remind me of that?' Abigail resisted the urge to pull the sheet up over her head. She was desperate to retain her dignity. She just didn't quite know how.

'It was *my* performance you disparaged!' Gifford felt as if he'd been kicked in the stomach by the hated stallion.

His emotions were raw and exposed. For the first time in months he'd felt relaxed. At peace with himself and the rest of the world. Abigail had given herself to him so generously. Even her heedless comment about horses had filled him with tender amusement. He'd interpreted her words as a sign of her innocence and enchanting openness.

But now she'd withdrawn from him. Rejected his touch
and closed her thoughts to him. He was exiled from her
bed, no doubt from the confines of her room—and it wasn't
even morning.

She waited, lying rigidly on her back, not saying anything.

Gifford got out of bed. It was still raining. He found his
wet breeches and pulled them on. It was an unpleasant experience. His hot flesh cringed from the cold, clammy cloth.

'We will talk in the morning,' he said stiffly. 'Goodnight,
Miss Summers.'

Abigail waited until she heard the door close, then she
rolled on to her side and drew her knees up to her chest. A
few seconds later she pulled the sheet over her head and
buried her face in the pillow to muffle the sound of her
tears.

She cried for a long time. The tears were a welcome
release for the tension of the past few days. But at last she
dried her eyes and took stock of the situation. Her emotions
were in a state of such tumult she wasn't sure what she
thought or felt. She knew only one thing for sure. She could
no longer allow Gifford Raven to arrange her life for her.
She would be forever grateful he had rescued her from
Charles Johnson. She had no doubt that Gifford was a com-
passionate, honourable man. The most honourable, com-
passionate, heroic man she'd ever met. But she was not
going to become his mistress—without even the courtesy
of an invitation!

How dare he tell her what to wear tomorrow!

She held tight to her indignation over that minor example
of his high-handedness to protect herself from deeper, more
painful emotions. He'd made love to her, but he didn't love
her. Abigail had discovered she was greedier than she'd
ever believed possible. She didn't just want his body—or
even the jewels and fine clothes he would no doubt lavish
on his mistress—she wanted his heart.

She rolled on to her back, listened to the rain, and

frowned thoughtfully up at the ceiling. Perhaps she should think of it as a sort of cutting-out action. The kind of naval manouevre Admiral Pullen had told her about, where an enemy ship anchored safely in one of its own harbours was captured by stealth. According to the admiral, Gifford had excelled in leading such dangerous missions. She wondered how she could apply such tactics to a more peaceful enterprise. She wanted to capture his heart…his love.

The following morning Abigail discovered, not greatly to her surprise, that her green dress was not only still soaking wet—it had also been torn beyond repair. She flushed with self-consciousness at the memory of *how* it had been ripped. In her own secret heart she had no hesitation in admitting how wonderful Gifford's lovemaking had been. She drew courage as well as reassurance from the memory of his tender caresses. But it shouldn't have happened. She shouldn't have let it happen. It was entirely her fault if Gifford believed she was prepared to sell herself for nice dresses and jewellery. Somehow she had to repair the damage her heedless behaviour had done.

Mrs Chesney had sent all Abigail's clothes to the inn, including the dresses she had inherited from Miss Wyndham; but in the circumstances it was clearly unthinkable that she wear one of Miss Wyndham's gowns. She chose instead her primrose muslin and piled her hair carefully under a modest cap. But when she was ready, she could barely find the courage to go downstairs to the parlour. To face Gifford…and Anthony.

Her cheeks burned at the thought of seeing Anthony. Would he guess what had taken place between her and his cousin? She hadn't given his presence a thought the previous night, but now she was ashamed to face him.

And she was afraid to face Gifford.

Despite the optimistic plans she had made she wanted to hide. To escape. To pretend the events of the last few days had never happened.

No. She laid a hand instinctively against the pit of her stomach. She could never regret what had happened last night. It was a memory she would treasure all her life.

But it was necessary for her self-respect to pretend it hadn't happened. Even though she felt sure the changes that had taken place in her must be obvious for all to see, she knew she had to walk down the stairs and look both men straight in the eye. Show them she was still in control of her future.

Her mouth was dry. Her throat so tight she could hardly swallow. Her heart raced. She felt sick with anxiety. She stood gripping the door handle for several minutes as she tried to summon the courage she needed to leave the bed-chamber.

At last she lifted her chin, opened the door, and prepared to confront the hazards of the world beyond the safety of her room. She descended the stairs one step at a time, then faltered outside the parlour. She could hear voices inside. She wasn't sure whether it would be easier to face Gifford and Anthony for the first time separately or together. If they were together, it would presumably limit what Gifford felt able to say to her—but would her self-consciousness at the knowledge Anthony was observing their interaction outweigh that advantage?

She swallowed and pushed open the parlour door.

At the sound of her entrance, both occupants of the parlour looked in her direction. She stopped quite still, her thoughts knocked out of kilter by the unexpected sight of Admiral Pullen rising and hurrying towards her.

'Miss Summers!' he exclaimed. 'Miss Summers! Have you recovered from your ordeal?'

'M-my ordeal?' Abigail stammered as he seized her hand in a warm, encouraging grasp. Her mind was full of Gifford and the way he'd made love to her. She'd almost forgotten that Charles Johnson had abducted her. 'Oh... Yes,' she assured the admiral. 'I am quite well.'

Despite herself, her eyes scanned the room for Gifford,

even though she'd seen immediately that only Anthony and
Admiral Pullen were present. Where was he?

She half-turned towards the door, even though the admiral still had hold of her and was still talking to her. She
barely comprehended what he was saying.

'Gifford went for a walk,' Anthony said quietly. Her eyes
jerked to his face. He smiled at her with all his customary
friendliness. 'May I pour you some tea?'

'Thank you.' Abigail finally remembered her manners
enough to pay attention to Admiral Pullen. 'I'm so sorry,'
she apologised. 'I confess, I am still a little distracted by
what happened.'

'And no wonder. Come and sit down.' The admiral
towed her to one of the parlour chairs. 'A terrible ordeal
for you. But you'll be pleased to know we've routed out
that nest of vipers!'

'What?' Abigail glanced from Anthony to Pullen in confusion. 'What do you mean?'

'We visited the Blue Buck yesterday!' Pullen announced
triumphantly. 'Anderson, Tidewell and myself, and a couple
of magistrates. Took along some stout-hearted fellows to
reinforce our orders. Wouldn't believe some of the things
we found. Closed the whole place down.'

'You did? Mr *Tidewell* went with you?' Abigail found it
difficult to imagine the precise lawyer taking part in a raid
upon the unsavoury inn.

'Very hot to join us, he was,' said the admiral with satisfaction. 'A good man in a tight spot.'

'Good grief,' said Abigail. With the best will in the
world, she found it quite difficult to imagine Mr Tidewell
fighting his way out of a tight spot. 'What about…?' She
hesitated, reluctant to ask the most important question.
'What about Charles?' she whispered. 'What…? Was…?'

'He wasn't there, confound him!' Admiral Pullen
punched his fist into the palm of his other hand. 'But we'll
catch the black-hearted—' He broke off, looking at Abigail

with gruff discomfort. 'Never fear, my dear,' he said. 'We'll catch him. He won't get away with what he did.'

Abigail didn't like to think about Charles. She'd been afraid of him when he had her in his power. She hated him. But she didn't want to think about him. She didn't want what he'd done to change the way she thought or acted. If she let that happen, he would still have power over her.

'I hope he is caught,' she said, trying to keep her voice and her emotions neutral. 'It would be terrible if he tried to do the same thing to someone else.'

'He will be caught,' said Anthony, his soft assurance in chilling contrast with the admiral's more excitable manner.

Abigail's gaze flew to his face. Despite the part he'd played in her rescue, she'd thought of Anthony as the more reserved, less aggressive of the two cousins. He smiled as he met her gaze, but his smile didn't reach his eyes.

'It may be a toss up whether Giff finds him first—or I do,' he said calmly. 'But Charles Johnson will be caught.'

Abigail looked away. She was disturbed by the cold hatred she'd seen in Anthony's face.

'How can you h-hate him so much?' she asked. 'You don't know him.'

'He put a rope around your neck and sold you!' Anthony replied, his normally well-modulated voice harsh. 'I don't need to know any more than that.' He stood up abruptly. 'I won't spoil your appetite any further,' he said, and left the parlour.

Abigail stared after him in consternation, then looked towards Admiral Pullen.

'I don't know the full story,' he said uncomfortably. 'But I do know that the privateers who captured Raven's ship put Hill in irons and planned to sell him at a slave auction. It seems he feels quite…strongly…about such matters.'

'Oh, my God!' Abigail had known from Gifford's first arrival in Bath that he suffered nightmares about some event in his past. She pictured again the moment she'd first seen Gifford and Anthony through the window. Gifford had been asleep, but Anthony had been awake and reading when his cousin shouted out his defiance at his nightmare enemy. She remembered Gifford's pointed comment to Anthony on the subject. Did Anthony suffer nightmares as well?

There was so much she didn't know about the two men. Perhaps if she knew more, she would find it easier to understand what Gifford really wanted from her—and how to win his love.

'Breakfast,' Admiral Pullen prompted her. 'You must keep your strength up. It's particularly important when you're facing a crisis. Though in your case, of course, the crisis is over,' he added cheerfully.

'It is?' Abigail stared at him.

'Oh, surely,' he said. 'Raven will take you to straight to London. No one there will know a thing about the past few days. By the time the Season starts you'll be ready to take your place with the other débutantes. Splendid.'

'But I'm not sure if I want to go to London,' Abigail protested, on the spur of the moment.

'Not go to London?' he echoed, gazing at her in amazement. 'Why ever not?'

'I think I would be more comfortable returning to Bath,' she said nervously. 'If I'm in familiar surroundings it will be…' Her voice faded away as she saw he was shaking his head vigorously.

'No, my dear, no, I really don't think that's a good idea,' he said firmly. 'What happened is something of a minor— quite large—scandal in Bath at the moment. I really don't think you would find it comfortable there right now.'

'Scandal?' Abigail said in amazement. 'How can it be a scandal? No one saw Charles steal me, and I was rescued the very same night. To be sure I've been away these past two days, but I could easily have been taken unwell. Should anyone ask I could simply say I had a bad head cold.'

'I'm afraid not,' said Pullen heavily. 'It's true no one saw Johnson abduct you. But the wine he left drugged the housemaid's young man, and she ran screaming into the street. Then, by all accounts, Raven had Mrs Chesney and Anderson interrogating all your neighbours to see if they'd witnessed anything...'

'He did what? All the neighbours know I was abducted!' Abigail gasped. 'Why didn't he just tell the town crier?'

'He didn't do that,' Pullen said. 'But he did have Mrs Chesney's relatives make enquiries along all the main roads out of Bath—to determine your route.'

'Oh, my God!' Abigail buried her face in her hands.

'I'm sorry to say, the whole of Bath is talking about the incident,' the admiral told her. 'So you see, I really don't think you'd find it comfortable to return there just now.'

Abigail groaned. 'I never thought to ask how he found me,' she said. 'I was just so grateful he did. Good grief! Can't he do anything without making a great noise about it?'

'He's never been one to worry about what other people think,' said the admiral. 'So you'll be going to London. I'm glad to have that settled. Would you like some of this excellent mutton?'

Chapter Thirteen

Her heart in her throat, Abigail went in search of Gifford. She'd considered the option of waiting tamely at the inn for him to return—but then he might take her by surprise and put her at a disadvantage. If she went to find him, he would be the one taken by surprise at her unexpected appearance—and that might give *her* the advantage.

She swallowed back her nervousness. Her reasoning might sound convincing, but she suspected Gifford Raven was very rarely taken at a disadvantage.

The sky was clear blue, the air fresh after the storm. Water collected in shining puddles in the yard and raindrops sparkled on the leaves of the apple trees. The path through the orchard was waterlogged and muddy. Abigail's skirts were quickly soaked through from the wet grass. She stepped out carefully, but with great resolution. She was going to carry the war straight into the enemy camp.

She looked up from negotiating a particularly large puddle. Gifford was six feet away, staring at her, his expression unreadable.

Tall. Formidable. Unconquerable. His black eye-patch seemed unusually forbidding in the morning sunlight.

Abigail's mind went completely blank. Her stomach somersaulted with anxiety. Her legs felt weak. She stared at him, unable to say a single word.

He was so handsome. So strong. So self-assured. And completely out of her reach. It was almost impossible to imagine this cold-eyed, autocratic man in the throes of the passion they'd experienced last night. This morning he seemed so distant.

'Take off the damn cap,' he growled at her.

'W-what?' Of all the things she'd anticipated he might say to her, that wasn't one of them.

'It's ugly. Take it off.' He braced his hands on his hips and glared at her.

'I will not!' Abigail was incensed that Raven seemed to feel he was already entitled to dictate what she wore. She wasn't his mistress yet.

'It's ridiculous,' he snapped. 'Quite inappropriate. My fiancée does not dress like a middle-aged spinster.'

'Your *w-what*?' Abigail's heart bounded with shock at Gifford's curt statement.

'We'll be married as soon as we reach London,' he told her grimly. 'It's not what I wanted, but in the circumstances it cannot be avoided.'

Abigail's budding hopes withered like unwatered seedlings. He didn't want her, he was just abiding by his honourable principles. Her disappointment was intense, a physical pain so strong she wanted to double up under the force of it.

Instead she lifted her chin proudly, refusing to let him see how deeply he'd hurt her.

'I don't w-want to marry you,' she said flatly. 'And I won't.'

A muscle twitched in his cheek. If he'd been a lesser man, she might have thought he'd flinched. No doubt he was merely expressing his displeasure at her mutinous behaviour, she thought miserably. Gifford Raven was a born autocrat. And his naval training had only intensified his tendency to take command.

'I'm sure you don't,' Gifford said grittily. 'But it is necessary. You will still have a Season in London. I meant for you to have the opportunity to dance and flirt at Almack's like the other débutantes. As it is, you may still dance—but I'm damned if I'll tolerate you flirting with another man.'

Abigail stared at him. Her thoughts were chaotic. Her emotions pinwheeled almost out of her control.

'Since I won't be your wife, I'll flirt with anyone I like!' she flung back at him.

'Not while I have breath!' In two quick strides he was in front of her, looming over her, his expression fierce and intense.

He didn't touch her, but he was so close she could feel the heat and power radiating from his virile body. It reminded her of the trembling, straining tension in his hard muscles when he'd been poised, unmoving, inside her.

She might have blushed at the unbidden memory that filled her mind at such an inopportune moment—except she remembered what he'd said then.

'I was trying not to hurt you.'

In the midst of his own, overwhelming passion he had been concerned for her well-being, and afterwards he had been so loving and gentle in the way he'd held her. He'd given her everything she'd needed except sweet words. And now he was angry at the idea of her flirting with another man.

Perhaps there was still hope.

She gathered up all her self-assurance and gave him a small, tight smile.

'I will consider your proposal,' she said unsteadily. 'But, in the meantime, I will wear what I choose, when I choose.'

'Consider—!' Gifford bit off the rest of his angry rejoinder. 'Dammit! Do you want to end up like that old hag you were living with?' The demand exploded out of him.

'Don't you dare speak so disrespectfully of Miss Wyndham!' Abigail fired back. She clapped the palms of her hands against his chest and tried to push him away.

Instantly Gifford caught her upper arms and held her

locked against him. Only by maintaining tension in her arms did she manage to keep him at a small distance.

Her treacherous body didn't want to be separated from Gifford, even by a few inches. Her arms wanted to relax so that she could lean against him. She resisted the urge and pressed her lips together, angry at her weakness.

'I meant no insult to Miss Wyndham,' Raven said grimly. 'It was your own situation that concerns me.'

'My situation is my affair—not yours,' Abigail said jerkily. 'You are not responsible for me—or anything I have done.'

'I'm responsible for my own actions, dammit!' Raven snarled. 'Whether you like it or not, I've never turned my back on my responsibilities.'

'I absolve you for…for anything you may have done that makes you feel responsible for me,' Abigail said with difficulty.

'Are you hoping to find another stallion who pleasures you better?' Raven demanded savagely.

It took several seconds before his meaning sank in. Abigail stared at him in growing shock and disbelief.

'Y-you think…!' she stammered, dumbfounded by the implications of his words. 'Oh, my God! You are so stupid I could box your ears!' she shouted at him. 'You are a *stupid* man!'

'That's the second time you've called me stupid.' Raven scowled at her, but some of the fierce tension gripping his body slowly ebbed out of him.

'Well, you are stupid,' she said stubbornly.

Then she remembered why she'd had occasion to call Gifford stupid before. He'd claimed that not many women would wish to dance with such a disfigured man. She was too confused and over-emotional to consider the significance of what he'd said then, but her arms relaxed enough that he was able to pull her closer to him.

'You are the first person I've met who has considered me lacking in intelligence,' he told her roughly.

'You're the first person I've met who doesn't like my cap,' Abigail retorted.

'It hides your hair,' he said irritably. 'It's far too flimsy to keep your head warm—should the weather turn colder. It serves no practical purpose.'

Despite her confusion and uncertainty, Abigail almost smiled. She thought Gifford had just paid her a compliment—in a roundabout, bad-tempered way. 'Many things serve no practical purpose,' she said.

'Hmm.' His gaze lowered from the rich Titian curls framing her face to her eyes—and then settled on her mouth.

Abigail's pulse rate—which had settled into a slightly calmer rhythm—instantly accelerated.

Gifford stared down at her soft, full lips. They parted slightly under his intense perusal. His body kicked with unruly desire as he saw the tip of her tongue flick nervously over her lower lip.

He wanted her. But he was still stinging from her cold rejection last night. He had been on the very brink of joining his body with hers, of driving them both into the temporary oblivion of utter ecstasy—and she'd thrust him away! She'd coldly ordered him from her bed as if she were a great courtesan grandly dispensing her favours!

Her rejection cut deep, hurting and humiliating him much more severely than he was willing to admit even to himself. He'd been fighting a battle with himself ever since he'd left her room.

One second he wanted to consign the fickle, cold-hearted wench to perdition, the next he was trying to understand why she'd denied him so unexpectedly.

He knew she wasn't experienced in the art of making love. He had felt her virginal barrier, and her gauche observation about horses had confirmed her innocence. He was also certain she'd enjoyed her initiation in his arms.

To be sure, a few doubts had occasionally crept into his mind as he strode through the dawn countryside, but he had heard—and felt—the moment she had shattered with pleasure beneath him. She had not been cold or overly modest then!

She'd even told him that the old hag Wyndham had told her there was much pleasure to be had in the arms of a well-made man! Gifford flattered himself he was as well made as any other man—whatever the old crone had meant by that dubious phrase.

When the haze of thwarted lust and bitter rejection had finally cleared somewhat from his mind he had concluded that Abigail must have been concerned about her reputation—her future security—when she'd ordered him from her bed. It was the obvious explanation for her change of mood. His conclusion had not improved his mood. Did Abigail really think he was the kind of conscienceless blackguard who'd take a woman's maidenhead and then abandon her?

Gifford had been angry, insulted—and apprehensive—when he'd unexpectedly come face to face with Abigail in the orchard. Apprehensive, because he couldn't be absolutely sure she would not reject him again. He didn't want her to be cold towards him. He wanted her to be warm and responsive.

Of course, he didn't *need* her to be warm and...loving. His mind shied away from the implications of that word. He wasn't looking for love. He was independent and self-sufficient in all his needs, but it did pique his pride that Abigail had so easily been able to forgo another flight into ecstasy in his arms.

Now she was graciously *considering* his offer of marriage! As if she had an option! Did she really think there would be a queue of more eligible bachelors waiting at the door of Almack's to vie for her hand?

He frowned down at her lips. Her forearms were still braced against his chest, denying him the satisfaction of feeling her full breasts pressed close to him. He resisted the temptation to move his hands from her upper arms to slide possessively across her back and down the curve of her waist to the pleasing roundness of her bottom.

He had no intention of revealing to her how irresistible he found her, when she clearly found him insultingly easy to resist.

Of course she would be surrounded by eager suitors if he allowed her to go to Almack's unwed. He could not imagine any man who gained sight of those soft pink lips, rosy cheeks, rich auburn hair and seductive green eyes not succumbing to her charms.

Not to mention her courage. Her resolution. Her wayward but delightful tongue.

He noticed that she was looking somewhat disgruntled. Leaning a little closer to him and lifting her chin a little more than the demands of pride might require.

The little witch wanted him to kiss her!

Triumphant, savage satisfaction pumped through Gifford's veins. Learn your opponent's weaknesses. The first and most important principle of any successful campaign— and now he knew Abigail's. She liked kissing him!

Well, he would withhold that pleasure until the contrary little vixen married him!

She was pouting now! He couldn't entirely blame her. He had been staring fixedly at her mouth for some minutes. She was probably wondering if he'd forgotten how to kiss.

Horses move more! Hah!

She'd just have to wait.

A few seconds later the aching need in Gifford's body prompted him to reconsider the terms of his surrender to Abigail's charms. Perhaps it would be acceptable to kiss her when she'd *agreed* to the marriage—rather than abstaining until the moment he got the ring on her finger. An event which would, after all, take place before witnesses.

'Consider quickly,' he growled.

'Consider what?' She looked at him in bemusement.

'My proposal, dammit! You're inflicting unnecessary hardship on both of us by your delay.'

'Hardship?' Abigail echoed. 'What hardship does my delay cause to you? I'm the one who—' Her mouth suddenly fell open into a soft round O of startled enlightenment. 'You boar! A rutting stag would show more delicacy in his courtship.'

'What do you know about stags?' Gifford demanded. 'Did you spend your entire childhood studying the mating habits of the larger mammals?'

'Of course not!' Abigail blushed furiously. 'You have no business saying such improper things to me.'

'May I remind you that it was not I who first introduced this subject into—'

Abigail put her hands over his mouth. That had the immediate effect of muffling his words—and the secondary effect of allowing him to pull her body flush with his.

He saw her eyes widen with awareness. He was still holding her upper arms, which meant they were standing breast to breast, but there was no contact between the lower parts of their bodies.

Gifford ground his teeth together in frustration as he considered the benefits and disadvantages of hauling her up against his throbbing erection. It would be a torturous form of pleasure at best—and also tend to confirm her accusation that he lacked delicacy in his courtship. Besides, she might coldly order him to release her. The humiliation of her rejection was still raw in his mind and his heart.

He forced himself to stand still. Not to increase the contact between them.

Abigail didn't move either.

He glowered at her, then bared his teeth against her palm and clicked them together menacingly.

She jerked her hands away from his mouth.

'You tried to bite me!' she exclaimed, shocked and indignant.

'I *didn't* bite you,' he replied impatiently. He'd have needed a rabbit's buck teeth to make any impression on her palm the way she'd held her hand flat against his mouth.

Then it occurred to him that, despite everything that had happened, she had never shown the slightest fear of him.

She'd told him to get out of her bed at a most critical point in their love-making with no anxiety that he might refuse. She hadn't been afraid he would force her. She wasn't afraid of him now—which was why she was so shocked that he'd even pretended to bite her.

It was obvious she trusted him. It was a start. Now all he had to do was manouevre her into marriage by with- holding the pleasures of his well-made body from her until she proved suitably amenable.

'Good,' he announced to the world at large, glad to have settled upon a course of action. 'The carriages should have arrived by now. We must make a start.'

'*Carriages?*' Abigail was pressed up against Gifford's chest. His large hands circled her upper arms. She could feel the potent, masculine tension in his body. His gaze had been fixed on her mouth until she'd almost screamed with frustration at his failure to kiss her—and now he was talk- ing about carriages!

'I ordered two,' he said. He released her arms and stepped away from her. 'One for the luggage and one for you and Anthony.'

'Me and Anthony?' Abigail looked at him in sudden alarm. 'What about you?' She had a sudden, terrifying no- tion of him going off alone to find Charles Johnson.

'Hate carriages,' he said tersely. 'I'll ride beside you.'

'Wouldn't Anthony prefer to ride too?' she asked curi- ously.

'Probably. His wound isn't serious, but I don't want him to over-exert himself,' Gifford replied. 'I told him you would be bored if we left you in the carriage by yourself.'

'You've told him he has to ride in the carriage to enter- tain me?' Abigail exclaimed indignantly. 'As if I'm a spoiled—'

'It was far more effective than telling him he should take care of his injury,' Gifford interrupted. 'He's of a mind he is now in full health and able to take up arms with the best of us.'

'He wasn't wearing his sling this morning,' Abigail remembered. She'd been so preoccupied by her own anxieties she hadn't given a thought to Anthony's minor injury. Even though he was fit and healthy it must still have taken its toll upon him.

'I suppose, what you mean is, I should entertain him,' she said. 'I dare say I can manage that. Providing an interesting distraction from tiresome realities is an important part of a companion's role. Miss Wyndham always said I was very good at entertaining—'

Gifford had been walking through the orchard path ahead of her. He stopped so abruptly she cannoned into him.

'What happened? Is there a puddle?' She tried to peer round him. 'Why on earth did you chose to go for a walk when everywhere is so muddy?'

Gifford spun round to face her. 'At least it isn't raining! And I'm wearing boots. What the devil have you got on your feet?'

'Pattens.' Abigail lifted her muddy skirts to show him. 'I'll have to change my dress before we leave.'

'Don't wear one of Miss Wyndham's,' Gifford said autocratically.

'I'll wear what I like!'

'Not in the carriage.' Gifford frowned at her. 'How do you intend to entertain Anthony?' he asked stiffly.

Abigail blinked at the unexpected question. 'I suppose I'll talk to him,' she said, bewildered. 'Although I believe I saw him yesterday playing with a small travelling chess set. Perhaps I should ask him to teach me chess. That should distract him from the idea that we're trying to curtail his activity. Do you think he would like to teach me chess?'

'Chess?' Gifford considered her suggestion. 'That will probably be acceptable,' he conceded. 'Well, don't dawdle. I want to get to London as soon as possible.'

He strode away, square-shouldered and stiff-backed, towards the inn.

Abigail followed more slowly, her thoughts in a jumble. She was heartbreakingly sure Gifford only wished to marry her from a misguided sense of honour. He had said quite clearly that marriage was not what he'd wanted.

But it was also obvious that he had enjoyed making love to her. It was his impatience to bed her again which had prompted his command that she should 'consider quickly'! Despite feeling a certain measure of indignation at his crudeness, Abigail was inclined to feel flattered rather than insulted by his openly expressed desire for her. Even in her secret dreams, she had never dared to hope she might inspire such passion in any man—let alone one as potent and charismatic as Gifford Raven.

Was physical pleasure enough to sustain a marriage? Many women made do with neither love nor passion. Was she greedy because she wanted both?

Abigail sighed. When she'd made up her plan to capture Gifford's heart it had never occurred to her that he might already have made up his own plan to marry her. It was tempting to acquiesce. But if she married him now, made herself readily available to him whenever he wanted her, he would never have to consider how he truly felt about her. She might well find he regarded her only as a pleasurable convenience, when what she wanted to be was his beloved wife.

She couldn't give in now. She had to give Gifford the time and opportunity to learn to love her.

Gifford conducted a private debate with himself as he rode ahead of the two carriages. He didn't want to confine himself in the coach with Abigail under Anthony's amused and observant gaze. But nor did he entirely trust Abigail out of his sight. She seemed to have no notion of what constituted seemly topics of conversation for a young female. Something would have to be done about that before he exposed her to wider society.

Good God! What if she suddenly expressed appreciation for the fine quality of a gentleman's coat and started stroking him! Just as she had stroked him the previous day when she'd thought his shirt needed ironing. Of course Gifford knew her action had been prompted by her innocence—and a female's natural, though to him somewhat inexplicable, obsession with the proper care of fine clothes.

Perhaps some kind of needlework, embroidery perhaps, would be a good way to keep her hands occupied. Then if she took a notion to stroke someone she might stab them with the needle.

He sighed, knowing his fancy was quite ridiculous. Abigail wasn't clumsy, and she wasn't lacking in wit. She charmed almost everyone who knew her. It hadn't escaped Gifford's notice that he'd been able to call upon the help of so many men when Johnson had abducted her.

She was a shade too direct and open in her dealings with him—but he admired her for it. He didn't want her to stop saying whatever came into her mind—he just didn't want her to share her intimate thoughts with anyone else.

He sighed again. She was right when she said he had no finesse. He was a fighting man, not a courtier. He was ill at ease in the drawing rooms and ballrooms of fashionable society. He had no notion of how to dance pleasing attendance upon a female.

But despite her cruel rejection when she'd ordered him from her bed, he was convinced that Abigail liked kissing him. He clung to the one advantage he knew he had. He might be no hand at making pretty speeches—but he'd given her a much more tangible, potent pleasure. Of course, he never should have made love to her—but, since he had, it was his duty to marry her.

Gifford prided himself upon the fact that he'd *never* been reluctant to do his duty, no matter how difficult the circumstances.

Chapter Fourteen

The rope tightened around Abigail's neck. She gasped and choked, unable to move as men's leering faces crowded around her. Hands clawed at her. She was trapped…

She jolted awake. For several seconds she still couldn't move. Trapped in the terrifying void between nightmarish sleep and rational consciousness.

The room was dark and unfamiliar. It wasn't the bed she had shared for two nights with Gifford. This was a far grander coaching inn. She rolled on to her back and rested her forearm across her eyes.

She was shaken to the core. Too frightened to slip back into sleep. Almost too scared to venture from the bed in case the ravaging phantoms burst out from the unfamiliar shadows to claim her.

She'd begged Gifford not to leave her side the first night he'd rescued her—and he hadn't. Last night he'd watched over her from a distance and followed her into the rain before bringing her safely back to her bed. Tonight she was alone. Tonight she had to face the demons by herself.

She forced herself to sit up, unreasonably afraid that her movement would draw the attention of unseen, hostile observers. Gifford had leapt from his bed with a great shout of defiance in a similar situation—but she lacked the courage for such a grand gesture.

She eased herself to the edge of the bed and gingerly extended her feet to the floor. She experienced a childish fear that ghostly hands would seize her ankles. She held her breath anxiously then, with sudden resolution, stood up. She looked around the shadowy room, then turned towards the door.

She bit her lip indecisively. Gifford had been watching over her last night. He'd even suspected she was sleepwalking. Would he be watching her tonight? Almost of their own volition, her feet padded silently over the floor towards the door. Lingering tendrils of her nightmare still coiled around her like taunting wraiths, invisible but malevolent.

She turned the key with stiff, cold fingers. She half-expected a hand to grab her from behind and drag her backwards as she slowly turned the doorhandle.

She opened the door the merest crack and peeked out into the hallway beyond. A man was sitting in a chair opposite. She saw his feet first. For one heart beat she thought it was Gifford. Then her gaze rose as he stood and came towards her, and she saw it was Anthony.

'Abigail?' he said softly, concern in his brown eyes. 'Is something wrong?'

'Oh.' She closed her own eyes, disappointment and confusion briefly overwhelming her.

'Abigail?' She felt him take her arm in a supportive grip.

'I'm sorry.' She opened her eyes again and gave him a weak smile. 'I'm being foolish. I had…I had a d-dream. It was so real.'

'I know,' he said gently. 'Were you looking for Giff? Shall I fetch him to you?'

'Gifford?' Abigail blinked. 'Why are you sitting outside my door?' she asked.

'You didn't think we'd leave you unguarded in a public inn?' Anthony said lightly. 'And Giff has to sleep some time.'

'Of course… Guarded?' Images from Abigail's nightmare surged back to the forefront of her mind. 'Do you th-think…do you think Charles will come back for me?' she whispered, her eyes darting anxiously up and down the hallway. She'd never given the possibility a thought before.

'No. No, I don't,' said Anthony, his voice deep and re-assuring. 'But Giff and I—perhaps our experiences have made us a little more cautious than most men, that's all. We're here, sweetheart. No one's going to hurt you.'

Abigail drew in a steadying breath and smiled at him. 'Thank you,' she said. 'Thank you for watching over me. I'm sorry you've been put to so much trouble.'

'No trouble at all,' said Anthony. 'Would you like me to fetch Giff?'

'No.' Abigail blushed at the implications of Anthony's question.

Besides, Gifford's manner towards her had been cold and distant since they'd embarked upon their journey. He hadn't travelled in the coach with her and Anthony, and he'd barely spoken to her that evening. She was afraid he was already regretting his hasty decision to marry her. He'd certainly given her no opportunity to try to arouse his tenderer feelings towards her.

'No. No, thank you,' she said to Anthony. 'I don't want you to disturb him. I think I can sleep now. Perhaps you can sleep in the carriage tomorrow,' she added, as an afterthought.

'Perhaps.' Anthony smiled. 'But I might disturb you and embarrass myself with my snores. Goodnight, Abigail.'

'Goodnight.' Abigail closed the door softly and returned to bed. She felt out of sorts because of her nightmare, her unsatisfactory conversation with Anthony, and her confusion over Gifford's true feelings towards her. But it was comforting to know that both men were guarding her so carefully.

Gifford stood on the quarterdeck of the *Unicorn*, his hands locked together behind his back.

He'd been lucky. The two privateers and their prize had

originally been sailing together. Gifford and half his men had been prisoners on one privateer while Anthony and the rest of the men had been hostages to Gifford's good behaviour on the other. The *Unicorn* had been put under the command of a crew of privateers. But the morning before he'd escaped from his own captivity a storm had blown up. It had lasted for most of the day and separated the three ships. Gifford had taken his chance, released himself and then his men from their imprisonment and together they'd captured the privateer.

Normally he treated enemy prisoners with consideration, but he had nothing but contempt for the dishonourable conduct of the privateers. He'd incarcerated them in the same stinking hold his men had so recently escaped from.

His luck had held. He'd had two days before the lookout had spotted the *Unicorn* on the horizon. Two days in which his men could return to some measure of fitness after their mistreatment, and he could learn how the unfamiliar ship sailed.

It had been a tense, expectant moment when the *Unicorn* was finally within gunshot. Gifford's men were proud of their ship and their captain. None of them could bear the thought of the *Unicorn* in the hands of such a despicable enemy. Every single man under Gifford's command had shared his determination. Either they retook the frigate—or they sent her to the bottom.

They'd recaptured her.

Gifford had taken ruthless advantage of the fact that the privateer prize crew on the *Unicorn* still thought the privateer vessel he was commanding was in friendly hands. By the time the privateers had discovered their error, the small prize crew in control of the *Unicorn* had been overwhelmed.

Now Gifford had two ships under his command. The *Unicorn* under his own captaincy, and the privateer vessel under the command of Lieutenant Fenton. But only half of his crew had been held prisoner with him. He was woefully short of men. He'd been able to grant Fenton only a skeleton crew, sufficient to sail the captured privateer, not to engage in battle.

But if he couldn't capture the second privateer by stealth, no matter how much he had already gained, he would still have lost. Because Anthony and the rest of his crew were hostages aboard the enemy vessel.

Gifford stood on the quarterdeck of the *Unicorn*, his scarred face stony as they chased down the remaining privateer. He was dressed, not in his own uniform, but in the clothes of a privateer. His hat was pulled low over his forehead, the shadow thrown by the brim partially concealing his distinctive eye-patch.

If he made a single mistake now, Anthony would be murdered. A man as close to him as his brother. Closer, in some ways. Gifford was several years older than his brother, Cole. He could remember, briefly, a world in which Cole did not exist. He could remember his first introduction to his red-faced baby brother. But Anthony was two years older than him. Anthony had always been part of Gifford's life. There had been the long period of separation after Gifford had joined the navy, but during these last couple of years, when Anthony had sailed with him, the bonds of their boyhood had been renewed.

Gifford clenched his jaw. The thought of Anthony manacled and sold into slavery was monstrous. The thought of Anthony dead in these circumstances was almost unbearable.

His stomach cramped as he heard the lookout's hail. His prey was in sight.

He gave a series of quick orders, reducing sail and making some essential alterations to the rigging and canvas to make it appear from a distance as if the *Unicorn* had suffered storm damage.

He didn't want to come within hailing range until shortly before nightfall, another two hours away, but he didn't want his slow progress to arouse the other captain's suspicions.

He had the privateer's signal book. And he had forced several of his prisoners—separately, and at knife point—to give him essential information to hoodwink the other captain. He'd also compelled two of those prisoners to help him make the masquerade convincing. They knew that, if they did anything to betray him, they were dead men.

As long as the other captain remained in a state of false security during daylight, Gifford would be able to mount a covert attack under the cover of darkness.

If the attack succeeded, he would have recaptured his own ship and gained two prizes into the bargain. If he failed—Anthony would die…

Anthony looked up from his small chess set to see Gifford approaching him. At least his cousin had taken the trouble to dress, but Anthony recognised the expression on his face. Gifford had had another nightmare.

'I can watch. You sleep,' Gifford said curtly.

Anthony didn't comment on his cousin's mood. He hesitated, wondering if he should mention Abigail's bad dream. Gifford had been very understanding of her anxieties immediately after her ordeal but, as his own tension had increased, he'd become increasingly overbearing in his dealings with her. Anthony had heard two versions of Gifford's marriage proposal. He was sure that both versions had been edited for his benefit. But he was also certain that it had been less of a proposal, and more of a ruthless command.

Perhaps if Gifford realised Abigail had anxieties of her own he would be gentler with her. Or perhaps he would see them as another burden he had to shoulder, and his need to control all her actions would just become stronger. Anthony decided not to interfere.

He stood up and offered Gifford the chess set. 'An interesting problem for you to while away the hours,' he said.

Gifford frowned down at the small board. 'It's mate in two moves,' he said dismissively.

'Is it? Goodnight.' Anthony strolled away to his bed-chamber, a grin on his face.

'Do…do *you* have nightmares?' Abigail asked, as the carriage rattled towards London. It was a very *personal* question to ask a man she knew so little of, but she didn't know how else to begin the conversation.

'Sometimes,' Anthony replied.

'Oh.' Abigail swallowed. She wanted to know why Gifford and Anthony both had nightmares—and what exactly they were about. But she didn't know how to ask. 'Gifford has bad dreams sometimes too,' she said breathlessly.

'I suspect they may not be quite the same as our bad dreams,' Anthony replied quietly.

'Not…why not?' Abigail locked her fingers together as she stared at Anthony.

'My nightmares, and probably yours, are about our own fate, about being helpless—enslaved,' Anthony said steadily. 'Gifford's nightmares—I think—ultimately revolve around the consequences for other people if he had failed.'

'Oh.' Abigail took a deep breath. 'Won't you tell me what happened?' she asked.

Anthony started from the beginning. He told her how the *Unicorn* had been sailing in company with another British frigate when two privateers had been spotted on the horizon. He told her of the brief, evenly matched battle between the four ships before Gifford had been knocked unconscious by flying debris. His fall had been witnessed by one of the lookouts on the other frigate. The other British captain had been instantly convinced of Gifford's death. Instead of remaining in the battle to provide support for the *Unicorn*, now fighting under the command of a relatively inexperienced first lieutenant, he'd withdrawn from the combat. No one on board the *Unicorn* had been aware of his flight until the smoke from a broadside had briefly cleared. Suddenly they had discovered they were facing the two enemy privateers alone.

Abigail pressed her hands to her cheeks in horror. 'That wasn't when he lost his eye?' she whispered. 'He said it was a great splinter.'

'No,' Anthony smiled reassuringly. 'He lost his eye years ago. He was only unconscious for a short while on this occasion. Long enough for the first lieutenant to surrender the *Unicorn* to the privateers, and for them to take us all prisoners. Giff was a prisoner of one privateer captain, I was prisoner of the other—on separate ships.'

'Why?' Abigail didn't understand. 'Why did they do that? You must have been so worried about him…?'

'I was.' Anthony's expression became grim. 'It was two weeks before I discovered if he was living or dead.'

'Two weeks? Do you have nightmares about that?'

Anthony looked at her, but he didn't answer.

'Then your nightmares are not only about yourself either. You are like Gifford,' said Abigail firmly.

'Hardly.' Anthony gave a short, unamused laugh. 'Gifford was told if he made any attempt to escape, or recapture the *Unicorn*, I—and all the rest of the men who were prisoners on the same ship with me—would be killed. That's why they separated us—to use me as a weapon against him.'

'What did he do?' Abigail whispered, appalled.

Anthony told her how Gifford had waited until a storm had separated the three ships, then escaped and released his men before capturing the privateer and retaking the *Unicorn*.

'He is so resolute,' she said in awe. 'Only think how wonderful it must have been for his men when he released them. It must have seemed like a miracle to them—that he had found a way to rescue them.'

'They'd have sailed into hell with him after that,' Anthony said. 'Mind you, most of them would have done so even before that. It's marvellous how he held the hearts and loyalty of as rough a crew of men as you're ever likely to see. He's not an easy commander. He doesn't give a damn about the men liking him. He doesn't have favourites. But they all believed in him. They all trusted him to lead them anywhere.'

'Of course they did.' Abigail saw Anthony's impassioned face through a haze of tears. She knew exactly how Gifford could inspire such devotion in another human being.

'I don't think he fully understands that.' Anthony smiled crookedly. 'Reasonable or not, he feels that he let us all down, that we should never have been taken prisoners at all.'

'How can it be his fault?' Abigail exclaimed indignantly. 'He cannot be held responsible for what other men do when he isn't even conscious!'

'He would say that he is responsible, even so,' said Anthony, 'because he should have trained those men well enough that they know what to do in an emergency.'

'He thinks he's God!' Abigail said in exasperation.

'I said something similar not long ago,' Anthony agreed.

'What about you?' Abigail asked. 'What happened to you? Was it…was it very dreadful?' She put a hand to her throat, remembering the feel of the rope around her neck—in her nightmare and in real life.

'Physically my situation was not particularly uncomfortable,' said Anthony calmly. 'There were five of us altogether on the *Unicorn* whom the privateers intended to sell to the American slave market.'

'Slaves…' Abigail pressed her hands against her lips and stared at Anthony.

'We were kept in irons, but otherwise in relatively clean, comfortable conditions,' he said, his voice absolutely flat. 'And exercised on deck every day to keep us in good health, to preserve our value at auction.'

'Oh, my God…' Abigail remembered Charles Johnson's taunts when he threatened to rape her, but ultimately preferred to keep her maidenhood intact to increase her price.

It was so hard to imagine the proud, intelligent man sitting opposite her, one of the finest men she'd ever known, kept in irons.

'It turned out to our advantage,' said Anthony. 'In the end.'

'Advantage?'

He smiled faintly. 'When we were exercised we had an opportunity to observe and memorise a great deal about the privateer vessel and crew. One of my companions had been an apprentice locksmith until he was taken up by the press gang. One night while our guard was sleeping he managed to pick the lock on his manacles. Once he'd…dispatched…the guard, he freed us all. Then it was just a question of freeing the rest of the crew—who were being held prisoner in a different part of the ship. Then we took the ship.'

Abigail leant her head against the padded headrest. They were moving ever nearer to London, but she had no interest in the unfamiliar countryside rolling past the window. All her attention was on the man sitting opposite her.

'There is a very strong likeness between you and Gifford,' she said. 'From prisoner to conqueror. Both of you achieved the same thing.'

'The cases were not at all the same,' Anthony objected. 'I was able to escape only because of the skills of another man. There were five of us when we set out to rescue the other prisoners. Gifford freed himself by his own efforts, and released his men unaided. There is no comparison.'

Abigail looked at him through narrowed eyes. She understood Anthony believed what he was saying. She just wasn't sure if she believed it was true.

'What happened after you'd captured the ship?' she asked. 'You told me you're an artist, not a sailor. Were there officers with you?'

'One marine sergeant. He knew nothing of seamanship. But we were lucky. We had several extremely competent able seamen with us among the prisoners—including my

locksmith friend. And an excellent quartermaster who'd often taken the helm of the *Unicorn*,' Anthony replied. 'His
seamanship was superb.'

'So you sat and twiddled your thumbs?' Abigail asked
demurely.

Anthony grinned. 'Taking the ship was only the first
stage in the plan,' he said. 'None of us were going to let it
rest there. The big problem, given our reduced crew, was
how we could possibly recapture the *Unicorn* and rescue
Giff. Fortunately Giff rendered all our plans unnecessary.
But there was a very tense couple of hours when we spotted
the *Unicorn* sailing down on us. We were very relieved
when we thought she'd suffered storm damage. We thought
it would give us more time to make our move.'

To Abigail's surprise, Anthony suddenly began to laugh.

'After all the high drama of the previous few days, the
climax was almost farcical!' he exclaimed. 'Both of us—
Giff and I—intended to board the other under cover of darkness. We both had our decoy privateer prisoners visible on
deck, terrorised into going about their normal business, in
an attempt to allay any suspicions of foul play. Neither of
us were anxious to come within hailing distance until close
to nightfall—but both of us tried to look as if we were eager
to regain contact. I have seldom played a more interesting
game of chess.'

'How did you resolve it?' Abigail asked, amused and
intrigued by the notion of the cousins trying to outwit each
other on the high seas. Anthony had just, possibly unintentionally, revealed that though the quartermaster had been
responsible for handling the ship, *he* had been in overall
command.

Anthony grimaced, looking annoyed. 'It was an obvious
and simple mistake—though perhaps understandable given
our shortage of able seamen,' he said. 'One of Giff's lookouts spotted my locksmith friend in the rigging. Giff was
surprised there was a black seaman working freely among
the privateers—given their anxiety to turn a quick profit.

There weren't any blacks in either of the privateer crews. There were a few more manoeuvres after that—but it all ended peacefully.'

'Thank you for telling me,' said Abigail. 'It is such an amazing story. I think you are both heroes. I am sorry you have bad dreams. Do you…do you *often* have them?'

'Not so often now,' Anthony assured her. 'I dreamt sometimes of finding myself on the auction block—though of course that never happened to me—but the dream comes less often now.'

'So did I,' Abigail whispered. 'I felt the rope and I saw those men…but it was just a dream. We are safe. You and Gifford rescued me. And you—*you* rescued yourself. I'm sure you inspired your companions to take effective action, just as you say Gifford inspired his crew. It doesn't matter whether you were the one who knew how to pick the lock— you were the one who had the resolution and determination to succeed. I'm sure of it!' She smiled dazzlingly at him.

Anthony caught his breath. Whether Giff was fully aware of it or not, he was a very lucky man. Abigail had all the courage, generosity and loyalty a man could seek in a wife.

'Be patient with him,' he said abruptly.

'Gifford?' Abigail looked startled.

'He feels more than he can easily express,' said Anthony. 'But he is not insensitive to…softer emotions. He enjoyed your music.'

'My music? How could he? I've never—'

'We heard you playing the pianoforte through the open window, the evening before Miss Wyndham died,' Anthony explained. 'It was a splendid performance. I'm looking forward to hearing you play again, when we reach London. There's a fine instrument in the house in Berkeley Square.'

'There's also Gifford's brother, and his sister-in-law,' Abigail replied, feeling a spurt of apprehension at meeting two important strangers under such unsettled circumstances.

'They'll like you,' Anthony said confidently. 'And I believe you will like them. Cole can be something of a gruff soldier—but you are growing used to the Raven tendency to issue orders by now. Honor's first husband was a soldier in Cole's regiment. When he was injured they were left behind the column. She carried her husband on her back towards safety, and then shot a wolf with his musket before Cole found them and took them to safety.'

'Good heavens!' Abigail exclaimed, daunted by Anthony's description of Gifford's sister-in-law. 'She must be very brave and…' She hesitated. The word hovering on her lips was formidable, but it didn't sound a very flattering thing to say about a lady she'd never met.

'She is brave. You have a great deal in common in that respect,' Anthony said. 'Cole and Honor only returned to England from the Peninsula a few months ago. She is still adjusting to her new life here. I think she will be glad to make a new friend.'

'I hope so,' said Abigail nervously. 'I'm flattered you enjoyed my music,' she added, remembering she had not thanked Anthony for his earlier compliment on her playing, 'you must have heard many much finer performances.'

'Perhaps executed with more technical skill—but not with any greater feeling for the music,' Anthony replied, smiling. 'You have great feeling for the music.'

'Oh. Thank you.' Abigail appreciated his compliment all the more for its honesty. She knew her fingers weren't always as agile as she'd like them to be. 'Tell me about the concerts you've attended—the musicians you've seen?' she requested.

For the next few miles Anthony entertained her with accounts of concerts he'd attended before he'd sailed on the *Unicorn* with Gifford. To Abigail's delight she discovered she had seen at least one of the same performers. George Bridgtower, a celebrated virtuoso violinist, had given a concert in the Pump Room which Abigail had been fortunate enough to attend.

Anthony had seen the violinist perform several times. For many years Bridgtower had been first violinist in the Prince

Regent's private orchestra, performing often at the Pavilion in Brighton.

'I heard Beethoven wrote a sonata for him, and they performed together in Vienna,' Abigail said.

'That is so, though unfortunately the two men fell out afterwards,' Anthony replied ruefully. 'But Mr Bridgtower is an exceptionally gifted musician. I very much enjoyed it when I had an opportunity to speak with him. A most rewarding experience,' he said, smiling at what was obviously a pleasant memory.

It occurred to Abigail that Anthony's meeting with George Bridgtower might have held particular significance for him. Like Anthony, the violinist was of mixed parentage—Bridgtower was the son of a Polish mother and a West Indian father. Anthony's meeting with the musician must have given him a rare opportunity to talk to someone with whom he had more in common than simply a love of great music.

'I didn't attend as many concerts as I would have wished in Bath,' Abigail said. 'But I'm glad Miss Wyndham persuaded one of her friends to escort me to that one. I hope I will be able to see many different musicians perform when I am in London,' she added hopefully. 'Do you suppose Gifford would like to attend a concert with me?'

Anthony grinned. 'If you ask him,' he replied. 'I do believe Giff might even brave the horrors of the concert hall for your sake.'

Chapter Fifteen

'Oh, my goodness!' Abigail breathed, somewhat over-awed by the impressive façade of the house in Berkeley Square.

Of course she knew Gifford was wealthy. She'd even taken advantage of that fact when she'd been seeking suitable positions for Miss Wyndham's staff. But she was far more familiar with him in his guise of overbearing pirate—a man who wasn't above washing his own shirt in a bucket should the need arise—than as the owner of such a grand house.

'What's the matter?' Gifford had just assisted her from the carriage. He looked down at her in concern.

'Nothing,' she assured him, clinging to the support of his arm a few seconds longer. 'What a very fine house.'

'My father liked it,' said Gifford, leading her up the steps. 'I hope you—ah, Kemp!' he broke off as the door was flung open. 'How are you?'

'All the better now you've won my bet for me, sir! Excuse me, sir! Ma'am.' The butler cast a wary, apologetic glance at Abigail. 'I'm afraid I forgot myself. Major and Mrs Raven are in the blue drawing room.'

'Kemp, this is Miss Summers,' Gifford introduced her cheerfully. 'She'll be staying with us. The baggage is in the second carriage. We'll go straight up to my brother and sister-in-law. Oh, and Kemp,' he added, as the butler turned towards the front door, 'I'm glad my failure to remain in Bath an entire month has put you in pocket.'

'I forgot all about your bet!' Abigail whispered as they mounted the grand staircase. 'Does rescuing me count as an adventure?'

'I'm afraid so,' said Anthony, from two treads below them. 'I'm still awaiting settlement. I'm not sure who was foolish enough to take Kemp's wager!'

'Oh, but that's not fair!' Abigail stopped on the stairs, turning to glance between the two men. 'It was a rescue, not an adventure! He didn't walk on stilts through the Pump Room, or anything!'

'You consider stilt-walking adventurous?' Gifford raised his eyebrow.

'I couldn't think of a more appropriate example on the spur of the moment,' Abigail said impatiently. 'You know what I mean. I don't think this should count,' she continued earnestly to Anthony. She might be at odds with Gifford, but she still wanted him to receive fair play. 'He didn't do anything at all adventurous until I was abducted, and that wasn't his fault. I think he should be given another chance. I'm sure he is quite capable of spending a month in Bath without having an adventure.'

Anthony grinned. 'But the fact remains that he didn't,' he pointed out. 'Not only that, even before he rescued you he behaved in ways liable to call adventure down upon him.'

'He didn't!' Abigail said indignantly. 'When did he do that? He was very well behaved.'

Anthony laughed.

Gifford glared at them. 'May we proceed?' he said stiffly.

'I still think you should have another chance,' Abigail told him, but she did walk up a few more steps.

She stopped abruptly and swung round again, swaying slightly on the wide staircase. Gifford's arm shot out to support her.

'Does Kemp know what happened?' she whispered anxiously, looking down into the hall, where the butler was supervising the arrival of their luggage.

'Only that I didn't manage to spend a full month in Bath,' Gifford reassured her gently.

'Oh. Oh, good.' Abigail half-turned to continue ascending the stairs. Then she looked back at him. 'W-what about your brother?' she whispered. 'And…and Mrs Raven? Do…do they…?'

Gifford shook his head.

'Well, then.' Abigail touched the brim of her bonnet nervously, then smoothed her hands over her skirts. 'That's good,' she said firmly, though her smile wavered uncertainly. 'I am looking forward to meeting them.'

Gifford took her hand in a reassuringly firm grasp. He drew it through his arm and led her up the stairs to the drawing room.

Abigail was grateful for his strong, confident presence at her side. She couldn't help being apprehensive about the forthcoming introductions. From Anthony's descriptions, Cole and Honor Raven sounded a most formidable couple. Abigail could hardly believe they would consider her an appropriate wife for Gifford.

The first, rather frivolous, thought she had as she entered was that the blue drawing room was indeed blue. Then she saw a tall, powerfully built man stand up at their entrance and forgot all about the furnishings. He was an impressive figure, almost as tall as Gifford. Unlike Gifford he had brown hair, but he had the same fierce, piercing blue gaze. The similarity between the two brothers was unmistakable.

Abigail's stomach fluttered with nervousness. She had expected Gifford's brother to be a daunting man, and he was. His wife also rose to greet them. Abigail blinked. She was hardly able to credit that this fragile, almost ethereal lady had been able to carry a man on her back. She was a few inches taller than Abigail, blonde, slender and graceful, despite the fact that she was clearly with child.

Abigail immediately felt clumsy and dumpy—and rather dowdy in her well-worn companion's clothes. Perhaps she should have worn one of Miss Wyndham's dresses, but it was too late to worry about it now.

'Miss Summers, my fiancée,' Gifford introduced her.

Abigail curtsied nervously, then shook hands with Major Raven and his wife. She saw that both of them were studying her with surprised interest, but no hostility.

'How do you do?' she said. 'I am so pleased to meet you both, but I am afraid there is a small misapprehension. I am not...that is, Sir Gifford has very kindly...most *graciously*...asked me to marry him. But...but I have not yet given him my reply.'

She held her breath after she'd finished speaking, worried that she had been unnecessarily honest, but Gifford's introduction had aggravated her. Despite the high price he had bid for her, he did not own her, and she didn't like the idea that he would try to force her into marriage by acting as if it was already agreed.

Cole's eyebrows shot up. He glanced curiously at his brother's angry, closed expression and a smile twitched his lips.

'I see you're starting as you mean to go on,' he said to Abigail, a gleam in his blue eyes. 'It's important to show a balky animal who is master right from the beginning.'

'*Cole!*' Honor exclaimed, shocked. 'Pay no attention to him,' she adjured Abigail. 'He spent many years in the cavalry before he joined the 52nd. Sometimes it still influences his language. You must be tired after your journey. Won't you sit down?'

'Thank you.' Abigail perched on the edge of a chair, anxiously aware of Gifford's glowering bad humour and Cole's poorly disguised amusement. She struggled to think of something to say which might lighten the mood. 'The journey wasn't tiring,' she assured them. 'The carriage was so comfortable, and we came by easy stages.'

'No doubt Giff wanted to enjoy the scenery,' said Cole

blandly. 'He has been out of England for many years, you know?'

'Yes, I did.' Abigail swallowed. She could feel Gifford's simmering annoyance, even though he was standing several feet away from her. She also detected an underlying implication to Cole's unexceptional remark. Was he suggesting that Gifford had been admiring *her* along the journey? How embarrassing!

'You served in both the cavalry and infantry?' she said, desperate to divert the conversation.

'I did,' he agreed.

'I have never met a cavalry officer before,' she gabbled. 'You must be an excellent horseman. I am very fond of horses myself—but I have not often had the opportunity to ride—'

Gifford made an odd choking sound and grabbed her hand, hauling her up from the chair.

She gasped, and stared up at him in consternation. 'What's wrong?'

'I'll show you the pianoforte!' he growled. 'Abigail is very partial to the instrument,' he threw over his shoulder by way of explanation to his startled relatives.

'But, Gifford, I'm sure she'd like to rest first,' Honor protested, as he dragged Abigail over to the door. 'What on earth's the matter with him?' she said in disbelief, as the door closed behind Gifford and Abigail.

Anthony laughed. 'It seems that Giff can keep a cool head in virtually any situation—except where Miss Summers is concerned. I have no idea what set him off just then, but no doubt the situation will resolve itself satisfactorily.'

Gifford pulled Abigail along the hallway to a large room furnished with both a harp and a pianoforte.

'Here it is!' he pointed at it. 'You will like to play it!' he informed her tersely.

'I expect I will,' Abigail replied in bewilderment. 'But

surely it wasn't necessary to make such a furore over showing it to me.'

Gifford planted his hands on his hips and scowled at her.
'I wouldn't have needed to if you'd kept to unexceptional
topics of conversation. Why the devil did you start talking
to Cole about your liking for horses?'

Abigail's mouth fell open in surprise. 'He was in the
cavalry,' she exclaimed. 'I've never met a soldier before. I
didn't know what else to talk to him about.'

'You could have discussed the Spanish countryside with
him!' Gifford said impatiently.

'I don't know anything about Spain!' Abigail retorted in
astonishment. 'He would have thought me very odd if I'd
asked him to give me a lecture on the flora and fauna of
the Peninsula only a minute after we'd been introduced.'

Gifford's gaze narrowed dangerously. 'Not half as odd
as he must have thought it when you declared a fondness
for riding,' he said fiercely.

Abigail stared at him with some perturbation. Had the
lingering torment he obviously felt over the capture of the
Unicorn finally deranged his wits? What on earth was
wrong with expressing a liking for horses…?

Then she realised why he was so heated on the subject.
She bit her lip. The situation was embarrassing—but also
somewhat humorous.

'I suppose you think it's funny,' he snarled, seeing the
smile she couldn't quite suppress.

'No, no,' she hastened to assure. 'Of course not. I'm
sure…I'm sure…'

It was no good, she couldn't contain her amusement. She
covered her face with both hands as her pent-up emotions
found relief in laughter.

'Dammit! This is no laughing matter,' Gifford rasped.

Abigail peeked at his crimson, angry face through her
fingers and succumbed to another bout of laughter.

'Will you stop that!' he ordered, a hint of desperation as
well as annoyance in his voice. 'It serves no purpose to

become hysterical. You must simply take care to be more modest in your speech in future.'

Abigail bit her lip and brushed tears from her cheeks.

'Oh, Gifford.' She laid her hand flat on his broad chest and looked up into his fierce expression. 'I wasn't being immodest,' she assured him. 'I know very well the most respectable of ladies are fond of riding in Hyde Park. Many ladies hunt with no detriment to their reputation. You only found what I said shocking because you have formed an unfortunate association of ideas between horses and… and…'

'Well, if I have, who's fault is that?' he said belligerently. 'What the devil did you mean by saying you're not my fiancée? You know damn well you must marry me.'

Abigail sighed, her desire to laugh well and truly extinguished. 'I don't know anything of the sort,' she replied. She looked around the room. 'Shall I play for you?' she asked. She hoped that perhaps music might ease Gifford's palpable tension, not to mention his black mood.

'If you wish.' He moved restlessly away from her.

'Would you prefer Mozart or Haydn?' she asked, opening the instrument.

'How the devil should I know?' he demanded, prowling around the room.

'Oh.' Abigail was disconcerted by his impatient response. 'I know several sea shanties if you would prefer one,' she offered.

'No, no. Play something of your own choice,' he said.

'Very well.' Abigail hesitated for a few moments, wondering if perhaps she should suggest they return to the others. It was surely most unusual to arrive at a house and then perform a recital for her host without even having a chance to remove her bonnet. But Gifford tended to do things his own way, and he didn't seem in the mood for conventional social intercourse.

She took a deep, calming breath, cleared her mind and

began to play. As always, the music provided an exhilarating release for her own emotions.

Gifford sat down. He was furious—as much with himself as with Abigail. He'd lost control of the situation and he hated it.

Abigail's immediate denial that she was his fiancée had embarrassed him—and alarmed him. He didn't understand why he should be afraid for such a foolish reason, but his fear made him angry. Besides his bad temper, he was also somewhat discomfited by his own behaviour in dragging her from the drawing room. He wasn't quite sure how he'd managed to manoeuvre them into this unlikely and rather ridiculous situation. Abigail had behaved badly—embarrassing him in front of his family, by claiming they were not betrothed—but he had made the situation worse. Cole and Anthony were no doubt having great sport at his expense. He would have to manage things better in future.

He heaved a sigh, leant his head back, and let the music wash over him and through him. The tension in his muscles slowly eased. It seemed to him that there was both passion and gentleness in Abigail's performance, but he did not have a great deal of knowledge on the subject—only an emotional response to the music.

He liked the way she played. He hoped she would play for him often when they were married—he wasn't prepared even to consider the possibility that she might not marry him. He would ask her to tell him the names of the various pieces, then he would not be so ignorant when she asked for his preferences. Perhaps he would take her to some concerts. She would like that.

The last notes faded away and Abigail laid her hands in her lap. She waited for Gifford's response. She hardly expected him to applaud, but it would be nice if he said something encouraging.

'When you have chosen the house you prefer, I will have your pianoforte sent round by sea,' he said abruptly.

'I don't understand.' She twisted around to look at him.

'I don't like London,' he said. 'The air is foul and it's too crowded. We will stay for the Season,' he added quickly. 'So you may attend the balls. For the rest of the year I prefer to live elsewhere. When I have shown you my other houses, you may select the one you prefer—and then I'll have the pianoforte sent there. You'll obviously wish to have it where you spend most of your time.'

'Obviously,' Abigail echoed, gazing at him. 'Are you…are you suggesting you will allow me to choose where we live?' she asked tentatively.

Or was he telling her that he would leave her alone in one of his residences while he travelled wherever he pleased?

'As long as you don't choose London,' he reminded her. 'Besides, Cole and Honor seem well established here, and I can't see myself sharing a house permanently with my brother. He can be damnably annoying at times. We'll visit them. Do you mind spending most of the year in the country? We could take a house by the sea if you prefer. Brighton, perhaps.'

'Would you prefer that?' Abigail asked cautiously, startled by his suggestion.

He frowned. 'I don't know,' he said. 'Perhaps we should visit Brighton and see what we think.' He stood up and held out his hand to her. 'I'm hungry. Dinner should be served soon. You'd better take off your bonnet. Honor will show you which room you're in.'

Abigail allowed him to lead her from the music room. She was dazed by his announcement. Unless she had completely misunderstood him, he had just told her he would give her a free rein to decide where they lived when…*if*…they were married. Her father would never have made such a concession to her mother's preferences. Even her stepmother, who had provided him with the longed-for son and heir, had never been accorded such indulgent treatment.

It amazed Abigail that Gifford, a man more prone to issue

orders than anyone she had ever known, should be so willing to consider her wishes in such an important matter. Perhaps she was making a mistake in being so determined to hold out for a demonstration of warmer emotion from him. In virtually every way that counted—except when he'd made his hurtful announcement that she had to marry him, even though it wasn't what he wanted—he had been extremely considerate of her feelings.

She was very thoughtful as she dressed for dinner. After a few minutes of contemplation she decided to wear one of Miss Wyndham's gowns. It was a soft, lustrous cream silk, cut lower across her bosom than any dress she'd previously worn—though not scandalously so. It revealed the merest hint of her cleavage. She left off her cap, which had apparently incited Gifford's loathing. Instead she pinned up her hair in a simple style which framed her face with soft curls. Two fine combs, decorated with seed pearls, had been packed with the silk gown, obviously intended to be worn with it. Abigail placed the combs carefully in her hair, and stared at her reflection in the mirror.

Never in her life—certainly not since her mother's death—had she dressed in such a grand style. She was hardly beautiful, and she couldn't pretend to be in the first blush of youth, but perhaps she wouldn't be entirely out of place in such elegant company. Her hopeful smile was a little tremulous as she self-consciously adjusted one of her burnished curls. Perhaps her improved appearance might encourage Gifford to see her not only as his responsibility—as someone who incited his lust and his exasperation in apparently equal measure—but as someone he could love.

Gifford instinctively rose as Abigail entered the drawing room. Both Anthony and Cole did likewise, but Gifford was too stunned by Abigail's appearance to notice. She glanced around a little uncertainly, as if she wasn't quite sure she was in the right place. Gifford was dimly aware of this indication of her shyness, but he was far more immediately conscious of the overwhelming jolt of desire he felt when he saw her.

Her cheeks were becomingly rosy. When he took her hand, her lips parted a fraction as she looked up at him for guidance. The soft cream silk of her bodice gently revealed the curves of her bosom. When he looked down he could see the tantalising shadow that lay between her breasts. His self-imposed exile from her company during the journey to London had imposed a severe strain upon him. Now his palm ached with the need to take the weight of her breasts in his hand. Only his belated awareness that they were not alone, that Anthony was actually speaking to Abigail, stilled his gesture towards her.

The next moment anger coursed through him. The last time he had seen her dressed so revealingly in public she had been on sale at the Blue Buck Inn. What the devil did she mean, coming down to dinner in such an appallingly fast gown? Anyone would think she was a member of the demi-monde—not his intended bride!

His anger quickly faded as he realised that it must be one of Miss Wyndham's dresses. Abigail was obviously too innocent to know that the gown wasn't suitable. Fortunately only his close family had witnessed her faux pas, but he would have to make sure she received gentle advice on the matter before she went out in public. He glanced at Honor wondering if she would be a suitable mentor for Abigail. He didn't know Cole's wife very well, but what he did know of her, he liked.

His eyes narrowed as, for the first time, he noticed that Honor's dress was cut in a very similar way to Abigail's. The discovery startled him, not least because he'd already spent several minutes talking to Honor without thinking there was anything unseemly about her attire.

'Is something wrong, Giff?' Cole asked, an edge on his voice.

Gifford suddenly realised he'd been frowning at his brother's wife and, not unnaturally, Cole wasn't pleased.

'No, not at all,' he said quickly. 'I was wondering whether Honor might like to take Abigail shopping—I know nothing of fashionable milliners and mantua makers. But I would not wish you to overtax yourself,' he addressed himself directly to his sister-in-law, mindful of her delicate condition.

She laughed. 'I'm more robust than I look,' she replied cheerfully. 'After nearly four years of campaigning, I hope I can survive a morning's shopping expedition. If you would like that, Miss Summers?'

'Please, call me Abigail. I would be *very* happy to go shopping with you,' Abigail assured her. 'I've never visited London before, I'm very curious to see what it has to offer. But I must warn you at once—I only wish to look, not to buy. I do not actually *need* anything more than I already have. So please don't organise a special trip just for my sake.'

'I like to look, too,' Honor replied, smiling. 'Let us arrange something as soon as you have recovered from your journey. Perhaps in a day or two's time?'

'Oh, I'm recovered already,' Abigail said blithely. 'Let us go at whatever time is convenient for you. I have no other engagements in London.'

'You have one,' Gifford growled.

Abigail blinked at him. 'Indeed I haven't,' she replied, obviously confused. 'Outside of this room, I don't know anyone who lives in London. Except for Mr Anderson, of course, but he is not here—'

'To me!' Gifford said impatiently. 'You are engaged to me.'

'Oh!' Abigail blushed and looked down at her hands, folded in her lap. She was acutely aware of the tension in the room. Everyone was looking at her and Gifford. She glanced briefly in his direction and saw that his expression was dark with displeasure. She flushed with embarrassment, but she couldn't think of anything to say to smooth things over.

'Tomorrow morning,' Honor said quickly. 'Why don't we go shopping tomorrow morning? We can visit my mother afterwards. She is the proprietor of the Belle Savage coaching inn, on Ludgate Hill. The Belle is always so busy, with so many guests and coaches continually arriving and departing, there is always something to see.'

'Oh, yes, th-thank you.' Abigail's relieved smile lit up her face. 'I would like that.'

Gifford gritted his teeth, angry and frustrated that the prospect of shopping with his sister-in-law clearly delighted Abigail a great deal more than the prospect of marriage to him.

It had been a spur-of-the-moment decision to suggest the two women should go shopping together, but now he discovered *he* wanted the pleasure of introducing Abigail to the sights of London.

'Not tomorrow,' he said abruptly. 'You may go shopping the next day. I have other plans for tomorrow.'

'You do?' Abigail looked at him, surprise and a certain amount of hopefulness in her eyes. 'Involving me?'

Gifford suddenly realised that all his relatives were watching the interchange with considerable interest. As captain of the *Unicorn* he was used to having everyone hang on his words, but now he found he didn't much care for the phenomenon when it was his personal, private business everyone wanted to hear about.

'Damned impertinence!' he muttered.

Cole gave a snort of laughter which he converted into an unconvincing cough when Honor frowned warningly at him.

Anthony maintained a bland expression.

Abigail fidgeted on the edge of her chair, looking both confused and uncomfortably self-conscious.

Fortunately, before anyone had time to say anything else, Kemp arrived to announce that dinner was ready.

* * *

After dinner Abigail and Honor took tea in the blue draw-ing room. Abigail rapidly lost her shyness in Honor's com-pany. Gifford's sister-in-law possessed a natural charm which made her an entertaining, yet reassuring, companion. She didn't ask Abigail any awkwardly personal questions, something Abigail had been rather dreading. She did speak briefly of what an unimaginable relief it had been to Cole to discover his brother and cousin had survived the priva-teers' attack.

'Cole was told that Gifford and Anthony were dead,' Honor explained. 'He sold out of the army and came back to England to take up his new duties as head of the family—then Gifford and Anthony reappeared on the very day of our wedding.'

She smiled, tears shimmering in her eyes, at the memory. 'I have never seen Cole so happy,' she said. 'You must not think, because he teases Gifford sometimes, he is not sin-cerely attached to him. He was devastated when he thought his brother was dead.'

'They both seem to have a very forceful…ah… unconventional…way of expressing themselves some-times,' Abigail said tentatively. 'I don't mean in any way to sound critical,' she added hastily.

Honor laughed. 'Unconventional is a mild description of the way they can occasionally behave,' she agreed. 'Their father raised them to consider problems logically, to think for themselves at all times, and not to be swayed from re-lying upon their own judgement by the force of public opin-ion.'

'*Logical!*' Abigail exclaimed. 'Gifford is one of the most illogical people I've ever met!'

'Male logic is often indistinguishable from complete ir-rationality,' Honor readily agreed. 'At least according to my mother.'

'Anthony seems a little more sensible,' Abigail said fairly. 'He plays chess. That's a very logical game.'

'Perhaps, but there's nothing logical about his paintings,'

Honor replied. 'No, that's not fair. His draughtsmanship, his awareness of perspective, of other technical considerations, are all excellent. But there is such depth of colour and emotion in his work. I've spent hours looking at the pictures he brought back from his voyage with Gifford.'

'May I see them?' Abigail asked eagerly. 'Do you think he would mind?'

Honor stood up. 'Many of them have already been hung in the large drawing room. I'm sure he'd have no objection to you seeing those—any visitor to the house may do so. Would you like to look at them now?'

'Yes, please.' Abigail followed Honor along a wide landing, marvelling again at the magnificence of the house. Were Gifford's other houses equally fine—or were they even grander? She was fascinated by the novelty of her surroundings, but no longer overawed by them. It was the man who mattered to her—not his possessions.

Chapter Sixteen

'The ladies are in the large drawing room, sir,' Kemp told Gifford. 'Admiring Mr Anthony's paintings.' He forestalled Gifford's next question.

'We'll join them,' said Gifford briskly. The three men had lingered at the table, not to savour their port, but to discuss the problem of finding and dealing with Charles Johnson.

Gifford had told Abigail the truth when he'd said that his brother and sister-in-law knew nothing about her mistreatment at the hands of Miss Wyndham's great-nephew. But that had been when they had first arrived. Since then he'd given Cole the bare outline of what had occurred because he needed his brother's help. Gifford intended to hunt Johnson down, but that might mean leaving Abigail alone in London. In his absence, he wanted Cole to protect her.

'I hope he does call here for his money,' Cole declared, a deadly gleam in his eyes. He was as enraged by what Johnson had done as the other two men.

'It's unlikely,' said Gifford, 'but not impossible. Kemp, if any gentleman calls for Miss Summers bring him immediately to one of us—whichever of us is at home. But give the gentleman the impression that you *are* taking him to Miss Summers. Lull him into a false sense of security.'

'Yes, sir,' said Kemp. 'Any gentleman in particular, sir? Or all gentlemen?'

'All gentlemen,' said Gifford firmly.

Abigail was fascinated by Anthony's paintings. She admired all of them, but the one which drew her gaze again and again was a picture of Gifford standing on the quarterdeck of the *Unicorn*.

He was wearing his uniform, his hands linked loosely behind his back, his feet braced against the movement of the ship. He looked confident and in command. A man at peace with himself in his true element.

It hurt Abigail to realise that Gifford had never been truly at peace with himself, all the time she had known him. Except...

Just once. Immediately after he had made love to her. She remembered how relaxed he had been as he held her in his arms.

Not for the first time she wondered if she was going about her mission to win Gifford's heart the wrong way. If she married him, he would no doubt make love to her every night—her cheeks grew warm at the thought—and afterwards he would be quiet and peaceful. Perhaps if he felt quiet and peaceful every night for several weeks, he would become more even-tempered the rest of the time—and *that* might encourage him to feel affection for her.

Abigail wished she knew more about men, but it wasn't a subject on which she could easily seek advice. She also wished she might have an opportunity to spend time alone with Gifford, so that she could gauge his feelings for her more precisely. Recently it seemed as if they were surrounded by curious witnesses every time they met.

She heard the door open and looked around to see Gifford come into the room, followed by his brother and cousin. They were all impressive men. Tall, broadshouldered, and fiercely masculine. But only Gifford held her attention.

He wore his formal evening dress with as much assurance as he'd once worn his uniform. Her heart rate accelerated as he came towards her. He moved like a tiger. Soft-footed but unimaginably powerful. His gaze was hot and hungry as it swept over her body. Her breath caught. She felt nervous but excited. She wasn't afraid of Gifford. She'd never been afraid of him.

'Abigail likes your pictures,' Honor said to Anthony. Her voice jolted Abigail back into an awareness of her surroundings.

'They are truly wonderful!' she exclaimed, sounding more vehement than she'd intended because she was uncomfortably flustered by the direction her errant thoughts had taken. She turned away from Gifford and focussed all her attention on his cousin.

'Thank you,' Anthony replied, looking both amused and pleased.

'Honor says that you have many sketches of your voyage,' Abigail continued breathlessly. 'I would very much like to see them—if you don't object.'

'Not at all. You may see all my sketches if, in return, you will allow me to paint you,' Anthony returned.

'Paint me?' Abigail gasped. 'Whatever for?'

'Possibly in the character of Boadicea,' Anthony mused, studying Abigail with his head on one side.

'Under no circumstances!' Gifford said categorically. 'Paint her at the pianoforte.'

'A somewhat commonplace pose that would not do justice to her courage, her beauty, or the fiery resolution that sometimes flashes in her fine eyes.'

'You are not painting her dressed in a sheet!' Gifford said forcefully.

'Certainly not. I would wear my normal clothes.' Anthony maintained a straight face. 'We can have a special costume made for Abigail. I think she should hold a spear.'

Abigail finally found her voice.

'Stop provoking him!' she ordered Anthony, well aware

he was trying to bait his cousin. 'And you can both stop talking about me as if I'm not here.' She put her hands on her waist and glared impartially at the two men. 'If...*if*,' she emphasised, 'I agree to be painted I shall choose my own pose and my own garments. I will not be painted wearing a sheet—and I definitely won't hold a spear. Good heavens! I would look utterly ridiculously carrying a spear.'

'I find it quite easy to picture you with a spear,' Cole observed from the background. 'I must admit, the significance of the sheet eludes me.'

Abigail flushed scarlet with embarrassment.

'Everyone be quiet!' Gifford ordered, a note of sharp warning in his voice.

He reached out and stroked his fingers gently down the side of Abigail's neck and along the curve of her shoulder, accessible to him because of the relatively low cut of her gown.

Abigail's breath locked in her throat. He touched her with such casual, yet delicate intimacy. She stared up at him, unable to take her eyes from his face.

'You should have your portrait painted,' he told her quietly. 'Anthony has painted all of us. But you may choose a pose you are comfortable with. It is very tedious remaining still for so long, but it isn't otherwise an unpleasant experience.'

Abigail swallowed. She was aware that they weren't alone, but she couldn't look away from him. 'I think most people would be honoured to be painted by Anthony,' she whispered. 'He is a very fine artist.'

'Hmm.' Gifford's gaze fastened on her mouth for several seconds before he managed to wrench it away. 'Let her choose her pose,' he commanded Anthony. 'But I still think it would be most appropriate if she is seated at the pianoforte.'

Abigail walked restlessly around her bedchamber. She was tired, but her mind was too busy to allow her to sleep.

The situation between her and Gifford was unresolved and unsatisfactory. She wished she could sit down and speak to him quietly about the future, but he didn't seem inclined to discuss anything with her. He simply gave her orders. It was very frustrating.

On impulse she decided to have another look at his portrait. If she couldn't have a conversation with the man himself, perhaps she would gain inspiration from his image. It was a very lifelike portrait, painted by someone who knew Gifford extremely well. Perhaps it would help her gain an insight into his character.

She went down to the large drawing room. She was surprised so many candles were still burning. She knew Honor had retired to bed some time ago and she'd assumed the others had done the same. She hesitated in the doorway and heard Gifford's voice.

'We know the location of his family estate, but not of his current lodgings in London. Tidewell was only able to give us the direction of his previous lodgings. In the circumstances—'

'You're talking about Charles!' Abigail exclaimed. Gifford, Anthony and Cole were all present, and they all stood to attention as she walked into the room. 'You're talking about Charles without me!' Her voice rose, partly because she was genuinely indignant, but mainly because she felt unreasonably hurt at being excluded from the deliberations.

'It's not necessary for you to be bothered with this,' Gifford said stiffly.

'Not necessary? I'm the one he sold! Of course it's necessary for me to know what you mean to do.'

Abigail glanced from one man to the other, and saw that they all wore the same closed, hard, ruthless expression. She remembered what Anthony had said several days ago, that it would be a toss up whether he or Gifford found Charles Johnson first.

'What do you mean to do with him when you find him?' she asked grittily.

Gifford pressed his lips together. He didn't say anything and his gaze was cold and dangerous when he looked at her.

Abigail was chilled by his expression, frightened by the implications of his silence.

'He must stand trial,' she said croakily.

'If this comes to trial there will be a scandal,' Gifford said flatly. 'It would be impossible for you to remain untouched by it. You might have to give evidence in open court. It is unthinkable that you should be called upon to do so.'

'It is unthinkable for you to seek retribution by any other means,' Abigail said fiercely.

'You don't know what you are talking about,' Gifford retorted.

'Yes, I do.' Abigail advanced further into the room. 'I know that aboard your ship you have the power of life or death over your men. You can order them to engage in a hopeless battle at your whim. You can have them flogged if they disobey you. But we are not on the *Unicorn* now. It is not for you to assign Charles's punishment—it is for judge and jury. He must stand trial.'

'Are you willing to give evidence? To become the subject of the worst scandal of the Season? Of the year?' Gifford demanded fiercely.

Abigail squared her shoulders. In truth, the idea horrified her. But she was determined not to let Gifford take Charles's death upon his conscience. Nor did she want it upon her own conscience.

'Yes,' she said.

'Well, I'm not willing to let you,' he countered ruthlessly.

'I am the one he sold. I am the one who has a right to decide what to do about it,' Abigail replied. 'If—no!' She planted her hand firmly on his chest as he drew in a breath to speak. 'I haven't finished.'

Gifford closed his mouth and watched her grimly.

'If you overrule my wishes,' she said slowly, thinking out her argument as she made it, 'if you disallow my preferences…then you are acting as if you truly did buy me. As if you have a right to dispose of my body as you wish— or to discount the thoughts in my head or the emotions in my heart as if they are of no consequence. Because you own me. But you don't. You don't own me. I belong to myself and I can make up my own mind.'

Intense silence followed her words. Gifford looked down into her face, and at the hand she still braced assertively— yet strangely possessively—against his chest. He could see the resolution in her eyes, her fierce determination that her opinion would be heard.

He had never been willing to debate his decisions but, in appropriate circumstances, he had always encouraged his junior officers to express their views. He was training them to be competent officers, not a crowd of sycophants.

Abigail was not one of his subordinates but, when she defended her views so steadfastly and with such dignity, he felt proud of her. The burden of responsibility on his shoulders eased a little as he realised how willing she was to share responsibility for deciding Charles Johnson's fate. Ultimately, as befitted a man in his position, Gifford would make up his own mind what he would do about Johnson. But it was…liberating…to be reminded of Abigail's courage.

And her hand on his chest. That felt strangely like an anchor, holding him securely when sometimes it felt like he was adrift on an unfriendly ocean, endlessly confronted by enemies both phantom and real. A man could grow weary of everlasting battle.

He realised he had been silent for a long time.

'You are willing to face the consequences of Johnson coming to trial?' he said gruffly.

'Yes.' She held his gaze unwaveringly.

Gifford's chest heaved in a great sigh.

'So be it,' he said.

Abigail looked around at Anthony and Cole. 'You must agree too,' she said.

Both men nodded, then confirmed their agreement aloud.

'Good.' She sighed herself. Truth be told, she was afraid of the scandal, but she was more afraid of the possible consequences if she didn't hold firm to her beliefs. She felt as if she'd just confronted a tiger. She wasn't scared of Gifford, but his personality was so strong she hadn't been sure she would be able to hold her ground against him.

She decided it was best he didn't know that. He was already far too sure of himself.

'In that case I will tell you the direction of Charles's most recent lodgings,' she said instead.

'You know where he lives?' Gifford seized her upper arms in his hands. 'How? Why didn't you tell me immediately?'

Abigail pressed both hands against his chest. She half-expected him to shake her in his exasperated impatience—but he didn't. He held her in a firm but not painful grip and stared down at her. She could feel the tense anticipation in his powerful body as he waited for her response.

'Miss Wyndham corresponded with him regularly,' she said breathlessly. 'But her hands were too painful with rheumatism to hold the pen. I wrote at her dictation.'

'The direction?' Gifford demanded.

Abigail repeated it. 'I have no idea what kind of place it is,' she said. 'Charles always claimed it to be very fashionable. But the Blue Buck didn't seem fashionable to me. Perhaps this place will be similar. You must—' she tapped her fingers against Gifford's chest for emphasis '—be very careful.'

'I'm always careful,' he said, an odd expression on his face.

'Good.' She nodded once, very firmly. 'Well, then.' She stepped back from him and, after a momentary hesitation, he let her go. 'I will go to bed. Goodnight, everyone.'

She was already halfway to the stairs when Gifford caught up with her.

'Abby?' He put his hand on her arm to turn her. 'I thought you'd already gone to bed. Why did you come down again?'

She looked up at him, wondering what to say. She was still shaken from their clash of wills a few moments earlier. She wasn't ready for another tense encounter with him. Not when so much was at stake.

'I wanted to l-look at Anthony's paintings,' she said, quite truthfully.

'Oh.' For a second or two she thought he looked disappointed, dejected even, at her answer. Dejection was not an emotion she associated with Gifford Raven, but it passed so quickly she thought she must be mistaken.

'Particularly the one where you are standing on the quarterdeck of the *Unicorn*,' she said. 'It is so much easier to imagine your life at sea now that I've seen that. I must look at it again in daylight. Anthony is a very fine artist.'

'Yes, he is,' said Gifford absently. His gaze was upon her auburn curls shining in the candlelight. 'He must paint one picture of you with your hair down—but not for public display.' He stroked her cheek with one gentle fingertip, then caressed her lower lip with his thumb.

Abigail's heart began to race. Instinctively she swayed towards him. His gaze focussed on her mouth and he started to bend his head…

Then muttered a curse under his breath and abruptly straightened up.

'Goodnight,' he said hoarsely. 'I won't be able to show you the sights of London tomorrow morning, but don't go out with Honor. Maybe later in the day we can…dammit! Goodnight.'

He turned and strode away from her, leaving Abigail to stare after him, at first with bewilderment, but then with growing indignation. The man was far too free with his orders and far too contrary about when he kissed her! He caressed her in public, then refused to kiss her in private.

But he had agreed that Charles Johnson should stand trial.

And he had called her Abby again. Her emotions had been so overtaxed when he'd first shortened her name she had not fully appreciated how much like an endearment it sounded. But now when Gifford called her *Abby* it felt almost as if he had called her *sweetheart*. She hugged that cheering thought close to her heart as she climbed the stairs to her bedchamber.

Abigail was playing the pianoforte when Gifford opened the door to the music room. He paused in the entrance, watching her and listening to the music. He frowned as he realised she had her back to him. When she was engrossed in her playing it would be easy for someone to walk up behind her and startle her.

The harp had been his mother's, and no one had played it for nearly thirty years. His father had purchased the pianoforte, not to play it, but because he was fascinated by the construction of the new-fangled instrument. Until Abigail's arrival, no one living in the house had played either of the instruments. The room wasn't arranged for the comfort or peace of mind of a musician.

Gifford quietly closed the door and went to give Kemp orders to rearrange the furniture. He couldn't abide a situation in which his back was exposed, and he didn't imagine that Abigail was any different. He wanted the pianoforte repositioned so that she would be able to see immediately if anyone opened the door.

When he returned she had stopped playing. She heard the door open and turned towards him.

'You're back!' She sprang up and hurried over to him, an anxious expression on her face. 'Did you find him? What happened?'

He took both her hands in his, and looked down into her wide green eyes.

'Let's sit down,' he said.

'Oh, God! Is it bad news?' she asked, scanning his face worriedly.

'I don't believe so.'

'Not bad news?' Abigail let him lead her over the to the sofa. His expression was serious, almost solemn, but he didn't seem angry. 'What happened? Did you find Charles?'

'Not exactly.' Gifford replied. His grip tightened on her hands. 'Charles Johnson is dead,' he said.

'*What?*' Abigail stared at him in disbelief. 'Dead? But you—?'

'I didn't kill him,' Gifford said curtly. 'I gave you my word last night.'

'I know.' Abigail felt dazed. 'I don't understand,' she said. 'How did he die?'

'He was murdered,' said Gifford more gently. 'His body was discovered in his lodgings two days ago. No one knows who killed him.'

'Charles is dead?' Abigail repeated. The news was so shocking and so unexpected she couldn't fully comprehend it.

'Yes.'

'Someone killed him?'

'Yes.'

'How?'

Gifford hesitated.

'How did they kill him?' Abigail insisted. She needed details. Information that would help her turn these disconnected facts into a believable picture.

'He was garrotted,' Gifford said reluctantly. She saw that he was watching her worriedly. He didn't know how she would react at this news.

'Why?'

'I don't know,' said Gifford.

'Oh.' Abigail felt numb. She had carefully avoided thinking too much about Charles—now he was dead. She hadn't wanted to harbour evil will towards him—but evil had befallen him. And none of it made any sense.

She tugged her hands from Gifford's grasp and covered her face.

'Abby?' He moved closer and she felt his comforting touch on her back.

She took several steadying breaths, as chaotic emotion suddenly crashed through her. Tears filled her eyes and blocked her throat. She swallowed and lifted her head.

'No trial,' she whispered. 'There'll be no trial.'

'No trial. No scandal,' Gifford said, satisfaction mingling with the reassurance in his voice.

Abigail closed her eyes. Her head fell forward as her whole body slumped with relief. Gifford pulled her close to him. She rested her head on his shoulder, grateful for his solid strength. She hadn't realised exactly how much she dreaded the prospect of a public trial, of confronting Charles again across a court room, until the need to do so no longer existed.

'I'm so glad,' she murmured. 'That there won't be a trial. I shouldn't…I shouldn't be glad that Charles is dead—' she remembered how he'd caressed her breast with his pistol and shuddered '—but I am.'

Gifford's hold on her tightened in response to her shudder. 'So am I,' he said harshly. 'You have no reason to feel guilty. And no need to think of the matter again.'

'But we don't know why he was killed.' Abigail lifted her head to look at him. 'And what about Sampson? Gifford?' she prompted him, when he didn't immediately answer.

'We don't know where he is at the moment, but we do have an idea how to find him,' he said at last. 'We must go out again tonight—but there is nothing for you to worry yourself about.'

Abigail pushed herself away from him. 'I will not be

excluded from matters that closely concern me,' she said stiffly. 'I am not so feeble I cannot withstand a little worry.'

'Very well,' said Gifford coolly. 'Johnson discharged his previous manservant just before he returned to Bath to abduct you, hiring Sampson in his place. We've been told that the discharged servant returned to London independently and that he may know where to find Sampson. This evening Anthony is going to visit an alehouse where we've been told the dismissed servant has friends and often visits. If we find him he may be able to tell us where we can find Sampson.'

'What will you do with Sampson if you do find him?' Abigail asked.

Gifford pressed his lips together. 'It may be difficult to make a convincing case against him, now that his master is dead,' he said. 'He can always claim he was acting under orders, possibly even under duress. But I'm damned if I'm going to let him escape unscathed.'

'You won't…you won't k-…you won't…' Abigail was so disturbed she couldn't force the words past her lips.

'I won't kill him,' Gifford said icily. 'You made your views clear enough in relation to his master. But he will be punished.'

'Yes.' Abigail didn't protest any further. She'd been just as fearful of Sampson as she had been of Charles. Her nightmares had included both men. She sighed. There was so much she and Gifford needed to resolve, yet it seemed impossible to talk about their situation until all the consequences of her abduction had been dealt with. 'I will be glad when this is all over,' she said.

Anthony stepped over the threshold of the alehouse and looked around. Nearly all of the faces around him were black. Most of the men drinking in the taproom were probably servants, a few of them might be independent tradesmen and some were poor labourers. There was a significant black community in London, with its own taverns and other places of entertainment.

Anthony had visited such places before, though he felt as much of an outsider here as he often did in the drawing rooms of the *ton*. He'd been most at home on the *Unicorn*, for all the men and officers had accepted him entirely on his own merits, despite the fact he'd never previously been to sea. But that period of his life was over. Now he had to find a new goal for himself. In the meantime, he needed to find Charles Johnson's discharged manservant.

He ordered a tankard of ale and when he'd been served he enquired for the man he was seeking.

'Why do you want him?' the tapman asked warily.

'He may be able to help me find a mutual...enemy,' Anthony replied coolly.

A few minutes later he was joined by an even more suspicious man dressed in the rather shabby clothes of a gentleman's gentleman. He bought Johnson's ex-servant a drink and it was soon clear he hadn't exaggerated when he'd claimed to the tapman that Sampson was their mutual enemy. Johnson's mistreated valet had hated his late master and he harboured no warm feelings towards Sampson. It wasn't long before Anthony had all the information he needed.

'A very satisfactory conclusion to the whole business,' said Gifford. He was sitting with Cole and Anthony in the library.

'And a grim warning to anyone foolish enough to borrow large sums of money from Saul Dunlin,' said Anthony. 'Not a fellow I have any personal ambition to meet. But it may be worth remembering his name. To avoid him. Sampson was even more afraid of the man than he was of Gifford once we'd finally tracked him down.'

'Dunlin is a moneylender?' Cole clarified. 'Why the devil did Johnson borrow money from such a dangerous character? Desperate though he was, surely there were better alternatives?'

'According to the servant he discharged shortly before he abducted Abigail, Johnson's estate was already heavily mortgaged,' Gifford replied. 'He was a compulsive gambler, and the more reputable moneylenders he'd previously dealt with had refused him any further credit. As long as he still had the prospect of inheriting Miss Wyndham's famous—but non-existent jewels—he could hold Dunlin at bay with promises and piecemeal repayments. Once he'd discovered there were no jewels he became desperate.'

'So he tried to sell Miss Summers,' Cole said, his lip curling in disgust.

'He *did* sell Abigail,' Gifford replied grimly. 'I bought her. *Sampson* told us Johnson even considered calling here, in Berkeley Square, for payment—he was so frantic for cash. But then he made a few enquiries about me.'

'So he raced back to London and staked everything on one last, desperate game of piquet,' said Anthony. 'According to what his ex-servant told us, Johnson had never previously staked his estates—he really did have aspirations to be a country gentleman. But, in the end, he had no other option but risk everything—and he lost. Which will be a nice tangle for the fellow who won. If he wants to claim his winnings he'll have to pay off the mortgage!'

'So Johnson couldn't repay Dunlin, and the moneylender decided to make an example of him,' Gifford took up the tale, 'though I think that would be exceptionally hard to prove. Sampson told us the story, but I doubt he'd repeat it to a magistrate. Saul Dunlin seems to have a very long and powerful reach in certain parts of London.'

'You won't pursue him?' Cole looked at his brother through narrowed eyes.

'No.' Gifford stretched out his long legs in front of him. 'I have no personal quarrel with him, and he saved Abigail from the distress of a public trial.'

'She is a very determined woman,' said Cole, respect in

his voice. 'I was impressed by her resolution on the matter. I must admit, I was having difficulty thinking of a way to satisfy her insistence on bringing Johnson to trial without allowing her name to be made public.'

'So was I,' Gifford admitted. 'Fortunately it wasn't necessary, but I dare say we would have found a way. Johnson no doubt committed other crimes—in addition to amassing monumental debts—which we could have made use of.'

Anthony laughed. 'Poor Abigail,' he said. 'I don't think she fully appreciates how devious you can be—so forthright as you often seem. But she's very quick-witted. She'll learn.'

'What of Sampson?' Cole asked. 'You didn't let him go free?'

'He's been pressed,' Gifford replied. 'The navy now has a new landsman, able—though not entirely willing—to do his duty. As I said before, a very satisfactory conclusion to the whole business, though there are still one or two loose ends to tie up.'

Anthony groaned. 'Leave it to Malcolm,' he begged. 'I'm sure he'll find a very neat solution to the problem.'

'What the devil are you talking about?' Cole demanded.

'The…gentleman…who bid against Giff for Abigail at the Blue Buck,' Anthony explained. 'He must be wealthy because he pushed the bidding so high—though, like Giff, he may not have intended to pay. But Malcolm is in a far better position than any of us to find a way, quite legally, to punish him for his insolence. If Giff calls him out, even over a spurious quarrel, it's likely to cause the very scandal we're trying to avoid.'

Gifford sighed. 'Much as it goes against the grain, I believe you are right,' he said. 'Scandal must unquestionably be avoided. Tomorrow I shall show Abigail some of the sights of London,' he added, with a pleasant sense of anticipation.

Chapter Seventeen

'Mr Tidewell and Admiral Pullen, sir,' Kemp announced.

Gifford swung around to see the butler usher the two men into the blue drawing room.

Mr Tidewell looked confused. 'I beg your pardon, I am afraid there is a misunderstanding,' he said. 'I understood Miss Summers was here.'

Gifford grinned. 'A precaution,' he explained, shaking hands with his unexpected visitors. 'Kemp is under orders to bring any gentlemen calling for Miss Summers directly to me. Kemp, please ask Miss Summers to join us, and bring some refreshments.'

'Do you have news of Johnson?' the admiral asked, as soon as they were alone.

'Yes.' Gifford quickly brought them up to date. 'You are fortunate to catch us still at home,' he concluded. 'I'd intended to show Miss Summers some of the sights of London this morning.'

'Then I'm glad we called so early,' Mr Tidewell replied, just as Abigail came into the room.

'Mr Tidewell! Admiral Pullen!' She hurried towards them, a smile lighting up her face as she held out her hands to them. 'I am so pleased to see you both. Are you well?'

'Very well, thank you. I'm glad to find you in such good

spirits,' Mr Tidewell replied. 'You look charming, my dear.'

'Thank you.' Abigail blushed. She wasn't used to receiving compliments from the usually businesslike lawyer. 'Have you only just arrived in town?' she asked, noticing the well-worn valise by his feet. 'Do you have somewhere to stay?' Then she bit her lip and glanced apologetically at Gifford. It was hardly her place to invite Mr Tidewell and the admiral to become his guests.

But Gifford immediately endorsed her suggestion. 'I hope you will stay here while you're in London,' he said.

'There is really no need, sir.' For once the lawyer looked flustered. 'My sister lives in Westminster. But I do thank you for your hospitality.'

'I'll be glad to accept your kind invitation,' Admiral Pullen said. 'If it won't inconvenience you.'

'You could never be an inconvenience,' Abigail assured him warmly, then bit her lip. Once again she felt she had overstepped the boundaries of propriety, but Gifford didn't seem offended that she'd taken the role of hostess upon herself.

'Why don't we sit down, while you tell us what brings you to London?' he said.

'Do I need to give you an account of what happened at the Blue Buck?' Abigail asked, a little worriedly. 'For the magistrates?' She could think of no other reason why the lawyer should have made the journey to London. Admiral Pullen was probably here because he was an old friend of Gifford's.

'Oh no, that won't be necessary,' Mr Tidewell looked shocked. 'I have come upon quite a different matter. At Miss Wyndham's request.'

'Miss Wyndham?' Abigail exclaimed, glancing instinctively towards Gifford in her surprise. 'But she's dead!'

'Perhaps I should say I am here in fulfilment of Miss Wyndham's wishes,' Mr Tidewell clarified.

He opened the shabby valise and withdrew some documents.

'Miss Wyndham's last will and testament was somewhat complicated,' he vouchsafed. 'The document I read to you after the funeral only contained a portion of her final wishes.'

'But…but…' Abigail stammered. 'You told Charles…'

'I know.' Mr Tidewell sighed. 'This is a complex matter, and I cannot help feeling grateful he is dead,' he said heavily. 'It simplifies things tremendously. I did everything I could to ensure he wouldn't be able to contest Miss Wyndham's last wishes—but they were most unusual. There could have been difficulties. Though I'm sure you could have relied upon Sir Gifford and Mr Anderson's advice if the matter *had* come to court.'

'What *were* Miss Wyndham's last wishes?' Gifford asked.

'Ah.' Mr Tidewell opened the documents and looked down his nose at them. 'Briefly, I was to observe Mr Johnson's behaviour *after* Miss Wyndham's death—and during the reading of her *initial* wishes—to see whether he acted in a way consonant with an affectionate relative and an honourable gentleman. In particular, I was to note whether he showed concern for the welfare of Miss Wyndham's staff, and for Miss Summers herself—'

'He clearly failed *that* test!' Gifford interrupted, his expression ferocious, even though the object of his anger was well beyond his reach.

'Indeed, sir,' said Mr Tidewell drily. 'I was also to observe whether he accepted his limited bequest with a good grace…'

'The blackguard wasn't capable of grace!' Gifford leapt from his chair and began to stride around the room. 'What the devil did the old—did Miss Wyndham mean by such a ridiculous request?'

'Miss Wyndham was a generous, warm-hearted lady,' said Mr Tidewell coldly. 'She wanted the best for those she

left behind—and she wanted to *believe* the best of her only
surviving relative. Even though she couldn't help having
doubts about his true motives for visiting her.'

'I apologise,' Gifford said curtly. He pushed his hand
through his hair. 'I did not mean to speak ill of Miss Wyndham. She chose her friends well.' His quick glance encompassed all the other occupants of the drawing room. 'She is
not to blame for the sins of her relatives.'

Mr Tidewell nodded, acknowledging Gifford's apology.
'I am still not sure of the wisdom of Miss Wyndham's
requests,' he said. 'But none of us could have predicted
how badly Johnson would react to finding he inherited nothing of consequence.'

'Since he *didn't* show concern for the welfare of the staff
or behave with a good grace—what were you supposed to
do next?' Gifford asked.

'Wait until he left Bath,' Mr Tidewell replied.

'*Wait?*'

'Miss Wyndham was a trifle quixotic, but she was also
a realist beneath her romantic notions,' said Mr Tidewell.
'She knew that if Johnson behaved badly during the reading
of the *first* part of the will, he was likely to behave even
worse after he'd heard the second part, and possibly have
his own lawyers contest it. As I said, I made it as legally
unassailable as I could—but it is really most unusual. I'm
not sure it would stand up to close examination by greater
legal minds than mine.'

Abigail gripped her hands together to prevent them from
trembling. 'Mr Tidewell, please could you tell us the contents of the second part of Miss Wyndham's will,' she
asked.

The lawyer's convoluted explanations were filling her
with anxiety. She'd experienced too much uncertainty over
the past few days. She wanted to *know* what Miss Wyndham had said—not simply guess.

'If Johnson had behaved favourably, the remainder of
Miss Wyndham's estate was to be divided equally between

he two of you,' Mr Tidewell said. 'Between you, Miss
Summers, and Charles Johnson. If, however, he behaved
badly—as he did—you were to receive the entirety. As I
now present it to you.'

He stood up as he spoke and moved to the table, carrying
he valise. As Abigail watched in growing disbelief, he laid
one extravagant, exquisite piece of jewellery after another
on the polished surface. Diamonds. Rubies. Sapphires. Em-
ralds. All glittered brilliantly in the morning light. Three
heavily jewelled necklaces were laid out before Abigail,
with matching ear-rings. There was a diamond-studded
bracelet, innumerable brooches and ear-rings, combs set
with gems, finger rings, a cross on a gold chain, and two
ong ropes of pearls.

Abigail pressed both hands to her mouth, unable to credit
he evidence of her own eyes.

'I have a complete list of the jewels,' Mr Tidewell said
in his dry, precise voice. To Abigail it sounded as if he was
a great distance away. 'Signed by Miss Wyndham and wit-
essed by Admiral Pullen and Mr Sudbury, JP. You may
check the pieces against the list to verify nothing is missing.
I am sorry I did not bring them to you in a more appropriate
container. I thought they would be safer in my old valise.
I must admit I am relieved I can now pass responsibility
or them into your hands, sir,' he concluded, giving the list
to Gifford.

'It's a queen's ransom.' Gifford came to stand behind
Abigail.

'Miss Wyndham was much beloved,' said Mr Tidewell,
his voice revealing he also was somewhat in awe of the
sparkling magnificence laid out before them. 'She told me
that every piece was made new for her. Especially for her.
A symbol of her lover's great affection for her. She always
refused to sell them, because of what they meant to her—
but she did have suggestions for how Miss Summers might
make use of them.'

'What did she say?' Gifford asked.

'She thought it would be most practical if Miss Summer sold a few of the pieces to provide her with immediat capital—and kept the rest to wear, and as her dowry. Sh also hoped that Miss Summers would provide a home an employment for her household. I was in some difficultie over that request, since Miss Summers managed to mak provision for the staff even before the first will was read, Mr Tidewell confessed. 'But she certainly acted in the spiri of Miss Wyndham's wishes, even though not in exactly th way she'd envisaged.'

Abigail listened to Mr Tidewell's explanation, withou fully comprehending his words. She reached out, very del icately, and touched a diamond. It was hard and cold be neath her fingertip. Real. She leant over the table top, gentl touching one gem after another with the very tip of he finger.

'I've never seen real diamonds before,' she whispered 'Sapphires. Emeralds. So big. So many.'

'They are all gems of the first water,' said Mr Tidewell 'I confess, I am grateful you now have the advice of Si Gifford and Mr Anderson. I was concerned I would nc have the experience to negotiate a fair price for you—whe you decide which pieces to sell.'

'If Johnson behaved badly when he heard the first set o Miss Wyndham's wishes, you were to wait until he'd lef Bath before revealing to Miss Summers the full extent o her inheritance?' Gifford queried.

'Yes, sir,' the lawyer agreed. 'That was Miss Wyndham' idea, to avoid any possible awkwardness.'

'Good God!' Gifford exclaimed. 'The consequences i Johnson had found out! He could have accused you an Pullen of conspiring to cheat him of his inheritance—an God knows what else!'

'I know, sir,' Mr Tidewell said feelingly. 'It gave m many sleepless nights. That's why I persuaded Miss Wynd ham to tell Mr Sudbury what she wanted. Mr Sudbury is magistrate and has no personal connection with any of us–

though he has a reputation of great probity. As you can see, he witnessed the list I had made up of the jewels. I hoped that would provide some protection for all of us. Not least Miss Summers, who knew nothing of what Miss Wyndham intended. Mr Sudbury was one of the magistrates who went with us to the Blue Buck a few days ago. He did not feel there was any need to accompany us to London, but he desired me to assure you he is entirely at your disposal, sir, if you—or Miss Summers—wish to discuss this matter with him.'

Abigail barely heard the conversation. She touched one of the ropes of pearls, hesitated, then lifted them from the table. Their soft lustre seemed slightly less forbidding than the glittering brightness of the other jewels.

'She gave them all to me?' she whispered. Tears suddenly filled her eyes. 'And I can't thank her.' Her voice quavered and broke on the words. 'I can't ever thank her.' She bent her head and lifted the pearls to her lips. Tears slipped unheeded down her cheeks.

Gifford put his hands on her shoulders, squeezing reassuringly.

'She was thanking *you*.' Mr Tidewell audibly swallowed. 'She left a letter for you. She dictated it to me. I will give it to you. But…she made you her heiress in recognition that you had devoted nine years of your young life to her— willingly, and with a generous heart.'

'But I had no choice,' Abigail protested, brushing her tears away. 'I made no great sacrifice for her. I had to work, and she was an easy mistress.'

'But you loved her,' said Mr Tidewell, visibly moved. 'And she loved you. Well.' He cleared his throat. 'I believe my errand here is complete. I will leave you my sister's direction in case you should need me. I will be in town for a few days. Good morning to all of you.'

'Thank you.' Gifford shook the lawyer's hand. 'Thank you, Mr Tidewell. I believe Miss Wyndham would be pleased with how well you executed her wishes.'

The lawyer flushed. 'She was a grand old lady,' he said gruffly. 'I will miss her.'

'So will I.' Abigail smiled at him mistily. 'Thank you,' she said.

The rest of the day passed in a daze for Abigail. Everyone came to admire the magnificent jewels and congratulate her on her good fortune. Admiral Pullen was particularly delighted.

'You are a true heiress! A *worthy* heiress!' he declared emphatically. 'No one could ever have doubted the goodness and beauty of your character. Now you will bestow grace upon the jewels whenever you wear them. Splendid!' He subsided suddenly, slightly red in the face after his outburst, but very pleased with the situation.

'An heiress?' Abigail touched an emerald gingerly. She still hadn't picked up any of the jewellery apart from the rope of pearls.

Despite their intense curiosity, in deference to her, no one else had touched them at all. Honor sat in a chair next to the table to admire the jewels, while Gifford, Anthony and Cole all bent over the tabletop with their hands clasped behind their backs as they scrutinised Abigail's inheritance.

'Are they very valuable?' she asked hesitantly.

Everyone looked at her in astonishment.

'You could buy a fine country estate, throw in a carriage and four, and still have a comfortable income for the rest of your life!' Admiral Pullen exclaimed. 'If you sold them—which, of course, you won't need to now. You may wear any of them whenever you choose.'

'Oh. Oh, my.' Abigail was too distracted to catch Pullen's meaning. 'I thought…I thought…'

'What did you think?' Honor prompted her gently.

Abigail shook her head in an attempt to clear it. 'It doesn't matter,' she said, 'my mind is a little muddled.' She sank into a chair beside Honor.

She'd been thinking that Miss Wyndham hadn't given

her the dresses so that she could become a rich man's mistress. Miss Wyndham really had meant for Abigail to have a Season in London just like any respectable young lady.

Her eyes misted again. 'I wonder if Bessie knew,' she said suddenly.

'Bessie?' Honor queried.

'Miss Wyndham's maid,' Abigail explained. 'She was so adamant at the will reading that all the jewellery had been sold—so Miss Wyndham could lend Charles the money he was always asking for. But she *never* gave him that much. I know. I managed the accounts for her.'

'Bessie may not have known how much they're worth,' Gifford said. 'As you apparently don't.' He smiled briefly, but his expression was oddly reserved, as if he didn't share in the general excitement.

'She may not even have seen them very often,' said Admiral Pullen. 'Miss Wyndham told me she hadn't worn any of the jewels in public for forty-odd years, and not even in private for nearly thirty years. Bessie was only her maid for the last twenty-three years.'

'She spent so much time stitching these clothes for me,' Abigail said, touching the elegant walking gown she was wearing. 'I didn't fully appreciate the extent of the alterations at first. But she must have unpicked every single gown and made it up afresh.'

'Seems a bit of a wasted effort, if you could just go out and buy new ones as soon as you received your full inheritance,' Cole commented.

'Of course it wasn't!' Honor exclaimed. 'It was a gift of the heart. Besides showing an excellent sense of economy.'

'Miss Wyndham wanted me to take care of Bessie and the others,' Abigail said. 'I know Mr Anderson has already found positions for them—but Bessie could be my maid now, couldn't she?' she looked up at Gifford eagerly.

'I've already sent for her,' he said curtly. 'Apparently she found the journey into Oxfordshire rather exhausting.

She isn't used to travelling. But as soon as she has recovered from that journey she'll come to London.'

'Poor Bessie,' Abigail said remorsefully. 'I didn't mean for her to racket all round the countryside. You've already sent for her?' she added, frowning in confusion.

'Certainly,' Gifford said. 'You are in need of a maid, and your affection for each other cannot be questioned. It was always my intention she should continue to serve you—whatever the future holds for you.'

On which announcement he turned and walked out of the room.

'Has he ever considered a career on the stage?' Honor asked, in the startled silence that followed Gifford's departure. 'I've never known anyone with such a facility for dramatic entrances and exits. Has anyone told you about the grand entrance he made to our wedding?' she asked Abigail. 'Lazarus can have had no more impact on his audience.'

'I…yes…' Abigail struggled to maintain her composure. 'Anthony told me about it.'

She swallowed back tears which had nothing to do with Miss Wyndham's generosity. Apparently she was an heiress—but Gifford had just walked out on her.

He'd said he would drive her around London this morning, show her all the sights she'd only heard or read about. She'd been looking forward to spending time alone with him. She'd had such high hopes for the day—and now he'd gone. She wanted to sit quietly and talk to him about everything that had happened, marvel with him at Miss Wyndham's convoluted last wishes. But he'd gone.

He'd left her with his relatives and her old friend, Admiral Pullen. She liked all of them. At any other time she would have found the obvious love between Cole and Honor heartwarming. Despite Cole's occasional tendency to say outrageous things which shocked his graceful wife, he took great care of her, and Honor obviously adored him. Their love had made a great impression upon Abigail—but the accord between them highlighted the confusion in her own relationship with Gifford.

Everyone was so pleased for her inheritance. She did her best to respond appropriately to her good fortune, but it was difficult to be truly enthusiastic about the jewellery. She didn't want diamonds and rubies. She wanted to know why Gifford had walked away from her.

After a while she slipped out of the room, leaving the others to admire Miss Wyndham's jewels.

Anthony found her later in the large drawing room, gazing up at the painting of Gifford standing on the quarterdeck of the *Unicorn*.

'You've left a fortune lying on the table,' he said, smiling at her crookedly.

'Oh.' She blinked distractedly. 'I don't know what to do with all of it. It's very splendid,' she added hastily, in case he should think she was ungrateful. 'But I never had any jewels before, and Mr Tidewell took his valise away with him.'

Anthony grinned. 'I think we'll be able to find a more appropriate place to keep them,' he said. 'Cole is already considering how best to ensure they remain safe.'

'That's very kind of him,' Abigail said, glancing wistfully at Gifford's picture. 'Kemp said he went out,' she said. 'I expect he had business of his own to attend to. Now he doesn't have to worry about me anymore. Now Charles is dead.'

'Perhaps,' Anthony said non-committally. 'Perhaps this would be a good opportunity for me to make some preliminary sketches for your portrait.'

'Oh?' Abigail looked at him doubtfully.

'I could paint you wearing one of your new necklaces,' Anthony suggested. Abigail was still holding the rope of pearls between her fingers, almost as if it were a rosary.

'Oh, no!' she said immediately. 'Oh, no, I don't think I want you to do that.' She bit her lip, casting another glance at Gifford's picture. Anthony waited. 'They are Miss Wyndham's jewels,' she said at last. 'Made especially for her. Mr Tidewell said so. Her lover gave them to her—as…as *symbols* of his love. I don't w-want you to p-paint me wearing her jewels.'

'Then I won't,' said Anthony gently. 'Why don't we go into the music room? Gifford may well be right. I should paint you at the pianoforte.'

'Very well.' Abigail let him guide her away from Gifford's portrait and out of the large drawing room.

Gifford returned to Berkeley Square late in the afternoon. He asked Kemp to send Abigail to him in the library.

She responded to the summons, her heart beating fast with nervous apprehension and hope. As soon as she saw his grim expression fear swamped her. She was hardly able to force a few words of greeting from her lips.

'Sit down,' he ordered.

She perched on the edge of an upright chair, her hands locked together in her lap. She stared up at him, filled with foreboding. He wasn't simmering with volcanic anger, as she had so often seen him. Nor was he in a relaxed good humour. His scarred face was stern and austere. Perhaps this was how he looked when he gave orders that might lead to men's deaths.

'Abigail, you are now an heiress,' he said grimly.

'Yes.' She watched him carefully.

'In a position to have the pick of the most eligible bachelors,' he continued.

'I *am*?' That aspect of the situation hadn't occurred to Abigail. The only bachelor she was interested in was currently looming over her with a flinty expression on his face.

'In the circumstances, I believe we should delay any official announcement of our betrothal,' he announced.

'Delay?' Confusion added to Abigail's distress. It seemed clear that Gifford was taking this opportunity to extricate himself from a marriage that he had, from the first, openly declared he didn't want. But why bother delaying the decision?

'Obviously, if you are carrying my child, there can be no question that you must marry me,' he said grittily. 'But—'

'I'm not,' Abigail interrupted, blushing hotly.

Gifford pinned her with a burning stare. 'It's far too soon for you to know that.'

'It isn't!' she protested. Mortification consumed her whole body at her immodest announcement, but it was intolerable that this nightmare should be protracted any longer than necessary.

'Oh.' Gifford continued to stare at her. 'Are you sure?' he demanded.

'I'm not *ignorant*! Of course I'm sure!' she flared back at him. In truth, she wasn't sure, but it was unthinkable that they should ever repeat this conversation.

He jerked his gaze away from her, then turned his back on her. She gazed at his broad shoulders, determined not to let the tears prickling her eyes fall onto her cheeks.

She knew that Gifford's sense of honour had compelled him to rescue her from Charles Johnson. Then he had been overcome by his fierce passions—no doubt provoked by her own heedless actions. She was as responsible as he was for what had happened between them the night of the thunderstorm. She'd hoped so desperately that he would come to love her as she loved him, but it wasn't fair to trap him into a marriage he clearly didn't want. She held her head up and waited with dignity for him to deliver the *coup de grâce*.

'Then there is no need for us to be married,' he said, his back still towards her. 'You may dance at Almack's with a light…free…heart. There will be no scandal attached to your name. As Pullen says, you will be a fine catch.'

'I don't want to be a fine catch!' Abigail's throat burned with unshed tears.

'You've made your objections to marriage very plain

over the past few days,' Gifford said coldly, turning back to face her. 'No doubt you'll change your mind when confronted with a more personable man. In the meantime, I hope you will remain in Berkeley Square as my guest. Honor and Cole are fixed here permanently. I will be returning to sea very shortly.'

'Returning…? You have another commission already?' Abigail whispered.

Gifford flushed. 'I mean to visit the Admiralty tomorrow,' he said. 'I've served their lordships well in the past. I'm sure they will have work for me.'

'So am I.' Despair filled Abigail.

She stared at him mutely for several seconds. He stared back equally intently—then abruptly broke the connection between them. He looked down at the floor. Thick, heavy silence filled the library, oppressing Abigail until she thought she would suffocate beneath it.

Life suddenly returned to her benumbed limbs. She stood up. 'I hope you receive a commission worthy of you,' she said huskily. 'Excuse me.'

She hurried out of the library, terrified her feelings would overcome her before she'd escaped Gifford's presence. He didn't want to marry her. He'd never made any pretense about that. He wanted to return to sea. And she wanted him to be happy—no matter how much it hurt her.

Chapter Eighteen

Gifford walked. He didn't care about direction or destination. He had no idea where he was going. He had done what he believed to be right, but now he was anchorless and rudderless.

Abigail didn't want to marry him. She had always been adamant on the subject. He remembered with painful clarity what she'd said to him in the apple orchard: *I don't want to marry you—and I won't.*

He'd hoped she would become more agreeable to the idea with time, but virtually her first words on arriving in London had been to deny any betrothal between them. She'd never said anything subsequently to suggest she'd changed her mind.

And now she was an heiress.

With every glittering piece of jewellery that Mr Tidewell had laid upon the table, Gifford had felt Abigail slipping further and further out of his grasp. She didn't need him anymore. Just as Admiral Pullen had said, Abigail now had everything a woman required to be a social success. She was brave, kind-hearted, beautiful and charming—and now she was wealthy.

Gifford had taken the only honourable course open to him. It was right that she should be free to shine unencum-

bered upon the social stage. Of course, if she'd been carrying his child, that would have been a different matter...

But she wasn't. Gifford's hands clenched into fists. In
the circumstances his fierce disappointment at her confident
denial was unreasonable—but beyond his control.

He walked on.

Hours later he found himself standing on Westminster
Bridge. Night had fallen and the Thames was black beneath
him. The tide flowed swiftly to the sea. His own ultimate
destination. He had no desire to remain in England now.

He leant against the bridge and briefly closed his good
eye. The wind gusting along the river ruffled his hair and
tugged at his clothes. It was September already. Autumn
was in the air. He remembered the hot August night he'd
first seen Abigail's silhouette—and she'd seen a good deal
more than that of him.

Later she'd called him a 'well-made man', he recalled.
That was a pleasant memory. All his memories of Abigail
were pleasant except for the moment she'd ordered him
from her bed—and those occasions when she'd declared her
unwillingness to marry him.

A well-made man. He smiled at the words. Whatever else
she'd said to him, he did believe she'd enjoyed his love-
making. *Horses move more.* He still couldn't credit she'd
said *that*!

He stared unseeingly at the river, remembering all the
times he'd spoken to Abigail in Bath before Miss Wyndham
had died and Charles Johnson had interfered so diabolically
in Abigail's life.

He frowned as he recalled a conversation with Abigail
in the Pump Room about the book of hers he'd read. He'd
been appalled at the petty restrictions placed upon the lives
of women. He could even remember the words he'd used:
*You have no choice. No genuine freedom of action. You
must wait modestly to see if a man favours you. And if his*

conduct confuses you, you must appear unconscious and pretend indifference.

Abigail had laughed at him then, but she hadn't laughed very often recently.

He thrust his fingers through his hair, uncomfortable and disturbed by the direction of his thoughts. He had made love to Abigail, knowing deep in his heart that marriage must be the inevitable consequence of his action—but he had never told Abigail what sharing her bed meant to him.

Seen from Abigail's perspective, had his conduct been confusing?

She had made it very clear when they were talking about Charles Johnson's fate that she would never surrender her freedom of choice or her right to make decisions concerning her own future. Was she pretending indifference to him—refusing to marry him—simply because he'd tried to deny her the right to choose?

He hadn't asked her to marry him—he'd told her! And Abigail had consistently demonstrated she wasn't good at taking orders. Perhaps what she wanted was to be courted!

Gifford spun on his heel and began to stride back towards Berkeley Square. He'd never accepted defeat before, he wouldn't do so this time.

It was past midnight when he arrived at the house. Everyone was in bed. His jaw clenched in frustration that he must delay his plans until morning, but he was determined to behave towards Abigail with utmost chivalry. He wasn't entirely sure what that might entail, but he remembered his father talking to Anthony about the tradition of courtly love during medieval times. He took a detour into the library in the hope he might find a book on the subject.

Unfortunately there were thousands of leather-bound volumes in his father's library. Anthony—and probably even Cole—would have known exactly where to look, but Gifford was completely flummoxed. He scowled at the book-lined shelves that stretched from floor to ceiling on every available wall. The answer to his question might well be here, but there was no possibility he would ever find it. He was damned if he'd ask Anthony to show him the book he needed!

He stalked out of the library and up the stairs to his bedchamber. He would have to approach the problem from a different angle. Abigail probably wouldn't mind overmuch if he didn't adhere strictly to the rules of chivalry. She would be satisfied—he hoped—if he expressed the *spirit* of courtly love when he addressed her.

He stripped off his clothes and climbed into bed. He covered himself with a sheet and lay on his back, his hands stacked behind his head as he gave careful thought to the problem.

A few minutes later he heard a faint sound as someone turned his doorhandle. He turned his head sharply, his body tensing as he watched the door slowly open. To his utter disbelief, Abigail slipped through the narrow gap and stood staring at him.

He stared back. His instant thought was that she had been hurt or frightened by something—or someone, but she displayed no signs of panic.

She fumbled behind her and pushed the door shut, her gaze fixed on his face, then leant against it. She held a candle in one hand. Its flickering light illuminated her wide eyes and tumbling hair. Gifford was peripherally aware that she was wearing some kind of pale, silky robe, but all his attention was on her face as he tried to make sense of her presence in his room.

His heart hammered against his ribs as he watched her warily approaching the bed. At last she was standing on the opposite side to him. He saw that she was trembling. Hot wax spilled down the side of the candle as it tilted precariously in her hand. They gazed at each other for several tense, uncertain moments.

Gifford removed one hand from behind his head and wordlessly pulled the sheet back. He saw Abigail swallow nervously. She turned and put the candle holder down, then she pushed her robe off her shoulders and let it fall to the floor. Gifford swallowed. His mouth was dry with excitement, hope and a large portion of confusion.

Abigail crawled cautiously onto the bed. She sat beside him, her legs tucked under her, and looked at him. He looked back. Her Titian hair fell all around her shoulders, rich against the pale cream of her nightgown. He could see the rapid rise and fall of her breasts beneath the silk and knew that she was extremely nervous.

He would have said something, but his throat was too tight to speak. He wanted to touch her, but he kept his hands safely tucked behind his head. He was scared if he did or said the wrong thing he would frighten her away, like a wild animal.

She bit her lip and stretched out her hand towards him. He watched it come closer. Her fingers trembled. She touched his chest very lightly, then instantly snatched her hand away, rather as if she was testing to see if a kettle was hot. When he didn't move, she touched him again, this time letting her fingertips rest on him a little longer.

At last she rested her hand gently on his chest and smiled tremulously at him. He removed his hand from beneath his head and pulled her down beside him. A moment later her head rested on his shoulder as she snuggled up against him.

Excitement, satisfaction and triumph surged through Gifford's body. Abigail was in his bed! She was in his arms! Now all he had to do was make sure she stayed there.

He could feel her trembling. He stroked her hair with one hand and with his other hand he caressed the soft skin of her arm, which rested on his chest. For good measure—and because he wanted to—he turned his head and brushed his lips against her forehead. She quivered responsively. He kissed her again, hoping she'd lift her head so he could kiss her properly, but she just rubbed her cheek against his shoulder.

The silence extended. She obviously wasn't going to say anything. It was clearly up to him to sort out the fiddly details of their situation, and whether her intentions towards him were honourable. The date of the wedding…minor considerations of that nature.

'Are you…?' He paused and cleared his throat. 'Are you sleepwalking?' he asked, with hoarse caution.

'N-no,' she whispered.

'Are you…?' He stopped again. 'Are you…? Do you intend to exile me from the bed at any…crucial… moments?' he asked edgily.

'*Exile?*' She lifted her head, her green eyes wide and startled as she stared at him. 'No!'

He was uncomfortable with her close scrutiny. He guided her head firmly back to rest on his shoulder. Apparently she hadn't realised how devastating her rejection had been at such a sensitive moment. That was probably a good thing— as long as she didn't do it again.

He inhaled carefully, strengthening his resolve for the last and most important thing he had to say.

'You understand that if you remain in my bed one second longer…' he paused for emphasis, and to ensure that his voice was full of authority '…one second longer, you will be duty-bound to marry me.'

He held his breath. Every muscle in his body was rigid with tension.

Abigail didn't move. At last she nodded, her hair tickling his chin as she made the affirmative gesture.

Gifford exhaled. His body went slack with relief. He was glad they were in bed. The impact of her agreement was so profound he doubted he would have had the strength to stand.

Abigail would marry him! Abigail would be his wife!

Relief turned to exultation as renewed energy flowed

through him. He fisted his hand in her hair, gently obliging her to lift her head. Then he kissed her.

Abigail kissed him back. He wanted to marry her. He didn't just want to kiss her and make love to her. He truly wanted to marry her!

His body was hot and urgent against hers. She clutched him, drowning joyfully in the intensity of his passion. He fumbled with her nightgown and pulled it up to her waist. He stroked her hips, her thighs. She tingled and burned, as quickly aroused as he was. She'd missed him, yearned for him, and now she could have him.

He rolled her on to her back and lifted himself over her. She stroked his chest, his shoulders, the taut muscles in his arms. He paused, looking down at her. She looked back, her gaze already hazy with passion, wondering why he hesitated. Then she remembered he'd thought of her rejection as exile.

Exile had seemed such a strange word to use in this context, yet the implications were glorious. He'd told her that her bed—and her body—were home to him.

She lifted her knees, rubbing the inside of her thighs against the outside of his, and felt him shudder in response. Then she wrapped her arms and legs around him and drew him home.

'Abby, why did you come to my room tonight?' Gifford murmured, some time later.

'Don't you think I should have?' Abigail lifted her head and looked at him.

'Yes.' He slipped his hand beneath the weight of her hair, holding it back from her face as he pulled her closer for a kiss.

'I was talking to Anthony,' she said breathlessly, when she could finally speak.

'He told you to come to my bed!' Gifford exclaimed in disbelief.

'No, no,' she assured him hastily. 'We didn't talk about this…us…um…'

'What did you talk about?' he asked.

'Well…' She played with the curls on his chest.

He closed his hand around hers. 'Stop distracting me,' he growled, although the gleam in his eye was very far from menacing. 'Tell me what Anthony said.'

'It was about how you *always* consider the consequences before you act,' Abigail said. 'And sometimes—we were talking in particular about when the privateers captured you, you understand?' she interrupted herself, looking at Gifford anxiously. 'But I think perhaps, really, we were talking about us—you and me. I think he is a bit exasperated with us. But he was very tactful.'

'He's so damned tactful I don't know what he said yet!' Gifford exclaimed. 'What do you mean, he's exasperated with us?'

'He didn't *say* anything about being exasperated,' Abigail said scrupulously. 'I simply received the impression he might be. And I've already told you what he said. He said,' she repeated, 'that you always consider the consequences before you do anything. And sometimes…*sometimes*, although a consequence might, at first sight, seem to be a…a…a punishment, in fact it could be a…a *reward*. Only it doesn't always seem like it at first. But…but…'

'I see,' said Gifford. 'You believe I made love to you, so you'd have no choice but marry me?'

'Well…' Abigail hesitated. Put like that, it hardly seemed credible, yet he did want to marry her, he'd made it a condition of her remaining in his bed for a single second longer. 'Kemp told me you'd had the pianoforte moved—so no one could startle me,' she said. 'And always, *always* you have been kind to me. Your hands are kind.' She blushed and swallowed nervously. 'But I told you to get out of my bed. I thought perhaps…perhaps that was why you were a bit…a bit *angry* with me the next day. I didn't think of that at the time,' she confessed in a small voice.

'When I ordered you to marry me?'

'Yes. You said…you said it wasn't what you wanted!' Abigail's voice rose slightly as she remembered how much that had hurt.

'Abby.' Gifford groaned and pulled her down for another tender kiss. His hands on her body were so gentle and loving she almost cried.

'I meant I'd planned for you to have a Season,' he explained regretfully. 'That's what I told myself I wanted for you—but what I really wanted…was just you. I didn't fully realise it at the time, but I think I was afraid if I simply asked you—you might turn me down. So I took away your choices. Then I felt guilty. So…'

He pressed his lips together. There was both regret and sadness in his expression as he looked at her. 'I'm sorry,' he said. 'I'm so sorry, Abby.'

'Oh.' Tears misted in Abigail's eyes. 'I don't care about the Season,' she said unsteadily. 'I only wanted…' Her voice faltered and she laid her head back down on his chest.

Gifford held her in a warm, reassuring embrace.

'Me?' he asked softly, after a while.

She nodded mutely.

He brushed his lips against her hair, then found her hand and laced his fingers through hers.

'Why did you say ''no''?' he asked after a while. 'If you wanted me. You could have had me any time. All you had to do was walk into my bedchamber. I'm clay in your hands.'

Abigail smiled a little reprehensibly and turned her head to kiss his chest. 'No, you're not,' she murmured. 'Clay is soft. And you're…'

Gifford tightened his hold on her. 'Why did you say ''no''?' he repeated. 'I thought it was because you were angry with me for being so high-handed. For not giving you a choice. Was that it?'

'Partly. But mainly it was because I wanted…I decided it would be a cutting-out operation,' Abigail explained rapidly, before she lost her nerve. 'For your heart—'

'You wanted to cut my heart out!' Gifford exclaimed incredulously.

'*No!*' Abigail lifted her head and frowned at him. 'You know that's not want I meant. Don't be provoking.'

He smiled a little, very tenderly and stroked her cheek with gentle fingers. 'Then what?' he asked softly.

'I knew…I believed you liked *making* love to me,' she said, blushing. 'But I wanted you to…I wanted you to…to l-l…'

She couldn't say it. She placed her head on his chest once more and hoped he knew what she wanted him to say.

'I do,' Gifford said after a few moments. 'I do love you. I will always love you. With my body, I thee worship. I'm all yours. My body, my heart, my soul…they're all for you.'

Overwhelming happiness flooded like sunshine through Abigail. It was the most powerful emotion she'd ever experienced.

'I love you too,' she whispered. 'I love you so much. I couldn't manage without you. You know I thought—when I first heard Miss Wyndham left her gowns to me—I thought she meant I was to wear them to attract a rich lover. But I didn't want to do that. Then when Mr Tidewell told us about the jewels, I knew that wasn't what she'd intended and I was pleased. But then when you said you wouldn't marry me because I was an heiress I hated all the jewellery.'

'I hated Miss Wyndham's jewels from the moment Tidewell started hauling them out of the damned valise,' Gifford admitted gruffly. 'I thought…you wouldn't need me anymore now you're wealthy.'

'That is very silly.' Abigail propped herself up on an

elbow to look down at him. 'In fact, I'm sorry to be rude, but it is just plain *stupid*,' she said forcefully. But she softened the impact of her words by hugging him tightly and leaning over to give him a quick affirmative kiss. 'I don't care how rich you are, or how many houses you've got. I love *you*. I love you so much that before I came to you tonight I decided that if you didn't want to marry me—if you only wanted me for your mistress—I would be happy with that. Because if you didn't want me—nothing else mattered. I love you for your heart…and your soul—'

'Don't forget my well-made body,' Gifford interjected with a cocky grin.

Abigail pushed him indignantly. 'Don't make fun—' She broke off abruptly, then gently touched his damp cheek. 'You're crying,' she whispered, awed.

Gifford swallowed and tried to turn his head aside, but Abigail cupped her palm against his cheek and wouldn't let him. His fierce blue gaze was softened by tears. For a moment he refused to look at her, but then he lifted his gaze to meet her eyes. His expression was stripped of all its usual arrogant reserve. His face was full of tenderness, love—and an unexpected vulnerability.

Abigail was overwhelmed. She'd never once considered that Gifford might have suffered as much as she had during their period of misunderstanding.

'I'm sorry,' she murmured huskily. 'I'm so sorry. I should have agreed to marry you straight away. It would have saved so much heartache.'

'Would it?' Gifford covered her hand with his. 'It would have spared me heartache—but what of you? If I'd never told you…?'

'You have told me.' Tears welled up in Abigail's own eyes. 'You have *shown* me you love me—over and over in so many ways. I should have been more perceptive…'

Despite the lingering brightness in his good eye, Gifford grinned as he stroked the tears from Abigail's cheeks.

'Are you intent on quite unmanning me?' he asked, softly jesting. 'If you'd been any more perceptive you would have realised how often I was tongue-tied in your presence. Completely love-struck and reduced to barking orders at you to hide my lack of address.' He smiled ruefully. 'Earlier tonight I went to look in the library for a book on courtly love—King Arthur and his knights and so forth,' he confessed. 'To teach me how to romance you properly. But I couldn't find one.'

'Gifford!' Abigail was amazed at his admission. 'You don't need a *book*. You're already the perfect knight—'

'Baronet,' Gifford corrected, but he looked more than pleased by Abigail's praise.

'Don't quibble,' she told him severely. 'Every lady needs a champion, and you are my perfect champion. And I love you so much.' Her voice softened on the last few words.

Gifford drew her down for his kiss. Abigail tasted the salt of their mutual tears on their lips. It was a long, slow kiss in which they both confided and confirmed their love for each other.

At last Abigail rested her head on his shoulder and they lay in contented silence for several minutes.

'We must be married at once,' Gifford said briskly at last, sounding much more like his usual, authoritative self. 'It's a fortunate thing Tidewell and Pullen are both in town. Do you wish one of them to give you away?'

'Of course not!' Abigail sat up. Then, deciding that wasn't a sufficiently commanding position, she straddled Gifford. She blushed a little at her boldness, but he didn't seem to object. In fact he seemed rather pleased by her action. She looked down at him firmly. 'I do not belong to either Mr Tidewell *or* Admiral Pullen. Therefore they cannot *give* me away. I'm not a bunch of roses. I will give myself to you,' she told him generously.

'Really?' Gifford put his hands behind his head in much

the same position he'd been in when she'd first entered the room. 'Show me?' he invited wickedly.

Abigail bit her lip thoughtfully as she considered the situation. 'You might have to help me,' she said at last. 'I'm not quite sure...'

Gifford grinned briefly, but his expression was very tender as he reached for her. 'I'll always help you,' he assured her.

'Yes. Oh, wait! I'm sorry!' Abigail saw the flare of apprehension in his gaze as she interrupted their love-making and kissed him apologetically. 'I'm sorry,' she said again, pressing her breasts against him, and resting her forearms on his chest as she looked down at him. 'I just... You said you'd go to the Admiralty tomorrow!' she burst out. 'For a ship. I just remembered. Are you...? Do you want...? I would *never* want to hinder you...but...but...couldn't I go with you? Like Anthony did? Please! I don't want you to leave me behind.'

'I'm not going to seek another commission,' he said quietly. 'I can't leave you now—and I'm not taking you to war with me. Do you realise...' his gaze refocused slightly as he looked into the past '...I have spent eighteen years of my life almost continually at sea. And for all of that time—except for the brief peace over ten years ago—England has been at war. Every morning before dawn the ship is piped to quarters, so that if the new day reveals an enemy on the horizon we are immediately ready to go into battle. Every morning before dawn, whether midshipman or captain, I have roused up ready to fight—though weeks might go by before the fight takes place.'

He paused and refocused on Abigail. He smiled at her and she could feel a new sense of peace and certainty within him.

'More than half my life has been spent at war,' he said. 'I'm weary of war. I want to make love to you at dawn.

Then walk across dew-covered fields and startle a rabbit from cover—not an enemy frigate.'

Abigail smiled at him, happy tears shimmering in her eyes. 'I expect you will sometimes enjoy a solitary stroll,' she said. 'But—if you should happen to want me to accompany you occasionally—can we have breakfast first? I'm not very alert first thing in the morning.'

Gifford grinned. 'I give you my permission to stay in our cosy bed while I brave the belligerent rabbits, lazybones.' He skimmed his hands down her body, then repositioned her slightly. 'You mentioned you might need some help in giving yourself to me,' he reminded her. 'May I make some suggestions—just to help you begin?'

*   *   *   *   *   *